MARGARET KENNEDY

was born on 23 April 1896 in Hyde Park Gate, Kensington. Her father was a barrister and she was the eldest of four children. She was educated at Cheltenham Ladies' College and Somerville College, Oxford where she read Modern History. Her first published work was *A Century of Revolution* (1922), a textbook on modern European history. Her first novel was *The Ladies of Lyndon* (1923), preceding by only a year her major popular and critical success, *The Constant Nymph*, the novel which made her famous.

In 1925 she married David Davies, a barrister who became a Q.C., a County Court Judge and was knighted in 1953. They lived in Kensington (apart from wartime evacuation to St Ives in Cornwall) and they had one son and two daughters. Five plays by Margaret Kennedy were produced on the London stage, of which *The Constant Nymph*, written with Basil Dean and starring Edna Best, Noel Coward and John Gielgud, won great acclaim, as did *Escape Me Never* with Elizabeth Bergner. Both plays were successfully filmed. Fourteen more novels were published between 1927 and 1964, with a twelve-year gap between 1938 and 1950 when Margaret Kennedy was chiefly engaged in film work. Her first two novels after the war, *The Feast* (1950) and *Lucy Carmichael* (1951), were highly praised by British and American critics; the next, *Troy Chimneys* (1953), was awarded the James Tait Black memorial prize. Her short biography of Jane Austen was published in 1950 and she wrote another critical work, *The Outlaws on Parnassus* (1958), a study of the art of fiction.

After her husband's death in 1964 Margaret Kennedy moved to Woodstock, Oxfordshire where she lived until her death on 31 July 1967. Of her novels, Virago publish *The Ladies of Lyndon* and *Together and Apart* (1936).

Alas ! They had been friends in youth ;
But whispering tongues can poison truth ;
And constancy lives in realms above ;
And life is thorny ; and youth is vain ;
And to be wroth with one we love,
Doth work like madness in the brain.

*   *   *   *

Each spake words of high disdain
And insult to his heart's best brother :
They parted—ne'er to meet again !
But never either found another
To free the hollow heart from paining—
They stood aloof, the scars remaining,
Like cliffs which had been rent asunder ;
A dreary sea now flows between ;
But neither heat, nor frost, nor thunder,
Shall wholly do away, I ween,
With marks of that which once hath been.

COLERIDGE (from *Christabel*)

Margaret Kennedy

TOGETHER AND APART

With a new Introduction by
JULIA BIRLEY

To
ROSE MACAULAY

Published by VIRAGO PRESS Limited 1981
Ely House, 37 Dover Street, London WIX 4HS

First published by Cassell & Co. Ltd 1936

Printed in Finland by Werner Söderström Oy
a member of Finnprint

British Cataloguing in Publication Data

Kennedy, Margaret
  Together and apart.
  I. Title
  823'.912[F]   PR6021.E65

  ISBN 0-86068-216-1

CONTENTS

PART I—TOGETHER

	PAGE
TOGETHER	3
THE GRANDMOTHERS	9
THE WIFE	23
THE HUSBAND	29
THE PROTÉGÉE	42
ON THE BEACH	52
AT THE STATION	63
INTERFERENCE	66
THE LOOK	72
INDISCRETION	77
THE FRIENDS	89
A WASTED MORNING	94
THE RETURN	103
THE QUARREL	108
MIDNIGHT	114
MORNING	119
THE END OF THE HOLIDAYS	125

PART II—WRATH

WRATH	137

PART III—APART

ON RIVER CLIFF	161
THE ACCOLADE	172
FATHER AND DAUGHTER	183
ALONE	194
MOTHER AND SON	201
INTERIOR DECORATION	209
HAPPINESS	215
THE TURNING POINT	223
TRUTH	231
THE ESCALATOR	241
DECREE ABSOLUTE	247

PART IV—TIME AND CHANGE

KENNETH	259
MARK	268
ALEC	281
ELIZA	295
JOY	307
MAX AND BETSY	316
YEARS UNBORN	330

INTRODUCTION

At an upmarket charity bazaar in the early 1930s, the fortune teller was a major attraction. 'She's astounding', patrons muttered as they left the tent. 'She knows things I haven't told to anyone.'

She certainly knew her job. A few people compared notes afterwards; they found that the men had all been told that their wives did not really understand them, and they would soon have much more money. Women were assured that they would have more money, and that someone long lost but never forgotten would shortly reappear in their lives. One of the group however was Margaret Kennedy, and her experience was different. The clairvoyante had begun her routine, paused, frowned at the cards and exclaimed: 'I think you are just on the brink of a terrible mistake. This decision you've taken – I must urge you to reconsider it before it's too late. You'll regret it all your life. Things won't turn out as you expect. A powerful woman is your enemy, you know that already. Your children too – they'll get involved . . .'

The novelist listened in fascination. The warning had no application for herself, but was curiously relevant to the pile of manuscript notes on the table at home, and the imaginary situation that was never far from her mind. In 1936 this reached its public form as *Together and Apart*.

When my mother first recounted this incident, we children were enchanted, and believed every word of it. Thirty or forty years later, it seems to me, as with all her good stories, that if it is not true, it ought to have been. It has artistic truth. For of all her novels, *Together and Apart* is for me the most compellingly believable. Not that the 'realism' is stronger; it must seem mild indeed in the 1980s. But in spite of the disappearance of the bohemians, artists and musicians who lend colour to all the previous books, the story gathers such an independent momentum as it passes from scene to vivid scene, that, just as in 'real life', the reader grows increasingly involved in what must be happening offstage. If another mind could catch an inkling of it before it came to be written down, it would surely present itself not as fiction at all, but as something actual and concrete.

Again, *Together and Apart*, which is the seventh of the sixteen novels, is the most firmly rooted in contemporary time. It is hard to generalise about these, since Margaret Kennedy hardly ever repeated herself, and each one breaks new ground; some are set in the immediate or more distant past, while some, like the uniquely successful *Constant Nymph*, seem dateless. But in the conversations of the Canning family and their friends, I catch an authentic echo of the voices of my childhood, accents now subtly changed, or wholly obliterated. Alec and Betsy Canning belonged to my mother's own age group and social milieu. The grandmother even lived on Campden Hill, not half a mile from our old home. Their holiday house, 'Pandy Madoc', was imaginary, but its setting 'Afon Arian' is the Mawddach estuary in Wales, where we stayed every summer. In earlier and later books, Margaret Kennedy never borrowed quite so freely on what lay to hand at the time of writing.

It may seem surprising that at the height of maturity, and after the wide poetic ranges of *The Constant Nymph* and *Escape Me Never*, she should choose to limit herself to this narrow ground. Her starting points were not quite a matter of choice. They discovered themselves in the form of a picture, a situation, the name of a house, which held some significance that begged to be exploited. *Together and Apart* was conceived one sleepy afternoon on an escalator of London's underground. A man was coming up and a woman going down. She could not read their expressions, only that, as they passed, there was a movement of recognition, then each turned and held the other's gaze as long as they remained in sight. How many stories could have grown from such a seed! There must have been a special challenge in this one. Its immediate predecessor, *A Long Time Ago*, was a hilarious evocation of an Edwardian houseparty invaded by an amorous prima donna. It has a mellow glow of the past, of Ireland and childhood holidays. Perhaps Margaret Kennedy felt it important, this time, to present sex and marriage in the more murky light of common day. At this period she and my father were puzzled and distressed by what amounted to an epidemic of divorce among their acquaintance. The grandly desolate lines of Coleridge which she chose as an epigraph express her sense of the emotional waste and destruction in the lives of ordinary people. When we meet the Cannings on the brink of their divorce, they are as banal and recognisable as if they had walked out of some snapshot album of the 1930s, unearthed by somebody's grandmother to beguile a wet afternoon. Their way of life is just like their neighbours', there are maids to make beds and answer doors, and the children go to boarding school. Their own concerns are all-important to them, and the outside world only impinges now and again. Alec and Betsy have given a home to a Jewish refugee family, who play a small but significant role in the drama. Their son's intellectual friend Mark is already aware of a crisis in civilisation, while Max St Mullins, Betsy's saintly and absurd cousin, is devoted to the great causes of the day, unemployment relief, disarmament and so on. But Betsy's discontent, her fear that life is slipping away, has nothing to do with Europe's approaching cataclysm. A later generation would call it a clear case of mid-life crisis.

'Happiness, always promised for tomorrow, never far from yesterday, found no lodging in her heart . . . Only she, upon whom they all depended, must be kept so active and so restless that now she was thirty-seven, would soon be forty, would soon be dead, without ever getting her rights.'

She plans a neat demolition of the marriage, unaware of

the sexual time-bomb ticking away inside it. The explosion is satisfyingly sensational; the worst casualties not quite those we expect. There is Betsy's magnificently hateful mother-in-law (a type who appears in several of the early novels) dealing the final, crushing blow from her death-bed, quite unconsciously. Strong men have been known to weep over the death of Tessa, the Constant Nymph. Destructive old Emily Canning makes me reach for a handkerchief just as promptly.

Together and Apart has of course an appealing schoolgirl of its own. In counterpoint to the sombre themes of middle-aged betrayal and disintegration runs that of fourteen-year-old Eliza, no Constant Nymph, rather fat and inclined to be bossy and self-deceiving like her mother. Her visit to her brother's school, and her re-encounter with Mark, 'the friend she could never have because she was not a boy', is a fine dramatic turning point; it was drawn from contemporary Winchester, where the youthful urbanity of Richard Crossman had made a great impression on my mother, as he dispensed prefectorial hospitality in his study. From this point Eliza wins entire sympathy, so that one longs for her to have her chance, and shares her too-precarious happiness in the quiet final scene.

I think all connoisseurs of Margaret Kennedy's novels would put this one among the first half dozen. For my taste, though it lacks *The Constant Nymph's* special charisma, it must rank alongside it as a powerful story with a poetry of its own. Proust maintained that a book is the product of a different self from the one that other people know. In my mother's case, a subtly different persona seemed to us to emerge with each new theme, and the only constant was the craftsmanship. Literary judges might venture to decide which novel best realised her special gift. I merely feel sure that if she made Eliza more like the girl down the road than Tessa, then she had her reasons. The kind of life this book presents has passed into history – had already done so, in fact, by the time I was old enough to read it – along with the Margaret Kennedy who wrote it, and the Margaret Kennedy I knew. Now at last a new generation has a chance to learn the pleasure I have had from it all my life. One can only be grateful for such chances in 1981.

Julia Birley, London 1980

Julia Birley is Margaret Kennedy's daughter

TOGETHER AND APART

TOGETHER

I

Letter from Betsy Canning to her mother.

Pandy Madoc,
North Wales,
August 8th.

DEAREST MOTHER,

I'm sorry the Engadine isn't being a success, but I'm not surprised. Why on earth did you trust the Gordons to choose a hotel? You might have known better. How is father's lumbago? For heaven's sake don't go on sleeping in damp beds till you both have pneumonia. Move to somewhere more comfortable. You are both too old to camp out in mouldy little inns.

Here it is lovely—fine and hot. All the children are back from school, and we have a school friend of Kenneth's staying, Mark Hannay, so the house is pretty full. We can't overflow into the cottage, because Alec, in an expansive moment, has lent it to the Blochs. You know? He's that very clever Jew who designed the sets for the German production of *Caroline*. That's how Alec got to know him. Now they are persecuted, and had to escape in the middle of the night or something, in the clothes they stood up in. Absolutely penniless and swarms of rather uninviting children. He is trying to get work over here. I feel one ought to be sorry for them. But being persecuted doesn't make people nicer somehow, and I do wish Alec had told me before he offered them the cottage ; it's very inconvenient—right in the middle of the summer holidays.

Well now Mother, listen. I have something to tell you that you won't like at all. In fact, I'm afraid that it will be a terrible shock and you will hate it at first. But do try to get used to the idea and bring father round to it.

Alec and I are parting company. We are going to get a divorce.

I know this will horrify you : the more so because I have, perhaps mistakenly, tried very hard to conceal our unhappiness during these last years. I didn't, naturally, want anybody to know while there was still a chance of keeping things going. But the fact is, we have been quite miserable, *both of us*. We simply are unsuited to one another and unable to get on. How much of this have you guessed ?

Life is so different from what we expected when we first married. Alec has quite changed, and he needs a different sort of wife. I never wanted all this money and success. I married a very nice but quite undistinguished civil servant. With my money we had quite enough to live on in a comfortable and civilised way. We had plenty of friends, our little circle, people like ourselves, amusing and well bred, not rich, but decently well off. Alec says now that they bored him. But he didn't say so at the time.

I must say it's rather hard on me that he took so long to find out what he really wanted. He says it's all his mother's fault, and that she bullied him so that he was past thirty before it ever occurred to him to call his soul his own. I dare say this is true, but I have to suffer for it.

If I had known I was marrying a professional librettist I should never have taken it on. I always loved the things which he and Johnnie Graham wrote together : I do think he is inspired when he writes words for Johnnie's music. But I never imagined that they were going to turn into the Gilbert and Sullivan of this generation, and, when they got their first operetta produced, I was always against it. I would so much rather it had just been a hobby. I wanted it to be produced by amateurs, by their friends. When it was such an enormous success, of course I was pleased in a way, but I felt even then that there was something just a little vulgar about it all. And when, after the success of the second opera, he gave up the Civil Service, I was horrified.

Of course he has made a lot of money and is, I suppose, quite famous. But I never could feel that it was a worth-while profession for an educated man like Alec. It isn't as if he and Johnnie were producing great works of art. They don't pretend to be ; they say themselves that they are only out to provide entertainment. I cannot respect Alec as much as I did when he was at the Ministry doing an obscure, dull, but useful job, " helping to get the world washed and dressed." And he knows it. Can you under-stand this, you and father ? I know you would never have breathed a word of it to me, but I always felt that you weren't quite happy about it in your heart of hearts— that you thought it a pity when he left the Ministry.

We no longer have the same friends. He seems to be completely submerged in the stage world. He is so popular and so genial. Everybody likes him and he likes every-body. Our house is perpetually crammed with people with whom I have nothing in common, who simply regard me as " Alec's wife " if they even know me by sight, which often they don't, I really believe. They've never heard of father, or, if they have, the word " professor " merely suggests to them a sort of stage cartoon, an absent-minded old man with a beard and a butterfly net. They *are* the most complete set of Yahoos ; however, they're Alec's friends, and he has a right to his own tastes, though how a man of his brains and sensibilities can like to hobnob with such a crew is something which I cannot understand. *My* friends, as you can imagine, don't mix with them at all well.

Reading this over, I feel it sounds rather like a list of grievances, as if I were the only sufferer. But indeed Alec has suffered equally. I'm not the right woman for him any more, and he can't be happy with me. I will tell you two things to prove this which I would never have told you if we had not decided to make a break. He does, now, drink a good deal more than he ought. Not that he's ever *drunk*, I mean ; but in London he does drink all the time—he lives in a sort of genial, gregarious, alcoholic mist, not *quite* himself. That's why I'm always so thankful to get him away into the country. It's much better there. And the other thing : for some years there has been another woman. He has been pretty openly unfaithful to me. Had you heard any gossip about this ? Of course, as long as we lived together I never discussed it with anybody. I ignored it. And, mind you, I don't blame him. But I think it all goes to show that I am not the right wife for him.

Then why didn't I divorce him before ? Because of the children. I felt they ought to have a home, that we must all stay together as long as any decent appearance of harmony could be kept up. And now, *because* of the children, I have changed my mind. I now think that *they* would be happier if Alec and I gave up this miserable attempt. They are getting old enough to feel the strain and the tension, especially Kenneth, who quite realizes that Alec doesn't always treat me considerately, and resents it violently. A father and son can mean so much to one another ; it would be terrible if they become permanently alienated. I don't want the children to grow up with a distorted idea of marriage, got from the spectacle of parents who can't get on. I think the time has come to be quite open with them about it. I shall say :

" Your father and I have made a mistake. It's a pity,

but people do make these mistakes sometimes, and if they are candid and sensible it can be set right. It is nobody's fault. We are not suited to one another, but we have not quarrelled, and nobody is going to be angry or bitter. We are going to part in a friendly and civilized way. You will see quite as much of both of us in the future as you always have, and everybody will be happier all round."

Now, mother darling, do try to look at this quite rationally. Don't just cry out that a divorce in the family is a disgrace and that such a thing has never happened to us before. Who is going to suffer ? Doesn't it mean a better life for everybody ? Isn't it really sensible ? Alec can marry the woman who really suits him, I can live my own life with my own friends, and the children will grow up free from resentment and bewilderment. I know it's very sad that my marriage is a failure. But what's the good of pretending that it isn't ? We have both tried to made it a success and it doesn't work.

I'm writing to tell you now because we have decided to end it all rather quickly. Alec is going off on Wednesday with the Hamiltons, on their yacht, as he does every summer. He is never coming back, and he's going to write to me and say so, and send me the necessary evidence, so that I can divorce him. (Naturally I wouldn't dream of dragging the other woman into it. It will be a pure matter of form.) Perhaps you had better burn this letter. Anyway, don't show it to father ; just tell him what I've said and try to make him see it in a sensible light. Leave out this bit about the evidence—that we have settled it all beforehand, I mean. He is so conscientious about things like income tax, etc., he might think it was collusion.

Now I must stop, as the post is just going, though I feel as if there was a great deal more to say. Do try to understand. And please don't blame Alec. It has been quite as much my fault.

Your very loving
BETSY.

P.S.—Alec's mother knows nothing of this. We shan't tell her till it is too late for her to interfere.

Telegram from Mrs. Hewitt to her daughter.

engadine horrified letter am returning england immediately entreat do nothing irrevocable till I see you expect me wales wednesday evening have said nothing to father mother.

THE GRANDMOTHERS

EMILY CANNING, mother of Alec, was a widow and lived on Campden Hill with one old servant. But her existence was not lonely or inactive. She had a large circle of friends, varied interests, and a craving for power which preserved her from the lethargy of old age.

The desire to influence and to dominate, to play a leading part in the lives of other people, had always been her ruling passion : her talents and capacities were such that she had been able to indulge in it freely. She had beauty, charm and wit. She had the gift of creating drama, of raising the emotional temperature, of charging any relationship with an intense personal feeling. To be a friend was, for her, to be a partisan. A difference of opinion was disloyalty. People of both sexes and all ages fell easily in love with her. Those who did not were provoked to an irrational, a too violent dislike. But very few were able to remain entirely indifferent to her, or to preserve their peace of mind if once she had crossed their orbit.

She had one quality which is not infrequently found in characters of this type—the gift of second sight. Her feats of divination were well authenticated ; even her enemies admitted them, while to her friends they were a source of pride. She had seen several genuine ghosts. Sometimes, when the telephone rang, she knew who was trying to speak to her before she had taken off the receiver. She had premonitions about unexpected letters or visits, and her dreams were, beyond all doubt, prophetic.

On Tuesday night, or rather very early on Wednesday,

9

she had a most remarkable dream. It seemed to be morning and a person was bringing in her breakfast tray. But this person was not old Maggie, her maid ; it was Henrietta Hewitt, mother of Alec's wife, once her friend and now, for many years, an enemy.

Mrs. Canning was furious at this intrusion, but pretended to take no notice of it and began to eat her breakfast. Presently, however, she was forced to raise her eyes. Henrietta's face was hanging over the end of the bed. The body seemed to have vanished ; that long, stupid, mulish face hung solitary in the air, like a mask. It looked pinched and grey. Eyes and nose were red and the pale lips were working. A torrent of words came out of the mouth, every one of which was inaudible. Tears poured down the haggard cheeks. But no sound came to Mrs. Canning, who stared and said coldly :

" I think you will regret this."

Which she had said before at the end of their great fight years ago. And now she could hear faint snatches of words :

". . . So ill . . . my temperature is going up . . . up . . . so ill . . . cold wind . . . I can't go on . . . I can't. . . ."

" I'll make you sorry for this," cried Mrs. Canning fiercely.

Suddenly she threw a large card-case which was there. The face made a ghastly, shrill twittering noise and vanished. In an abrupt transition to the waking world she was sitting up and staring at the foot of the bed, where no face was. Morning, early sunlight, filled the room. London sparrows were making a terrific noise, twittering in the plane tree outside the window.

After a few seconds she threw off the nightmare bewilderment and realized that she had been dreaming. The clock on her dressing-table stood at a quarter to six.

She lay back on her pillows, and thought how odd a dream it was, and wished, as all dreamers do, to tell somebody about it immediately. Gradually the conviction gained upon her that this was one of her prophetic dreams. To-day she would certainly receive a visit from Henrietta, and the unlikelihood of the thing only made her the more positive. She began to be agreeably excited, already telling the story of it to her friends.

" I hadn't the least reason to suppose she was coming. I knew the Hewitts were in Switzerland. And . . . as you know . . . there is no love lost between us . . . oh, yes . . . it's all old history now . . . one tries to forget it . . . but Henrietta was unforgivable . . . she behaved abominably. . . ."

Twelve years ago Henrietta, her friend, her ally, had suddenly turned against her. She had come and said the most monstrous things, come with a card-case, too, which was the height of absurdity between intimates and co-grandmothers. The hen-witted creature must have thought that this touch of formality would give her confidence. An inveterate fidget, she kept turning it round and round in her hands as she talked, giving her antagonist a chance for a jibe.

" I see you hold all the cards," Mrs. Canning had exclaimed.

Whereat poor Henrietta had flushed and started and dropped her case on the floor. She was easily routed. But unfortunately the jibe had a double edge. She did hold all the cards. From a spate of ill-chosen, incoherent words her meaning became clear.

". . . Young people do resent interference. One must let them make their own mistakes, though, of course, Betsy has always been a very practical girl ; still, there are many occasions when I've wished she would let me advise her : that nursery-maid, for instance, I could have told her. I've had so much experience of girls from orphanages, I mean, it's only one instance, and indeed, dear Emily, you mustn't think that I don't sympathize and understand. We mothers are all the same, and it does seem very hard, because we only want to help. But, you see, in Wales there is very good bathing."

"My dear, I quite believe it. But are we talking of Wales?"

"Oh, yes. That's why I came. You see, this cottage is quite a bargain . . . right on the coast, an ideal holiday house. Betsy knows it; she's stayed there. It belongs to our friends the Aylmers. You may have met them? Dr. Aylmer, of Corpus . . ."

"They want to buy it?" interrupted Mrs. Canning sharply.

"They . . . they've bought it."

They had. And sent Henrietta with a card case to say so. They had behaved so badly that they were ashamed, and took shelter behind Betsy's imbecile mother.

None of Mrs. Canning's friends could believe their ears when they heard of it. For the whole world knew that she was planning to give them a perfect holiday house, a delightful old place in Gloucestershire. It was, in name, to be her house. She would live there, in two rooms, and run it for them; but they were to come whenever they liked, and send the children whenever the nursery party was in need of a change of air. They would have no holiday expenses and Betsy would be freed from the burdens of housekeeping, so that it was an ideal arrangement for them.

Now she learnt from Henrietta that they had never liked the plan. They wanted a cottage of their own. Of course, in a way, she had known that, but they were wrong to want it, and she had managed to ignore their tentative objections. For this reason she had hurried on the negotiations for the purchase of Marstock Hall without consulting them, hoping to have concluded the whole business before they had time to protest.

In her dismay she made a serious blunder. She said:

"They can't. It's impossible. I've bought Marstock Hall."

This was not, unfortunately, true. She had been put to great trouble and expense. She had been down to Gloucestershire several times, had paid a surveyor, and had put the Bedford Gardens house in the hands of an agent. All her friends had been apprised of her intended removal from London and had duly commented upon Alec's luck in possessing such a mother. But she had not, actually, signed any agreement, and it was still possible to withdraw from the purchase. This she was obliged, in the end, to admit. To be thus put out of countenance made her more angry than anything else could.

" Why have they sent you ? " she asked.

Henrietta explained that she had not been sent. She had come unprompted, because poor Betsy was really dreading the explanation, and it was bad for her to be upset while she was nursing dear little Daphne.

" You bully people so, Emily dear. You always have, ever since you were a child. I must say it, because I think it is having a very bad effect on Alec and Betsy. I know you mean the very best, it's only because you're fond of them, but you not only criticize people, you try to actually force them. . . . Betsy is very independent, and you can't expect Alec to put your wishes first now he's married. You spoil their happiness. . . ."

Wrath must vent itself. If no other breast is available it will plunge a dagger into its own. Mrs. Canning felt herself pass the sentinels of conscience with a fatal, light-hearted ecstasy. She was quite free. Nothing, no scruple, held her back, and she could say what she liked.

" Perhaps," she began, almost gaily, " you would like to hear some criticisms of Betsy. . . ."

" Oh, no, no . . . no, I shouldn't," protested Betsy's mother.

" I don't mean merely mine. It may surprise you to know that I'm not the only person who considers her very conceited and very selfish. In fact most of our friends . . . please don't imagine that everybody thinks Alec as lucky as you do. She's hopelessly spoilt. You've allowed her to grow up with a fantastic idea of her own importance. Of course she's very pretty, and, being her father's daughter, people have made much of her. But . . ."

" Oh dear, oh dear," wailed Henrietta, bowing under the storm. " I knew you'd be very angry, Emily. I'm sure I don't wonder. It's so disappointing for you, and they ought to have been firmer . . ."

" I'm not angry," Emily asserted, " I merely feel you ought to know."

Conscious of frantic folly, but entirely delivered into the hands of her bad angel, she repeated every unkind thing which she had ever heard about her daughter-in-law.

" . . . and as for May Cameron, who is quite devoted to you and Arthur, I can assure you that, when she heard of the engagement, she was in despair. She said to me, quite candidly : ' Alec is much too good for her. His whole life will be sacrificed.' I said : ' Oh, she'll improve.' And May said : ' No. The conceit is too ingrained. They've taught that girl to regard herself as something infinitely rare and precious. She'll always regard him as a sort of Prince Consort.' "

" May Cameron . . . said that ? " gasped Henrietta.

Wrath was satisfied by Henrietta's sick, heart-shattered look. The wound had been dealt and the giddy frenzy subsided. Mrs. Canning had got what she wanted, if to give pain had really been her desire. Henrietta was creeping away.

Something else must be said—something that would bring them back from the timeless regions of passion to the actual occasion. The interview should end on some calm and rational pronouncement. She said, as they parted :

" I think you will regret this."

So Henrietta went home, grievously wounded, but with an unsullied conscience. She had been quite honest, quite sincere, in her attempt to speak out. No malice had inspired her ; she only wished to do her duty. To forgive

May Cameron had seemed at first impossible, and, in great indignation, she had told her husband so. But he had convinced her that this was unreasonable. Betsy, he said, was extremely conceited. A fault which had long been obvious to her parents could hardly be overlooked by their friends. Had Henrietta never criticized the Cameron girls? Had she not frequently commented upon their thick ankles and their tendency to acne? Would not May Cameron resent this if she knew? Thus he induced her to forgive her friend. She did so, felt a great deal happier, began to be more sorry than ever for poor Emily, and forgot the whole incident.

Emily Canning fared worse, for her conscience could not help her. She, who had lied about Marstock Hall, who had recklessly betrayed many confidences, could not forget so easily. Moreover, she had nobody to tell her that she was being unreasonable. Her partisan friends were violently indignant on her behalf. But nobody could comfort her, or know how sorry she was to think that she had said such cruel things to Henrietta.

And now no ordinary justice could redress the balance between them. Only what she called poetic justice, by which she meant some unexpected turn of events which should prove that she had been, after all, in the right. She had said that they would regret it. If ever they showed signs of doing so, if ever they were forced to come to her for help or advice, that would be poetic justice.

I only wanted to devote my whole life to them, she thought. But they aren't grateful. They won't let me. . . . I'm so very lonely. They don't seem to think of that.

A heavy footstep passed her doorway and went down the stairs.

Maggie, she thought, glancing again at the clock.

Time had passed. It was after seven.

Lazy old thing! She thinks I shan't know how late she is. I'll go down and tickle her up.

*   *   *   *   *

This maid and mistress adored one another and squabbled continually. Maggie was doing the hall. When she heard Mrs. Canning's door open she stuck out her lower lip and resolved instantly not to be tickled up. A slight skirmish before breakfast was not unusual, for Emily Canning was a bad sleeper, woke early, and was bored unless she could be up and doing.

" Good morning, Maggie ! " came a voice from the top of the stairs.

" Good morning'm."

The two old women eyed one another warily. Maggie was sixty-five, fat, rosy and asthmatic. Her mistress, though three years older, had retained a slim and girlish grace. In this dim light she might have been taken for quite a young woman. A white dressing gown wrapped her softly, and her face was just a pale triangle in which her green eyes flashed with an unquenchable fire. A black chenille net hid the tell-tale grey of her hair.

She opened fire :

" I suppose it's because you are late this morning that you ruin my nice floor. Just look how streaky the polish is ! "

" It's the mop," said Maggie. " They go like that when they're worn out."

" It was new in the spring."

" No'm. Excuse me. Not new it wasn't. You got it at the St. Mary Abbott's jumble."

" You put on too much polish."

" I have to. The more wore out it is, the more polish I have to put on. And then again, the more polish I put on the more wore out it gets."

Mrs. Canning lost time while she wondered if this was true. Maggie nipped in with an indulgent offer of a cup of tea. . . .

" I've been awake a long time," said Mrs. Canning. " I . . ."

She remembered her dream and realized that she must

put it immediately on record. Horrid old Maggie had shown signs of disbelief, occasionally, when she boasted of her own supernatural powers. If she mentioned this dream and it came true, as she was sure it would, there would be an end to that nonsense. The question of the mop could be shelved.

" Mrs. Hewitt may be coming here to-day," she said briskly. " Possibly to breakfast. Have we any bacon ? "

Maggie, who also knew that the Hewitts were in Switzerland, controlled her countenance with some difficulty.

" Yes'm," she said. " Four rashers."

" I have had such a vivid dream that I feel sure there is something in it. She is on her way to see me."

" Yes'm."

" Oh, Maggie ! You are an odious woman, really. I do think you might be a little bit surprised."

" I'm ever so surprised."

" I know you don't believe in my dreams. But you will admit that it will be very strange if she really does come this morning."

" Very strange indeed, 'm."

" You'll admit there's something in it ? "

" I never said there was nothing in it," declared Maggie. " But I do say that you add on to it afterwards. . . ."

The front door bell rang and she moved away down the hall to answer it. Mrs. Canning, scuttling up the stairs out of sight, remained listening.

She could hear Maggie removing the door chain which was put up at night. Now the door was open. There was a mumble of talk. Somebody was being ushered into the house.

" She's been expecting you, 'm," Maggie was saying.

Mrs. Canning gave a little excited skip. She was psychic ! She was ! This proved it. This would make a wonderful tale.

Peeping over the bannisters she saw Henrietta's mule face in the hall, exactly as she had dreamt of it, except that it was now surmounted by a sad-looking hat. All resentment, all memory of old injuries, vanished for the moment. She flew down the stairs, full of kindly welcome, and so pleased with herself, so overjoyed that she had trusted to her instinct and prophesied to Maggie. Now she had a witness, and Maggie would have to eat humble pie. Oh, she was pleased with herself. Dear Henrietta ! But how ill . . . how frightfully ill. . . .

" Emily ! Don't come very near me. I've got influenza."

" Oh, you poor thing ! "

" My temperature has been going up all night. I won't stay. . . . I'm going to a nursing home. It's the only thing. You remember that place in Devonshire Street where Arthur went when he had his operation, very conveniently there was a telephone in my bedroom at the hotel so I rang them up, but I had to see you, I couldn't talk to you over the telephone, you never feel it's really private. I can't go on. I can't go to Wales. The Paddington Hotel it was ; I went straight there when I got to London last night because I meant to catch the 11.5 this morning. Keep well away. You might put a handkerchief over your face with disinfectant. Of course it may not be catching, only a chill. The beds were very damp in Switzerland."

Henrietta had sunk down upon a chair in the hall. She kept waving the other two away, refusing to go upstairs into the drawing-room.

" I'd better not move about much," she explained.

Fever had made her a little light-headed. But at last they got her on to the drawing-room sofa, and Maggie went off to make a cup of tea. She would not, even then, explain herself until Mrs. Canning had sprinkled lysol over a large handkerchief and put it on as a kind of mask. This was annoying.

What guys we both look, thought Emily. But I can make it sound very funny when I tell it. And I dreamt

about the temperature. Yes, I did. But I forgot to tell Maggie, idiot that I was. Now she'll say that I've added it on afterwards.

Then, as Henrietta babbled on about going to Wales, a sudden fear snatched at her heart.

" The most dreadful thing. . . . I rushed back by the next train. . . ."

" Henrietta ! Are they hurt ? Are they ill ? Is anyone . . ."

" No, no, nothing *dreadful.*"

This distinction was perfectly clear to Mrs. Canning, who once more prepared to enjoy herself. But, as Maggie came in with the tea at that moment, she thought that she had better chalk up her score as a prophetess.

" I knew you were coming. You appeared to me in a dream last night. I told Maggie. Didn't I, Maggie ? "

" What ? " asked Henrietta plaintively. " I can't hear you inside that handkerchief."

" I dreamt you were coming."

" How odd ! Do keep that handkerchief over your mouth. I can hear if you speak distinctly."

As soon as Maggie had left them Henrietta came to the point.

" They say they're going to be divorced."

" Oh ! What ? Not divorced ? It's not true ! "

" Yes ! Yes ! Betsy wrote and told me."

" But why ? Why ? Is it because of that Mrs. Thing ? She can't ! Not after all these years. She must have known. She must have condoned it."

" Mrs. Thing ? "

" Mrs. Adams."

" Who is . . . oh, I see. I didn't know her name. Betsy didn't mention it."

" Then it is because of her ? "

" No. Not altogether. It was a very great shock to me. I knew nothing about it, not a word."

" Really, Henrietta ?   But everyone knows.   It's been going on for ages."

" I think it's dreadful for Betsy.   Surely you don't . . ."

" Of course I don't.   I blame Alec very much for it. But one can't interfere, can one ? "

This little dig was lost upon Henrietta who merely said :

" I suppose not.   Mrs. Adams . . . what . . . what sort of person . . . ? "

" I've only seen her once," said Mrs. Canning.   " She was pointed out to me at the theatre.   Very young, very fair, and as hard as nails.   They tell me she's a wanton creature.   There are plenty of others besides Alec.   But she made up her mind to get him and got him.   It was on her side rather than his.   He could have been kept out of it perfectly well, if only Betsy . . ."

" But he wants to marry her."

" Good heavens !   He can't.   How awful.   Henrietta ! It must be stopped.   He mustn't be allowed to do anything so frantic.   Does Betsy say . . . what does she say exactly ? "

Mrs. Hewitt felt her head go round.   Her throat was so sore that she could scarcely speak.   To remember what, exactly, Betsy had said became more and more difficult. She fumbled in her handbag and found the letter, and then, while she was looking for her glasses, Emily took it away. A faint misgiving assailed her, for she half remembered that Betsy had not written very kindly about Alec's mother.   But she was too ill to protest.   If Emily would read the letter it might be better.   There would then be quite an interval when no speech, or thought, or effort would be demanded.   One could lie back and suffer.

Her malady seemed to advance in definite stages, like a car changing gear.   All night, while she lay tossing and debating, she had been unbearably hot.   Now she was cold.   She had never been so cold.

A voice reached her ear. She opened her eyes once more to look at the mobbed head of Emily. An angry, impatient voice came out from behind the handkerchief.

" This is all nonsense. It's as plain as a pikestaff. He doesn't want the divorce. It's she . . . she's persuaded him . . ."

" You think so ? "

" Indeed I do. There's something behind all this. Something she doesn't care to admit. She talks of being free to lead her own life with her friends . . . oh, she's going to get more out of it than that. She's talked him into it. He's so weak, poor Alec."

" But it must be stopped," wailed Mrs. Hewitt, who had begun to shiver violently.

" Certainly it must. Do they know you are coming ? "

" Yes, I wired. But I can't possibly go. I . . . you . . . must wire again. . . ."

" That's all right. Don't worry, Henrietta. Leave it all to me."

The triumph in Mrs. Canning's voice rang out unmistakably, through the handkerchief. She could not but see the hand of Providence in all this. For poor Henrietta would have been quite the wrong person to deal with such a situation. She would most certainly have made a mess of it. She would have argued with Alec and Betsy, uniting them against her by tackling them together, when the obvious stratagem would be to divide them. This plan of a divorce was the outcome of some friendly agreement... Therefore, they must be made to quarrel. Alec must be provoked into such resentment that he would refuse to give his wife her freedom. He had been talked into it, probably, against his better judgment. As soon as one knew what was behind it all, what Betsy was really after, he could be talked out of it. Did Alec know ? Had she been quite candid with him ? If she had not, and he found it out . . .

Whatever it is, thought Mrs. Canning, I'll find it out. I'll show her up.

She looked at her suffering companion who was now in the throes of a severe rigor. I think you will regret this, she had said, and she was right. All this came of letting Betsy get so spoilt. This, she thought, is Poetic Justice.

THE WIFE

BETSY stood in the hall, staring ruefully at her mother's telegram. It should not, surely, have taken so long to come, even from Switzerland. *Expect me Wales Wednesday evening.* Now it was Wednesday morning. In eight hours' time—in less—the battle would begin.

Deeply did she now regret that most premature letter. She had written it in order to avoid just this very thing— an immediate invasion of protesting kinsfolk. Her parents were to be abroad for the whole of the Long Vacation, and she had counted upon their reluctance, so irritating upon other occasions, to make any change in their plans. They might be expected to write, frequently and at length, but it had seemed unlikely that they would become seriously troublesome before the autumn, when their advice would be too late. That, as she had explained to Alec, was why he had to desert her in the month of August, when nobody was at hand to interfere.

But she should have waited until he was actually out of the house. It was bad enough that everything had been postponed, and that an unexpected consignment of work from Johnnie Graham had forced him to cancel his yachting trip, so that he was not going, after all, to desert her for at least three weeks. To have him hanging round Pandy Madoc would be a sore trial to her nerves. Most likely his resolution would weaken and he would begin again to say that he did not want to be divorced. There would be more arguments, more scenes. All her hard work must be done over again, for she had only just screwed him up to it, and had counted upon getting the

23

thing done quickly. He was so lazy, so lethargic. He shirked any kind of effort or decision. He had admitted that he ought to go, and that she had a right to her freedom. It was pure laziness which had made him so reluctant to take the necessary steps. And now her mother was coming to encourage him, to give him any number of reasons for remaining inert.

She could not think what to do. She had a slight headache and there was so much to be done that she could not begin. She just stood there, folding the telegram into little strips, like a fan.

Light, pouring in from the open front door, lay in a triangle on the black and white squares of the hall, turning white to a creamy yellow. Outside it was blue and hot : one of those timeless days when there are no shadows, and gulls hover motionless over a sea which remains, hour upon hour, at half tide. It was a day to lie on the beach and hear the lazy mew of a gull, the indolent flop of a wave, and see the horizon lost in a shimmering haze ; not a day to think and scheme and bustle, but just to lie in the sun, and lie in the sun, and go into the sea, and feel cool water on warm flesh, and come out, and feel the hot sun on cool flesh, and lie dreaming until time came back with the shadows. Outside the house it was that sort of day. But not inside, where so much had to be done. In every room a clock was ticking. Do this ! Do that ! Hurry ! Make up your mind ! So that she never dared to stop, not for a minute.

It's not fair, she thought.

It never had been. All her life the essential unfairness of things had oppressed her. As a child she had complained of it loudly ; it had seemed so monstrous that no impartial scheme of justice, no natural law, existed which should ensure that Betsy Hewitt got her rights. She still felt it to be monstrous, though she had learnt to keep the sentiment to herself. Not Alec, not her mother, not anybody in particular, but life had betrayed her. Now she was thirty-seven and she had never known real happiness. She had been cheated. Life had left her always hungry, always craving for something and unable to put a name to it. She was perpetually craving for something that never happened. She looked forward to events, they happened, they were past, and it was as if nothing at all had occurred. Experience evaded her. Never once had she lived in the moment, never captured that eternal instant between the past and the future which is now.

This was surely unfair, for she had done nothing to deserve it. She had been at the greatest pains to safeguard her own happiness. Ever since her early teens, when she first realized that unlucky people are seldom interesting, she had made up her mind to be fortunate. She had then resolved to make no mistakes ; to be healthy, popular, solvent and well treated. And so, on the whole, she was. Good luck had attended her. Childbirth did not hurt her nearly as much as it seemed to hurt most of her friends. Her cooks did not give notice, her water pipes never froze, her children were seldom ailing, and she was always able to pay her bills. The friction between Alec and herself might have developed into tragedy had she allowed it to do so. But she had not ; she had been fair and sensible. So that if ever anybody deserved to be happy it was she, who had taken such care to avoid misfortune.

Complacency upheld her. As long as she could remain very busy she was satisfied. But if ever she paused, even for a moment, complacency would vanish and she would once more know herself to be cheated. Happiness, always promised for to-morrow, never far from yesterday, found no lodging in her heart. It was not fair.

Still, she did not know what she wanted, unless it was to go out and lie in the sun instead of being so busy. Nobody else had such a burden to bear. Alec was happy, and the children, and the maids. They did not have to think and plan and order a car to meet the London train that afternoon. Only she, upon whom they all depended, must be kept so active and so restless that now she was thirty-seven, would soon be forty, would soon be dead, without ever getting her rights.

A child was running on the gravel outside, heavily thudding up the drive. It could not be Kenneth or Daphne, for they ran lightly; it must be Eliza, who was going through an awkward stage which no Eurhythmics, no course at the Ballet School, could mitigate. Presently she came clattering into the house like a young bullock, and Betsy's irritation rose a point.

" I can't think," she complained, " how you can manage to make such a noise in sand-shoes. Really your feet might be made of—of granite."

Eliza halted abruptly and scowled at her feet. They annoyed her quite as much as they annoyed her mother. The whole of her body annoyed her. She could neither control nor ignore it, and of late it had rapidly changed for the worse. It grew more conspicuous every day. It stuck out behind so that she was forbidden to wear shorts any more. It stuck out in front so that all her jerseys were too tight. Indelicate grown-up people did not hesitate to call attention to this. They would look significantly at her chest and say that she had shot up. Shot out was what they meant. Nor was it any comfort to know that these and other disgusting, humiliating changes were a step towards womanhood. They felt like a step away from it. Nobody, shackled with such a body, could hope to achieve any poise or assurance. Many grown women could wear shorts without looking ridiculous. Her mother did not stick out anywhere, nor did Joy Benson, the holiday governess. Nobody in the whole of Wales had a body like Eliza's.

" If you would only run on your toes . . ."

" I do. Is our lunch ready ? "

" How should I know ? Surely you can see to that for yourselves ! If you want sandwiches, go and cut them."

" What are the maids for ? "

Their glances met and clashed. Frequently, and for
no obvious reason, they were opposed to one another.
Betsy would feel that this awkward, swarthy child did not
belong to her any more, was alien both in body and spirit,
and could never have been the dear little baby whom she
had once borne and nursed. Eliza, half aware of this,
was exasperated by all her mother's superior advantages,
her authority, her quick mind and sharp tongue, her slim
elegance, all of which seemed to separate them. Yet they
were more alike than they realized. Eliza, twenty years
hence, would be the image of Betsy. Her mouth was
larger, her eyes a deeper grey, and her brows straight, not
delicately arched. But she was her mother's daughter.

" The maids," said Betsy, " have plenty to do without
waiting on you children. You'll get your own sandwiches."

" Oh, all right. Just as you say."

" Precisely, my child. This happens to be my house."

" Oh, is it ? I thought it was father's."

" Then don't behave as if it was yours."

Eliza hunched her shoulders with a jerk.

" Is that," asked Betsy, " meant to be an airy shrug ? "

It was, and Eliza collapsed. She was no match for her
mother.

" Run along, dear. You are all going down to the
beach for the day aren't you ? You'll find a loaf and a
knife in the kitchen."

Eliza did not run, nor did she go to the kitchen. She
went upstairs very slowly, kicking the stair-rods all the way.

Betsy, watching her, remembered to be just and sensible.
She remained luckier than most mothers. For all girls
go through this stage, more or less, and many have spotty
faces, which Eliza had not.

That nice, clear, brown skin is a great blessing, she
thought. It's the only thing she's got from me, poor
child. And egotism at that age isn't incurable. One was
an egotist oneself . . .

Now here was Kenneth coming in and, in his turn, demanding sandwiches. Her face grew kind and tender ; she had a glance for him which belonged to nobody else in the world. She could not look at him or hear him speak without a pang of pleasure. For Kenneth had never changed or grown away from her. He was still her baby, her firstborn, her bright and lovely boy.

" You lazy little things," she protested. " Why can't you cut your own sandwiches ! "

" Because we are spoilt, Mrs. C. That's why. Somebody always cuts them for us."

" Well, to-day you'll cut them yourselves."

" What's the matter ? Why have you got your warpath face on ? What's that telegram ? "

He was eager with sympathy, but he did not wait for an answer. His friend, Mark Hannay, called to him, out in the garden, and he rushed away, shouting.

But he saw I was upset, she thought. So loving ! How can one's children be so different ? He's a great comfort to me. A comfort ? What for ? I'm not unhappy. Only slightly worried. This telegram . . . oh, damn !

THE HUSBAND

PANDY MADOC, the old mill cottage which the Cannings had bought from Dr. Aylmer, had lent its name to the new house. For Alec had secured several acres of hill-side, above the mill, and, when he grew rich, built lavishly. In one of his disastrous spasms of good-nature he gave a free hand to a friend, an architect who needed a job. Neither he nor Betsy liked the result. Their new house was modern, roomy and commodious, but they both thought it ugly. It had the bleakness of a sanatorium; the flat roofs, all at different levels, suggested beds for consumptives. It seemed to consist entirely of windows, grudgingly connected by meagre intervals of fabric, which they had painted a deep ochre, to tone with the bracken and gorse of the hill-side. But by no device could they make it look like part of the landscape.

The garden went up in steep terraces, and there were no trees, save in the deep ravine where the stream ran which had once turned the mill. The main road skirted the base of the slope, running close to the sea, and a drive circled down from the house to join it. Here at the bottom were more buildings, also painted yellow, a garage, a power-house and the old mill cottage. High up the hill, on the topmost terrace, stood the garden house where Alec was supposed to work.

To this retreat he would ascend, directly after breakfast, but he seldom actually began to work until at least an hour later. The interval was spent in a condition which he described as starting up. Only very gradually could he bring himself to face the formidable effort of invention. First he must smoke a pipe, sharpen a few pencils, read the newspaper, and sometimes do part of a cross-word puzzle. This was the moment when it was most likely that he would answer letters. In the need to postpone that first disgusting plunge, he would snatch at the dullest occupation. Yet at some time in the morning he would come to grips with his task. Before the afternoon, words of a kind would be scribbled on a page which had been blank.

Johnnie Graham's new score lay scattered about the room. In all their productions they had worked upon the same plan. They would settle the plot and the scenario together. Then Graham would go away and write music which he sent piecemeal to Alec, who concocted words so apt, so smoothly married to the tunes, that most people imagined the librettist to have inspired the composer. In actual fact he could do nothing unless Johnnie had done something first ; it was Johnnie's creation that set him off. He would accept no work unless Graham was to partner him, but the demand for their joint productions was sufficient to keep them both very busy.

They had been friends all their lives. They had been in Palestine together during the War, and afterwards they had worked in the same department of the Civil Service. It was not until they were both past thirty that they had begun to exploit their combined talent for profit or to regard it as their profession. Alec admired Johnnie immensely. He would exclaim with delight and wonder when a new score arrived. Johnnie, on the other hand, admired nobody, not even himself. At school he had been a dreary little boy with chilblains. Success and fame had not improved his circulation or raised his spirits. Nobody could discover whence came the grace and gaiety which transfused his work, or imagine the state of existence into which he must retire when composing. He brought no enthusiasm back with him from those airy regions, and never commented upon Alec's contribution unless he wanted to change something. Silence was his only form of praise.

In the spring they had discussed a new light opera on Byron in Venice. When Alec first suggested the idea, Johnnie showed more eagerness than usual. He said :

" Unpleasant fellow, Byron ! " and added, with a faint relish, " he'll do very well."

" He can be treated as a romantic figure," Alec pointed out.

" What ? Same thing. Better put it in Venice. Fat, he was, by the time he'd got to Venice. Gives you more choice of singers."

" I'd thought of putting in Lady Caroline——"

" No, no, no ! You don't want too much story. It's a bore. We'll have a carnival or something, and a girl dressed up as a boy—ugh ! A silly girl . . . a virgin . . ."

" Why dressed as a boy ? "

" They like it. And then another woman, older, in petticoats, a wanton. They all get mixed up. Misunderstandings. Everybody behaves very well, though. They forgive and renounce and all that. Girl doesn't lose her honour—ugh ! Marries an honest gondolier. . . . Byron sets out for Greece, or goes off with the wanton. We'll settle which later. Ugh ! "

" It sounds like something I've heard before," objected Alec.

" Oh, no, no ! I don't think so. No, it won't."

Johnnie meant that his part of it would not. For Alec's part he cared less than nothing.

They had agreed to write it in the autumn, but Johnnie's Muse took hold of him before that, and the first act arrived at Pandy Madoc in the beginning of August with a request that Alec should get to work immediately. Such a change of plan was not convenient, but Johnnie, who had always ruled their collaborations, could not bear to be kept waiting

when once he had begun.   Alec read the score and found,
as usual, that it had set him off.   The rubbishy plot
began to assume a shape entirely of its own.   He could
do something with it, and his yachting expedition must be
cancelled.

He liked work, though he loathed effort.   The two were
separable in his mind.   He liked the idea of his task whenever he was not actually engaged upon it.   But there was
something indecent, to his mind, about the labour involved.
Deep below the surface of his thought, in some obscene
tarn, lay the words, the ideas, that he wanted.   He would
send down a line and haul them up, and it was the process
of hauling which he found so indecent.   For hours together
his line would come up empty.   Sometimes it brought up
rubbish, and sometimes it became entangled with the scum
on the top of the pond.   Both rubbish and scum were
deceptive ; they could often resemble a genuine catch.
But, if he persisted, the right object would come up in
the end.   He knew it to be right, though it surprised him,
though he had never seen it before.

Once landed upon the bank, it was no longer indecent.
He could shape and polish the bright treasure and assign
to it its proper place.   There were days when he did no
hauling at all, but spent his time disposing of yesterday's
catch.   And there were other days when the exertion of
hauling became too intolerable and he fell back upon the
rubbish, faking it as he had learnt to do and incorporating
chunks of it into his fabric.   This he did without com-
punction, for otherwise the work would never be finished,
and nobody seemed to notice the difference.   Only if too
much fake was included in his script there was a danger
that Johnnie might send it all back with a large " NO "
scrawled across it.

To-day was to be a hauling day.   The idea so disgusted
him that he even thought of writing a nice long letter to
his mother.   He would have to write to her some day soon,
and tell her that he was going to be divorced.   A divorce

seemed to be very like a marriage in many ways ; relations
would be hurt unless they were warned of it beforehand.
But it was too soon to write about that, and he could not
think of anything else to say. So he gave up the idea, and
wrote instead to one or two people who had asked for his
autograph. Then he went on to the terrace to smoke a
last pipe.

Already the sun was almost too fierce. A light haze
lay on the sea, hiding the mighty curve of Cardigan Bay.
Some little breeze must haunt the upper air, for the pine
trees behind the garden house were sighing softly, but no
breath of it touched the terrace. He sat on the hot stones
of the wall, as happy as a lizard.

The machine in the power house, down by the mill, was
working away for dear life. Chuff ! Chuff ! it said,
Chuff ! Chuff ! It reminded him of a certain type of
woman. Betsy was like that, and his mother too. Admirable creatures ! Happy as long as they could be in a bustle.
Upstairs and downstairs they went, chuff-chuffing away, in a
manner which he had found irritating when he was younger.
But he had learnt, long ago, to remain aloof, to disregard it.

Now there was Betsy chuff-chuffing out of the house on
some errand of life or death. She was making for the
terrace steps, as though she might be coming up to the
garden house. This meant a real emergency, for she never
disturbed him when he was supposed to be at work. He
was going to be asked to do something or other, or even,
which was worse, to give an opinion. He grew apprehensive.

But a respite was promised in the person of Mrs. Lloyd,
the rector's wife, who now approached round the curve of
the drive. Betsy was forced to turn back. He hoped
that they would go into the house and remain there for a
long time, chuff-chuffing together. They remained, however, in the drive. Mrs. Lloyd, by the look of her, was
asking for something and Betsy was expressing a desire to
oblige. Neither listened to the other ; they were too busy

saying the same thing over and over again in different words.

And now all the children surged out of the house, carrying bathing towels and luncheon baskets. They clustered round Betsy, pelting her with demands, And Mrs. Lloyd was saying to be sure, how much they had grown. She must be saying it in some particularly annoying way, for they were staring at the ground, and kicking the gravel about in a frenzy of embarrassment. Mark Hannay, their young guest, stood a little apart, pinching the buds on the fuschia bushes, and pretending not to hear. At last Betsy released them. She settled their demands and they plunged off down the hill by the steep path through the garden. But now the two women must say, all over again, everything that they had already said. Alec could never quite make out how many times a woman has to repeat herself in order to express the measure of her goodwill. But one thing was clear to him. This repetition was a kind of politeness. To say a thing once, and once only, was impossible except when speaking to inferiors.

The children were at the bottom of the hill. They darted across the road, climbed a stile, and sped away over the fields towards the sand dunes and the sea. They had fallen into their natural order, the two girls in front, the two boys behind.

Betsy and Mrs. Lloyd were approaching their coda. They had begun to move, or rather, Betsy had, just a little, so as to encourage her companion. Neither wished to be standing there. All business between them had been transacted long ago and each had a thousand things to do. But to part was apparently the hardest thing in the world. Inch by inch they edged themselves asunder, still talking. In another minute poor Betsy would think that she was free.

But she would be mistaken. A fresh infliction was in store for her. A strange, squat figure had emerged from the fuschia bushes—Frau Bloch, from the cottage at the bottom of the hill. She was waiting with a meek per-secuted air, until Betsy should notice her. In spite of the blazing sun she wore her fur coat. Nobody had ever seen her without it, and the Cannings supposed it to be the coat in which she stood up when she and her family escaped from Hitler.

Alec could not see Betsy's face, when, having got rid of Mrs. Lloyd, she turned to deal with a fresh demand. But he was amused to observe that, this time, there was far less repetition. They were not trying to be polite. Betsy hated the Blochs, who were not sufficiently grateful for the loan of a cottage and who were always coming up to complain of it. He could hardly blame her ; they were unpleasant people and he could not think how it was that he had ever come to offer them shelter. Bloch ought to have seen that he was drunk when he did so, and should not have held him to it.

Betsy had, as usual, the right to be annoyed, for it was her custom, in the summer, to use the cottage as a kind of annexe for guests. Now she found herself unexpectedly short of space and at any moment Frau Bloch was liable to come plunging out of the fuschia bushes, like some uncouth, furry beast, growling the news that " the frying pot vos brunt." Betsy had to stoop to hear what she said. A few brief exchanges disposed of the matter. The fur coat vanished into the bushes and Betsy straightened herself again.

But she did not immediately bustle off to deal with the next problem. Something seemed to have brought her to a standstill. Some emanation of bewilderment and despair reached Alec as he observed her, and he was aware of a pity which he had felt before, when looking on at her activities. He knew quite well that she was not happy, that she did not really enjoy all this busy bustle. He knew that she wanted to pause and that she needed someone who could make her drop it, stop it, be quiet. That he had never done so was his worst failure as a husband.

He had never tried. Mockingly, affectionately, he had always let her go her own way. With her, as with his mother, he had taken the line of least resistance. To be indulgent and easy going was, in him, not a virtue but a vice. He had never sincerely tackled the problem of their relationship or tried to rule her when she needed guidance. Yet he had once loved her, passionately, and was still very fond of her. The knowledge of her essential frustration could not but trouble him.

When, at last, she began to climb the terrace steps, he obeyed his better self and called down to her :

" Want me ? I'll come ! "

He rose from his wall. But she waved a letter or something and called out that she wanted to come up and talk. There was no point in going down only to climb up again. He re-seated himself and watched her zig-zag course from terrace to terrace up the hill. It was a pity that the first line of *Byron* should, just at that moment, have leaped out of the tarn. But that was always the way. At any sure approach of an interruption the fish would begin to rise as they never did when he wanted them.

" What did Ma Bloch want ? " he asked, when she joined him.

" Oh . . . the brutes have fused all their electric lights. Let's go inside. I'm getting sunstroke."

They went into the cool of the garden room and he glanced, with a pang, at the score lying scattered over the table. Just then he felt that he could have sat down and written something without any pain or grief at all. But that gleaming fish had vanished. Such treasures can never be captured twice.

" My mother is coming."

He dragged his mind away from that lost opening, and looked at the telegram which she proffered. She told her story warily, alert lest he should laugh at her for having brought all this on herself. But good nature is a virtue as well as a vice, and he was kind.

" It's a frightful bore," he agreed. " But I don't see that we can stop her coming now, do you ? "

" She's coming to argue with us. She wants to stop the divorce."

" If she does we'll tell her to shut up. We'll say nothing is decided, and she'll only do harm if she tries to poke her nose in. Only we'll put it more nicely."

" Oh, but," said Betsy quickly, " that wouldn't be true. We have decided, haven't we ? It's only postponed for three weeks, isn't it ? "

He hesitated. The prospect of this divorce was most distasteful to him. He had not the slightest wish for it. But Betsy had. She believed quite mistakenly, as he thought, that she would be happier. He knew that she would merely go on chuff-chuffing all by herself, getting worse as she grew older and wondering what was amiss.

" Haven't we decided ? " she asked again. " Haven't we agreed that it's the only thing to do ? "

" Ye—es. Since I can't manage to be a better husband.' This he said more to himself than to her.

" Oh, Alec ! I never said that you were a bad husband."

" But I am."

She smiled, pleased that he should say so, though she would never allow anybody else to suggest such a thing.

" And I . . ." she said, " have been a bad wife."

A good husband, he thought, would have ruled her. That would have been hard work, too hard for him. It would have meant concentration, struggle, a continual exercise of understanding and sympathy.

He had no doubt of his own superiority. He knew himself to be more reasonable, more equitable, to have a greater desire for integrity and a clearer mind. It was he, and not she, who should have directed their joint lives. But he doubted his power to assert all this. She was too nearly his equal, too civilized and sensitive. He could not rule her brutally, as though she had been an animal or a slave. And to direct her in any other way would exhaust the whole of his mind and spirit. Life was not long enough to attempt such a thing.

Yet he had married her and had undertaken thereby to cherish her, to be responsible for her happiness.

" It's been entirely my fault," he said slowly. " I'm so damned lazy. That's what's wrong."

" You can't change your nature now, at your time of life. And besides . . . even if you did try, even if you gave her up, do you think we'd get on any better ? "

He stared at her. What on earth . . . oh, good God ! She meant Chris Adams. She was thinking of his adultery, a thing so irrelevant that he had forgotten all about it.

" You'd much better marry her, really Alec. You'd probably be a good husband to her."

" My dear child, do get this into your head. I shall never marry Chris. I don't want to. She wouldn't have me if I did. She's got a husband of her own who suits her very well."

" He's a horrid man. Everybody says so."

" Besides, I've told you. It's all finished. She's gone to California. I don't suppose I'll ever see her again. It's been over for months."

" I just can't understand how you can have let her go out of your life like that. If you loved her . . ."

" I didn't. Love had nothing to do with it, ever."

That was a thing which she always refused to believe. It would have made everything so much easier if only Alec had genuinely and sincerely loved Mrs. Adams. Then he would have been asking for a divorce.

Betsy sighed, and sank wearily down upon the window seat.

" You know," said Alec, " you're tired out. That's what you are. In no state to make such an important decision. You get no peace here. Everything is on top of you, the children and the maids and the Blochs. . . .

No wonder you think you want a divorce. How can we make up our minds in such a hurly burly ? If we could get off quietly somewhere, and talk things over . . . why ? What's the matter ? "

She was leaning out of the window as if something had caught her attention.

" I thought I heard someone on the terrace. Oh ! It's Emil Bloch ! I do wish they wouldn't come up here. We never offered them the whole garden."

" He's not coming in ? " asked Alec apprehensively.

" No. He's going down the hill."

She watched the narrow, dark head of their guest as it vanished below the terrace, and added :

" I believe he was listening."

" Oh, I don't think he'd do that. Did you hear what I was saying ? "

" If my mother comes, where on earth am I to put her ? There's no room, with the Blochs at the cottage. You'll have to sleep up here, Alec. I'll have to put her in the spare room and Mark in your room."

" All right. Put away. Did you hear what I said ? "

" Of course I did."

" Then answer me. I may be a bad husband, but you have one shocking fault. I say something and you reply about something quite different. What did I say ? "

" That I ought to get away on my own and be quiet. I quite agree. I've thought so for years. But I don't very well see how it can be managed."

" Why not ? "

" Well . . . it's in the middle of the holidays."

" It's always something."

" How can I possibly go off by myself in the middle . . ."

" I don't mean by yourself. I mean with me."

" With you ? "

" We've never really . . . I've never . . . don't you think before we decide, that we ought to try, very hard, to understand one another. To get at the root of what's

been wrong and see if we can't do something ?   I feel I've
got a lot 1 want to say ; but it needs thinking out, and I
can't say it here.   Your mother would run the house and
look after the children."

" You mean go off now ?   Immediately ?   But what
about your work ?   I thought Johnnie said . . ."

" Oh, Johnnie can go to hell.   This is more important."

His eagerness took her by surprise.   She felt, for the
first time, that he wanted to keep her, that he valued her.
In their previous arguments she had felt that he merely
disliked the idea of a change.   She did not, for a moment,
know what to say.   To give herself time she assumed a
mulish expression.

" In fact," said Alec firmly, " I'm not going to agree to
this divorce unless you do."

" But we do understand one another.   There's nothing
more to say."

" I've got a lot more to say."

She wavered, feeling tired and weak.   He saw that he
had impressed her and that he must be quick to seize an
advantage.

" Take a day off and come down with me to the beach.
We'll settle what to do there.   You'll face your mother
much better after a restful day and a long bathe."

" Oh, I can't.   I've got so much to do."

" Don't do it."

" That's easy for you to say.   But . . ."

" I really mean this, dear.   I shan't agree to the divorce
unless I'm sure that you're in a fit condition to make up
your mind.   You aren't now.   You won't be t'll you've
had a rest.   So the sooner you'll agree to knock off, the
sooner we shall get the thing settled."

She protested feebly for a little while, and then gave in.
At the bottom of her heart she felt a twinge of curiosity :
she wanted to know what all these new things were, that
he was so anxious to say.

" I'll tell them to pack us some lunch," she said.

" Good.   We'll start in ten minutes."

She nodded and left him.   Outside, as she went down the garden, he heard her calling imperiously :

" Joy !   Joy ! "

THE PROTÉGÉE

A LONG legged, lovely creature came bounding up the hill. This was Joy Benson, who came with them to Wales every summer. Betsy paid her a pound a week for being a sort of holiday governess and handy girl ; it was not an agreeable situation, but she needed the money, for she had an invalid mother to support. For the rest of the year she taught at a Kindergarten in a provincial town. The Hewitts had known her father, years ago, and it was they who had paid for her education. They had been astonishingly generous.

Though undemonstrative, she had given nobody any reason to suppose that she was not appropriately grateful. Betsy, having known her from birth, took her loyalty for granted. Joy, she would have said, was a nice thing, but a little dull, low-spirited and solemn. Her name did not describe her nature. But she was beautiful. Her shining hair was the colour of a ripe cornfield, and the grace of her sturdy young body could hardly be obscured by the deplorable clothes which she wore, shapeless garments, hand woven and embroidered by putative peasants. In a bathing dress she deserved her name. Naked she might have posed for Aphrodite.

" I'm going out for the day with Alec," began Betsy, as soon as they were within earshot. " Tell Serena to cut sandwiches for us at once. My mother is coming this evening by the London train. Tell Eccles to meet her with the luggage grid as she always has enormous suitcases. Tell Blodwen to make up Alec's bed in the garden house, and move Mark Hannay into Alec's room, and get the spare room ready for my mother. See about clean paper in the chest of drawers, soap and towels. Blodwen forgets. And remember flowers for the dressing table."

" Oke," said Joy lugubriously.

" Don't say Oke, I've banned it in my house. The Blochs have fused the cottage lights. See about that. Mrs. Lloyd wants two dozen glasses for the fête ; I told her I thought we could lend them. Count them and see. Remember about the fish and send off the grocery order . . ."

Joy kept saying yes, her brown eyes fixed attentively upon Betsy's face. Yes . . . she said . . . yes . . . and if she was surprised that Mrs. Hewitt should be coming she did not show it.

" And then you'd better go down and join the children. You can't lunch here all by yourself. Tell Serena to cut extra sandwiches for you," concluded Betsy.

Joy departed with an acrobatic bound. To run and to leap at Betsy's command was clearly her duty. She sped through the tasks of the day like a melancholy ballerina ; her youth and her physical vitality kept her on her toes. First she ran to the kitchen and then upstairs in search of Blodwen, the housemaid. As they set about their duties each wondered why Mrs. Hewitt should be coming so unexpectedly, and why Alec and Betsy should be going off alone together for the day, a thing which hardly ever happened. Each followed a train of conjecture, one in English and the other in Welsh. They stripped Alec's bed and folded up the sheets, which were to be carried to the garden house. A faint masculine smell pervaded the bed and reached their nostrils. They both flushed slightly as they struggled to turn the heavy mattress, the golden head bobbing towards the black one in silent perturbation.

Blodwen remembered that it was her half day and that she was going out with her boy. She was mad about him.

Three o'clock they were to meet, and now, if they were all after taking their lunch out, there would be no washing up, and she would have time to wave her hair. But oh, how was she to wait till three o'clock ? Her dark eyes smouldered as she pulled the pillows out of their cases.

Joy wished that she could be alone there for a minute. She wanted to fling herself down and lie, stretched and quiet, on this bed where he had slept. It had been so hard to learn that he was not going away after all, just when she had braced herself to the thought of not seeing him any more that summer. Now for three weeks more they would be in the same house, often in the same room. He would speak to her, and sometimes even touch her. It was anguish. When he was away she could forget about it sometimes. But when he was there, in the house, she lived at fever point ; nothing was real, or had any meaning, save those brief moments of contact and recognition. She could not resist the impulse to wait and to hope.

Only when he had gone could she realise that her love was shameful, and that she must strive to regain her freedom. He did not love her and he never would. He scarcely knew that she was there. He was everything to her and she was nothing to him. But when he was near she could not bring herself to believe this, because there was something between them though he did not know it. He had kissed her once, in London, two years ago. Before that time she had been free, and cared not a straw for Betsy's husband, though she liked him well enough. But she went to them in Well Walk, where their London house was, to help Betsy during the Christmas holidays. And one night they played hide and seek in the dark with a lot of people who had come in from another party. The house was full of whispers and giggles, sudden shrieks, panic scuffles. Alec thought she was somebody else— one of the girls who had come in, a little drunk, from the other party. They had both slipped behind one of the

window curtains in the library. She had recognized his
voice, and, hearing stealthy footsteps in the room, she
clutched at him warningly. They stood rigid, very close
together, in the breathless dark. The footsteps creaked
away and Alec kissed her, whispering another name,
thinking that she was somebody else, the kind of person
who thought nothing of a kiss. He thought nothing of
it. But then something happened; a fire blazed up in
them both, not only in her, but in them both. Who
are you? he kept whispering, who are you? But
she never told him. She got away before he found
out.

Still, she had been something to him. For a few
seconds she had been everything; she had felt him gasp
and tremble, she had felt the sudden violent racing of his
heart. It had happened, and it could happen again.
And, though she knew it was very wicked, she could not
help hoping and waiting. Conscience and modesty for-
bade her to do more. She would never reveal herself;
never, of her own will provoke another moment of instinctive recognition. But she was not strong enough to van-
quish hope. Something might happen, some circumstance,
in which she was again completely passive, might bring
them together as they had been then.

Heavy-hearted and light-footed she ran upstairs and
downstairs. She counted the tumblers, and sent off the
grocery order, and picked a vase of flowers for Mrs.
Hewitt's dressing-table. The visit to the cottage she put
off till the end of the morning, as she could look in there
on her way down to join the children on the beach. It
was noon before she collected her bathing things and ran
out into the hazy, golden air. The smell of the sea mingled
with the smell of the gorse on the hillside. It came in
warm, aromatic waves. But the smell of the cottage was
stronger than either, a not unpleasant reek of onions and
furniture polish which had arrived with the Blochs. All
the windows were draped with eiderdowns, the next best

thing to the red feather mattresses which Frau Bloch would have preferred to hang out of her windows.

Joy stood uncertainly upon the doorstep, sniffing the strong blast of onions (or was it garlic?) which rushed out at her. Nobody seemed to be there. No sound of movement or foreign chatter came from inside. She knocked once or twice thinking that they had no business to go out and leave the front door wide open. People on the road, tramps, might stroll in and steal Betsy's things.

She knew where the fuse box was, and she thought that she might as well see what was wrong. It was not their house, and Betsy had told her to go. Wrinkling her nose a little, she stepped over the threshold. The living-room was like a pig sty. A number of charcoal drawings, designs for film sets, littered the table from which the morning meal had not yet been cleared. The edge of one of them was in the honey dish and she moved it mechanically, with a sniff of disapproval. Her unhappy, enslaved mind was roused for a moment to contemplate the Blochs. She saw that alien family, sitting round the table, conversing and thinking in German, perceiving everything strangely. But they did not interest her greatly. Nothing did, unless it touched upon her obsession. She lived in blinkers, in a condition of stupidity that was almost imbecile. The adventures of the mind, the avenues of escape, of speculation, imagination and reflection existed for her no longer.

One glance at the fuse box was enough. She climbed on to a chair and began to replace the fuses from a piece of wire that she had brought with her.

A voice from the kitchen startled her.

" Allo ? "

Footsteps padded and Emil Bloch appeared.

" Allo, Miss Benson ! "

" I came to see about the fuses. I knocked several times. I thought everybody was out."

" So ? "

He leaned against the doorpost and stared at her. He was a horrid rude man, a foreigner. But he wore an old blue shirt which had once belonged to Alec. So that she could not remain indifferent to him. That single circumstance had invested him with significance, and she glanced round at him now and then, as she snipped off lengths of fuse wire. Each time she encountered his detached, incomprehensible stare. It was like being regarded by an animal, a wolf. He frightened her a little. He had a gaunt, narrow face, a hungry mouth and very pointed teeth.

" Did you use an electric iron ? " she asked presently.

He shook his head.

" Because you shouldn't. The current isn't strong enough."

" So."

Suddenly he smiled. His expression became kind and genial, as though he liked her very much for some quite simple reason.

" You have a beautiful . . . corp . . ." he said slowly.

If he had said body she would have been offended. But the odd little word sounded innocent and naïve. She laughed, and he laughed too.

" Laigs very good," he added. " Very good . . . here . . ."

He slapped himself and looked at her enquiringly.

" Thighs," she told him, after a second's pause.

" Sighs . . ."

He repeated the word softly, almost wistfully, as she got down off the chair. She laughed again, nervously, because she did not know what to say.

" This is the first time I hear you laugh. It is bad for you . . . here . . . I think. You are in a bad . . . situation."

" Oh no . . . I . . . I'm very happy here. I . . ."

He silenced her with a gesture while he arranged another sentence in English.

" Soon . . . it will be better for you . . . they will make . . . a divorce . . ."

" What ? "

" Then, perhaps, he will take you away."

" What are you saying ? What do you mean ? "

" I think you loff Alec, isn't it ? "

She gave an astonished gasp and burst into tears. Emil, with puzzled concern on his narrow face, talked German very fast as if trying to pacify her.

" Oh . . ." she cried, between her sobs, " how did you know ? But it's not true. How did you know ? How can you think such a thing ? "

" How you speak to him . . . how you look at him . . . one or two times. . . . Don't be afraid. Nobody has said it. But it . . . jumps into my mind . . . mine only . . . I think, when there is divorce then they do not have to hide it any more, so I am glad for you. And for him."

" But you don't understand. You're quite wrong. He . . . he doesn't care anything about me. I'm nothing to him. He doesn't know . . ."

" So-o ? He knows not ? "

He was completely at a loss, having believed until that moment that this beautiful young girl was Alec's mistress.

A melancholy chill came over him. He remembered once more that he was in a strange country where nothing was quite what it seemed to be, so that he, a clever man, could make stupid mistakes. He had meant to be kind and friendly to this girl, whom he had often pitied, seeing her so enslaved by love. He had a fellow feeling for her. Her situation could not be pleasant, in servitude to the *ungemuthliche* Betsy. But he had got it all wrong, because he was an exile, and there was no point of contact with these English, these foreigners, who meant to be cordial but remained disagreeable and obscure. The kindness departed from his face as he said :

" I'm sorry. I don't understand why they make a divorce, I don't understand anything."

" But they aren't. Really they aren't. You have misunderstood something."

" But yes, they are divorce. That I have heard."

" Who says so ? "

" To-day already. I have heard them speaking by the window, they speak of this all the time, how they divorce and the Old is coming to forbid such."

" The old . . . ? "

" The old lady . . . the mother. . . ."

Mrs. Hewitt ? thought Joy. Was that why . . . but it was impossible.

" I'm sure you misunderstood. They haven't quarrelled. Why . . . they've just gone out on a picnic."

He shrugged his shoulders and laughed unpleasantly.

" That is, perhaps, an English custom."

" Eavesdropping isn't an English custom," she said quickly.

" Please ? "

" It's dishonourable."

" What is that please ? "

" To overhear private conversation . . . nobody does . . . in England . . . no gentleman, I mean. . . ."

" So ? I make that too difficult, for now, to be an English gentleman. . . ."

" Why should they want to divorce ? They're quite happy."

" As you say ? Mrs. Betsy is perhaps wishing for better. I think she will be to marry Lord St. Mullins."

" Lord St. Mullins ! "

Joy had never seen this cousin of Betsy's, who had recently and somewhat unexpectedly, succeeded to a peerage. But she had heard of him often, for he was a family joke. Nobody mentioned him without a guffaw.

Max Buttevant he had been, before the death of various uncles and cousins had translated him ; a crank, a pacifist, a conscientious objector, the hero of innumerable ridiculous anecdotes.

" Oh, you're quite wrong. What on earth makes you think so ? "

He pondered and arranged his words.

" In June, soon after we arrive here, she is staying alone at the house. He is coming here, every day, I say so, every day to see her. Very often I am seeing them together."

" I dare say. He was staying over at Tan-y-Vron, with his sister. Of course he came here. He's Betsy's cousin."

" He loffs her," asserted Bloch positively. " And he is very rich, isn't it ? High born also."

" You've absolutely misunderstood. It's impossible."

" Maybe. As you say, I don't understand anything."

" You mustn't say such things to anyone. Not anyone."

He nodded but she felt that he was not to be trusted. He was a foreigner and no gentleman.

" Not about a divorce, that's all quite a mistake, I'm sure . . . or . . . or about me, how I cried just now . . . it was nothing . . . silly. . . . Don't tell anybody."

" If you wish."

They regarded one another suspiciously. He believed that she was lying. He knew what he had heard. He had ears. He had eyes. Never had he seen a man more blatantly in love than Lord St. Mullins.

Silently he stood aside to let her get out of the house.

In the garden she stooped to tighten the strap of her sandal. She heard his voice suddenly speaking to someone inside. A raucous growl answered him. It was Frau Bloch, who must have been in the house all the time, in the kitchen, next door. They had not been alone. She had been listening in the kitchen, while they talked and when Joy cried.

He was telling something—a long, angry sounding monologue. Joy thought she heard her own name, repeated several times. The brutes were discussing her. And then came something about Lord St. Mullins. They were awful people, sinister and full of ill will. They were foreigners.

ON THE BEACH

THE children were coming out of the sea for the fourth time that morning. So low was the tide that the coast had almost disappeared beyond a huge, hazy expanse of sand and shallow pools. Daphne rose from a last wallow in the small shrill waves which fringed the bay, and screwed up her eyes, searching the distant dunes for the place where they had left their luncheon baskets. A spot of orange guided her: it must be the rubber float which they carried up there after their third bathe. She set off in that direction, running swiftly over the smooth sand, cautiously over the ribbed sand, and splashing through the pools, which felt quite hot against her ankles after the bracing cold of the sea.

Eliza followed her. They went on and on over the beach, and soon got quite far away from the sea, but the dunes seemed to come no nearer. Slim Daphne ran with her chin up, her reddish mop of curls flying out behind her. Fat Eliza padded along thoughtfully, poking her head forward in a search for razor shells.

Suddenly Daphne stopped, gazed, and turned back, calling :

" I say ! Joy's there."

" Where ? " asked Eliza, catching her up.

" By our lunch things."

" Oh curse ! "

They both turned to tell the boys, who had only just come out of the sea and were walking so slowly that they seemed almost stationary. They were still too far off for a shout to reach them.

So it always was, on any expedition. Daphne and Eliza would go first, dashing up hill and down dale, intent upon getting somewhere. Mark and Kenneth, absorbed in a discussion which never stopped, would go where they were led, scarcely aware of the road. All places were one to them. They crossed the sands as though they had been crossing their school cloisters. Even in bathing suits they had certain clerkly traits, a forward hitch of the shoulders as though long scholars' gowns should have been streaming out behind them on the salt wind. Yet, when the mood came on them, they could be wildly active, swimming across the bay, and racing one another up the mountains.

With a sigh the two girls sat down on the sand to wait for them. Imperceptibly they drew nearer. Mark, without once looking up, was steering straight towards their picnic place. Kenneth went where he went, dancing along beside him, earnest and agitated. Kenneth looked thin and small in a bathing suit, and his fair hair, which no water could flatten, stood up on end. His bright, shifting glances went this way and that, into Mark's face, back at the sea, across to the dunes. Mark, nearly two years older, was of a sturdier build ; the sea had matted his dark hair right down over his eyes, which made his head look a little too small.

At last they came within earshot and Daphne called out her unwelcome news. But she could not claim their attention for more than a second. They glanced briefly at the intruder sitting far away on the dunes, and returned to their discussion. The girls rose and walked on beside them, listening impatiently.

"The third dimension, in space," said Mark, "has got a time element in it somewhere. Take an ordinary photograph. It's perfectly flat . . . two dimensional. Look at it through a stereoscope and you get an illusion of three dimensions. It has acquired depth. Very well then. What happens ? It looks frightfully wrong and artificial somehow. Doesn't it ? Much further from the truth than the flat picture. Everything in it is dead—the figures are absolutely frozen . . . petrified. Why ? Because when you've got space you want time. And there isn't time in a photograph."

" You mean a snapshot, not a time exposure," interposed Daphne."

Kenneth gave her a quenching look and Mark went on as though she had not spoken.

" You can't conceive of time without space or of space without time."

" I never said you could," replied Kenneth. " I merely say that . . . that our thoughts . . . aren't bound by them. If I want to think of last week I don't have to think myself back through hour after hour till I get to the day I want. I can think of last year as quickly as I can think of yesterday. If I want to think of the dining-room at home, I don't have to think myself all the way across the sands and the fields and the road and up the hill. I'm there in a second."

" Not your astral body," put in Daphne again. " If you want to make your astral body go anywhere you have to think every yard of the way."

The boys both fell on her. They were so contemptuous that Eliza would have burst into tears. But Daphne was not afraid of them. She had read all about astral bodies in a magazine and to their taunts she made the same serene response :

" It's been proved. There was an old man who wanted to get into a certain library and it was locked. So he sent his astral body inside and it read the book he wanted and did the work ever so much better than he would have if he'd gone himself."

" And after that," suggested Kenneth, " I suppose he never went anywhere again. He just lolled in bed and sent his astral body out to fag for him."

" It didn't say," replied Daphne, quite unabashed.

They amused themselves by trying to rout her. Eliza, who had understood a little of what they were saying, longed to put in a word, but dared not for fear she should be snubbed. It was a frequent source of astonishment to Eliza to discover that she, who had the rudiments of a mind, must walk beside them in nervous silence while Daphne, frivolous and mindless as a flower, could attract their mocking attention.

As they came nearer to the luncheon place they walked more slowly, as if to put off the moment when Joy must be included in their group. None of them liked her, though they would have found it hard to say why. Her dutiful obedience to Betsy made her a tiresome companion; she often tried to assert authority over them, believing herself to be Betsy's representative. And they were not deceived, as older people might have been, by her buoyant activity; they had a good deal of that themselves. They, too, could run and leap. Her low spirits were perfectly obvious to them, and they felt instinctively that there was something wrong with her.

When at length they reached the sandbank they greeted her without enthusiasm and flung themselves down among the bents and grasses. The sandwiches were divided and they all began to munch in silence. Far away the sea whispered. Seabirds ran about on the wet sand as if they had taken refuge there from the dazzling sky. The five people on the dunes had each gone back into a private world. Their existences went on separately as though they had been miles apart instead of lying in a row, almost touching one another.

Mark continued his reflections upon time and space. He was trying to reach some conclusion which evaded him. For five minutes he sat with a half-bitten sandwich in his hand, so much engrossed that he forgot to eat. The distant sea and the bright air were not quite out of his consciousness; they combined to give him a sensation of pleasant well-being.

Daphne lay on her stomach because she wanted to tan her back. She believed that she was thinking. A lot of little pictures passed through her mind. The girls at school were admiring her back. She was browner than anybody else. But it said in a book that too many violet rays might melt the marrow in your bones. She saw it bubbling. And Miss Troutbeck, the matron at school, whom she now saw on a rostrum in a science class-room, said that sunbathing could be overdone. Elsie Mottram's pink face interposed, saying that Trouty was pre-war, definitely. And some girls giggled because Trouty said you got pneumonia if you shaved under your arms. That was not a nice joke, but those girls in room six were like that. They're just kids—they don't know, they said ; and Jean, who was Daphne's best friend, said thank you, we don't want to ; it won't happen to us for simply ages. So they went down to the pantry to scrounge some biscuits and a prefect saw them, which made one think of ghosts because that prefect knew somebody who had seen a ghost. But the word is frightful because it reminds me that I may be going to hell. Maisie Renshaw blasphemed against the Holy Ghost. He that blasphemeth against the Holy Ghost—well, I only laughed. Somebody said spook meant the same as ghost. And Maisie's voice came from behind the cubicle curtains : what about the Holy Spook ? So we all laughed. Have we all blasphemed ? Jean says no, and her father is a clergyman. She says only Maisie has. He said strawberry ices are indicated when he took us out to tea. Only why do they wear a cross on their watch-chain, sort of on their stomach really, which isn't very reverent ? Why can't they have it sort of on a chain round their necks ?

Eliza's thoughts were more connected. She was saying something very clever, to which Mark and Kenneth were listening with attentive admiration. Daphne was not there. Mark said : You have put it very well. You have expressed that idea much better than I could. Or he might even say : I never thought of that. But what exactly had she said ? Was there anything which she knew that they did not ? How did they come to know so much more ? Didn't she sit at a desk for hours on end having education poured into her ? Well, she had a better French accent. But why were boys so different ? Their life was so different at St. Clere's among the Welsh Marches. They had cloisters and libraries, and on Sundays they walked on River Cliff, out into the country. They talked a slang which dated from Chaucer. Their life was lordly and free, while hers was spent in a hen-roost built of pitch-pine and sham gothic. She would have given anything to be a boy and have a friend like Mark.

Kenneth had thought of a joke which he was longing to exploit. But it would need a feed-line. Somebody must say what a bore it was that Joy had been sent to superintend their lunch, and he would say that surely they could all be " nurtured and fed without the aid of Joy." He would pretend that he had just thought of it. The girls were so sottish that they would not, probably, recognize the quotation. But Mark would, because Emily Brontë was in fashion among the intelligentzia at St. Clere's. Mark might laugh, and Mark's approval was rapture. Mark was absolutely perfect, so that Kenneth's heart was uplifted just to see him sitting there, frowning away at his half-bitten sandwich. He was so amazingly beautiful. It was incredible that one man should unite so many perfections—be in the school six, and Chapel Prefect and have read pretty nearly everything. Some people thought that he threw his weight about. Some of the masters seemed to think so. They said that Parkin, who was all right but knew nothing about anything except botany, would make a better head of the school next year. But surely a man has the right to be arrogant if he is absolutely unique ! " Without the aid of Joy." Was it, after all, really funny ? Or good form ? Mark might think it caddish to make jokes about a girl like Joy, a sort of servant, really ; Mark was always very courteous to her, helping her carry things and opening the door, as if she had been a guest in the house. But then Mark's manners were perfect and he never said caddish things by mistake, as Kenneth sometimes did.

Joy ate up her lunch and sat staring out to sea with eyes that saw nothing of all that space and loveliness. Her thoughts were like waves, rushing perpetually up to a given point and then receding. A divorce ! If it were true . . . why, then . . . but it was not true. It couldn't be. It was perfectly impossible. It was wrong and wicked to imagine such a thing. Only, if it had been true, why, then, if a thing like that could happen, then other things could happen, and he wouldn't be Betsy's husband any more, and so . . . but there wasn't the slightest chance, the least likelihood. People quarrel when they get divorced. They don't go off on a picnic. The Blochs would imagine anything, ungrateful pigs . . . disloyal to listen to them . . . only why is Mrs. Hewitt coming ? Perhaps it's true. Can it possibly be true ? No, no, no . . . it can't.

The sun had moved. It was going down towards the sea. The colour of water and sand had changed from white to a soft gold and the incoming tide had a new tune.

Betsy roused as if from a deep sleep. She began to trickle handfuls of dry, hot sand through her fingers, playing that old, old game that has been played with sand since the world was made. She felt profoundly peaceful and rested as she lay there, letting herself be swung round, with all sentient and insentient things, towards the shadow and the coolness of night. She would have liked to lie on there till the hot sand was cold. In the end it was Alec who remembered the time and began to talk of trains.

" I suppose," he suggested reluctantly, " that we ought to think of meeting your mother."

She agreed, but made no effort to move. He had to

fetch her shoes and strap them on for her, and roll up their bathing things. She lay there, quite passive.

All day he had been turning over the thoughts in his mind and bracing himself to certain decisions. But he had said nothing because he felt that it might be wiser to let her lie quite still. So seldom was she content to do that. Now he observed, as he emptied the sand out of his own shoes:

" We haven't settled what exactly are we going to say to your mother. I'm sticking to what I said—that we've got to go off alone together for a little while before I agree to anything. If, after that, you are quite sure you want to part, I'll do exactly as you wish. Shall we thank her very much for coming, and ask her to run the house while we go? We'll give her to understand that our private affairs can't be discussed till we come back."

Betsy thought: If I go away with him I shall end by giving the whole thing up. He is going to be much too nice about it. And then she thought: Well, why not give it up?

She said:

" But I still don't see what more there is to discuss."

" I want to be sure what you are going to do with yourself after I've given up the right to look after you. I've not always taken sufficient pains about your happiness, but that's no reason why I shouldn't do so now. It isn't as if you wanted to marry anyone else. Won't you be rather lonely? "

" Oh, no, not more than I've always been."

" How do you . . . imagine your life . . . afterwards? "

Very much happier was how she had imagined it. And not lonely at all. Of course she would marry again some time. And the other man, whoever he was, would love her better than Alec ever had, would worship and cherish her. She was experienced now; she knew how to make herself prized. She would not throw everything away a second time, giving all she had to give with both hands, as she had done when she was a girl. The other man should never be too sure of her, never take her for granted.

Did Alec really think that nobody would want to marry her ? There were plenty ; Max Buttevant, Max St. Mullins for one. Poor Max was most touching in his wild adoration. She might even marry him. She would have to see how she felt when she was free, and so she had told him before he went off to China.

Then why not tell Alec so ? she thought. Why not tell him that Max wants to marry me ? Why don't I want to ? He'll wonder how we came to be discussing it. He'll think it's all much more definite than it is. After all, I don't know. I'm not sure that I want to marry Max.

She looked at Alec, so unsuspicious and friendly, and thought : I shall be rather a bitch if I do marry Max, if I haven't said anything, especially if we go away like this.

She sighed and Alec rolled over till he could touch her hand and say :

" You don't really want it, you silly darling."

" Perhaps . . . I . . . don't."

If she gave it up then she would never have to feel that she had been rather a bitch.

He thought : We are getting on nicely. That's as far as we'll go to-day. Mrs. Hewitt isn't as big a fool as she looks. I'll give her a tip how things are, and get Betsy away. And afterwards . . . pull up my socks, drink less, get out of all this racket, make Betsy feel she's loved . . . but stand no nonsense ; make her drop this martyred frame of mind . . . make her pull herself together too. Oh, my God ! What a grind !

Then he stretched out both hands and pulled her to her feet. They began to walk quickly, enjoying movement after those long hours of repose. It was cooler and clearer : a slight breeze had sprung up. The mountains, sweeping back from the sea, had their afternoon colours and blue clefts of shadow were creeping up their sides.

The train would come down to the coast along the great

estuary of the Afon Arian, which ran far inland between its mountain walls. Alec and Betsy crossed a little cove, rounded a peninsula of sandhills and came to Morvah Bay, where they found the children and Joy playing rounders on the sand with the Bloch boys. When Betsy called to ask if anyone was coming to the station to meet Grandmother the circle broke up with cries of astonishment.

" Didn't you know she was coming ? Didn't Joy tell you ? "

Joy had not thought of telling them, and Betsy commented mentally, for the hundredth time, upon the girl's inertia.

" Put on your shoes quickly," she commanded. " Joy, you go home and see about tea. Mark! Would you like . . ."

Mark quickly offered to carry the baskets and towels for Joy. He felt that he would be in the way at the station. The children sat down to put on their shoes, goaded into haste by Betsy, though there was really plenty of time.

Joy ran about in an eager, excited way, collecting towels. She felt that Alec's eyes were upon her. Her bathing dress, which she still wore, annoyed Betsy. It was not quite suitable. In her position she should have known that a one-piece suit was the right thing ; the brief little bodice and briefer shorts gave an entirely wrong impression. Kenneth was, after all, nearly sixteen, and Mark older. It might do them harm to see so many of Joy's ribs.

Alec also glanced at the girl, watching the play of muscles on her brown back as she bent over the bundles. He approved of the bathing dress. But he did not look at her for long, though he thought her very beautiful. Her position in his household, her youth and her modesty acted as a kind of brake on his thoughts. He looked at her and then looked away, across the sea at the faint shape

of Bardsey Island, now emerging from the haze. And his
face grew a little sad : he had been touched by that grief
which attends upon beauty, an austere pity for something
which is tender, evanescent and solitary.

Betsy gave orders and gathered her brood together.
Outwardly she bustled, but inwardly she was at peace,
calmer than she had been for many months. She felt
strangely light-hearted and hopeful. Of the dangers which
encompassed her, of all the combustible material which
lay strewn about that beach, she comprehended nothing
at all. Blithely she went her way like a sleep-walker who
strays upon the edge of an abyss. Blind chance might
preserve her, but she would never know it. Only if chance
betrayed her would she wake.

AT THE STATION

IT seemed that the little Blochs were determined to come with them. They straggled after the Cannings up the lane, gabbling together in their outlandish tongue. Betsy tried in vain to send them home and Eliza explained that they were going to the station for their own amusement. It was their favourite haunt. They preferred it to the sea or the mountains, perhaps because they felt that it was the nearest point to home—the place of arrival and departure. They would be down there at seven in the morning, scuffling up and down the platforms and rattling at the slot machines, and often they remained for the whole of the day. The porters were very kind to them and taught them Welsh, which they now understood better than English.

Emil Bloch haunted the place, too. There was a bench at the very end of the platform, with a view up the estuary, where he would sit huddled for hours together. The bitter thoughts of the exile racked him. This evening, however, he had not come to brood, but to witness the arrival of the Old. He wanted to find out what was really happening among the Cannings.

The sight of Alec and Betsy, surrounded by their children, took him slightly aback. They looked so like a united and happy family that he began to doubt if he had after all understood what they were saying in the garden-house. Smiling his shy, hungry smile, he went to greet them and asked as many questions as they would answer. No doubt they would think him impertinent, but they would forgive this in a poor, ignorant foreigner. Yes, they said, they

63

were expecting Betsy's mother and her visit was quite unexpected.

" Vy does she come ? " he asked innocently.

The children's eyes endorsed this question.

" On some family business," said Alec. " Look ! There's the train."

Far up the estuary, rounding the base of a hill, crept a trail of white smoke. But the diversion did not quench Emil for long. He returned to the attack :

" Not . . . I hope . . . something bad ? Not bad news ? "

" Oh, no," said Betsy. " Children, just run and see if the car is here."

Kenneth and Eliza raced to the railings and peered into the station yard. The car was there, and the luggage grid.

" Why is she coming, anyway ? " muttered Kenneth.

" I think," said Eliza, " that mother and father have had a row or something."

" Oh, rot ! "

" Well . . . they do, don't they ? "

Kenneth could not deny it. He could not remember when it was that he had first got this impression that his father was a naughty boy and his mother most justly aggrieved. But it had been in the air for so long that both he and Eliza had come to accept it as natural. Possibly all parents might be like that.

" Why do you think so ? " he asked. " To-day, I mean."

" When I went this morning to see about lunch she was looking sort of . . . martyred . . . as she does when he's done something to annoy her. You know ! "

" No, I don't. You shut up. Piano legs ! "

Kenneth worshipped his mother and resented Eliza's occasional disloyalties. Of his father he was extremely critical, especially since he discovered that Mark did not think very highly of the Canning and Graham musical plays.

The puff of smoke was now much larger. It vanished among a clump of trees two miles away. When it emerged all the little Blochs came stampeding out of the parcels office and crowded round the Cannings. Betsy, exasperated, caught Alec's eye; he grinned and tucked her hand under his arm. Mrs. Hewitt should see them thus and make what she liked of it.

The train rumbled into the station and stopped. No flurried, mulish face looked out of any window. The Cannings hastened up and down, distracted, and it was Emil Bloch who at last drew their attention to an elegant little person who had just made a leisurely exit from the hindmost coach.

" Is not there," he said, " the lady . . . the mother . . ."

She came towards them, smiling at their amazement. All through the long journey she had been laughing to herself, picturing their faces when the wrong mother got out of the train. It was exactly as she had imagined. They were astonished, and then they were alarmed. They were panic-stricken.

Before she had finished embracing them Alec had had time to think that a braver man would pack her straight off back to London by the very next train. And Betsy's dismay hardened into an obstinate fury.

What has she come for ? What ? To interfere ? If she says one word—*one word* . . . I won't be bullied . . . whatever she wants I shall do the opposite . . . just let her say one single word. . . .

INTERFERENCE

BUT Mrs. Canning said nothing. And they began, very soon, to wonder why she had come. It appeared that she knew nothing of Betsy's letter or its contents. Poor Henrietta Hewitt had, she said, turned up at her house that morning, too ill to explain anything.

" Really I was most worried about her. She could scarcely speak. I got her into a nursing home and promised I'd see to everything without really knowing what it was I'd got to see to. She seemed quite frantic at the idea of not being able to get on here, but couldn't tell me what the crisis was—only that you and Alec were going somewhere on a yacht. She was very nearly delirious, poor thing. She kept going on about this yacht. So I thought, if a grandmother was wanted, I might do instead. I could run the house for you while you're cruising. But I really think we ought to ring up the home this evening, and find out how she is, before you go."

The report from the nursing home was grave. Mrs. Hewitt's temperature had continued to soar, and the doctor was inclined to think that she had typhoid fever. Betsy, in a panic, caught the morning train for London. Later she telephoned that her mother was very dangerously ill, and that she could not possibly return for several days.

Alec could not but feel that catastrophe had been averted. He had feared a fatal clash between Betsy and her mother-in-law, and, as long as these two could be kept apart, he did not care which of them went to London. For himself he felt no alarm. His mother knew nothing about the divorce, apparently, so that he had no battles to fight. He could get back to work with a free mind, and, as soon as Betsy's mother was better, he would insist upon a conjugal holiday.

He might have remembered that open attack was seldom part of his mother's strategy. Long experience had taught her to anticipate the mysterious perversity of the human mind. She knew that most people do not like to be helped, advised or influenced. It was years since she had argued with anyone. She had learnt to use force rather than persuasion, and she had become an adept at imposing her will upon rebellious subjects. Avoiding any declared intention, she would begin by shaking the nerves of her victims by constant small skirmishes on side issues ; she would undermine the fabric of their resistance, provoke them to lose their tempers for no obvious reason, surround them with a hostile audience, cut off all avenues of retreat, and finally, when the crisis came, leave them to discover that they were in no position to attack.

In this campaign her way was clear, and Providence had played into her hands by dispatching Betsy to London.

She must, in the first place, make herself extremely agreeable to everyone at Pandy Madoc. Her visit must be a success, and the household, under her management, must wear its happiest face. All her charm must be exerted, so that when Betsy came back and began to lose her temper over trifles the tide of popular sympathy would be against her.

Secondly, she must find out everything that she could, every detail that might have some bearing on the case. It was possible that Betsy had taken somebody into her confidence. She might have several partizans. These must be discovered, pumped and persuaded to change sides, to proffer criticism and disapprobation when Betsy turned to them for support.

Not until all this had been done would she tackle Alec. And then she would surprise him with all that she knew. If she was lucky she would, by that time, know so much that she would not need to mention Mrs. Hewitt and the letter. Perhaps she would be able to tell him something that would annoy him very much. Betsy would learn, she would have to learn, that his patience was not inexhaustible.

The first part of her task was easy. She could always make herself liked if she chose. She was indulgent and sympathetic, gave very little trouble in the house, and permitted the maids to go to a local dance which Betsy had banned. Lobsters were ordered daily instead of once a week; peaches abounded. The ice-cream man was told to call every evening. No restraint whatever was put upon the children; even Daphne was allowed to go to bed when she liked.

Contrary to all expectation she made friends with the Blochs, who improved greatly in consequence. She could talk fluent and idiomatic German, which was a welcome change for them after the primitive baby talk which was all that Alec and Betsy could manage. They had not conversed with anybody except themselves for months. She got Frau Bloch out of the fur coat and brought her up to the house to sing Schubert. It had only taken her three days to discover that the woman had a very fine voice and excellent musical taste. Alec could not help feeling that Betsy might have discovered it. But then Betsy had never been fair to the Blochs. They were not such dreadful people after all; his mother liked them, and seemed quite to understand why he had offered them the cottage. There were many good points about his mother. She was the only woman in the world who gave him enough lobster, which agreed with him perfectly, whatever Betsy might say.

But the Blochs were not, as Mrs. Canning very soon decided, likely to have received confidences from Betsy. There had been no love lost in that quarter, and she must look elsewhere for partizans. The little errand girl, little Joy Benson, was a much more probable ally. The child was a Hewitt belonging, and seemed to be devoted to Betsy.

It was more than likely that she knew something. To a girl of that age, inexperienced and violently prejudiced, Betsy's case might seem a good one. She must be enlightened.

And so it was that Mrs. Canning opened the second part of her campaign by a conversation with Joy. They had driven up together to a lake, high in the mountains. The rest of the party were to walk there, but Joy had been smilingly requested to come and help with the preparations for a picnic lunch. As they sat in the heather, by the lake side, some hints were dropped and some questions asked.

" Poor Mrs. Hewitt ! You must be worried about her. You're almost as much her daughter as Betsy is. You know, I wouldn't tell anyone else about this, only you are so much one of the family, but she frightened me terribly when she appeared at my house that morning. It may have been a sort of delirium, but she had got the most terrible idea into her head. I haven't dared to speak of it to Alec and Betsy. She was quite convinced that they were on the verge of getting a divorce ! "

Joy said nothing. Her blank stare conveyed nothing.

" You knew nothing about it ? Betsy had told you nothing ? "

" No, Mrs. Canning."

" I hardly like to speak of it. When people are as ill as that they get ideas. . . . But I do feel, if there is any truth in it, that Betsy's friends ought to help her."

" Yes, Mrs. Canning."

Oh, bless the girl ! Why must she go on : No, Mrs. Canning ! Yes, Mrs. Canning ! Betsy should have got her out of it.

" She mustn't be allowed to sacrifice her happiness. From what Mrs. Hewitt said, I gathered she feels she isn't the right wife for Alec. She doesn't understand his work, or care for it, and she thinks he would be happier free. Now—quite apart from this particular instance—speaking generally—how do you look at a situation like that ?   How does your generation look at it ? "

Mrs. Canning's smile was enchanting as she thus took counsel with youth. But Joy did not understand the compliment. She flushed scarlet and said that she did not know.

Whereupon she was told that the younger generation do not approve of divorce for the middle-aged. For themselves, to whom trial and error is permissible, it is a solution. But at Betsy's time of life (she's thirty-eight, remember) it could only be called a confession of failure. The young, clear-eyed and scornful, have little sympathy for failures.

This point of view was bound to enrage Betsy if only Joy could be induced to adopt it. But the girl was very stupid. She said nothing to the point, and merely asked, after a short pause, if Alec wished to be divorced. When told that he did not she said :

" Then she can't, can she ? "

" She might persuade him. She might make him feel that he ought."

" But . . . how could they . . . unless . . . I mean wouldn't one of them have to . . . wouldn't he have to . . ."

" Oh, yes. That is what is so dreadful. She would have to prove that he had been unfaithful."

" And . . . has he ? " breathed Joy faintly.

" Of course not. It's all very sordid. He would have to go to an hotel, I believe, with some woman, and stay there for a week-end. Some woman who was nothing to him."

Mrs. Canning was surprised to find the girl so ignorant. Perhaps that bathing dress, with no middle, had misled her. If she had known she would not have taken such pains to invent the views of the clear-eyed, scornful younger generation.

" You mean he's got to ? " exclaimed Joy. " Got to . . . go . . . away with somebody ? "

" It's the law," said Mrs. Canning, adding : " Of course, nothing would happen."

This statement, though sweeping, did not seem entirely adequate. But it was difficult to make oneself plainer without indelicacy.

The girl did not look particularly surprised. Mrs. Canning would have given a good deal to know why she was so thoughtful.

" Hadn't you," she asked suddenly, " any idea of all this ? You hadn't heard a word of it ? "

" Oh . . . yes . . ."

" What ? But you said that Betsy never . . ."

" Not from Betsy. It was Mr. Bloch."

" Mr. Bloch ? Good heavens ! Do they know ? What did they say ? "

" He asked me about it once. I said I didn't know. I didn't think there was anything in it. I thought it was just that they don't understand English."

Now it was Mrs. Canning's turn to be surprised.

THE LOOK

A DISTANT shout woke echoes across the lake. The walking party had arrived. Over the shoulder of a green hill a little fringe of figures appeared against the sky. For a moment they stood bunched together, and then they separated as each scrambled down the grassy slope at his own pace.

Alec waited at the top of the ridge for Eliza, who was some way behind. He had noticed, or thought that he had noticed, that she had dropped back on purpose. Probably the boys had been snubbing her.

On former holidays she and Kenneth had been allies, and Daphne had had to play second fiddle. But, since the arrival of Mark, Eliza had been cast off. Her days were full of small rebuffs and disappointments, so that Alec, who saw it all, was often sorry for her. She had still a child's trustful unawareness of situation. Holidays were supposed to be enjoyable, and she did her best to preserve that faith, accepting each check as an isolated incident, not seeing that a change had taken place in Kenneth and herself. Every morning she would prepare to enjoy herself, undeterred by the fact that she had not done so on any previous day. Later she would be tagging along a little behind the others, bewildered and glum, but quite prepared to be happy if only they would allow it.

Alec felt that he ought to be able to help her ; but he did not know what to say. It would not do to tell her that she would in time revenge herself upon these arrogant boys, and that they one day would find themselves at the

72

mercy of little girls whom they now despised. Their cleverness would not save them from that.

Fat, earnest, hopeful Eliza would change, inevitably, into a woman whom he did not know. He was sorry, for he liked her very well as she was. Of the three she was the only one who meant very much to him. The other two belonged to their mother entirely. But she had caught at his heart when she was but an hour old ; they put her into his arms, and she stared up at him as if expecting him to tell her what on earth had been happening. She still looked at him like that sometimes, giving him a spasm of tenderness and compassion. He was aware of her as a being, helpless and perplexed in a cold-hearted world, for whom his utmost foresight and protection could do very little. This sentiment assailed him now as he watched her toiling up the slope in pursuit of a brother who did not want her. When she reached the top he told her to wait and rest for a little, while he lighted his pipe. They flung themselves down upon the warm turf, and gazed at the chain of lakes below. The mountains, dappled with cloud shadows, swept back from this high valley. Their own lake, Llyn Alyn, had a small island floating on its silvery breast. Neither of them could view this prospect often enough. It could not be printed so clearly on their minds that they would recall it when they were far away. Little was left for all their greedy gazing —a mere memory of light and airy space, of colour so soft that it escaped the inward eye as does an image seen in a dream.

They were both thinking this, and presently Eliza said :

" Do you think it's true that Nature never did betray the heart that loved her ? "

" Lord, I don't know ! " said Alec. " Who says so ? "

" Wordsworth. We did him last term. It's his philosophy of life, you know. One of those quotations you have to work into an essay . . . that, and the meanest flower that blows. I wonder what is the meanest flower."

"Some kind of dandelion, I should think."

"Oh, no. They're too yellow. I should think chickweed. Fancy having thoughts too deep for tears over chickweed! But what do you suppose it means, exactly, about Nature not betraying?"

"Well . . . I suppose it means that if you like this sort of thing "—he indicated the noble expanse below—"you find you go on liking it more and more. You never suddenly discover that it's all rot . . ."

"And so it's a consolation when your heart is broken."

"Possibly. If you're ass enough to get a broken heart."

Eliza looked pained, for she thought that it would be interesting to have a broken heart. In fact she sometimes felt as if she could hardly wait to be grown up and have one. Some day, she was sure, a great tragedy would come into her life, which would make her mysterious and important. People would say: Eliza—no—Elizabeth Canning has been through the depths. . . .

"Ken and Mark have got down to the road," she said wistfully. "Just look at them jabbering away. . . .

Alec grunted. He felt ashamed that he did not like young Hannay more, for the boy was obviously a nice boy, well-mannered and intelligent. He was a good friend for Kenneth, who was vain, weak and unstable, whatever his mother might say. It was something quite personal and petty that rankled in Alec's mind ; he felt sometimes that his young guest was silently weighing him up and that the result was unflattering. Not that Mark ever gave him any ground for thinking this. But occasionally he got a glimpse of himself as this youngster might perhaps be seeing him : middle-aged, beginning to put on weight, not quite as quick in mind or body as he had been, a little too rakishly good-looking, abominably lazy and quite content with the second-rate.

"We must catch them up before they get to the lake," suggested Eliza. "It would be awful if they bathed without us!"

She was determined to pursue them. These young whipper-snappers meant more to her than he did. They were compatriots and he was not. She hurried him down the hill at breakneck pace, but when they reached the lake it was already dotted with swimming heads.

Mrs. Canning sat by herself on the heathery shore, and she said as she handed them their towels :

" They say the water is very warm."

Alec looked at her sharply. There was a dangerous sparkle in her eye.

" Mother ! You aren't dreaming of . . . you haven't got a bathing dress, anyway."

" I could manage with my chemise."

" Sheer lunacy ! Think of the last time, when you would bathe at Arisaig. Why, you were ill for weeks. Your lumbago . . ."

" It wasn't bathing that made me ill at Arisaig. It was having to play bridge."

" Mother . . . I implore you . . ."

" Oh, very well ! Very well ! I won't."

For a moment she was shaking with rage. It was unbearable to be old, to have to sit and watch other people, when her heart was not old at all.

Alec went behind a wall and put on his bathing dress. If Betsy had been there she would have remembered to bring some rope-soled shoes to protect his feet from the stones. For the drawback to this lake was the difficulty of entering the water, the prospect of a long wade over the rocks which were painfully sharp and covered with slime.

He was glad to see, when he emerged from his shelter, that the others had all swum round beyond the island. Nobody would witness his ungainly hobblings, flounderings and groans. For he always felt elderly and foolish when going into this lake.

As he stood by the water's edge, wondering at which point to assay the horrid journey, a voice hailed him. He turned and saw Joy waving a pair of bathing shoes, and he sent her a shout of gratitude. She came leaping over the heather. She had got on her funny bathing dress, but she had not been into the water yet, and her yellow hair flew out behind her. He thought how nice it was to have this lovely creature ministering to him. He had a genial vision of himself as some Eastern potentate ; he had only to clap his hands and beautiful brown girls came tearing up to do his will.

She gave him the shoes and stood before him, panting, her young breasts rising and falling quickly beneath the little bodice. He knelt down and tied on the shoes. With those things on his feet he felt new confidence. When he stood up she was still there, and still looking at him. She met his eyes.

" Go away," he said hastily. " I'm not going to have anyone watching me or I shall come to grief even with these things on."

She smiled and turned away. She ran straight into the lake, over the treacherous stones as though they had been a smooth carpet, and flung herself into the deep water. Her yellow head shot away towards the island.

Alec followed, with anxious care, wobbling and cursing at every step. At last it was deep enough for him to lower himself cautiously, lie prone and strike out. The bottom sheered away. The silky water wrapped him round, softer, more enervating than the sea.

He swam slowly, for he was thoughtful. Just now he had been very much surprised. At one moment he told himself that there was nothing in it. At the next he was certain that there was everything in it.

She did, he thought. She certainly did. Young Joy gave me a look just now.

INDISCRETION

AFTER three weeks at Pandy Madoc, it was inevitable that Mark Hannay should find himself a trifle bored. Kenneth's adoration isolated them. Hardly a word was he allowed to exchange with anyone else ; it was as if the two boys were marooned upon an enchanted island of intimacy, and this island, though pleasant, was small. They had swum, they had fished, they had climbed mountains and ridden for miles along the sands. Now there was nothing left save to do all these things over and over again. Kenneth's powers of reason and argument were limited. He was beaten too easily, and too often he was betrayed by an anxiety to please or to impress. They were not equals. Mark began to hanker for a change of company.

One night, after dinner, they wandered out into the garden to watch the sunset. A store of unexhausted energy disturbed them. They had been very active that day but they were not ready for repose ; they both felt that they would like to go on and do something new. Mark extinguished the idea of another bathe so curtly that Kenneth was dismayed. The possibility of an end to this idyllic interlude had always haunted him. Now, as he looked into the cold, handsome face of his friend, he experienced a dreadful pang of anxiety.

" Well, you say . . ." he exclaimed. " What shall we do ? "

Mark did not answer. He was listening. From the open windows of the drawing-room a faint, tentative strumming stole out into the bloomy air of sunset.

" Who is that ? "

" That ! Oh . . . only Eliza."

Mark listened attentively for a few seconds and then said, in some surprise :

" She plays well."

Music was a pleasure which they could not share, though Kenneth had done his best to imitate Mark's enthusiasm. When Frau Bloch came up to sing he stifled his yawns and stood, with his friend, beside the piano, gravely intent. Some volumes of *lieder* lay about on the piano and Mark sometimes tried to pick out the songs which had most delighted him. Now Eliza was doing the same thing, but with much more success.

" Brahms," said Mark smiling. " *Wie Melodien.* . . ."

" We might go down to the Institute and have a hundred up," suggested Kenneth.

" No, let's go in and make Eliza play some more."

" She can't play. She can only strum."

" Oh, she's not bad. I say ! "

Eliza had begun to sing. Her little voice, easy and untrained, soared up like a bird taking flight. Mark turned and went into the house.

Dusk filled the drawing-room. Light from the rosy sky outside lay in quiet pools here and there, on mirrors, bowls and polished tables. A blur of cigarette smoke hung over Joy, who sprawled in the shadows. Eliza had lighted one candle and put it on the piano. In its soft radiance her face, bent towards the music, had lost its childish uncertainty : it was intent and noble, stamped with a presage of what she might become. Mark looked at her and then went to stand behind her where he could see the music. At first she did not hear him. When she became aware of his presence she lost confidence, played a wrong note, and stopped. Maturity eluded her. She shrank once more into a clumsy, groping child.

" Go on," said Mark.

" Oh, I can't."

" You can do it much better than I can," he said gently.

He began to turn over the volumes on the piano and to speak of other songs. Kenneth, watching jealously, saw an astonishing change in his manner. The arrogance and formidability were gone, and without them he seemed to be quite a different person. He was talking to Eliza in a simple, unguarded way, as if she had been an equal. He might almost have been pleading with her—trying to lure back the creature she had been a moment ago.

Eliza's voice, shy and uncertain, demanded if he had ever tried to play *Am Wasser Zu Singen*. She could play it but to sing it at the same time was too difficult.

" Then hum it," said Mark, finding the song and putting it on the stand for her. " I'll hum it too."

She began to play and hum. Mark joined in like a cheerful bumble bee. The imperfections of the perform- ance troubled neither of them for their minds were fixed upon an imaginary rendering, this song as it might be sung in a perfect world.

Kenneth stood irresolute. To join them was impos- sible, for he could not hum in tune. Nor could he pretend to listen with any pleasure to such a peculiar noise. His mother ought to have been there to sit on Eliza, who could not really play and was much too ready to butt in. But there was only Joy, mooning away as usual, more like a piece of furniture than a human being. He clattered across the room and asked her loudly where everybody was.

" I don't know," said Joy rousing herself. " I think Daphne is writing letters in the schoolroom. Your father has gone down to the inn to ask why the beer didn't come."

" Where's Grandmamma ? "

" Gone down to see the Blochs."

There was a pause in the music and Kenneth called out ironically to know if he and Joy were expected to applaud. But the pair at the piano took no notice. They started again. Eventually he wandered off into the garden, racked by an anguished jealousy which he knew to be ridiculous.

Joy followed him a few minutes later. She wanted to be in the garden when Alec came up from the inn. No fixed plan of action guided her, but she had taken to doing things like this. Whenever she could she placed herself in his way and forced him to be aware of her. It was an impulse which she could not control and which had been released that day when she sat with Mrs. Canning by the shores of Llyn Alyn.

No thought of the future troubled her. She did not ask herself what she would do with him if she got him. It was almost as if she expected to die as soon as that fulfilment had been tasted. Nor did she reason on the subject. Reason, such fragments of it as were left to her, merely stood in the way.

It was cool and dark in the garden. An immense, clear sky, far deeper and more spacious than the sky of day time, spread its tent over the watchful earth. She climbed to the second terrace and leant her elbows on the wall which still had a lingering warmth from the sun which had baked it all day. A smell of night stocks reached her. Cool air fanned her bare shoulders.

For a moment the doors of her prison house were unbarred and she emerged to draw a breath of freedom. Her lost self faintly summoned her. There might have been another Joy, not rotting in captivity, not a slave, but free to possess the world, free to laugh, see, hear and know. A nice, honest creature, this lost self could have been, capable of fortitude and wisdom. But in these chains she must dwindle and die. Overpowered with shame she could only whisper :

"Forget him . . . go away . . . put an end to it . . . you're mad . . . this isn't love . . . it's horrible . . . be brave and end it . . ."

Footsteps came up through the garden. She could see the end of his cigar moving like a firefly down below. Now he was on her terrace, his head and shoulders outlined against the sky. He had stopped and seen

her, where she leant against the wall. He was not going
to pass on. He was coming to lean on the wall beside
her.

Down at the inn he had met some friends and had had
several drinks. If he had had one drink less, he would
have gone straight on. But he was in that easy mood
when indiscretions are committed, and the girl puzzled
him. He had been thinking about her lately. Whereas,
in the past, he had seldom been aware of her, she seemed
now to be always before him. Nor could he decide whether
this was a mere accident or whether she was doing it on
purpose.

" You seem to be very thoughtful," he said.

This opening he immediately regretted, for he had meant
to avoid personalities. There was no harm in leaning
beside her on the terrace, but he must be careful what he
said.

" I was thinking," said Joy, " that I shall be sorry not
to come here next summer."

" Why ?   Aren't you coming next summer ? "

" I don't know if I'll be able to.   I'm thinking of taking
a new job, in the autumn.   I'm sick of teaching.   A
friend, a girl I know, wants me to go and help her run a sort
of book shop in Chelsea.   I rather think I will."

" What does Betsy think of it ?   Have you told her ? "

" No.   I haven't told anybody."

" And . . . your mother ? "

" She's going to live with her sister any way.   That's
quite settled.   I shall be glad to have rather more freedom.
I think one ought to live one's own life, don't you ? "

Alec reflected that Betsy and the Hewitts would probably
disapprove. Joy had been trained, at their expense, to
teach in a kindergarten and make a home for her mother.
And then it struck him that he would not see her again
very often. She would no longer come to Pandy Madoc
in the summer and Betsy, offended, might not invite her
to Well Walk. Very soon she would not be his employee

any more, but a queer girl, a disturbing girl, whom he had never quite understood, who seemed to be modest, but who sometimes gave him looks.

The silence went on too long and he broke it to make, in spite of himself, another personal remark.

" Aren't you catching cold ? "

" No," she said, hugging her bare arms together. " I'm quite warm."

His moral censor warned him urgently to stop and go away as he sought confirmation for this statement.

" H'm . . . yes . . . you are ! "

Stop it you fool ! Don't touch her ! Let go of her elbow !

" You women," he exclaimed, " are extraordinary. I can't think why you don't all die of pneumonia. That dress you have on, muslin isn't it . . ."

" Chiffon . . ."

" There's no warmth in it. Now, I have on a cloth coat and I'm none too warm."

" Silk is supposed to be the warmest thing there is," said Joy distractedly, as his grip on her arm tightened.

" No. It's the triumph of mind over matter."

He said this a little too pompously and made haste to add :

" Clothes, for us, are a mere covering. But not for you. You never think of them from the point of view of warmth or convenience : you're independent from those considerations . . ."

For some little time he went on talking of clothes though he knew that she was not listening. This impersonal and slightly solemn dissertation seemed to minimize the significance of what he was doing. So long as he could keep it up his arm could remain where it was quite comfortably. It meant nothing. He had just wanted to know, that was all, and now he knew. Had he wished, he could have gone much farther. He could have gone as far as he liked. She was his if he wanted her. But he was not so drunk as all that. He knew when to stop. Gracefully, almost absent-mindedly, he would, in a moment, remove his arm and bid her good night.

Suddenly he laughed aloud. A ridiculous couplet had bounced into his mind : *He removed his arm from about her waist and she died . . . of the sudden cold.* Joy started and stiffened. The poor little thing was frightened by that brutal guffaw, and no wonder.

" Sorry . . ." he mumbled. " Darling . . . I'm sorry . . ."

Cad ! Kissing the governess !

She's not the governess. She runs a bookshop.

The quick breath of a furnace swept over him. His laughter, his curiosity and his tipsy assurance crumbled. He felt that he had never kissed anybody before, never experienced contact with another existence, never desired anything so much as he desired this girl. Except once . . .

" Was it you ? " he whispered. " You ? Behind the curtain ? "

" Yes . . ."

" Come up . . . come up to the garden house for a minute . . ."

And then, suddenly, he had pushed her away.

" Sorry," he said again. " I must be drunk."

There were footsteps, near by, retreating. Joy gasped and steadied herself against the wall. He realized that he had heard these steps, a moment ago, quite near on the terrace. Somebody was running away. He leant over the wall, peering into the darkness.

" Who is that ? " he called.

He dashed down to the lower terrace, but by that time the footsteps had gone. The garden seemed to be quite empty.

This sudden diversion had sobered him. Of the excitement which he had experienced not a trace was left. It was like an electric current, which has been switched off.

Anxiety and self-reproach took its place. He became conscious of extreme folly. Joy was leaning over the wall above him and he called out to her :

" Did you see who it was ? "

" No."

Nothing on earth would induce him to go back. He hesitated and then bade her good night.

" Good night, Alec."

As he hurried back to the house he tried to convince himself that the footsteps in the dark meant nothing. And he made vows for the future. No harm had been done, but he had learnt that he could not trust himself.

Betsy's fault, he told himself. She keeps me in a refrigerator, and then turns loose a violent girl like that at me. . . .

His mother was in the drawing-room, crouched over a patience board where she had just set out a game of Senior Wrangler. She gave him a sharp, curious glance and he felt as if his entrance had been too hasty and disordered.

" I've been down at the Pub," he explained. " I went to see about the beer and met the Garstangs. Has everybody gone to bed ? "

" I don't know," said Mrs. Canning. " I've only just come in myself."

" Oh ? Where have you been ? "

" Down at the Blochs. They asked me in for coffee and to see his designs for that film."

" Oh, really ? "

He reassured himself. It could not have been her feet on the terrace. She would never have run like that in the dark.

As she dealt out her first pack she said, casually :

" The poor Blochs ! They find English life so puzzling. I've been trying to explain Lord St. Mullins to them."

" Max ? Why ? Do they know him ? "

" Oh, yes. He was down here in June, you remember, staying with his sister over at Llanfair. The Blochs were at the cottage and they met him when he came to see Betsy."

" Oh, that was it. Well, I don't wonder he puzzled them. He needs a lot of explaining."

" They couldn't understand how Betsy's cousin could be an earl and she have no title. They seemed to think him very odd altogether."

" He is, don't you think ? "

" I don't think I've ever actually met him."

" Oh, mother, you must have. Why, he was at our wedding."

' I don't remember him. I remember a lot of Buttevant relations, Mrs. Pattison and the old Lord St. Mullins, the old uncle and the boy who was the heir then, the poor boy who was drowned, but I don't seem to remember . . ."

" If you'd once seen him you couldn't forget him."

She shook her head, looking elderly and vague.

" Why ? Does he look so queer ? "

" Oh, you know . . . he's a wizened little creature, with a squeaky voice. Always chattering and waving his hands about."

" What age would he be now ? "

" Forty-ish. But he never grows any older. He was never young either. Always an elderly boy. I believe his parents were pretty old when he was born, which may account for it. You know how an apple looks, that shrivels before it's ripe ? "

" Is he nice ? " asked Mrs. Canning. " Apart from his appearance ? "

" Well . . . you can't dislike him, exactly. He's so warm hearted and so desperately sincere. You know he was madly in love with Betsy ? "

" Oh ? Was he ? "

Mrs. Canning dealt out her second pack. He went to mix himself a drink at the side table. She seemed to have forgotten his discomposed entrance and he hastened to distract her mind with further conversation.

" Yes. And when she turned him down he cried so much, poor little man, that she very nearly changed her mind. He's a fearful bore, really, but he has hundreds of friends because nobody has the heart to snub him. And then he's a crank : can't leave the world alone. Thinks it's his job to make it a better place. Goes about trying to stop atrocities. I must say he's as brave as a lion ; in the eye of God he must be worth a dozen of me. He'll go up to any ruffian, twice his size, and tell him he didn't ought to. One can't but admire him. He'll take any risk."

" What is Betsy's view of him ? "

" Oh, she laughs at him, but I think she's rather fond of him, too. He regards her as a kind of goddess, which must be a very endearing trait."

" Very ! And you . . . you like him on the whole ? "

" Yes . . . on the whole. But he's got no sense of proportion. He goes on about his causes in season and out of season. You ask him to dinner and he brings a lot of exhibits with him, genuine instruments of torture that he's brought back from somewhere, or photographs of vermin in slums. Makes you sick in the middle of dinner. He tries to be matey with me because I'm Betsy's husband, but we haven't a thing in common. He will cross-examine me about the theatre, if the stage hands get unemployment pay, and how many cubic feet of air the chorus have in their dressing-rooms. Of course I can't tell him."

" Does he like being an earl ? "

" I think he does rather. He likes speaking in the House of Lords. It's a place where he can talk without being interrupted. He never could get into the Commons in the old days. He was always trying and always forfeiting his deposit. And he enjoys all that money, I think. Not that he spends any of it on himself. But he likes giving it away."

Mrs. Canning looked up quickly.

" Oh ? Is there much money ? I should have thought with three sets of death duties, so close together . . ."

"No, there weren't three. Only one. The heirs died off first, you remember, and he inherited straight from that old uncle you met. Oh yes, he's horribly rich. Owns three seaside resorts."

The patience had come out. Mrs. Canning began to stack up the cards and put them away.

"Then," she said lightly, "if Betsy hadn't refused him, she'd have been a countess by now, and very rich."

"Yes. Poor Betsy! She did miss a chance. But no self-respecting woman could marry Max."

"Where is this place . . . Llanfair . . . where his sister lives? Mrs. Pattison?"

"Isobel's house? Oh, it's down south, along the coast. About fifteen miles or so."

"I was wondering if I ought to call on her, while I'm here. It might be civil."

"Oh, I don't think you need unless you'd like to."

"She and Betsy are great friends, aren't they?"

"Well no. I wouldn't say that. Of course they've known each other all their lives. They're cousins. They like each other as much as most cousins do."

She rose, collected her cards, her work and her spectacles, and wished him good night. As he went to open the door for her she said:

"I think I'll call. I'd like to meet her again."

When she had gone he began to feel that he had been talking too much. He had done so to cover his own nervous disarray, but he was not quite sure that he had been successful.

And he was surprised that his mother had never met Max. At the time he had been chattering so much that he had never paused to examine the unlikelihood of it. Now he did so and became convinced that she was mistaken. She must have met Max repeatedly. She could not have helped doing so.

But she was growing old and her memory was failing. She often made odd little mistakes. Betsy, who was prejudiced, asserted that there was always some motive behind these innocent confusions. He could not think this was a case in point ; there could be no possible motive here. She must genuinely have forgotten, and he had no grounds for feeling that he had been pumped. Yet, if he had not been off his guard, distracted, not quite sober, he would have talked less. Not that he could remember having said anything particularly indiscreet. But indiscretion, that evening, seemed to charge the air, and he was far from happy.

THE FRIENDS

MARK was brushing his teeth when he heard Kenneth run upstairs, pause, and knock at the door.

" Come in ! " he called pleasantly. " Where on earth have you been all this time ? "

" In the garden," said Kenneth, shutting the door.

" Eating worms ? "

" Shut up ! "

Mark turned round quickly and saw that his friend was still in a black mood. That must be set right. Young Kenneth must not be allowed to fly off the handle so easily.

" Why did you go off like that ? " he demanded. " We wanted to play poker and we couldn't find you."

" I thought you were singing."

" Not all night, you ass. You know, you ought to be more tolerant of other people's amusements. I dare say we did make a shocking noise, but we didn't do it for long. You must take your turn at being left out of things occasionally. Eliza has to, and she doesn't sulk."

" And when do you have to ? "

Mark laughed.

" I don't have to. I'm so broadminded."

Kenneth sat down listlessly on the bed. He was looking quite green and Mark began to realize that this was beyond a childish huff. Something had gone seriously wrong. He asked, in a kinder voice, if anything was the matter.

" Nothing."

" Got a belly ache ? "

" No."

" Well, you look as if you had."

" Do I ? "

" Get off my bed, if you don't mind, because I want to get into it."

There was a pause. Mark waited for information, but Kenneth merely hung about the room until he lost patience.

" Either you say what's on your mind or go away."

" I couldn't ever tell anybody," declared Kenneth, beginning to shiver.

Yet he had obviously come there to tell Mark. He was sick, furious and excited.

" Oh well," said Mark, risking a guess. " Don't make such a fuss about it. I suppose you fell over a couple in the dark."

" How did you know ? "

" Is that it ? "

" Yes."

Now they were on safe ground. Mark thought he knew how to deal with his.

" It happened to me once," he said, " when I was quite a kid. In a ruined cottage. . . . I was sick in the car going home. Say what you like, it's not pretty . . . no. . . ."

He lay back on his pillows and stared at the ceiling. Actually he was not nearly as sure of himself as he wished to appear. His mind was an excessively well regimented domain. Everything in it was neatly labelled and pigeon-holed. No problems were left lying about unsolved. But it did not rule, as he would have liked to think, supreme over the neighbouring countries. It hung, like a little star, in the midst of chaos. Outside there was a dark region of shapeless seething impulses and passions which he dared not explore. To bring those tumultuous forces into light and order was a task beyond his reason to accomplish, so that he generally pretended they were not there. Laughter was his best safeguard ; a part of his tidy mind was given over to ribaldry and thither he retreated when threatened by the unknown.

He now wanted to laugh and to make Kenneth laugh.
A good rude giggle would put everything right. He said
in the voice of the housemaster who had prepared them
both for confirmation :

" You understand what happens, eh boys ? Perfectly
wholesome ! Perfectly natural ! Don't *laugh*, Wedder-
burn ! This . . . is . . . not . . . a . . . joke ! "

" I don't think it is," said Kenneth. " I see nothing
funny about it."

He began to retch. Nobody could be further from
laughter than he was.

" I say," said Mark in alarm. " You can't cat over my
bed. Go and drink some water."

He jumped out of bed and brought some water himself,
in a tooth glass. Kenneth took it with a croak of thanks.

" Do buck up," urged Mark. " What were they doing,
anyway ? "

" K-kissing."

" Kissing. Good God ! Is that all ? "

Kenneth swallowed some more water and blurted it
out.

" It was my father . . . and Joy. . . ."

There was a freezing silence. Mark was appalled. No
joke could possibly be made out of this. The sympathy
melted from his face and his expression became severe.

" I see," he said at last. " Well . . . you can't do
anything about it. So if I were you I'd cut off to bed
and forget about it."

" He's a filthy old swine. He makes me sick."

" I'm sorry, but I don't want to hear about it. He's
your father, not mine."

" If he was your father, what would you think ? "

Mark had not the slightest idea. He had never known
his own father, who had been killed in the war. His
mother too had died when he was quite small and he had
grown up alone, with no family life, never taking anything
or anybody for granted. He knew very little about love

or affection. His mind had ripened early but his heart
had been undernourished.

"Very funny, isn't it?" insisted Kenneth. "Frightful
joke. I suppose you'd roar with laughter if it was your
father."

"No. Of course I shouldn't. Don't be an idiot."

"Then what would you do?"

That he did not know was all that Mark could have
said. The situation shocked him profoundly. But he did
not like to admit either of these facts, or to surrender his
own reputation for infallibility. Kenneth had always
regarded him as a mentor and to confess himself at a loss
would not have been pleasant. Vanity, no less than
disgust, prompted him to evade the issue.

He hesitated. He knew that he was being asked for
help, and he was very much aware of Kenneth's instability.
That was a thing which he had recognized long ago : the
boy might easily go to pieces unless somebody took pains
to keep him straight. He had repaid Kenneth's adoration
by accepting a certain moral responsibility for him. If he
rejected this appeal he would be failing his friend.

He did reject it, simply because he found no authori-
tative pronouncement in any of his pigeonholes. He could
produce no formula. And he was too inexperienced, too
immature, to know that no formula was required, and
that an apt generalization will mend no wounded hearts.
Sympathy was all that was needed, but he had much to
learn before he could understand that.

"I can't discuss your father's morals," he said. "It's
impossible. Don't make such a fuss about it, anyway.
I don't see it's your business."

"Oh, isn't it? You said yourself you were sick once
. . . and that wasn't anybody to do with you I suppose."

"That was quite different. They weren't merely
kissing."

Kenneth went and put the glass down on the washstand.
Then, half-turned away from Mark, he said in a low voice :

" But did it . . . make you feel you wanted to do the same thing yourself . . . in spite of feeling sick ? "

" Oh shut up," said Mark furiously. " Think of something else. Everybody is the same. But you forget about it unless you're a rotter."

" Perhaps I am a rotter. It may be hereditary."

Mark's comment on this was brief.

" Anyway," said Kenneth, going out of the room, " I think you've been beastly about it."

A WASTED MORNING

THE news from London was reassuring. Mrs. Hewitt was said to be out of danger and Professor Hewitt had come to take charge of her, so that Betsy was hoping to get back to Pandy Madoc quite soon. But there was, in Betsy's letters, an undercurrent of anxiety which Alec could not fail to perceive. They were full of unspoken questions. She wanted to know what his mother was up to. He indicated, in his replies, that his mother was up to nothing at all, as far as he could see.

" She's extraordinarily placid," he wrote, " and I've never known her to take life so easily. She lets us all do what we like, if you can believe such a thing.

" If anything, she's a bit too easy going ; it's quite time you came back and took up the reins. Liberty is one thing and licence is another. Indulgence doesn't spoil me ; I can stand any amount of it. But I like to see other people toeing the line.

" The maids are getting abominably slack. Blodwen has gone back to her habit of only putting one shoe in my room at a time, so that I can never find a pair. And the children are getting out of hand. Ken has been quite impossible these last few days, sulky and offensive to a degree. It may be that he misses Mark Hannay, who went off on Tuesday. But he's going through a most unpleasant phase. He lost the key of the garage this morning. Pure laziness ! He put it in his pocket, instead of taking the trouble to return it to its proper place. Then went bathing and lost it on the beach. We had to send to Morvah for a man to cut a new key. When I ticked him off he wouldn't apologize—was unbearably insolent. I found myself saying all the sort of things I never expected to say to my children : ' I dislike your tone, etc.' A nasty scene. But he'll settle down when you come back. He isn't the only one of us who needs you badly.

" Betsy dear, you were right about lobsters not agreeing with me. Shall I never learn that you know best ? Mother has fed us lobsters every day for a week and I never want to see one again. I've been thoroughly out of sorts but took bismuth in large quantities and am now all right again. But do please come home soon, for it's mouldy without you."

He was working very hard indeed and saw little of his family save at breakfast and supper. This was partly in response to pressure from Johnnie Graham, and partly in order to keep away from Joy. For several days he had never seen her except at meals and was beginning to hope that the incident had been closed.

One morning, however, when he went up to the garden house after breakfast, he found a letter lying on his desk. As he read it his imagined security came crashing about his ears.

DEAR ALEC (it said),

Mrs. Canning has told me that you and Betsy are going to be divorced. She says that you have to go off with some woman for a little while, to get the evidence.

Is this true ? And if you must go off with somebody will you let that person be me ? I must tell you that I love you so much that I think I shall die if I am never to see you again. You are the whole of life to me. Of course I know that you do not, and never can, love me like this. But, after what happened the other night, I don't feel that you would mind going away with me for a little while, and afterwards I should never bother you, or ask for anything, or ever expect to see you again. I should have had a little bit of happiness and that is more than many people have. I would rather have just a little time with you and then try to start life all over again, than go on for ever with nothing. I should be miserable afterwards, but my life would have some meaning and now it has no meaning. I should prefer that kind of misery to this.

Please do not think that I am too young. I understand what I am doing perfectly and it will not ruin my life. As you know, I am leaving my job and going to run this book shop. My friend will not mind about my private life because she has done it too.

I am writing this because it will be easier for both of us if you want to say no. If you write it, not say it, I mean. But do not, do not say no unless you really feel you don't like me well enough. And do not be angry with me for writing. I am in such despair. I cannot bear it any longer. You won't look at me or speak to me, but you have no right to be angry.

JOY.

There were so many bombs dropped in this letter that Alec could scarcely make up his mind which had shattered him most.

The opening sentence, with its certain evidence of his mother's duplicity, stunned him. She had been aware, all the time, of his breach with Betsy and had actually gossiped about it. There was no end to the harm she might have done. For all that he knew, she might now be spreading the news to Isobel Pattison with whom she had gone to lunch.

And as for Joy. . . .

This was a perfect nightmare. For more than an hour he banged about the room, cursing all women, even Betsy, who had brought this upon him by her untimely letter to Switzerland. He was so furious that he did not, at first, contemplate making any kind of answer to Joy. She deserved none. He would ignore her outrageous proposal and it was to be hoped that she would guess, from his silence, what he thought of her.

But, after a while, other considerations occurred to him. If he did not reply she might, perhaps, think that he was making up his mind. They would have to meet at meal times with the burden of this unanswered letter between them. Besides he ought not to allow his mother's gossip to go uncontradicted. Perhaps he had better write a short, stern note, denying the likelihood of a divorce and making the girl, if possible, ashamed of herself. He flung himself into his chair, seized a pen, and wrote :

DEAR JOY,
My mother is mistaken. Betsy and I are not going to be divorced so that this situation does not arise. . . .

Need he, he wondered, say any more than that ? Would she realize the implied rebuff ? Or must he say that in no circumstance would he have listened to her suggestion ?

Remembering all that had occurred upon the garden terrace, he began to feel that some sort of explanation was necessary. Look at it how he would, the blame was mostly his. While admitting this, he must try to bring her to her senses, to put the whole thing in a more rational light. She must not be allowed to go through life with such an exaggerated idea of the importance of a kiss.

He read through her letter again and was moved, for the first time, to a sort of compassion for the pain in it. Shock had prevented him from feeling this before. He had been so much occupied with his own troubles that he had not fully grasped her state of mind. Now he was obliged to admit that she suffered, that she believed herself to love him, and that he had given her undeniable encouragement. Such a mistake in so young a girl was not unpardonable, nor was it his place to scold her. He ought rather to help her if he could, and to word his reply so as not to hurt her feelings. The mere fact of rejection would be humiliating enough ; he must try to save her from unnecessary bitterness. For he was twenty years older than she and more experienced ; it lay with him to clear the matter up.

With more muttered oaths he addressed her again :

" But, my dear Joy . . ."

Was that too kind ? He did not think so.

". . . I couldn't, in any circumstances, listen to your suggestion for a moment. In the first place, I don't think you quite understand the custom in these matters among decent people. The divorce law, it's true, requires evidence of infidelity ; but this is a mere matter of form. It generally means no more than a week-end spent in some hotel. . . ."

Oh, Lord ! Oh, Lord ! Is that enough ? Will she understand ? I don't have to use the word adultery, do I ? This is simply underlining the fact that she's offered to . . .

" But there is no actual infidelity . . ."

Collusion, in fact, my dear Joy ! So nice to have to explain it to you. And so prudent, supposing I was going to be divorced. Oh, Betsy ! I could wring your neck for this !

" And in the second place I couldn't possibly allow you to be mixed up in it. I should be behaving scandalously. You are so young and Betsy's friend, and part of my ' family ' in the Roman sense of the word.

" In the third place, I must try to convince you that your feeling for me is not as important or permanent as you think it is. I am older and more experienced, and I am sure that this is so. Of course I am touched and grateful . . ."

Am I ? No. Yes. Perhaps I am. Poor little thing !

". . . and I feel that it is partly my fault because I lost my head the other night. I have no excuse to offer for that. I behaved very badly, and I am ashamed of myself. But do please believe that, in a very few years . . ."

Years ? That sounds very conceited. She won't forget me for years ?

". . . in a very few months . . ."

A little hard-hearted perhaps ? As if I wasn't taking her seriously enough ?

". . . in a much shorter time than you now suppose you will have completely forgotten me. Everybody begins by loving the wrong person : the first shot is always wide. Sooner or later you'll find the right man. What you see in me is really some quality for which you are unconsciously looking in him. So that you aren't entirely on the wrong tack. When you find him you will know what I mean. He'll remind you of me, a little, but he'll be a hundred per cent nicer. So that you must not make yourself miserable over this, my dear, and try to realize that the happiest people begin by making mistakes. I am very glad that you have told me, and you must not be sorry that you have done so because . . ."

He could not, for the life of him, see any reason why she should not feel sorry. She had offered herself to him. She had been rejected. Nothing really could soften that.

He read his letter over from the beginning, and it struck him as odiously false. It shirked the main issue—the strong physical attraction of which they were both aware. This existed, and he was trying to pretend that it did not. He was a coward and a hypocrite.

Taking another sheet of paper, he wrote as follows :

" I am not going off with anybody. If I were I should enjoy going off with you. You attract me very much, and I should get a considerable kick out of it as long as I could feel sure that it would land me in no obligations towards you. For I believe that, for both of us, the attraction would not last for long and that we should have very little in common when it was over. But it would be good fun while it lasted.

"It would be, however, both wrong and foolish, and I hope I should have the strength of mind to resist the temptation. Therefore let us put the idea of it out of our minds. That is the best possible thing that we can do for ourselves, for each other, and for everybody dear to us."

This was candid, to the point, and, in a queer way, far less insulting to her. But it could not be sent. Such words might be spoken, but they could never be committed to paper. He had some relics of prudence. Perhaps, after all, he had better talk to her.

He tore up all that he had written, and her letter, too, and burnt the pieces in the grate. It was half-past twelve and he had got nowhere. A day's work lay untouched upon his desk. The whole morning had been ruined by these blasted women. At luncheon he would have to meet her, which he could not possibly do until the matter had been settled. He must go to the golf club for the day.

On his way down the hill he remembered that he could not have the car. His mother had taken it over to Llanfair. So that he must go to the club on a bicycle, which, on that hilly coast, was almost as bad as walking. His rage boiled over. Like most good-tempered men, he had little control over himself when really put out. He felt it to be quite monstrous that he, Alec Canning, a distinguished man who had earned enough money to own a large Buick, should be obliged to push a bicycle for five miles upon a grilling day because a pack of intolerable women had driven him out of his home.

The key to the bicycle shed hung, or should hang, on a nail behind the front door. He turned into the house to get it and ran slap into Joy, who was doing the flowers in the hall. They exchanged one panic-stricken glance.

"I'm going to the golf club," he said hastily. "Where's the key of the bicycle shed?"

"On the nail. Isn't it on the nail?"

" No, it's not. It's not on the nail."

" Oh, isn't it ? "

" No, it's not."

" Perhaps Ken took it."

" God in heaven ! Where is he ? "

" I don't know. Gone to Morvah."

She had never seen Alec in a rage before, and she was
bewildered.

" Can't I . . ." she said wildly, ". . . can't I run
and . . ."

" What ? "

" Get another key ? "

" Get another key ? Where from ? "

It was a ridiculous thing to say, but she had wished
to appear helpful. Her futility, her white, startled face,
were like a match to powder. He exploded :

" What nonsense ! What utter nonsense ! How can
you talk such nonsense ? . . . I've had about as much
nonsense as I can stand."

" Oh, Alec ! Are you very angry with me ? Why are
you so angry ? "

" Why ? Why ? Isn't it enough that my mother
should have been spreading this story . . . these
lies . . ."

" Then it's not true ? "

" Of course it's not. Not a word of truth in it."

" Oh ! oh ! But how could I know ? How
could . . ."

" And then you must needs pester me . . ."

" Alec ! Oh, Alec ! "

". . . with this abominable suggestion ! Oh, it was my
fault. Oh, yes ! I know it was my fault. I shouldn't
have kissed you. But you asked for it. . . ."

" I only . . ."

" For God's sake go away. Clear out and go away.
Leave me alone. I never want to see you or think of you
again. If you had any decency you'd go. . . ."

She hid her face in her hands and cowered away from him as though he was beating her. She stood, shrinking and cowering, for a long time after he had finished speaking, after he had gone.

THE RETURN

IN the early afternoon the fine day clouded to a melancholy softness. The string of mountains across the bay was blue and clear, and the dove-grey sea stretched away to them without a wave or a shadow. Betsy, on her way up the hill from the station, kept stopping and looking about her; in the train she had been restless and agitated, but this quiet evening soothed her. She was very glad to be at home and she felt as if sky, sea and earth were making her welcome. She had thought so much about her reception in the house, wondering what Mrs. Canning had been doing, what Alec would say, and what would happen next. But she had forgotten that she was coming back to a place that she had loved for many years. Now she was going to love it more, be more ready to hear its gentle voice, because it was one of the things that she was going to keep. If she gave up this impatient craving for freedom and resigned herself to duty, she would at least have this to help her. And she would have a tranquil mind with which to enjoy it.

And up there, up at the house, she thought, there is nothing very difficult to be done. No one is against me, They all love me. There is no fighting. Even she is fond of me and wishes me well. We both want the same thing. But I must stay in this peaceful frame of mind. I must not let her upset me. I must try to be wise and loving; I must keep this peace in my heart. I am sad now. But all peace has something sad in it. To accept is more difficult than to fight. . . .

Everybody seemed to be out when she got to Pandy Madoc. The doors stood open and the rooms lay empty in the quiet grey light. She looked into the drawing-room and saw an untidy heap of music lying on the open piano ; the room bore traces of an alien occupation. Some of the chairs had been moved. The window seat was littered with canvas and embroidery wools. The book-cases had not been dusted properly. She took in these tiny details with a faint uneasiness, for they were all eloquent of the woman who had been living there while she was away. It was as if Emily Canning could stamp herself indelibly upon any place where she had been.

But it could all be put straight very quickly, in five minutes, thought Betsy, going back into the hall, where there was an unpleasant smell of dead flowers. With rising irritation she saw that all the flower-bowls and vases were scattered in disorder on the hall table. Most of them were half filled with dirty water. On a heap of newspaper lay a mass of decaying, stinking vegetation, ready to be thrown away. Somebody must have begun to do the flowers and then left them, hours ago, for the freshly cut bunches of sweet peas and roses were already withered, poor things !

Betsy, who hated bad smells, turned away with an impulse to get out once more into the fresh air, to re-capture the mood of her arrival. But a slight movement on the stairs arrested her. She looked up and saw Mrs. Canning peering over the bannisters, bright-eyed and furtive, like some animal peeping out of its burrow. The hidden presence in the house had come alive.

" Betsy ! "

" Hallo ! I'm back, you see ! "

I must be loving and wise, she reminded herself, and she smiled as kindly as she could.

Mrs. Canning came running down into the hall.

" But, my dear, we never knew you were coming to-day ! Did you telegraph ? "

"No," said Betsy, still smiling. "I thought I'd give you all a surprise."

"Your mother? How is she?"

"Very, very much better. Quite out of danger. The report this morning was so good that I just jumped into the train and came home."

"But . . . you poor thing! Nobody met you."

"That's all right. I walked up. I liked the walk after sitting in the train all day. My suit-case can be fetched up from the station any time. How is everybody? Where are they all?"

"I don't know. Alec seems to have gone over to the golf links."

"Oh, has he?" asked Betsy in surprise. "When he's so hard at work? Is he stuck or something?"

"I don't know. I've been out all day, lunching with Mrs. Pattison."

"Oh!"

Something in Mrs. Canning's tone suggested that she could have said a great deal more if she liked. Betsy felt the old defensive uneasiness, the need to be on her guard and to make little plots in order to frustrate other little plots. But if she was to be loving and wise she must ignore that feeling. She asked casually if there was any news.

"Oh . . . Joyce Thing . . . your sub-scrub . . ."

"Joy Benson?"

"She says she has a headache. I've just been up to her room. I don't know what the matter can be. She looks as if she's been crying herself silly. But she calls it a headache."

"Oh," said Betsy, looking at the flower-table, "so that's why . . . oh, well! I'll go up and find out what's the matter."

But at that moment Kenneth appeared in the doorway. At the sight of his mother he gave a joyful cry and flung himself upon her. She hugged him almost fiercely. Alec's account of him had alarmed her, and she saw in a moment

that things had been going badly with him. Then Eliza
and Daphne came bounding in. The hall was full of
chatter and the house woke up from its grey repose. The
maids in the kitchen began to make domestic noises.
Footsteps ran up and downstairs, doors banged and taps
ran in the bathrooms.

Mrs. Canning went into the drawing-room and sat in the
window-seat, working at her tapestry. She was making
a cover for Betsy's piano stool in a very striking design
which she had copied from a piece in South Kensington
Museum. Like all her undertakings, it was original and
charming, and at first sight provoked admiration. But
she lacked the patience to carry it out properly. The
stitches were uneven, the rows slanted in different direc-
tions and the colours were wrongly shaded. None of the
groundwork had been done, only the more amusing parts
of the pattern, and it was probable that the piece would
end its days in the bottom of a certain Florentine chest,
along with many other half-finished embroideries, some
of them fifty years old. For she meant to finish them all
some time, and so could not bear to throw any of them
away. But instead she kept launching herself upon new
enterprises, as a child of ten might do. The contents of
that drawer were proof that a child of ten can be a wife,
a mother, a grandmother, an arbitress in the lives of other
people, and can delude the world into believing that she
is an experienced woman of sixty-eight.

A step on the gravel outside made her look up. Alec
was coming wearily through the garden. His day's golfing
could not have done him much good, for he looked quite
fagged out. She called to him through the window, and
when he came close she saw that he was in one of his
awful insane tempers. They only happened once in ten
years, so that in between she was apt to forget that they
could ever happen. But she knew the signs of them well
enough—an odd, unseeing look about the eyes.

" Betsy's back," she told him.

" Oh ! " he said. " Good ! "

He did not, however, say it with any great interest. His blind, angry eyes were directed towards his mother, and he added :

" I want a word with you some time."

She quailed for a moment and then remembered that she, too, wanted a word with him. He was angry with her, but she had a very good defence up her sleeve.

" Yes, dear," she said quietly. " But it's a quarter to eight. If you want a bath you must hurry."

He went on, round the house, and she continued to sew. From time to time she stopped pushing her needle through the stiff canvas and looked out at the grey sky and the grey sea and the fringe of mountains hanging between them. There would be no sunset. It was all melting into a gentle dusk.

THE QUARREL

MRS. CANNING'S rule was over and the children were sent to bed early. Betsy followed them almost at once, for she was tired and ill at ease. Serenity had deserted her; it had begun to crumble the moment she got into the house.

There was something evil in the air, hanging about like a bad smell. She felt it, though she could not locate it. Half a dozen small things worried her, but these could easily be set right and could have no possible connection with one another. The house was dirty and untidy. The staff had grown slack. Joy had a headache. Kenneth was sulky. And Alec was not himself at all—still suffering, probably, from an excess of lobsters and bismuth. But none of these things, not all of them together, could account for this premonition of disaster.

Alone, in the seclusion of her bedroom, she held it at bay. This uneasiness, she told herself, was nothing new, nothing extraordinary. The mere presence of her mother-in-law was sufficient to create it. When Mrs. Canning was in the house little things became charged with a disproportionate significance; nobody was quite frank, and unexplained resentments sprang up. It meant nothing; it was simply that her temperament produced a kind of chemical reaction in the people about her.

Yet, thought Betsy, as she brushed her hair, she is not evil. She can be brave and generous. She is deeply attached to us all. But she has no truth. She simply doesn't know what truth is. When you fight her you fight with shadows . . . but soon she will go away. She will die some day. Yes . . . I shall be glad when she dies. . . . I wish that wasn't true, but there it is. Shall I be glad ? Or shall I be sorry that I didn't love her better ? When people die we see them in a different proportion. Just because they are dead and we are alive. We think of them as passive and ourselves as active . . . we feel that we should have been the ones to act and to tune up the relation-ship. . . . But perhaps there is still time. If I try very hard we may be friends yet. . . ."

In the drawing-room, immediately below, she could hear the rise and fall of voices. Alec and his mother were talking. She wondered how long they would be, and if she would have time to put cream on her face before they came upstairs. Alec had come back, since the departure of Mark Hannay, to sleep in his own room, and she hoped that he would drop in and have a little gossip with her before going to bed. But she did not want him to find her all creamy, for this was the first night of the new life. Nothing very much would happen. They would talk, and laugh, and make a few plans—that was all. But it would be the first step towards the readjustment of their lives.

Leaning towards the glass, she studied her face intently, trying to define the changes that seventeen years had wrought. They were, in sum, very small. It was still a young face, for she had taken care of her looks. But the girl who had married Alec . . . she was gone, swallowed up in the years. Time was rushing past and so much of it had been wasted. Soon she would be old. And some day they would both be dead, she and Alec, lying quiet and separate in their graves. That vanished girl had known nothing of time. All life was before her and she had known nothing—poor pitiable, enviable fool. Now time was everything. Every hour brought one nearer to the end.

A door closed, down below. She heard Mrs. Canning come upstairs and go into the spare room. She put down the pot of cold cream that she had picked up, and sat still, listening. But it was a long time before she heard his feet on the stairs, so long that she had begun to be a little indignant. For they had scarcely exchanged three words together alone yet, and he must know that she would be waiting for him. She told him to come in quite sharply when he last he knocked at her door.

" Betsy, what is this about Max Buttevant ? "

Her heart seemed to tumble downstairs. It couldn't be true. He hadn't said it.

" What ? What do you mean ? "

" Max St. Mullins, I mean. Is it true you've promised to marry him as soon as you've got rid of me ? "

" Who says so ? "

" Is it true ? "

" No. No, it's not true. Who says so ? "

" Isobel Pattison told my mother so this afternoon."

" She must be mad."

Betsy got up and began to put away some clothes in her wardrobe. She wanted time to find her feet again. She felt that she could get through this safely if only she had a little time. For she had plenty of things to say. She had thought it all out long ago, what she should say if Alec ever found out about Max. This ought not to have knocked the wind out of her so completely.

" Isobel says that he told her all about it before he went to China. He seemed to regard it as a settled thing— that you would get your freedom while he was away, and marry him later."

" He had no right to. I gave him no right."

" Did you ever discuss it with him—our divorce ? No . . . how could you ? He'd gone to China before it came up. Did he ask you to marry him ? What did you say ? Was that what put the idea of divorce into your head ? "

" Your mother has been making mischief. You are most unfair to listen to her. You promised you wouldn't discuss my affairs with her. It's disloyal. . . ."

" Please answer my questions. She has made an accusation against you. I want to know if it's true."

" Why shouldn't I marry Max ? If I was free it would be a perfectly respectable thing to do."

" I don't question that. I merely want to know why this is the first I've heard of it. Have you discussed with him, at any time, the possibility of you getting your freedom ? "

" Yes . . . I have . . . but . . ."

" When ? "

" In June. When he was down here."

" And you didn't ask me for your freedom till July."

" No. Because you weren't here. I made up my mind in June, and told you about it as soon as you came down."

" But you discussed it with him first ? "

" Yes. I told him I was thinking of it."

" Why ? "

" We are cousins . . . he is very fond of me. . . ."

" Did he ask you to marry him ? "

" Yes. Yes, he did. But . . ."

" Was this the first time he had asked you ? He's been in love with you for years. Why does he suddenly . . ."

" If you want to know, it was because he had only just heard about you and Chris Adams. He is not the sort of person who hears much gossip. He always thought we were perfectly happy together ; he hadn't the faintest idea of the real state of things. When he did discover it he was horrified, and begged me to leave you. . . ."

" And so you thought you would leave me. It was all his idea."

" Not at all. I was getting sick of you myself. I would have made up my mind just the same if he hadn't been there. He has nothing to do with it."

" Oh, hasn't he ? But he asked you to marry him and he thinks you're going to. Did you say that you wouldn't ? What did you say ? "

" I said we couldn't discuss it till I was free. I might want to marry him. I might not."

" And not a word of this to me ! Not a word ! "

" Why should I have told you ? It was all so indefinite. How could I know what I'd want to do in a couple of years' time ? It would have made it sound so much more definite than it was, if I told you. I never imagined that you would object to my remarrying, if we got a divorce. I shouldn't mind it if you did. I want you to. What we do when we are free is our own concern."

They were facing one another now, both reckless with anger.

" Then the reasons you gave me were pure humbug."

" No, they weren't."

" You felt the real reason wouldn't sound so good."

" You're grossly unfair. I won't be cross-examined. . . . I won't be treated like this. I . . ."

" Your insincerity is past praying for. I give it up. You pose as an injured wife, you play on my feelings, talk about the children . . . and all the time you . . . quite calmly . . . a man you don't love . . . you know you don't love him . . . you couldn't . . . but you want to be Lady St. Mullins, and so . . ."

" He loves me. He loves me and you don't. You never have. You only want to keep me because . . ."

" Well, do you want to marry him, or don't you ? "

" That's my business."

" It's mine too. If you do, we part on the spot. You've got to come out in the open now."

" I've told you. . . . I couldn't make up my mind till . . ."

" You think I'm going to hang about, waiting till you've made up your mind if you want to chuck me for that little monkey ? You'll make it up now."

" She told you to say that."

" No, she didn't."

" Setting this trap for me ! Going round behind my

back . . . collecting evidence . . . making me out so . . .
I shall never forgive you for listening to her."

" I don't ask you to forgive me. I had to find out the
truth, hadn't I ? "

" I've nothing to be ashamed of."

" You think not ? Haven't you lied to me, again and
again ? "

" I have not. I won't be bullied like this. You and
your mother . . . you can tell her she's done herself no
good by this. If you think this is the way to keep me . . ."

" What do you want ? Shall I go ? Make way for
him ? All right. I don't care. I'll go. I'll go to-
morrow. You're not worth . . ."

" Yes—go ! Go ! "

" I'll never come back if I do."

" I don't want you back. I want to be rid of you.
You've insulted me and called me a liar. If you don't
go, I shall."

" Right you are. Good-bye."

" Good-bye."

MIDNIGHT

A SWITCH clicked and the big room in the garden-
house sprang into light. It had the dreary, impersonal
look of a room revisited after it has been left for the night.
Its daily life had been suspended, the warmth of humanity
was extinguished. The untidy litter on the desk, the
pipes, the letter files, the scribbled sheets of foolscap, spoke
neither of yesterday nor of to-morrow.

Alec, still moving with the somnambulistic precision of
a man in a rage, went across to the desk and began to
collect his possessions. He had come up to find the score
of *Byron*, his manuscript, some unanswered letters and
a cheque-book. For he was packing his things. He had
begun to do so the moment he left Betsy's room ; he had
gone straight to the box-room and pulled out a couple of
suit-cases. There was a train at seven o'clock next morning and he meant to take it. He was determined to do
something violent and irrevocable.

Betsy's face was always before him, not as he had seen
it just now, for he had been too blind to look at her, but
melancholy and appealing, as it had been when she first
came to him, in this very room, and begged for her freedom.
He lashed himself, remembering every word that she had
then said, her false friendliness, her appeal to his generosity.
She was a bitch, and he was sorry that he had not told her
so ; a sly, cold-blooded, heartless bitch. If she had had
a lover he could have forgiven it. But she cared nothing
for Max, nothing for anybody, bitch that she was, daughter
of the horse-leech. . . .

But he was done with her now. She would get no more

from him save leave to go to hell her own way. He wasn't going to worry. She could sell herself to that little monkey on a stick, go to bed with him, sell her precious body that she made such a fuss about. It would be an easy bargain for her, the fellow was as good as a eunuch, but she'd like that, it would suit her down to the ground. Much cry and little wool was her idea of a bargain. Now he'd found her out he wasn't going to worry. There were other women in the world and better ones. Plenty of them. Oh, yes, he could get on very well without her.

The sheets of his manuscript were all mixed up, and, as he sorted them, he began to whistle softly, because he was so calm, because going away meant so little to him. Why he whistled a hymn tune he did not know ; it was the first tune that came into his mind out of that dark store-house where it had lurked for more than forty years in company with heaven knows what spasm of infantile jealousy :

> " Jerusalem the golden
> With milk and honey blest ! "

To Joy, crouching among the divan cushions, the whistling was horrible.

The same tune came over and over again as he rustled the sheets of foolscap. She was petrified with fright. She lay there, scarcely breathing, and prayed that he would soon stop and go away :

> " Beneath thy contemplation
> Sink heart and voice opprest ! "

When first the light dazzled her and he was there, walking about the room, she had thought he must have come on purpose to find her. He had pursued her up here in his anger. She had cowered away helplessly, waiting for him to speak. Only gradually had she become aware that he thought himself alone, and then it was too late to move.

He had not once looked at the dark corner where she lay. He was busy all the time at his desk.

"Jerusalem the golden . . ."

Sometimes it stopped for a moment as he paused to glance over a letter or a sheet of notes. Then, in the silence, she could hear moths banging themselves about the room. They had fluttered in from the darkness outside, when the light was switched on. There was a sound of tearing paper and the tune began again :

"Jerusalem the golden,
With milk and honey . . ."

It broke off.

He was staring over at her corner in a startled way. He took two or three quick steps forward and stopped. His blind eyes looked at and through her.

"What are you doing here ? "

"I . . . I . . ."

"What have you come here for ? "

"I didn't mean to. I never thought you would come up here so late. I didn't, honestly. I thought you'd gone to bed . . . I really did. I'm going away, as you told me to. I'm going to-morrow. I never meant to see you again. When you came in I didn't know what to do. I hoped you would go away and not see me."

"Why did you come up here ? "

"Please, Alec . . ."

"You were lying here in the dark when I came in ? "

She was still too frightened to move. She crouched there, peering up at him. The words were dragged out of her, one by one.

"I was only . . . sort of . . . saying good-bye . . . to you . . . and your room, and all your things . . . because I thought I should never see you again. . . . I . . . always

wanted . . . I wanted to lie down here . . . for a minute
. . . where you've slept . . . that was all."

" I see."

He went back to his desk and began to shuffle his papers
into a small portfolio. His hands shook a little, but he
said evenly :

" I'm not angry. Not with you. Not for this."

Reassured, she sat up and pushed the hair out of her
eyes, murmuring :

" I would have gone if I could have got away without
you seeing me."

He looked up and down his desk to see if he had forgotten anything. He spoke with his back half turned to
her :

" My mother seems to have been right, after all. Betsy
wants to be rid of me, so I'm clearing out."

Joy, in the act of dragging herself to her feet, sat down
again with a plump and gaped at him.

" What ? "

" I say I'm off. For good."

" You're going away ? "

" Yes."

He turned round and looked at her. She still felt as if
he did not see her. Ever since he came into the room he
had been like a stranger, like Alec's body possessed by
someone else. Then, picking up his portfolio, he went
towards the door. He stretched his hand out towards the
switch.

The switch clicked and the room vanished. She
could hear no movement. She could not tell if he had
gone out or if he was still there. In the darkness she
said :

" Take me with you."

And did not know if he had heard it or not. She would
not have dared to say it if she knew.

There was absolute silence. The darkness pressed down
on her. Then a slight movement told her he was still

there. The door clicked and a key turned. There were little noises as he came back into the room.

He was feeling his way among the furniture. The whistling began again, shrill and very soft, as he pulled a curtain across the glimmering square of a window:

> " Jerusalem the golden
> With milk and honey blest ! "

She flung herself down, hiding her head under the cushions, so as not to hear it.

MORNING

BLODWEN brought Alec's note to Betsy with her early tea. It was quite short, and merely told her that he had gone by the early train and that his address had better be care of his club for the moment.

She read it with composure. She had slept very well, and awoke in the curious immobility which comes immediately after shock. She was like a person who has fallen downstairs and who lies pensive for a while at the bottom before locating injuries. Nothing, for the moment, hurt.

Alec had gone. It had been at her own desire, therefore it could not be described as a disaster. She did not pity herself. Nobody would have the right to pity her. This was only what she had been planning for months, though she had, to be sure, wavered a little just lately. And that horrible scene last night had no real significance in their lives. The sooner she could forget about it the better, because they were not parting on account of that quarrel. They had agreed to part, and to entertain regret would be childish. There was not more to regret upon this morning than upon any other morning.

Only she felt wretchedly tired, as if she had been up all night instead of sensibly asleep. She would have liked to lie still and do nothing ; but there was the world to face, and she must show it immediately how little pity she needed. She must give her own sensible account of the matter, repeating it again and again, until all memory of last night was submerged.

Mastering her fatigue, she jumped out of bed and took

a cold shower bath. She took some trouble over her face. To put on rouge in the morning was not her custom, especially in the country; but to-day she went to work, very carefully indeed, and achieved a result that might have deceived anybody.

But will it, she wondered, deceive Her? Is it likely that I should come down looking *better* than usual? Perhaps a little less . . . the train is going away all this time . . . he is there. I am here. Well, and what of it? I'm quite happy. Yes, but is he? Isn't he angry and miserable? Oh, don't let him be! Make him see it as I do . . . all for the best. Because I must care about what he is feeling. We are still friends, I hope. . . . There! That's most becoming.

She was in the dining-room, brisk, cool and competent, as the gong rang. But nobody was there to see her, and she felt as if she had got her public expression ready a little too soon. The children were always late, but Joy should have been there punctually. And then she remembered Joy's headache, or whatever it was. All those things left over from yesterday must still be attended to, and she was tired. She turned a haggard face, in spite of the rouge, to greet her mother-in-law.

Emily Canning had taken no pains to hide the traces of a bad night. For nine hours she had been turning and tossing and wondering if everything was going to be all right. She had heard Alec go into Betsy's room and had taken heart from the fact that he had not stayed there very long. He could not have been cozened out of his indignation in that brief period. Betsy was capable of anything; she could have explained the sun out of the sky, no doubt, but it would have taken her half the night to explain her conduct on this occasion. To all appearances she had had very little to say for herself, and everything would be well if only Alec had been firm. It was a pity that he had been so angry, but that was the worst of Alec—he would never assert himself unless and until he had lost his temper.

Was she wise to have struck so soon? The hours crept
by. No night had ever been so long. Her anxiety became
uncontrollable; she could not bear to take breakfast in
bed but must hurry down to see what had happened. In
the face of Betsy's surprise she said, with an attempt at
gaiety :

" Oh, I was awake, so I got up."

" Porridge," suggested Betsy. " Coffee ? "

" Oh, thank you. I'd like some porridge."

Betsy handed her the cream jug, and said lightly :

" Alec has gone off."

" Gone off ? Gone off, where ? "

" I don't know," said Betsy, turning to carve herself
some ham. " We settled it last night. I gather you
knew a little about it, that we've agreed to part, I mean.
Now that I'm back, and my anxiety about mother is over,
there seems nothing to wait for. So we decided to get it
over and he's gone."

Mrs. Canning made no comment. She was pouring the
cream over her plate, over the table cloth. When Betsy
turned round there was a great pool of cream on the table.
The old woman was staring at it ruefully, with her mouth
open.

" Never mind," said Betsy quickly. " I can wipe it
up in a minute."

She got a napkin and mopped up the cream and put an
inverted saucer under the wet patch on the cloth. The
breakfast table became dishevelled and squalid. Mrs.
Canning looked on, her old mouth still foolishly open.
All the vitality, all the cunning, had gone out of her face ;
it was shapeless and quivering, so that Betsy felt quite
ashamed, as if she had done something brutal.

Well, but she had to know. She had to be told. I
didn't mean—I didn't know she could be hurt like this.
Oh, why must people be old ? It's most unfair.

" I thought," suggested Betsy, " that we might all go
over to the sheep dog trials to-day."

Mrs. Canning repeated :

" Sheepog triars . . ." in a voice so slurred that it did not seem to belong to her.

Then she controlled her heavy tongue and got it to ask distinctly :

" Did you quarrel ? "

" What ? "

" Did you and Alec quarrel last night ? "

" No," asserted Betsy. " Oh, no. It's nothing of that sort."

" But he's left you."

" We've agreed to part. It's all right. Really it is. We're both quite happy about it. We've been discussing it for weeks."

" No ! No ! You've quarrelled. I made you quarrel.'

" No, really, Mrs. Canning. It's got nothing to do with you. We've done what we've done, because we wanted to."

" I made you quarrel. I made him angry with you. I thought, if he was angry, he wouldn't listen to this nonsense of yours. I wanted to stop this divorce."

" You couldn't have stopped it."

They faced one another miserably, over the messy table. All their lives they had been antagonists, and now, now that Betsy had won, there was no triumph.

The defeat of old age is never triumphant. It is too final. They both felt as though Emily Canning had been dismissed to her grave. She had lived too long. Betsy felt a fantastic desire to comfort her, to convince her that she still counted for something in the world. If her will was not still a force with which other people had to reckon, then the poor old thing might as well be dead.

" Oh, Mrs. Canning, you'll see . . . you'll understand. Alec will be ever so much happier. You'll be glad it has happened. Don't fail us, or be against us. We shall want your help more than ever. You can do so much for us now ; there are difficult times ahead of us, and we shall rely on you so much to support us."

" I think this will kill me."

" It will be so bad for the children if they think something dreadful has happened.   We must take it calmly."

" Oh, the poor children ! " quavered Mrs. Canning. " Poor little things !   What will happen to them ? "

" I must discuss with you what I'm going to say to them."

" How could he agree to do such a thing ?   He ought to have thought of his children."

" But they won't suffer.   They'll take it all as a matter of course.   Children do, if a thing is explained to them properly.   We shall share them.   There won't be any sordid squabbles about that, or money.   The whole thing can be arranged in a friendly way if only . . ."

Betsy broke off to greet Daphne, who, at that moment, rushed in.

" Why, darling !   Your hair is all wet.   Have you been bathing already ? "

" Yes.   All of us.   I say !   Where have father and Joy gone to ? "

" Father has gone to London.   And as for Joy . . ."

" London ? " exclaimed Eliza, as she came in.   " Whatever have they gone to London for ? "

" Joy hasn't gone anywhere.   Father has gone off on business.   Really, Eliza !   Your hair is dripping.   Did you bathe with no caps at all ? "

" But Joy has gone.   She was at the station," protested Eliza.

" Joy was ? "

Daphne explained :

" The Bloch boys saw them.   Father and Joy, getting into the seven o'clock train.   And we met them in the road, the Bloch boys, I mean, and they told us."

" They saw *Joy* ?   What on earth . . ."

Mrs. Canning sprang to her feet with a cry.

" Then it's true.   It's true.   That girl . . . they warned me . . . Frau Bloch said something . . . but, of course,

I didn't believe it for a moment. I said Alec would never . . . but it must have been true. Oh, Betsy ! "

" But she can't . . ."

" Didn't you know they'd gone ? " asked Eliza.

" Betsy . . . you must stop it. You must fetch them back."

" I don't understand. I don't believe it. There must be some mistake."

" Mother ! What is it ? "

" It's perfectly impossible," declared Betsy. " Nothing can make me believe . . ."

Her face belied her words. The rouge stood out on her ashy cheeks like a fine red dust. She turned blindly and stumbled towards the door, but there she met Kenneth who had already been upstairs, and said, with a face as white as hers :

" It's true, mother. She's gone. I've been up to look. She's left all her things packed. She's gone with him."

He hugged her tightly with his thin arms, as if to protect her, adding :

" I knew about it before."

" Knew about what, Ken ? "

" About him and Joy. They're pigs. You divorce him, darling. Forget about him. I'll look after you."

Eliza and Daphne were so much confused that at first they only got the impression that something frightful had happened to Kenneth. Later they learnt that something frightful had happened to everybody.

THE END OF THE HOLIDAYS

SOMETHING frightful had happened but nobody talked about it. Mrs. Canning went back to London in floods of tears. Their mother kept smiling all the time so that it was dreadful to look at her. She said that it was none of their business, because it would make no difference in their lives. It was just something between herself and their father.

In September her great friend, Mrs. Trotter, came to stay and there were endless discussions behind closed doors. Mrs. Trotter's face was long, but her eyes sparkled, and it was impossible not to see that she was enjoying herself. She treated their mother as if she had been a convalescent, petting and spoiling her, and reproving the children if they were noisy. At any mention of their father she looked mysterious and spoke well of him in the tone of one who is performing a duty. She wrote enough letters to fill up the post basket every day.

Eliza and Kenneth discussed it once, but they fell out so dreadfully that they were sorry they had done so.

" If you're on his side," said Kenneth. " I never want to speak to you again."

" I'm not on his side. I only said we can't know why he did it."

" I know why," muttered Kenneth.

" I suppose he asked your leave and explained all about it."

" Don't be a fool. You're so childish . . . I don't suppose you really understand what he's done."

" Of course I understand," she said indignantly. She

blushed and looked solemn, adding: " I suppose you think he has defiled his marriage couch ? "

Kenneth, in spite of his wretchedness, burst into a fit of laughter. A couch, to both of them, meant something made of black horsehair and strewn with antimacassars, such as they had seen in sea-side lodging-houses. But Eliza used the word because marriage couches were mentioned frequently in the *Alcestis* which she had begun to read in the summer term.

. " You're nothing but a baby," he said, his laughter subsiding. " You don't begin to understand."

" I do," said Eliza huffily. " I know all about marriage and all that. Mother told me ages ago, and I've been to lectures at school. But what I mean is . . . he just *couldn't* have done a thing like that. I don't believe it. Why should everybody jump to conclusions ? Why, just because he went away in the train with Joy . . ."

" She's a whore," said Kenneth.

It excited him to say so and he flushed scarlet. But the word did not shock Eliza to the same extent for she was surprised and interested to learn that it was pronounced that way. Still, she felt herself obliged to reprove him.

" You're disgusting. And you don't know anything about it."

" Yes, I do. I knew about it before anybody did, as a matter of fact. They were doing it all the time, before they went away. They used to go up to the garden house and do it."

" That's a lie. You ought to be struck dead for telling such lies. He wouldn't ever . . ."

" It's true. I saw them together once . . . he was kissing her and asking her to come up to the garden house. I knew what he meant all right. I knew what for."

" I won't listen. It's not true. It's just your horrible ideas. Nobody else thinks so."

" Mother does."

" She does not."

" She does, for I told her."

" You did? You said a thing like that? I do think you are . . . oh, you make me sick ! "

" Well, she believed me. I could see she did."

" Then she makes me sick. She's as bad as you, when he's her own husband. I expect he went away because she was so horrid to him."

" If you say that I'll hit you."

" And now she wants to get everybody on her side."

" Every decent person would be, naturally. She's going to divorce him. She couldn't do that unless she was in the right."

This was a knock-out for Eliza who burst into tears.

" I hope they won't let her," she sobbed. " They oughtn't to. It's very unfair. If they do, it will only be because she tells a lot of lies that she knows aren't true, because she can't really believe them, and you made them up."

Kenneth took two steps towards her and checked himself.

" I can't hit you," he said slowly, " because we're too old. But I'll never speak to you again."

And for the rest of the holidays he never did speak to her nor she to him. Daphne became their go between, and they avoided one another's company as far as possible.

Daphne did not suffer as they did. She understood very little of what had happened and had no wish to understand more. Her father had run away, he had behaved queerly : to have a queer father, to be queer in any way, was a dreadful misfortune. Nobody at school must ever be allowed to know of it ; if they knew, then she would be a little different from other people. She would be pushed out of the happy, safe herd, into the limbo of peculiarity, among the freaks. Nobody else, nobody who counted, had a queer father. One knew what a father ought to be :

rich, important, and, if possible, good looking. He was a recognized authority. I am a Conservative because Daddy is a Conservative. Daddy says the League of Nations ought to be scrapped. At school she always spoke of him as Daddy, because everybody did, anxiously concealing the fact that he was Father at home. One could boast discreetly of his wealth and success. A poor father was almost as bad as a queer one. Daddy says I can take up music if I like, but he wants me to have a good time. He wouldn't like me to go in for it professionally. It isn't as if I would ever have to earn my own living. Daddy gave Mummie a simply marvellous diamond and platinum bracelet. And, if he was good looking, one showed him off on Speech Day. In the past Alec had been a perfectly adequate father. He was rich and famous. The other girls admired him very much. Since he had no politics Daphne was able to say that he was a Conservative.

Now he had gone and done something queer. Her great fear was that Jean Hodgekin, who had come to stay with her, might get wind of it. Jean was her best friend, but there are some things which no friendship can survive. She was constantly on the watch lest a chance word from the others should betray the shameful secret.

Jean, however, was not a perceptive child. She came from a dull home and a solemn family so that the depression prevailing at Pandy Madoc did not strike her particularly. From Daphne's way of talking she had expected, somehow, to find that the Cannings ragged an awful lot, but this was not so, and she was relieved because she did not much like being ragged. That Eliza and Kenneth never spoke was queer, but then Eliza was a freak, even though she was Daphne's sister. Everybody at school thought so. And Kenneth was sort of sarcastic. She said as much to Daphne on the last day of the holidays, and Daphne, in excuse, mentioned that he was supposed to be brainy.

" Daddy," pronounced Jean, " says that being clever is no excuse for being sarcastic."

" Well . . . clever people always sort of try to be."

" Daddy says clever people are constructive not destructive. He says it's easy to criticize and destroy everything but what are you going to put in its place ? "

" In what's place ? "

" In what you are being sarcastic about. Kenneth ought to just try being a child widow for five minutes."

" A child what ? "

" A child widow in Southern India. He was being sarcastic about missionaries. So I said you just try being a child widow. So he said he'd love to. So I said no you wouldn't. They'd take away all your jewellery and shave your head and make you do all the house work and only give you one coarse meal a day. And they would burn you, only the British Raj wouldn't let them. Well, I mean how can he say that missionaries don't do a lot of good ? I said in Bombay they don't even bury their dead. They put them in Towers of Silence for the birds to eat. It's disgusting. And he said well, anyway, that's being kind to the birds."

" He just likes arguing," explained Daphne.

Jean thought this a perverse taste. It was rude to argue. Nice people never did because they all thought alike.

She flattened her nose against the schoolroom window. It rained in sheets. It had rained every day since she came to Wales.

The sea was a confusion of grey and white and there was no horizon.

" Let's tell some more Chinese tortures," said Daphne, reverting to their principal intellectual entertainment. " It's your turn."

" No, it isn't."

" Yes it is. I told the one yesterday about making ants walk down your throat."

" Well . . . I don't know any more good ones. Not Chinese ones. Only one Betty Morrison told me, and that was the Inquisition."

" Betty Morrison ! You don't mean Betty Morrison ? "

" Oh, no," said Jean, with delightful irony, " I mean Princess Margaret Rose."

" But I thought you thought Betty Morrison was a freak."

" She's not bad if you squash her pretty often."

" Everybody thought she was awful when she was new."

" New girls are always sort of freaks. Then they seem to get all right somehow."

This was quite true. Mere newness was a detestable quality and the girl who had it was an outcast. Some new girls were humble, and some were bumptious, but they were all freaks until one got used to seeing them about.

" Well, what torture did she tell you ? "

" About the room that gets smaller. Do you know it ? "

" No. Go on ! "

" They put you in a nice room and give you lovely food," began Jean, with a zest. " And you think it's going to be nice, but it isn't. . . ."

Eliza bounced into the schoolroom and flung open the lid of the piano. She was going to practise for at least two hours and if anybody found the noise disturbing they could just go away.

Daphne and Jean responded to her flounce in the only possible manner. They exchanged mysterious looks and were silent, as if they had been talking secrets. Curled up together in the window seat they began to whisper, their little smooth, round heads close together. Smothered bursts of giggling punctuated Eliza's scales. They were not talking about her, but their sidelong glances suggested that they might be.

She practised every scale and every arpeggio, in octaves, thirds and sixths, all through the sharps and all through the flats. For the past three weeks she had practised so continually that her improvement was really marked. Already she had achieved a measure of control over her hands and fingers, and in this daily battle she was beginning to find a solid satisfaction. In order to play scales well she had to concentrate so hard that she need think of nothing else. Her unhappiness was forced out of her mind. To try to think of nice things, or to read an interesting book, was of no avail ; nothing pleasant was strong enough. Just because scales were horrid there was a useful sort of grip about them.

Presently she was alone. Daphne and Jean had grown tired of whispering in such a noise and had retreated upstairs. The next item in her programme was a little treat which she had been saving up for herself. She was learning the last movement of the Moonlight Sonata ; her heart was set upon conquering it because of something that Mark had said. He had mocked at the people who can only play the first movement with both pedals down and a soulful expression, and she had uneasily suspected herself to be that kind of person. But when he next came to Pandy Madoc he would get a great surprise. She would begin to play the first movement and he would look politely down his nose. Then she would play the second, which is so much more difficult than it looks, and he would nod approval. And then she would dash into the last movement and he would not be able to hide his astonishment.

This was her only way of bringing better times a little nearer. For she could not give up hope or think that God would allow this misery to last for ever. Somehow it would all come right. Her father would return, and everybody would be happy. There would be another summer at Pandy Madoc, a shining summer, when she and Mark and Ken would be three close friends and nothing would be changed except that she would be able to play the whole of the Moonlight Sonata without a stumble.

But it was heartbreakingly difficult. She could slur the upward rush of arpeggios by a discreet use of the loud pedal, so as to disguise a want of perfect smoothness. Would Mark notice that? Yes! He certainly would. And was life long enough for such a task?

Life, at the moment, seemed very long indeed. Four tedious years of childhood still lay in front of her, four years before she could be eighteen and grown up. When she was eighteen she could begin to live and have experiences. She could become an interesting, mysterious person who had been through a lot. That she was, even now, going through a good deal, did not occur to her. She lived inside childhood, like a grub inside a cocoon, and when she emerged into the bright, adult world she expected to be quite a different being. Nothing that happened now could have any bearing upon the future.

The rain sluiced down the window panes. She thumped away, counting loudly, until Kenneth's voice brought her to a standstill. He was peering round the door, his unhappy glance shifting this way and that, as if he had lost something.

" I say," he said awkwardly, " I'm off."

He was going back to school that morning.

She jumped up. The black abyss of their quarrel lay between them and she could say nothing to bridge the chasm. How could they part when so much was left to mend? She asked hurriedly if she might come in the car with him to the station.

" Mother's coming, and Mrs. Trotter."

" Oh! Then I don't expect there'll be much room."

They looked dumbly at one another. He came up to her and gave her a hasty kiss.

" Good-bye . . . you old Eliza! "

" Oh . . . Ken . . . good-bye . . ."

They clung together as they had clung years ago when they were first parted, when he went away to his preparatory school. Their grief then had taken them entirely by surprise. Neither had minded the separation until the last night of the holidays, when he had appeared, looking a little frightened and solemn, in the night nursery. He wanted to give her his old doll, Valerie, to take care of while he was away. Whereupon Eliza had opened her mouth quite square and howled. And he had howled too, while three-year-old Daphne peeped at them curiously through the bars of her crib. They made such a noise that their parents heard it and came hurrying upstairs. Betsy had soothed Kenneth, Alec petted Eliza, and Nannie comforted Daphne who, realizing that she was being left out of something, had begun to bellow.

Now they were too old to howl. Nor did they know what to make of one another. They were no longer part of the same thing : they were separate people, and the cosy unconscious growth of their joint selves had come to an end. Like fledglings fallen from the nest too soon, they shivered in the coldness, the isolation of this vast world. They longed for the smother of home, the contact of other downy creatures ; to squabble and peck at such close quarters that they had no quite separate being but seemed all to be one person. To love and understand one another, when thus set apart, was too difficult. They could not attempt it.

She hugged him. She kissed his cold cheek. He had been out in the rain, helping to put his luggage on the car. She felt the rough wet surface of his coat.

Their mother called from downstairs. He broke away and was gone.

PART II

WRATH

WRATH

(Being extracts from various letters bearing on the case of Canning *v.* Canning and Benson.)

Mrs. Graham to Mrs. Trotter.

St. Leonard's Terrace.
Sept. 20th.

MY DEAR ANGELA,

Johnnie and I have only just got back from Salzburg and we are absolutely stunned by the rumour which is going round about the Alecs. Yesterday we saw the Merricks, at the Vereker first night, and they told us that Alec and Betsy are parting company! Is this true? I do hope it isn't. It is said you have been staying at P.M. so will know. Do send me a line.

Johnnie is rather upset—more than I would have expected considering how airily he took the Chris Adams episode. Has Chris anything to do with this? The Merricks say no, she has gone to California. Johnnie says Alec ought not to allow his home to be broken up, and it is quite different from amusing himself outside within reason. He says if you marry a woman you stick to her, however much she bores you. He says no marriage would last a week otherwise. Complimentary, isn't he?

The Merricks say they think Betsy is the moving spirit. As you know they have always been somewhat pro-Alec. They think she is egotistical and conceited. Do for goodness sake write and tell me what is really happening, and if Betsy is sorry or pleased. I must know before I see her. Where is she? In Wales still?

Mrs. Trotter to Mrs. Graham.

Cambridge,
Sept. 23rd.

. . . My dear, I know all about it. But I'm afraid I can't give you the full details because I've promised Betsy not to tell anybody. But this I can tell you. Alec has behaved *disgracefully*. The Merricks wouldn't stand up for him like this if they knew everything. And as for their running Betsy down ! Well ! I always thought they were nice, but one lives and learns !

Betsy is in Oxford, with her people. She has been a perfect saint about it all, really wonderful. She won't allow Alec to be blamed, and says it is all to be done in a friendly way ! She doesn't want his friends to know how he has behaved, she doesn't want anyone to be put against him. This much I can tell you. In fact I ought to. It's nothing to do with Chris Adams. *She* is a back number.

But I really do think a man like Alec ought not to be allowed to get away with it like this. Here has Betsy given up all the best years of her life to be left at nearly forty with three children on her hands ! I do think it's absolutely disgusting. I never liked him, as you know, but I didn't think he was quite as bad as this. He never appreciated her. Right from the first he was inclined to neglect her for other women. The night Daphne was born he *took another woman out to the theatre !* I can tell you that because everybody knows it. And you remember how frightfully ill Betsy was ? I simply can't bear to think of all she has been through, not only with Chris Adams by any means, and nobody has ever heard her grumble, have they ? Not that he was ever really *horrid* to her ; she says he was always kind, in a way, except at the very end, when he was awful. But he is fearfully weak and vain. He can't say no, when women throw themselves at him, and of course there has been a good deal of that sort of thing, because he is successful and popular, and good-looking too, I suppose. *And* selfish ! My word ! The way he's always let her be sacrificed !

That old mother of his came between them and poisoned him against her. We've always known that old woman was a trial. Only Betsy would have stood it for so long.

Somebody ought to blow him up about it. Hasn't Johnnie got any influence ? Betsy is so completely miserable that I think she would take him back if he could be brought to his senses. Can't you or Johnnie do anything. You are his greatest friends. . . .

Postcard from Johnnie Graham to Alec.

Hart's Club, W.1.

Sept. 24th.

Can you lunch with me here Thursday 1 p.m. ?

Postcard from Alec to Johnnie Graham.

Hotel Trois Couronnes,

Vaucluse, Provence.

Sorry I couldn't lunch with you. Here till mid-October.

Johnnie Graham to Alec.

St. Leonard's Terrace.

Oct. 4th.

. . . What on earth are you doing at Vaucluse ? A beastly hole ! And what has happened to Byron ?

The women here are saying you have left your wife. If you don't come back soon you won't have a shred of character left.

Can I do anything ? You'll say it's no business of mine. But I'm your oldest friend and I'm not going to see you making a mess of things without trying to stop it. Of course I don't know what the trouble is, but they say Betsy is miserable and heart-broken ; not disinclined to make it up, by all accounts. If you like I will go and see her, and find out how the land lies.

You're too old for this sort of thing, you know. You

can't desert a woman of Betsy's age, after all these years. It's so discouraging for the rest of us who are staying the course. You've always given her too much rope, so you've only got yourself to thank if she kicks up her heels. For God's sake come back and take a firm line with her. Ten to one, it's that she wants.

Come back anyway, for I've got another Act finished. . . .

Alec to Johnnie Graham.

>   Les Baux,
>   Provence.
>   Oct. 10th.

. . . I'm here by Betsy's orders, and I don't think it would look right if I came back too soon. I've got to desert her well and thoroughly. She told me to. I'm sorry to hear that she is miserable and heart-broken; but it is now too late for her to change her mind. I very much doubt if she has done so. She had pretty definite plans for the future when I saw her last.

See her if you like. I don't know what her account of the business may be, but, whatever it is, I'm sure it's correct and I shan't contradict it. She will do me justice. She always has.

I'm sorry you should worry about my reputation. I had no idea divorce was such a black mark against one, in these days. Betsy has always assured me that it is not, and plenty of our friends seem to have survived it without much damage. Things will take their course and settle down. . . .

Mrs. Graham to Mrs. Trotter.

>   St. Leonard's Terrace.
>   Oct. 14th.

. . . We have just had a very strange letter from Alec, from Provence or somewhere. No time to tell you much, but he says that Betsy asked for the divorce, and told him to go, and that it's all her doing! Can there be anything

in this ? Johnnie thinks there is. He says A. is so lazy
he never would desert his wife unless he was pushed into
it. . . .

Mrs. Trotter to Mrs. Graham.

Cambridge.
Oct. 16th.

. . . Well! Of all the outrageous things! To start
putting the blame on Betsy! Alec ought to be taken out
and shot.

Now I'll tell you something that I did promise Betsy
not to tell. But you must keep it to yourself. In the
circumstances I do think her friends ought to defend her.
Only you can tell Johnnie of course.

Alec went off with another woman. You remember
that girl they called Joy, Mrs. Hewitt's niece or something,
who used to go to Wales with them every summer ? They
called her a governess but she wasn't really, she didn't
teach anything, only did odd jobs for Betsy. Well, it's
her ! Quite a young girl ! Betsy found out, after they'd
gone, that he'd been having an affair with her, so openly
that even the children knew about it. I mean, to put
it quite frankly, there is no doubt that he had seduced
her, or been seduced by her.

Now how can he say that Betsy told him to do such a
thing as that ? How dare he suggest it ? Is it likely,
I ask you ?

It has nearly killed Betsy. She feels, in a way, responsible. She says she oughtn't to have had the girl there,
knowing what Alec was with women. Of course, she says
herself, it was probably six of one and half a dozen of the
other. The girl was an obvious little slut and probably
asked for it. But still ! !

If Alec is going to take this line, Betsy *ought* not to
forgive him. I did hope they might be reconciled, in
spite of his conduct, as she is so frightfully unhappy.
But not after this. He ought to be absolutely cut and

dropped by all decent people, and I hope he will. It's too filthy. . . .

Alec to Johnnie Graham.

Southwick Court, W.2.
Oct. 25th.

. . . My address for the next few months is as above. I got back to England on Monday and have taken a furnished flat here, a rum sort of place with glass ceilings and steel furniture. But it will house me and my belongings till my plans are more settled. I've just sent off a lot of stuff to you by special messenger. When can I come along and talk about it ? . . .

Johnnie Graham to Alec.

Hart's Club, W.1.

. . . The MS. of Byron arrived all right, for which many thanks.

Frankly I don't know when you can come along and talk about it. Susie won't have you in the house, and I can't very well blame her, for I suppose the women have a right to their Trades Union.

I think, perhaps, we had better drop Byron for the time being. I don't feel like meeting you. I'm sorry, but I can't accept the fact that you've behaved like a cad. I've been too fond of you to shrug my shoulders at it, as I would if you were a mere acquaintance. Of course I know worse cads, and have worked with them, but they were people I didn't care a damn for.

I don't sit in judgment on you. It's your own affair. But I don't want to see you till I can take in the idea that you have seduced a helpless young girl, your depend-ant, and callously deserted your family. The work we do together is founded on intimacy, an understanding and sympathy which I can't feel now. I'm very sorry indeed. But you can't be so much changed that you don't under-stand what I mean. . . .

Mrs. Canning to Alec.

Bedford Gardens, W.8.
Oct. 27th.

. . . I rang up your flat this morning, but they said you were out. So I must write instead. Are you free, dear, on Friday evening? I want to give a little party and I very much want you to come. A few friends to dinner and some others to come in later. Eight o'clock. Black tie.

So many of your friends are anxious to see you, and one wants to contradict the very unkind rumours that are flying about, started, I fear, by the Hewitts. It is important that you should show that influential and sensible people are on your side. I have asked the Merricks who are very loyal to you and furious at what is being said. And should I ask the Grahams, do you think? Tell me who you would like to be asked. . . .

Alec to Mrs. Canning.

Southwick Court, W.2.

. . . They told me you had rung up, "they" being Joy, but I expect you didn't recognize her voice. This is a service flat and we have no maid. The telephone, if answered at all, is answered either by me or Joy.

My dear Mother, it is very nice of you to want to give a party for us. We shall be delighted to come. No, don't ask the Grahams. They have dropped me, and Byron is off. Johnnie is surprised at me and thinks I have polluted the Old School Tie. . . .

Mrs. Canning to Alec.

Bedford Gardens, W.8.
Oct. 29th.

. . . I am so glad that you can come on Friday, darling! But I am afraid I meant the invitation for you *only*. It would not be at all a wise thing for me to receive Miss Benson. Surely you must see that? I must have a long talk with you soon, please dear! I can't talk on the

telephone and I have a great deal to say ! When can you
come and see me ?

Alec to Mrs. Canning.

Southwick Court, W.2.
Oct. 29th.

. . . I'm very sorry about the party, but I'm afraid I can't
come unless Joy is asked. I don't go to houses where she
is not received. As to our having a talk ; Mother, it's no
use. I won't go back to Betsy and I won't leave Joy.
So what is the use of talking ? It will only distress you.
Of course I will come and see you, but only on condition
that we do not discuss my domestic affairs. And I'm
afraid you won't be able to keep off them, which is why I
have not been round to Bedford Gardens since I got
back. . . .

Mrs. Canning to Alec.

Bedford Gardens, W.8.
Oct. 30th.

. . . Your letter has distressed me terribly. My dearest
Alec, I am your mother, and I shall always stand by you.
But I think your conduct is much worse than wrong—it is
very foolish. Why must you insist upon living with her
in this blatant way ? You are putting yourself into such
a false position. Don't you see that it will give colour
to all the scandalous mis-representations that are flying
about ? Why can't you manage more discreetly ? Nobody
need even know that she is in London.

Nowadays people are very broadminded, but they are
just as fond of scandal as they ever were. You can do
almost anything you like, provided that you do it in the
right way. It is a terrible mistake to behave as if you
don't care what people think. Nobody is so popular that
he can afford to disregard public opinion. It may have
struck you as odd, I know it often has me, why some
people should be dropped by their friends and socially

discredited for some very slight irregularity, while others, most flagrant offenders, continue to be accepted every-where. It seems so inconsistent. But if you look into it you'll always find that people who have been dropped have had no *savoir vivre*. They have managed badly, giving the impression that they thought they could behave as they like, which is fatal. It is that, it is arrogance, which puts the world against you.

I don't suppose that anybody, outside the Hewitt circle, is particularly disposed to blame you. Divorce is nothing nowadays. But people do enjoy feeling that they have power, and, at the moment, you are at a slight dis-advantage with the world, and they feel it, and that they are being kind and loyal when they stand up for you. And you must let them feel that you recognize this. You mustn't demand their support in this take-it-or-leave-it way. It will offend them. They will say : why should this girl be forced on us ? If they seem disposed to recognize your *liaison* that would be quite another thing. Have I made this plain ?

Dearest, I am horrified at what you tell me about the Grahams. It would be the worst possible disaster if you were to quarrel with Johnnie. What would happen to your work ? You say you can't work with anybody else. Have you told them the real facts ? Do they know your side of it . . . ?

Alec to Mrs. Canning.

Southwick Court, W.2.

Oct. 31st.

. . . I don't know what facts Johnnie has got hold of. I told him to get them from Betsy and I am sure she has said nothing that was not true.

Your letter is full of worldly wisdom and I agree with every word of it. I'll keep it for Kenneth to read when he is twenty-one. But I'm afraid I can't follow your advice, and poke poor Joy away in a little flat round the corner.

I intend to marry her as soon as I am free to do so. She is expecting a child and I mean to do everything in my power to support and protect her. My obligations towards her are the most important thing that I have to consider.

In the meantime I expect my friends to treat her as if she is my wife. I have no use for people who cannot do that much for me, and who are ready to put the worst interpretation on my conduct. I suppose I shall find out how many people I can really rely on, and I am bracing myself for some shocks. . . .

Mrs. Graham to Mrs. Trotter.

St. Leonard's Terrace,
Nov. 3rd.

. . . What do you think? We've just had a long visit from old Mrs. Canning! Come to tell us Alec's side of it!

Well, of course, we had to be civil. She was awfully nice to us when we first married: in fact, she always has been nice. And you can't blame the poor old thing for standing up for her son. But I couldn't help a few little digs. She said she supposed we had got our account from the Hewitts. So I said, Oh, no! We haven't seen the Hewitts since it happened, but I gather *they* are taking it all with great dignity and are certainly not running about defending Betsy. I don't suppose they think she needs any defending!

But now, my dear, just *listen* to Alec's side. He is so chivalrous that he is taking all the blame when it is really Betsy's. The Joy girl had nothing to do with the divorce. She was a sort of afterthought. He had to run away with somebody, so he took her, though Mrs. C. agrees that it was not a happy choice. The real reason is that Betsy—*Betsy* wants to marry somebody else, so she bullied and coaxed Alec into giving her her freedom. And who do you suppose the other man is? The little grasshopper!

Mrs. C. didn't say so, but I took the liberty of putting two and two together, for she let out that he was (*a*) somebody who had been in love with Betsy for a long time ; (*b*) rich, and of an exalted social position ; (*c*) has relations living near Pandy Madoc. So who else could it be ?

Now what do you make of all this ? Can there be any sort of truth in it ? And if there isn't, oughtn't Betsy to be informed of what Alec and Co. are saying ?

I'm glad to say that none of it cut much ice with Johnnie. He merely says that, even if it's true, it doesn't justify Alec. He ought to have told Betsy that she damn well couldn't marry anyone else. And he was very disgusted at Mrs. Canning's line about the Joy-girl. She said the girl was asking for it, etc. Johnnie says that is the height of caddishness. A man who seduces a girl half his age and then tries to put the blame on her ought to be kicked. You know Johnnie is a bit sentimental and old-fashioned about girls.

Last item ! the Joy-girl is going to have a baby, so Alec thinks he has got to marry her. This defeats comment, don't you think ?

Mrs. Trotter to Mrs. Graham.

Cambridge,
Nov. 4th.

. . . Excuse a hasty scrawl. I am acting Charity in a Morality Play and the rehearsals literally go on all day and all night.

I have no words to say how *furious* your letter made me. I am *certain* that there isn't a *word* of truth in Alec's story. Don't we all know that Betsy has *always* laughed at the grasshopper. Re the expected infant, they'll look silly if it is born before May, won't they ? Yes, I think Betsy should be told. She is back at Well Walk now, isn't she ? I really think you had better go and drop her a hint anyway. You don't know who Alec and Co may be spreading this story to . . .

Post Card from Alec to Kenneth.

> Southwick Court, W.2.
> Nov. 5th.

When is your. half-term ? I thought of coming down for it.

Kenneth to Alec.

> St. Clere's College.
> Nov. 7th.

I'm spending half-term with my mother.

Mrs. Graham to Mrs. Trotter.

> St. Leonard's Terrace,
> Nov. 14th.

. . . Well, I've seen Betsy. I went to tea with her yesterday. She looked all colours ; so much upset that I can't help wondering ! The grasshopper was up in Wales this Summer. Of course she denied Alec's story at once.

I told her about the baby, too. She said very little and looked as if she was going to cry, for a minute, poor thing ! Then she did what we did, i.e. did sums in her head ; I could see she was thinking . . . well !

Whatever she may have felt and said, when you were up at Pandy Madoc in September, she is pretty bitter now. This very friendly agreement to part, we heard so much about, isn't exactly working. The grasshopper story and this suspiciously prompt baby have put an end to all that. . . .

Mrs. Pattison to Mrs. Canning.

> Tan y Vron,
> Llanfair.
> Nov. 16th.

. . . A friend, who has just been staying here, tells me that my brother is being widely talked about in connection with the Canning divorce. This has disturbed me very much. I gather that Alec's party is putting it about. I cannot help fearing that you may have forgotten that all I said to you last August was said in strict confidence. I should not have told you at all, but you seemed to be so sympathetic and so worried, and I was worried myself because, as I told you, I did not at all welcome the idea of such a marriage for Max. I do hope that I may rely upon you to deny this rumour. It is most unfair that Max should be brought into it when he is abroad and cannot defend himself.

I think it should be made perfectly clear to everybody that this quarrel has nothing to do with Max. Alec has deserted his wife for another woman; everybody knows that, and it is because of this that Betsy is divorcing him. . . .

Mrs. Canning to Mrs. Pattison.

Bedford Gardens, W.8.
Nov. 17th.

. . . I don't think you have anything with which to reproach yourself, or that our conversation had much to do with it. Betsy admitted to Alec, of her own accord, that she wished to marry your brother, and asked for her freedom. He has furnished her with the evidence she wanted and that is the truth of the matter . . .

Joy to Kenneth.

Southwick Court, W.2.
Nov. 16th.

. . . Your father was so much upset by your refusing to see him that I feel I must write to you. I have never seen him so much upset over anything. At first he did not want to tell me what had happened, but I insisted upon knowing.

I feel sure that you do not know what has really

happened. You must not believe people who try to put you against him. Nothing is his fault, he has behaved in a very fine and generous way. Your mother wanted to get rid of him, so that she might marry somebody else. If she had not wanted this, he would never have left her, though she never tried to make him happy.

I am doing everything I can to comfort him. We shall be married, I hope, sometime next year, and we hope that you and Eliza and Daphne will come and live with us, for part of the time, anyway ; of course we do not want to take you away from your mother altogether. I will do all I can to make it a happy home for you all. Your father and I love each other very much and it is wicked of people to say that I have ruined his life. Your mother is going to be happy with her new husband ; why should she grudge it to us ?

Your father does not know that I am writing to you and he would be angry if he knew. He will not say one word, to anyone, to defend himself. But I cannot allow people to poison your mind against him. . . .

Mrs. Graham to Mrs. Trotter.

St. Leonaid's Terrace,
Nov. 17th.

. . . I've been having a spot of bother with Johnnie. He got a sentimental " poor old Alec ! " spasm, and showed distinct signs of weakening. I think he felt a hankering to go back to work and couldn't face the idea of it without Alec. He began to say how can we really judge without knowing all the circumstances, etc. ?

But now, luckily, the Joy-girl has taken it upon herself to finally upset the apple-cart. She has been writing to the children, if you please ! Kenneth sent his mother, without comment, a letter he had got. They are trying to put him against his own mother, when she has been so determined, all along, that the children are not to be dragged into it. This gave Johnnie such a jolt that he is now quite implacable again.

Betsy is *livid*. She says now she will fight to the last ditch to get complete custody of the children. It would be one thing letting the children see him if he had behaved decently, but quite another if they are to be put against her. Besides, is the J—G a suitable person to have charge of little girls ?

She says she is going to cite her as co-respondent. Alec very coolly sent her some evidence, a hotel bill or something, which doesn't bring Joy's name in. I suppose he got somebody else for that occasion. But Betsy jolly well is going to bring Joy into it now, as she wants the Court to know that he oughtn't to have the children. . . .

Betsy to Mrs. Hewitt.

Well Walk, N.W.
Dec. 1st.

. . . I've decided to go abroad for the rest of the winter. I can't stand London any more and I want to get away. I want to be away till my case comes on. I'm going for a few days to Angela Trotter and then I go to Paris where Pen Priday has lent me a flat. Angela is going with me, to settle me in. She is the only really loyal friend I've got, as far as I can see. I don't feel you and Father are really sympathetic, though I know you are sorry for me. But you don't back me up, when it comes to the point ; Father has a natural bias, I suppose, towards the man's point of view. I should have thought anyone would agree that I am right to fight for my children.

I thought Ken might join me in Paris for the holidays. There would be just room in the flat for him, and we could go about together, and he is of an age to enjoy it. It will be good for him and nice for me ; I know quite a lot of interesting people there who will, I hope, have something to think about other than me and my affairs.

Can Daphne and Eliza go to you, poor sweets ? It will
be a little dismal for them not to have Ken and me at
Christmas, but there wouldn't be room for them, and, if
there was, I am really too far through to face the idea of
dragging about with the lot of them. And I know you
will love having them. . . .

Eliza to Kenneth.

> Barton House School,
> Wendover.
> Dec. 7th.

. . . Why have you never written this Term ? Did you
get my letters ? Daph got a P.C. from you. Do please
write.

Have you heard about the Hols ? We are going to
Gran's and you are going to Paris. How awful ! I
thought we should all be at home. We are always together
at Xmas. Do get mothei to change her mind. We can't
be sepperated at Xmas, when we have to decorate the
house and everything.

How is Mark ? Did he get the Grier Prize as you
thought he would ? If he has please congratulate him
from me. And tell him we went to a concert where
Elizabeth Lange sang some Brhams, Bhr, Barh, oh bother !
most frightfully well. . . .

Mrs. Trotter to Mrs. Graham.

> Rue St. Evian,
> Paris.
> Dec. 12th.

. . . I've got Betsy settled into her flat here and am
coming home on Monday. I'm glad I went, for she is on
the point of a nervous breakdown—not fit to cope with
anything, poor dear !

You would have thought she might hope for a little

respite here. Not a bit of it. The persecution has pursued her ! Hardly had we got into the place when Charles Merrick turned up. It seems he is over here on some engineering conference, and he turned out to have brought a message from Alec, who wanted to get into touch with Betsy and heard she was in Paris, and so got Charles to go and see her as a sort of ambassador. He asked her if she wouldn't agree to keep Joy's name out of it, and appealed to her not to try to get the children entirely away from Alec. The cheek of it ! What right has he to interfere in a matter which is entirely between Alec and Betsy ? It is not a matter for outsiders to discuss at all.

Alec, he says, has only just realized that she means to claim the children and has the face to say that it isn't fair, not in the bargain, etc. Also he wants something settled about money ; I suppose he thought he could trap Betsy into agreeing to take much less than she ought to get, so that he could give it all to Joy.

I'm glad to say Betsy was quite firm. She is going to stand out for as much alimony as she can possibly get, and never let him see the children till they are grown up. She says now she doesn't care who knows how badly he has behaved, so I can tell you a lot of things that I couldn't before. How he drinks, for one thing. Once, when he was drunk, he threw her down a whole flight of stairs. She says she can never tell *anybody* what awful things he said to her on the last night, before he deserted her. But I'll tell you the rest when we meet. . . .

Charles Merrick to Alec.

> Hotel St. Cyre
> Paris,
> Dec. 12th.

. . . I'm afraid it's no go. I've seen Betsy and she does mean to get the children. I said all I could, but it was no use. I'm more sorry than I can say. I think she might consider not bringing Joy into it, if you would undertake to make no effort to keep the children.

She is so extremely bitter that I can't understand it at all. It is not like her, and I fear that her friends have been injudicious and have worked her up into this state of mind. She looks very ill, I think, and her nerves are obviously all over the place. One can only hope that she may grow calmer and will change her mind before the divorce comes on, which can't be, I imagine, for some time yet.

I am very sorry that I have had so little success. . . .

Charles Merrick to his wife.

> Hotel St. Cyr,
> Paris.
> December 13th.

. . . As regards *l'affaire* Canning, it's no go.

Betsy is a harpy and a fury and a bitch. That's all I can say. I've seen her, and said what I could, and tried to keep my temper. But for pure spite it would be hard to find her match. I told her I was sure that Alec had no hand in those letters to the children. She didn't believe me. She didn't want to believe me.

Every petty grievance is raked up, even to little things that must have been forgiven and forgotten years ago. In 1920 he pushed her so that she fell downstairs. Good heavens! One push is surely allowed in every marriage. I nearly told her that I once knocked you out with a hot water bottle.

The kindest thing is to suppose that the poor thing is half off her head. She looks it. You know, I can't but think that she still cares for him, and that's what is at the bottom of this insane anger. " To be wroth with one we love, doth work like madness in the brain."

Oh, Meg, my dear darling, don't let us ever quarrel. It's hell upon earth for a man and his wife to get it in for one another. It isn't natural. It's like gangrene or cancer. It rots the whole system. Yet I've known people who could part good friends with no rancour. I suppose it's all right if there really is no love left. If there is—and in this case I believe there is—it mortifies and goes bad.

Try to go round and see Alec and Joy. I know she bores you, but they are both so down that it would be a good deed. Their friends ought to stand by them.

I hope to be back on Christmas Eve. Kiss the brats for me, and don't read in bed too late. . . .

Mrs. Merrick to her husband.

Victoria Road, S.W.
December 18th.

. . . I went round and sat with Alec and Joy last night, and I hope you will chalk it up to me, darling, for I did it to please you. Sat was about all we did. Conversation was sticky. Joy provided coffee, the worst I've ever drunk, but not until he had prodded her into doing it.

Those two are ghastly, stuck in that horrible flat in the middle of all that " unnatural " steel furniture. Why did he ever take such a place ? It's morbid of him.

She just sits like a lump, gazing at him with an expression of tragic devotion. One can see it's getting badly on his nerves. She is devoted to him, I dare say ; but I've a feeling that she knows perfectly well what a mess it all is, and that he is only sticking to her out of compassion. But she will never let him go. She'll cling to him like a limpet as long as they both live. She'll turn into an *exigeante* doormat, if you can imagine such an object.

You say Betsy is bitter. So is he ; not only against her, but against all the world. I think it has been a great shock to him to find that so many people have believed the worst of him. He had always been so popular and friendly ; all this malice is a revelation, and I think it has given him a sort of persecution mania. I'm sure he

sees slights now where none have been intended. And
he is inclined to say nasty things about people, sneering
and spiteful. He seems to want to make out that all
marriages are really failures and that people who maintain
otherwise are either fools or hypocrites. He was especially
nasty about the Grahams ; said that Johnnie had been
fed up with Susan for years but didn't dare say so, and
was too much of a coward to break away, and had, therefore, a grudge against anyone who had broken away.
I almost felt as if he disliked us for being so happy, and
wouldn't be sorry to know that our marriage wasn't really
working.

Just at the end he was rather more like himself. He
came down with me in the lift. It was a fine night, so
I said I'd walk along to find a taxi, so he came too and
took my arm, and said that it was nice of me to come.
He told me how rotten Joy was feeling. And really I
do feel sorry for her, poor thing. It must be dreadful
to be going to have a baby in such circumstances without
any of the pleasure and hope and pride, and no company
much except that bitter, disgruntled man.

He talked about the baby a little bit, and I got the
impression that he is feeling most terribly guilty and
ashamed. He said once or twice that it was all his fault.
I think he must have lost his head in some way. Though
he doesn't love her, he must have got into a sort of state
over her, and felt some very violent attraction, and not
tried to control it. I mean what he felt and did was not
checked by any kind of affection or consideration for her,
or even ordinary prudence. So now here's this baby,
wanted by nobody, who is going to be a person who can
feel and suffer as much as any of us. I do understand,
absolutely, why he feels that he must stick to her and it.
But it's more of a hate child than a love child.

Where has all this hatred come from ? It's like a storm
of evil that has broken over them. I don't see how any
of them can ever be happy again. You say it is love

gone bad. Do you think that is because they are all
denying the truth ? Love doesn't go bad, however unhappy it makes you, unless you poison it yourself. It
isn't the injuries and wrongs that they can't forgive ; it's
because they know, Alec and Betsy know, and Joy does
too, that in spite of everything, in spite of all they've
done and said to hurt each other, they can't bear to be
apart.

PART III
APART

ON RIVER CLIFF

S T. CLERE'S COLLEGE stands on the brow of a steep cliff above a tributary of the Severn. It looks out, across the river, at the mellow red brick of a little old town and a church which is one of the glories of the West. Behind it is a land of forest ridges and deep, fertile valleys ; about it, on every side, lie the Welsh hills and the English hills.

It has produced good scholars for six hundred years. The ancient monastery, built in the early part of the fourteenth century, became a sanctuary for learning ; in that wild land, the battlefield of two races, it was the only place where the arts of peace could be preserved. Thither repaired all the young clerks of the Welsh Marches, any boy who cared more for books than broken heads. And there they heard news of all that was happening beyond their own savage hills ; they met and talked with scholars from other lands. When they left St. Clere's it was to seek advancement in the church and a surprising number of them became bishops. But learning, not statesmanship, was their vocation, and not one of them became an archbishop or a cardinal. Nor was their foundation prolific in saints and martyrs. If they got themselves burnt or excommunicated it was for some form of heresy so recondite that only they and their opponents could understand it.

Henry VIII dissolved the monastery. The college became a secular grammar school, prospered exceedingly and grew into a great English institution. But the tone of the place remained unchanged. St. Clere's continued to produce a high percentage of bishops, deans, dons, schoolmasters, some notable judges and law lords and, when the Civil Service examinations became competitive, a great many permanent heads of departments. The crop of soldiers, doctors, poets, politicians, evangelists and criminals remained a scanty one. In the Middle Ages these cloisters and courts never sheltered voices crying in the wilderness ; they provided, rather, security for the rational communication of ideas. Six boys out of ten went on to a particular college at Oxford which had been richly endowed with the spoils of the old foundation, so that the associations, standards and way of thinking which they had formed at school persisted throughout their university career.

St. Clere's remains, on account of its situation, the most beautiful of English public schools. The outward changes have been as slight as the inner ones. All that can be seen dates from the fourteenth and fifteenth centuries. The chapel, the cloisters, the old convent buildings with their fine gatehouse form a noble pile along the top of River Cliff, and modern extensions are stowed away among the trees behind where they cannot spoil the view. The little town across the river is of later date. It grew up when times became peaceable and roads more safe. But, fortunately, it stopped growing in the reign of George IV, and does not, therefore, contain a single ugly building. Town, school, river and the surrounding hills are as lovely as a dream. And, like a dream, they are a little remote, a little unreal. They stand outside the hurry and stress of the modern world, just as the old convent stood aloof amid the turbulent life of the border.

Against this remoteness, this beauty, Mark Hannay had suddenly taken to hurling the most violent abuse. He had been head of the school for nearly a year, and for two terms had enjoyed that exalted position as much as anybody could. But in his last term at St. Clere's he went through a period of extraordinary mental discomposure.

It had occurred to him to look up the careers of former heads of the school in order to find out how many of them had become Prime Ministers. None of them had, and this dismayed him, for it was his intention some day to direct the affairs of the nation. He believed himself to have the requisite capacities. But now he began to wonder if it was, after all, a good thing to be head of St. Clere's, and from that to question whether St. Clere's itself was a good thing. His was a nature inevitably destined to undergo, at some time or other, the upheavals of sudden conversion. He underwent it now. The certainties of a lifetime seemed to crumble as he tested them. He began to abuse all that he had formerly admired, to exalt all that he had formerly despised. That he was capable of doing great things in the world he still believed; that he would ever do them could no longer be taken as a matter of course.

For some time he kept this mental turmoil to himself. But, at length, having reached some conclusions, he imparted them to his friend and rival, Adrian Parkin. It was on a Sunday afternoon in June when cuckoos shouted from every tree and the hawthorn was curdled with blossom. All the fields and hills were dotted with little black figures walking sedately in couples. Chubby juniors made wide circuits to avoid the path along the top of the cliff which immemorial tradition had forbidden to them. A certain nervousness overshadowed the Sunday promenade of these innocents; there were so many things which they must be careful not to do, and so many masters' wives wandering about. The little top-hats were seldom at rest for long.

But no nervousness attended Hannay and Parkin. In this small world they were gods. They strode along the middle of the sacred River Cliff, sublimely arrogant, saluting their female acquaintances courteously, but with a touch of condescension.

"My mind is quite made up," said Mark. "I'm not going to Oxford. What's the use? What's the use of getting a first in Mods and a first in Greats, or being President of the Union, if it comes to that ?   What happens afterwards ? "

Parkin did not reply.   His eye was on the flowery bank above them.   Here, or hereabouts, two years ago, he had found the ivy-leaved bell flower ; to his great disappointment, he had never seen it again.   Mark, however, did not want a reply.   His question had been rhetorical.

" Afterwards," he said, " it's one of three things.   I shall either capitalize my brains and go into the Civil Service, or gamble on them and go to the Bar, or funk the whole thing and become a don.   What else is there for any of us ? "

Parkin said that he thought he should like to go to Central America and look for orchids.   Mark disposed of this a little impatiently :

" Oh, yes, you're all right.   You aren't a typical St. Clere's man, and you're going to Cambridge, anyway.   I didn't mean you, I meant me."

" I know you did," said Parkin with a grin.

" What am I going to do ?   If I don't make up my mind now it will be too late.   I must know where I'm getting."

" I should have thought you'd do very well at the Bar."

" Do very well ! " said Mark, with the utmost contempt. " I dare say I should.   It's a nice gentlemanly profession, isn't it ?   And quite exciting because you don't know how it's going to turn out.   Quite a little adventure.   You either do very well and are overworked, or you don't do at all, and starve."

" You wouldn't have to starve."

Mark flushed.   The idea of his own wealth humiliated him.   He had fifty thousand pounds and Parkin had not a penny ; but the choice of a career was surely quite as important for him as it was for Parkin.   He fiercely resented the suggestion that it did not matter very much what he did, since he was bound to be a rich young man.

Only lately had the idea of money obtruded itself upon either of them ; it played a very small part in life at St. Clere's.

"You dress up," he said, ignoring the interpolation. "You put on a wig, and you play a game, rather like chess, with another fellow in a wig. I dare say I should enjoy it. I like problems. If I go to Oxford I should doubtless go to the Bar."

"The administration of justice isn't a game," argued Parkin. "It's a very important work that's got to be done by somebody."

"I shouldn't have to worry about justice, only about winning cases. It would be ages before I became a judge," said Mark modestly. "Besides, I want to make laws, not administer them."

"Then go into politics."

"I mean to. But will four years at Oxford give me the training that I want ? I don't believe it will."

"I should have thought that a liberal education . . ."

"Liberal Poppycock ! " exploded Mark, now well in his stride. "It's all nonsense. Don't you see what's happening ? What's the good of all this liberal education ? What has it done to us, to the upper middle classes ? It's been used as a sort of strait-jacket. What have we learnt that is going to help us to live ? To think ? And how far does thinking get us ? To a point at which we realize the entire futility of ever doing anything at all, since all action is highly illogical. We think so much that we get frozen up into a sort of mental constipation that keeps us quiet for the rest of our lives. There must be some better way of training the human intelligence. What's the matter ? "

Parkin had made a sudden dive at the bank. But he had been deceived.

"Nothing . . ." he said. "I thought it was . . . any-way, it's a bit early in the year still. Go on."

"You aren't listening."

" I'm listening like hell. What do you say is wrong with the upper middle classes ? "

" We don't lead. We don't break new ground. We ought to. We've got the capacity and the brains, but the energy . . . that's all been drained out of us by this precious liberal education. We go meekly into the job of getting our livings as pleasantly as we can, making it as much like a game as we can. Play up, play up, and play the game ! That's our attitude. . . ."

" I don't think so," said Parkin. " I've only once been told to play the game since I've been here, and that was by an old boy who preached in Chapel one evening about a mission to the Solomon Islands. You're flogging a dead horse."

" No, I'm not. We know the world is in a filthy state. We know we're drifting to glory ; we can see the smash ahead of us, but do we exert ourselves to stop it ? We can't. We're too frightened of change. We're too much rooted in the past. All our energy and intellect is securely tied up ; they've taken jolly good care of that."

" Who is *they* ? The governing body or who ? Do you really mean to say that there is a set of people somewhere who sit down solemnly and say : ' Now how can we stop Hannay from saving the nation ? ' I'm surprised at you."

" No. It's done unconsciously, of course. But you must admit that the average public schoolboy, here and elsewhere, is trained to carry on the present system as long as it will last. He isn't taught to be a leader."

" I should jolly well hope not. Just imagine it ! Several thousand leaders going down from the Universities every year ! Several thousand of 'em all waving pick-axes and out to break new ground. There wouldn't be any ground left."

" But we don't believe in the present system. We don't think the world is being run properly : only we're afraid that when the present system goes we'll go, and all we stand for. So we back it to save our skins. The only people who dare get a move on are people who've escaped a liberal education."

"That's true enough," agreed Parkin. "But I think it's always been so. Half-baked fanatics are effective, and get things done. Good things and bad things. The intellectual, the man with a trained mind, doesn't work for quick returns."

"Well, nowadays we've got to work for quick returns, or we'll all go to glory. That's why I feel I've got to make up my mind now. I'm not going to the University. I'm going to get a job on a tramp steamer. In the stokehold."

"Oh? How will you set about it? Getting a job like that?"

Mark was not quite sure. Nor could he explain very clearly how life in a stokehold was going to help him.

"Don't think I want to pose as Comrade Hannay. I mean to be myself, an intellectual, but an effective intellectual. I want to see how much of all I've learnt, up to now, will survive in quite a different kind of life. If it won't survive it's no use. Before it's too late, before I'm set, I want to put myself in a kind of melting pot."

"A stokehold ought to be that. What equipment will you need?"

"Only a sweat rag."

Parkin laughed so much that Mark was nettled.

"I suppose you think it's all rot."

"No. No I don't. I think I see what you mean. But why a stokehold? Isn't that a bit constricted? What you want is to knock about and meet all sorts. If I were in your shoes I should join the Army for a bit."

"You mean enlist as a private?"

"Yes. You'd see much more life that way."

"But that would tie me for years. I only want to think out an alternative for going to Oxford."

"It depends. You might go into the gunners, for instance. That need only mean three years with the colours and nine with the reserve. I know that because a boy in our village wanted to enlist and asked my advice and I looked up the details foɪ him. A line regiment would tie you up for seven years. I should find out about the R.F.A. if I were you."

" Are you serious ? "

" Perfectly serious. I think it would do you a lot of good."

Mark was struck by the suggestion, but did not entirely relish this last sentence.

" Do me a lot of good ? " he asked suspiciously. " What do you mean ? "

" Well . . . you'd meet all sorts, and you'd have to learn how to get on with them. That would be very useful, afterwards, when you get going with your pickaxe. If you get on with people they're more likely to listen to you."

" But I should have thought I did get on with people very well."

" You do here. You would at Oxford. With your own sort. You haven't much use for any other sort. I think three years as a private would do you a lot of good even if you went to the Bar afterwards. You seem to be quite sure you'd get work at the Bar, and only worry whether you'll enjoy doing it. I've a brother at the Bar, and what worries him is the difficulty of getting any work at all. If you can't get on with people, solicitors and so forth, they aren't likely to give you work."

" What's wrong with me ? Why should you think . . ."

" You can't forget your own superiority, and that puts people's backs up."

" I don't . . . " began Mark.

But he broke off, unable to contradict the accusation. From nobody else would he have accepted so much criticism. He had never known the wholesome humiliations of family life and had always been treated far too much like a grown-up person. It had never been anyone's business to advise or correct him. He had no home. His guardian, an elderly solicitor, looked after the fifty thousand pounds, read his school reports, and saw that he went to the dentist four times a year. When he was younger his guardian's housekeeper had been responsible for his clothes. If he had nowhere else to go he could always take shelter in his guardian's house at Wimbledon. But most of his holidays were spent in the homes of his friends where he was treated with consideration as a guest. So long as he remained pleasant, good tempered and well mannered, his arrogance would go uncensured.

He was angry with Parkin, but he was impressed. Their friendship had survived considerable stress, for they were rivals both in scholarship and in status. Many of the masters would have preferred to see Parkin head of the school, and Mark, knowing this, had been obliged to suppress many jealous qualms.

They had come to the end of River Cliff and turned through a small wicket gate which led to the college playing fields. Another pair of strollers stood aside to let the great men pass. One of them was Beddoes, a prefect, but no crony of theirs, a boy with so doubtful a reputation that most right-minded people thought it a scandal that he should be in the sixth at all. The other was Kenneth Canning.

When they were past and out of earshot Mark growled :
" There's a liberal education for you ! "

In the preceding term he had wanted to make some protest ; to take the extreme step of going to the head master and demanding that Beddoes should be deprived of office. But Parkin had dissuaded him, pointing out that they had no conclusive evidence.

" If it wasn't Beddoes," said Parkin, " it would be somebody else. You can't blame the school. There's three hundred decent men here and a dozen rotters, if as many. What can you do with a man who inevitably picks up with a rotter ? Canning is . . ."

He paused, remembering that Mark had once been fond of Kenneth.

" He's a young horror," said Mark grimly. " He wasn't, as long as I kept an eye on him."

" Well, you couldn't keep an eye on him for ever. He's got to stand on his own feet sometime. But he's the sort that goes wrong whatever school he's at. Just as some people pick up any germ that's going. The school's all right. It isn't the school that's done it. It's something wrong with him . . . his home or something."

" Yes, it is. It's his home. He's been having a bad time. His people were divorced the other day, you know."

" Yes. I'd heard. But he's not the only one."

" It all boiled up last summer when I was staying with them. He was in a bad way. He . . . he wanted to discuss it with me and I shut him up. I'm afraid I hurt his feelings. Any way I know he's been sore with me ever since."

" Oh ? Why did you shut him up ? "

To explain why was not very easy to Mark.

" Well, wouldn't you ? Discussing his people when I was staying in the house ? "

" Yes. I see. Beastly situation."

" Wouldn't you have refused to discuss it ? "

" Why it depends. If I'd thought it would do the poor chap any good to get it off his chest . . . what did he want ? Advice what to do or anything ? "

" No. Not exactly. He was frightfully upset."

" He just wanted to tell you about it ? "

" How could I listen ? What would you have done ? "

" I don't know," said Parkin diffidently. " If it was a friend of mine . . . well . . . if he wanted to talk I think I'd have listened . . . and . . . you know, sympathised and said how frightfully sorry I was. I mean . . . even if you can't say anything particularly useful, he might have got it off his mind."

" You think I ought . . ."

" Nobody could say what you ought to have done unless they were there."

They were passing the gates of the Sanatorium and Parkin turned aside, explaining that he must drop in and call on a friend with a broken collar bone.

Mark cut back across the fields towards the school. He was by now fully convinced of his own inferiority to Parkin, to anyone possessed of a warm heart. He loathed himself and he loathed the cold-blooded vanity which had betrayed him. For he knew quite well that he had allowed vanity to silence him when Kenneth asked for help. He had failed, he had been ineffective, in a very simple crisis, not from stupidity but from egotism.

And I can't blame the school, he thought, for my egotism. What am I going to do about it ? How can I get rid of it ? I shall never be worth anything unless I can get rid of it.

He hunched his gown up on his shoulders and passed under an archway into the cloister. His footsteps rang out on the echoing flags ; for hundreds of years those stones had echoed to the pacing of young feet. His trouble was as old as they were but he did not know it, or reflect that he was not probably the first boy to pass that way with a bad conscience.

THE ACCOLADE

ELIZA heard his footsteps before he came out of the cloister. The great quadrangle, where she stood, was empty and silent save for the cooing of pigeons on the cobbles. Mrs. Hewitt and the head master had just gone into the library to look at a new portrait. She should have gone with them but she had lingered behind, afraid lest Kenneth should be looking for them and miss them. The chapel tower soared up into the pale summer sky. She looked up and down and round about, wondering whether she was ever going to see Kenneth. Then she heard firm, quick footsteps coming along the cloisters and thought how much that sound seemed to belong to this place. And because St. Clere's meant Mark, for her, she was not surprised to see him come out into the sunlight from under the great arch. He was as she always saw him in her mind's eye: dark, vigorous, sombre, pacing along thoughtfully with his gown hunched up on his shoulders. She scarcely dared to speak to him, for fear of interrupting his august musings.

He turned, at her shy greeting, and she saw with dismay that he had not the faintest idea who she was. But he shook hands and enquired cordially after her health.

"Very well, thank you. I say . . . do you know where Ken is ? "

Now he remembered. But she had grown so much and looked so different that he had been at a loss. She was thinner. Her dress or something had changed her so that she might have been almost grown up. He thought :

Schubert . . . Pandy Madoc . . . Kenneth's sister . . . Eliza
. . . recalling these items in that order.

" Doesn't he know you're here ? "

" No. He didn't know I was coming. How can I find
him ? Dr. Blakiston told a boy to find him, but that was
ages ago. He keeps dragging us round and showing us
things, Dr. Blakiston, I mean, and they seem to have
forgotten we came here to see Ken—not a lot of pictures."

Mark reflected for a moment. Then he lifted up his
voice and bellowed :

" Fa-ag ! "

The shout echoed round the quadrangle. Feet clattered
on staircases and half a dozen little boys came pounding
up as fast as they could run. One, who came through
the gate house, was a good deal behind the rest. Mark
waited until the last comer had joined the panting group
and then addressed him.

" You ! "

The rest clattered away.

" Find Canning," said Mark, " and tell him that his
sister is here. He's somewhere on River Cliff. You'll catch
him if you run. You've my leave to go on River Cliff."

As the little boy set off Eliza asked :

" Do you always choose the last one who comes ? "

" Yes. It teaches them to hurry. How did you get
here ? Isn't anybody with you ? "

" It's my half term," she explained, " and I'm spending
it at Malvern with my grandmother, Mrs. Hewitt I mean.
She's doing a sort of cure there. So she asked me what
I'd like to do to-day and I said I'd like to come over and
see Ken, because it's quite near really, by motor bus.
But it was only decided at lunch-time so I couldn't let Ken
know."

" Where is your grandmother ? "

" Oh, she's in the library with Dr. Blakiston. They
are great friends, you know. He's asked us to tea but I
wish he hadn't, because I want to talk to Ken."

" I see.   Well, wouldn't you rather have tea with us ? "

" With you and Ken ? " exclaimed Eliza beaming.

" He hasn't got a study you know.   He's not in the sixth.   But we can use mine.   How is Daphne ?   She's not here, is she ? "

" No.   She's gone with a friend for half term.   Ken will come, won't he ? "

" Sure to."

At this point the head master and Mrs. Hewitt emerged from the library.   Mark went across to them and got leave to entertain the Cannings in his study.

" It's all right," he said, coming back to Eliza.   " They say you and Kenneth can have tea with me."

And he took her across towards the gate house.   He saw that she was excited and nervous.   She scarcely listened when he pointed out the glories of his study, a beautiful little panelled room which had always belonged, by right, to the head of the school.

" I know," she said.   " I've seen it before.   Listen ! If Ken doesn't come, if you'll tell me where to look, perhaps I'd better go after him myself. . . ."

" That boy is sure to find him.   It's impossible to miss anyone on River Cliff.   You wouldn't find him any quicker yourself."

" But supposing he won't come.   I'm so afraid that other boy, the boy Dr. Blakiston sent, did find him, and he just wouldn't come."

Mark looked his amazement.

" You see," she added, ". . . perhaps you didn't know . . . I haven't seen him since last summer.   Since Pandy Madoc and the end of the holidays last summer."

" Not seen him ?   But at Christmas and Easter . . ."

" No.   At Christmas he was in Paris with Mother. And at Easter I was in quarantine for mumps, so I stayed in our school San. all the holidays.   And he hasn't written either.   He hasn't answered my letters.   That's why I felt I simply must come.   Oh, Mark !   Do you know what is the matter with him ? You're his great friend. Has he said anything to you . . . about being angry with me ? "

" No, nothing. Not a word."

Her eyes searched his face anxiously.

" He's quite all right ? "

" Absolutely. As far as I know."

" I had a sort of feeling that he wasn't. You . . . you know what has happened to us, don't you, Mark ? "

" About your people ? The divorce ? Yes. I'm very sorry. I expect it's been an uncomfortable sort of time for everybody."

" It's been beastly. Did Ken tell you about it ? What is he choosing ? Did he say ? "

" Choosing ? "

" You know my mother is to have us till we are sixteen and then we can choose. Of course Ken is seventeen and I know he has chosen to stay with her. But, you see, I shall be sixteen next birthday. And I want rather . . . I'm not sure . . . I can't bear absolutely to give my father up. But I can't bear to give up Ken either. So I thought, if only Ken and I could talk about it sensibly, we might persuade them to sort of share us, so that we didn't have to be so broken up. Ken could get mother to agree, I'm sure he could. But I don't know how he feels and if he is still so violently on mother's side. Can't you tell me ? "

" I'm afraid I can't. He's said nothing about it to me."

" Oh ! I thought he would have. You're his great friend."

Mark felt obliged to explain that he and Kenneth were intimate friends no longer. Whereat she grew very pale and stared at him in deep dismay.

" I didn't know," she said at last. " I'm sorry. I'm sorry I've bothered you with all our affairs. I thought . . ."

" I only wish I could do something," exclaimed Mark.

She fished a handkerchief out of her neat handbag and blew her nose.

" Do you," she asked from behind her handkerchief, " know a song called *Dithyramb* ? "

" Oh, *Dithyramb*, " said Mark. " Yes. I've got a record of it here."

He hunted out the record from a cupboard and put it on his gramophone, talking meanwhile of this song and that, and not looking at Eliza until she should have had time to compose her features. When, at last, he did look at her he forgot what he was saying in a rush of sympathy.

" Do sit down," he urged, pushing forward a decrepit basket chair. " I'll get some tea. We won't wait for Kenneth. He'll be here by the time it's ready. And afterwards I'll leave you two in here, so that you can talk. I'll see that you aren't disturbed."

He went across to the door and again the demand for a fag went echoing across the quadrangle. The last comer was sent to boil a kettle.

" But Ken's all right ? " insisted Eliza as Mark rummaged in a cupboard for cake and biscuits.

Again he reassured her. They sat in silence, he on the table and she in the basket chair, listening to the record of *Dithyramb*. Before it was finished there was a sound of footsteps outside and Kenneth came in with another boy. Everything began to happen at once, the things she had expected and the things she had not expected. Her greetings and explanations were gone through with a perfunctory brightness because other people were there, listening, when she had expected to be alone with him. It was impossible to know if he was angry with her for coming. She had never imagined it like this.

He said, hurriedly :

" We'll go out into the town. We'll get some tea."

And Mark said, with equal haste :

" I've sent for tea. You'll have it here, won't you ? "

And there was a little pause which puzzled her. In spite of her private anxiety she perceived something of the tension between the boys. Kenneth hesitated, and then, as two fags brought in the tea, the other boy, Beddoes, sat down at the table with a laugh.

" All right," he said to Mark. " If you'd rather."

Mark did not look pleased. It was plain that he had meant his invitation for the Cannings only. But he said nothing and turned to Eliza, asking her if she would take charge of the teapot.

His study was on the ground floor, and a few minutes later a party of tourists, visiting the college, peeped curiously in through the open window. They got a pleasant glimpse of four young people putting away a substantial meal. The little schoolgirl, solemnly pouring out, was unexpected, and the intruders smiled as they took her in. They passed on, and a voice exclaimed :

" Did you see the li'll sister ? Wasn't she just too sweet for words ! "

Eliza remembered it afterwards, and was comforted to know that she had looked sweet. The rest of that tea-party was all a blur. She could never be sure when it was, how soon, that the confusion passed away and she began to take note of all those dreadful little changes in Kenneth, and to know that he was not any more the person who had been hourly in her mind, ever since they parted last summer at Pandy Madoc.

They were so small, these changes, that they meant nothing singly. His eyes were harder and his way of speaking slower, more deliberate. The flashing eagerness was gone, the quick glances, the crowing laughter. He was oddly languid. In eyes and voice there was a kind of jeering swagger, something guarded and disagreeable.

She looked across the table at Mark once, met his eye, and saw with a pang that he knew all about it. He knew that some dire thing had happened, beyond her power to foresee, and he had not been justified in assuring her that Kenneth was all right. Before the question in her eyes he flushed scarlet.

Beddoes did most of the talking, but she scarcely looked

at him. He was just a boy who had thrust himself in rather tactlessly, and she was too much worried to notice him. He seemed to be easy, talkative, and he was always asking for another cup of tea. It was a sudden flicker in Kenneth's eyes which propelled her at last towards enlightenment.

"The A.A. do it all for you," Beddoes was saying. "You drive straight on board."

What did that warning flicker mean? Why did Ken want to stop Beddoes?

"But don't you," she asked, "find the right-hand driving rather confusing?"

"I don't mind it. But in Sweden it's left-hand, as a matter of fact. And the roads are marvellous. You can do hours on end at seventy. Canning doesn't believe that, but he'll see for himself."

"I didn't say you couldn't in a decent car," put in Kenneth. "I merely say you couldn't do seventy anywhere in that old thing of yours. Fifty would shake her to bits."

"Very well, you wait. As a matter of fact I've almost got my father to say we can take the Bentley."

Light dawned on Eliza.

"Oh!" she exclaimed. "Is Ken going with you? To Sweden?"

It appeared that he was, for the whole of the summer holidays. This was no chance intruder but Kenneth's new friend, who had taken the place of Mark.

She looked at him keenly and met the utterly candid stare of inveterate dishonesty. Nobody could accuse Beddoes of not looking them straight in the face. Few people would have found fault with his appearance. He was fresh and healthy, he had blue eyes and fair hair, and the brutality of his mouth was not apparent when he was talking. Betsy had been charmed by him. But Eliza, strung up to a kind of hyper-æsthesia, had not a moment's doubt. She knew at once that he was vicious, cruel and a liar ; that he was to blame for the change in Kenneth. She knew it better than Mark did, for she grasped it instinctively without troubling to define the implications. Mark still wanted confirming evidence before he would believe what he suspected. Eliza needed no evidence. This Beddoes was horrid and he had made Kenneth horrid. To her it was as clear as daylight.

So that she scarcely knew what to say when tea was over and the others had gone, leaving her alone with Kenneth. She had screwed herself up for this interview, but all that she had been going to say went out of her head before the jeering eyes of this stranger. She could only exclaim :

" I'm sorry you've quarrelled with Mark."

" I haven't."

" Oh. I . . . thought you had."

" Did he say so ? "

" No. But I can see you aren't friends any more."

" He throws too much weight about," said Kenneth, adding suspiciously : " What's he been saying about me ? "

" Nothing. Why didn't you write to me ? Why didn't you answer any of my letters ? I've been so worried."

" I don't like writing letters."

" You always used to. I thought we'd made it up."

" Made up what ? "

" Our quarrel . . . last summer . . ."

" Oh, did we quarrel ? I don't remember."

" Oh, how can you ! "

He sprawled back in his chair and looked her up and down in silence.

" Are you really going to Sweden all the summer ? " she asked.

He nodded.

" Then I shan't see you again till Christmas."

" No. I dare say not."

" And I'm going to be sixteen in November."

" What has that got to do with it ? "

" You know. Perfectly well."

He did not trouble to deny it. But his look became more openly hostile.

" You'll choose father," he said at last.

" I don't know. That's why I wanted to talk to you. If it means that I shall never see you any more, Ken . . ."

" It certainly means that. You'll have to live with him altogether. Mother won't want you, and I shan't."

" Oh, Ken . . ."

" But hadn't you better make sure that he wants you first ? He's got Joy. They may think two is company."

" Oh ! Is . . . is Joy . . . there still ? "

" Of course she's there. She's his mistress, you fathead. If you live with him she'll be there, sleeping with him, and even you won't be able to pretend that she isn't. But go if you want to. You and she will have a nice time, pulling mother to pieces."

" We shan't. I shan't."

" They're a couple of pigs and you can go and pig it along with them. But don't think we'll ever want to see you again. We don't want any sows in Well Walk."

" You're a pig yourself, to say such things and think such things," cried Eliza. " Yes, you are. You're just a nasty little boy ; you've got ever so much nastier than you were. And I think that Beddoes is like a hog, so there. It's all his fault. I know it is."

" Shut up ! What d'you mean ? " cried Kenneth, jumping up.

" You pretend to be so disgusted at what other people do. What about you ? "

Kenneth called her by a name that she had never heard before, and flung out of the room.

Mark was hovering about in the quadrangle. He wanted to intercept anyone going to his study so that Eliza should be left in peace with Kenneth. But the interview was over much sooner than he had expected.

Kenneth emerged with a face of thunder, ignored Mark's " hallo," and went across to Beddoes's study. Greatly perturbed, Mark hurried back to Eliza. One glance at her face told him most of what had happened.

" Poor Eliza ! " he murmured.

" Oh, Mark, what shall I do ? "

" You had a row ? "

" He thinks I'm awful and disloyal. I don't know what to do. I get so muddled. I can't help loving my father the best. I can't help my feelings."

" What you feel," advised Mark, " is often wiser than what you think."

Only lately had he come to this conclusion himself, so he said it with much emphasis, and Eliza was impressed.

" I suppose," she said forlornly, " that I'd better go and find my grandmother."

" I'll take you."

He found her bag and her gloves for her. As they crossed the quadrangle she said :

" I don't like Beddoes."

" Don't you ? Why not ? "

" He's a cheat, isn't he ? "

" A cheat ? "

" Do you like him ? "

" Not much. But I've got nothing definite against him."

In the cloisters she said :

" It's been so awful, all this winter, having nobody to talk to about it. Because of course I couldn't talk to Daphne. But I always thought, well, anyway, it wasn't so bad for Ken because he had you. You see, if you've got a friend, then you tell them things, and you start trying to put it all sensibly, and that makes you get more sensible. And when there's been a quarrel in a family, then nobody is sensible, so you want a friend. Somebody who is outside. But I thought Ken was all right, and now he isn't."

" Yes," said Mark thoughtfully. " You must have been through a lot."

They had reached the head master's doorstep. She turned to him with a look of amazement, unable to credit her ears.

" But I think you're a first-rate creature," he added, ringing the bell. " I wish I was like you."

" What ? "

" Good-bye."

He nodded and turned away as the maid opened the door. Eliza had to go inside. She was so much astonished that she nearly fell over the doormat. Could she have heard such words from Mark, *from Mark*, the noblest of God's creatures, the friend she could never have because she was not a boy ?

A first-rate creature ! It hasn't happened to me. It couldn't. There isn't so much happiness . . .

She followed the maid into a room full of people. They smiled when they saw her radiant face, concluding that she must have spent a very happy afternoon.

FATHER AND DAUGHTER

THAT day was the first of the better days. Eliza travelled back to Malvern in a whirlwind of happiness, in spirits so high that she found plenty of courage for the next step.

Early on Monday morning she packed her suit-case and slipped out of the hotel, leaving the following note for her grandmother :

DEAR GRAN,

I have gone up to London for the day to see father. I will go back to school by the 5.40 from Baker Street, which is what all the London girls go by. Thank you very much for a lovely ½ term ; it was very good of you to have me. And please don't worry about me being alone in London. I have plenty of money and know my way about and will not get into conversation with strangers. Mother always lets me go about alone, really. I would have told you, only I know mother does not wish us to see him, so you would have had to say no. And I *must* see him !

Your very loving

ELIZA.

She did not know where her father lived now, but she thought that she could find out. When she got to London she found a public call-box, and rang up her other grandmother in Bedford Gardens.

" I want father's address," she explained.

Mrs. Canning, at the other end, was taken by surprise.

" Eliza ! Where are you ? Aren't you at school ? "

" No. It's my half term. Grandmamma, do please tell me where he is. Mother won't."

" Oh ! " said Emily Canning. " Oh, really ? How dis . . . oh, well, it's 97D, Gladstone Gardens, near Gloucester Road Station."

" Oh, thank you ! "

" Where are you ? "

" At Nuneaton."

" What ? "

" I hope you are quite well, grandmamma ? "

" Eliza, where did you say you were ? "

" At Torquay."

" What ? Where ? "

But Eliza had rung off.

Mrs. Canning began to be sorry that she had given the address so readily. She ought to have found out more, but the temptation to cross Betsy had been too strong. That Eliza should have foreseen this, should have exploited her, was incredible. She could not believe that any grandchild of hers could be capable of such duplicity. But the more she thought it over, the more uneasy she grew.

How abominably sly, she thought. This is quite a new trait in Eliza. Well . . . she must have got that tendency from Betsy. . . .

Gladstone Gardens was a dingy little square of tall houses which had been turned into flats just after the War, when any flat, however makeshift and uncomfortable, could be let at a high rent. Now it was a shabby, depressed neighbourhood—a middle-class slum. People on the down grade lived there. The communal front doors were neglected, there were no lifts, and the staircases smelt.

Eliza found No. 97, climbed up a great many flights, and presently came up short against a door put bang across a top stair. It had " D " on it, so that it must be the right one. But she was surprised, for there was something very mean, quite unlike her father, about the entry, the stairs and this door. She could not imagine how he came to be living in such a place.

She rang the bell, which was of the kind that makes a loud, angry noise immediately on the other side of the door. And, as she waited, she wondered how they managed when there was a party, with crowds of people trying to get up these steep little stairs and nowhere to stand while they waited to get in. For it was impossible to think of her father without thinking of parties.

Footsteps came clumping inside the flat. A surly-looking servant peered out at her, admitted that Mr. Canning was at home, and at length agreed to let her in. They had to insert themselves with care into the narrow hall while the door was being shut again.

" Will you wait in here, please ? " said the maid, opening a door.

Eliza passed into a room which was full of Eastern trophies. Ivory elephants walked along the mantelpiece above the gas fire. The stone-coloured walls were covered with weapons, embroideries and pictures on rice paper. There was a Buddha sitting in the corner, and on the hair carpet there was a tigerskin. Ladies, Burra Mems, photographed in presentation gowns, peered regretfully out of tarnished silver frames. She looked about her, quite bewildered, until her eye fell on the divan by the window. There, in a little wicker basket, lay something so astonishing that she nearly fainted.

Staring her eyes out, she moved slowly towards it. At last she knelt down and pulled the shawl back a very little way so as to see more.

It was asleep. It had such a *good* little face, composed and serious, that she was filled with awe. The tiny red hands were crossed devoutly beneath the chin. She knew why that was, for she had been to physiology lectures at school, and had learnt that a new-born child will always pack itself up into a neat little parcel, tucking away its arms and legs. Just so had it lain in its first tender home.

Birth, that most extraordinary event, was still quite close to it, making all life appear miraculous.

So deep was her wonder, her contemplation, that she did not hear her father come in. And he for a few seconds could not speak, because he failed to recognize this tall young stranger, and thought she was Betsy. Time seemed to have run backwards. Her face was turned away as she knelt beside the divan, but the line of her cheek, the shape of her head, the dark curls on her neck, all brought the young Betsy vividly before him.

But that girl was gone forever, as he knew in the next instant. No vicissitude could bring her back. Even if Betsy came. . . . But who was this ? He said something, he did not know what, and she turned round.

" Eliza ! "

She was too much excited to greet him.

" Oh, Father ! How . . . I never. . . . What a darling little baby ! "

He smiled.

" Didn't you know that you had a little brother ? "

" A brother ? "

The word was like an electric shock. Could there be any brother except Ken ?

" Was he . . . how old is he ? "

" Just a fortnight."

" Was he . . . born here ? "

" No. In a nursing home. We brought him here yesterday."

" Then . . . he's . . . Joy's little baby ? "

" Yes."

But how clever of Joy ! How strange that such a wonderful thing could happen to her ! What did she feel like ? Had she been frightfully excited ?

" He's so dark ! "

" Yes. Isn't he ! "

" Are you married to Joy then ? "

" No. I'm going to marry her as soon as . . . you can't

get married again immediately after a divorce you know. Not for six months."

" Oh, yes . . . the law . . ." said Eliza vaguely.

The law did so many things that she could not understand.

They realized that they had not kissed one another and they did so now. He said :

" It's lovely to see you again, Eliza. How did you . . . how is it that you've come ? "

Words departed from her. Fifteen cannot talk to forty-five. It was impossible for either to tell the other anything. Of all that had happened to them both, since they sat resting on the hills above Llyn Alyn, so little could be explained. They could only guess.

But she made a crude attempt and told him the most important thing, from her own point of view.

" I saw Mark yesterday."

" Mark ? Who's he ? "

" Mark Hannay. You know . . . Ken's friend."

Alec remembered, now, a handsome boy who talked a great deal. He could feel no interest in hearing about Mark Hannay.

" Only," said Eliza earnestly, " he and Ken aren't friends any more. Isn't it awful ? "

" How is Ken ? "

" I had tea with them yesterday," was all that she could say.

" Oh ? Were you at St. Clere's ? "

" Yes. It's my half term. Ken is going to Sweden this summer with a boy called Beddoes. I wish he wasn't."

" Oh, really ? But how did you get here ? "

" I got the address from grandmamma. Who is this photograph of ? "

" I don't know."

Eliza looked so much puzzled that he explained :

" These aren't my things. This is a furnished flat."

" Oh ! " she cried, in obvious relief. " Then you won't always be here ? "

" Good heavens, no ! We only took it because we wanted something in a hurry. We had to clear out of Southwick Court, as the owners were coming back. When Joy is all right again we'll find something more permanent."

" Oh. I see."

" You didn't think I'd gone and bought all these elephants ? "

She had. She had accepted all these queer things, these photographs of strangers, as part of the upheaval in their lives. Her father had gone and done so much that was unexpected and inexplicable. The elephants were not more surprising than the baby.

" It's cheap," said Alec. " And we can get rid of it any time. We only take it by the month."

Eliza made a dive after something that might explain it.

" Then are you poor ? " she asked.

" I'm short at the moment. Yes. I've done no work for nearly a year and there's nothing much coming in just now."

She registered this fact. Divorce sometimes made people poor. But her mother seemed to be quite rich still, and they had not left the house in Well Walk.

There were three or four sharp knocks on the wall.

" That's Joy," said Alec. " She wants me to bring her the baby. We put it in here because it's cooler."

He approached the basket and doubtfully pulled back the shawl.

" Oh, let me carry it," begged Eliza. " Do let me. I know how to. I did at the crêche. I'll be awfully careful."

He was glad to allow it, for he was terrified of picking the baby up. Her expert handling of the creature filled him with respect and amazement. She was a woman in command of a situation and, at the same time, a little girl enjoying an enormous treat. To carry the baby gave her intense delight : she stood looking at him as if the world could hold no greater treasure.

" What's his name ? " she asked suddenly.

" Peter."

" Oh ! "

She thought Peter was an awful name and so did Alec. That he would have gone and called a child that, of his own accord, was most unlikely. It must be Joy's doing.

Again she was bewildered. He could not be regarded as one who knew what he was about. She had expected to find him active, dominating and perfectly sure of himself. He had done something strange and violent : he had broken up the natural order of things. In her imagination he had acquired a rebellious energy. Not all at once could she readjust her ideas or see him as a man who has been swept away on a tidal wave and marooned in a place not of his own choosing.

There was another knock on the wall. She carried Peter, very carefully, into the next room.

Joy was sitting up in a tumbled bed. Her yellow hair stood up on end and a shabby green cardigan was huddled on over her nightgown. She looked tired and fragile. In the nursing home she had felt extremely well, but the move back to the flat had been exhausting. At the sight of Eliza she gaped and flushed. Eliza advanced cautiously and put the baby into her arms.

" You don't mind, do you, Joy ? I've carried little babies before. I know how. I did so want to."

" Why have you come ? " asked Joy confusedly.

" She's come to see us," said Alec. " She didn't know she had a brother and she's over the moon."

" Who brought her ? "

" I brought myself. It's my half term. Oh, look ! He's awake ! "

The baby began crying in angry little bleats. Joy hastily pulled down her nightdress and tried to feed it. But neither she nor it was clever at performing this simple function. It kept slipping down into the hollow of her elbow instead of lying composedly at her breast.

" You want ten million more pillows," exclaimed Eliza. " And a cushion under your arm."

She tucked in pillows, just as they had done at the nursing home, until Joy was comfortable. The baby began to suck tranquilly.

Alec and Eliza sat on either side of the bed, gazing at his little dark head. Eliza felt uncomfortable because her father was there, and thought that Joy might have managed the whole business more modestly. Then she remembered what Kenneth had said yesterday. She began to blush hotly. It must be true about her father and Joy. The marriage couch, that prim symbol with its antimacassars and horsehair, was here. She was actually sitting on it. But then the baby was here, too. The grossness, the brutality, of Kenneth's words meant just nothing at all. To apply them to this situation was impossible. Nothing to do with a baby could be bad.

Presently Alec took Joy's breakfast tray into the kitchen. As soon as he was out of the room Joy broke into reproaches.

" Why didn't you come before ? He's been longing to see you. I don't think it was very kind."

" I wasn't allowed," explained Eliza.

" Your mother wouldn't ? "

" It's the Law, you know. Till we are sixteen."

" It's wicked. I can't think how she can be so cruel. Isn't it enough that she has taken all his money ? "

" Has she ? "

" Of course she has. All his savings. Every penny he's got. Didn't you know ? "

" No, no, I didn't."

" Why did she let you come now ? "

" She didn't. I came without leave."

" Oh ? You did ? Oh, good ! "

Joy looked at her curiously and added in a kinder voice :

" I'm very glad you've come, dear ! I never wanted to come between him and his children. It has nearly broken my heart. She'll be furious with you, I suppose ? "

" I hope not," said Eliza. " I'm nearly sixteen."

" So you are. Then you're on his side ? "

That Eliza had a side of her own was something which nobody seemed to consider. She looked rather sulky, kicked the brass end of the bed, and said that she did not know.

" When you're sixteen . . . what will you choose ? "

" I don't know."

" I wish you'd come to us. I'd do everything I could . . . we always got on all right, didn't we ? You are his favourite, you know. He minded losing you most. If you knew all he's gone through . . . I can't explain now. You're too young to understand. But you will. And there's one thing that you ought to know. Your mother . . ."

" Oh, don't," burst out Eliza. " She's my mother. You mustn't say things about her. It's got nothing to do with who is in the right. I don't care about that. I don't want to know. If I come to you . . ."

" Then you are coming ? "

" I'll have to think about it."

When Alec came back Joy announced triumphantly :

" Eliza thinks she may come to us when she is sixteen."

" Oh ? " said Alec. " Do you ? Eliza ! Do you ! "

His delight prevented him from saying more, but he smiled broadly and so did Joy. They both looked at Eliza as though she had given them the promise of something infinitely precious.

She will come to us, thought Joy. And that will show them that his children are on his side. They will see that his children would rather live with us. I haven't ruined his life.

She will come to us, thought Alec, and everything will be better. She and Joy will be pals, and they'll fuss about with the baby, and I shall have some peace. So clever, the way she tucked in those pillows! She's a peach and a pearl. She'll make life bearable.

They want me for their own sakes, not mine, thought Eliza. Funny! I've been wondering if I'd like it, but they don't worry about that at all. But I shall like it. I shall look after the baby. *She* can't, the stupid owl! Fancy getting a shawl like that, full of holes where he might catch his fingers! Doesn't she know *anything*? My babies, my own babies, will have proper shawls. Oh, what fun that will be! How happy I am! A first-rate creature. . . . Oh, Mark! Oh, you Mark! You have made me happy. . . .

She hugged herself as she sat on the bed. She was very happy and Mark had made her so. That was as far as she had got towards knowing that all she ever wanted from life would have to come from Mark.

The doorbell buzzed angrily. The maid's feet went clumping along the passage. A chatter of voices broke out and Eliza jumped off the bed.

" Oh, goodness! That's grandmother! She's come after me. From Malvern! Oh my goodness! "

" Mrs. Hewitt? " exclaimed Alec.

Eliza poked her head round the door and said mildly :
" Here I am."

" Eliza! " cried Mrs. Hewitt. " This is very naughty. How could you do such a thing? What will your mother say? "

Too flustered to know what she was doing, she came storming into the bedroom.

" Look at our baby," said Eliza.

Henrietta Hewitt collapsed. Here she had got herself into the head-quarters of sin. And what did she see? A woman lying in bed with a new baby : a place where all comers should tread softly and speak gently.

To stalk out in silence and scold Eliza elsewhere was the proper thing to do. Alec and Joy were shameless trans-

gressors and their baby should have been treated as
though it were not there or not new. But for Henrietta
this was impossible. As well might a devout Catholic
pass the Host without genuflection. It was a new baby.
A little bastard, no doubt, and a terrible misfortune, but
new and therefore a gift from God.

She approached the bed ungraciously and peered at him,
expressing a hope that Joy had not had too bad a time.
Because, when it came to having " a time " one had to be
sorry for any woman, however sinful.

" A dear little baby . . . so neat . . ."

This compliment, peculiar to Henrietta's generation,
surprised Eliza and Joy. Alec remembered how much it
had always annoyed Betsy, and felt a strong desire to
laugh.

Inarticulate with embarrassment, humanity, compassion, shock, and a sense of disloyalty to Betsy, Henrietta
got herself and Eliza out of the flat. In the street she
began to scold. But Eliza was quite impossible. She
refused to be scolded and skipped along, chattering about
her new brother with a childish glee.

" You don't seem to understand," said Mrs. Hewitt at
last. " It's all very sad. Very dreadful. He oughtn't
to have been born at all, poor little child. Don't you know
that, dear ? "

" But you said yourself he was a dear little . . ."

" All babies are . . . one feels they are very sweet . .
but . . ."

" Very well then ! "

Mrs. Hewitt gave it up. She said with a sigh :

" We'd better lunch at Gorringes."

ALONE

EVERYBODY has one hidden, irrational terror : of thunder, of ghosts, of cancer, of fire, of being buried alive. Shame may disguise but cannot banish it ; reason may command but cannot silence it. Far below the level of consciousness the roots of fear draw nourishment from secret and forgotten sources.

Betsy was afraid of going to the dentist, not because she minded pain, but because once, as a child she had heard of a person who jumped when the drill went on to the nerve, so that the drill slipped and gashed his throat. She lived in dread lest the same thing might happen to herself.

But she was very much ashamed of this fantasy and had avowed it to nobody except Alec, a long time ago, when they were first married. He had been extremely sympathetic. He realized at once that a visit to the dentist must be much worse for her than for anybody else, and that she could not be helped by knowing that such an ordeal is the common lot. All through their life together, even after they became estranged, he did his best to help her. He insisted that she should go in time, before any great amount of drilling became necessary. If left to herself she would never have done so. Once every three months he made an appointment for her, and conducted her himself to the horrid tryst. He sat in the waiting room while it was going on, shared in her glee when it was over, and took her out to luncheon afterwards as a reward.

So now she had not been to the dentist for eighteen

months, because there was nobody to make her go. In the autumn, when she got her Decree Absolute, several teeth were aching slightly. She tried to think that it was some kind of neuralgia and chewed on the other side of her mouth. By Christmas they ached continually. In January she could stand it no longer. She rang up the dentist one day, in a fit of desperate courage, and made an appointment for the following morning.

The children were odiously callous at breakfast. They knew what was in front of her, though of course they could not possibly know all that she suffered. But they seemed to be pleased that she was going to the dentist, because incidentally she could take them all in the car with her and drop them at a skating rink in the Edgware Road. They wanted to be there by half-past ten and, when she objected that her appointment was at eleven, they were heartless enough to suggest that she might arrive a little early and read the magazines in the waiting room.

"Would *you* like to spend an unnecessary half hour in that waiting room?" she asked.

"Yes," said Kenneth. "I would. I like looking at the magazines. I never see them anywhere else. I like going to the dentist."

"You've never been hurt," snapped Betsy.

"Well, have you?"

She could not truthfully say that she had. Mr. Abercrombie was very clever.

"But he's going to hurt this time."

"Then it's your own fault," said Kenneth. "You ought to have gone before."

He was sulky because she would not drive him to the skating rink. His temper, all through the holidays, had been atrocious; he expected the whole house to be run for his convenience, and he often spoke to her in a bullying tone, which Alec would never have permitted. And all because she had refused to let him go to Switzerland with his friend Beddoes. But he had been away in Sweden all the summer, and it was only natural that she should want her children together at Christmas. She looked at his discontented face, and sighed. Last Christmas he had been with her in Paris, and he had been so sweet. Not all the agony of that time could ever make her forget how sweet he had been, how touchingly sympathetic, how understanding. No grown man could have looked after her better. For a boy of sixteen he had been wonderful.

Now he was squabbling childishly with Eliza, who had accused him of fainting when he had to be vaccinated.

" So you're not so awfully brave yourself. You needn't show off about liking to go to the dentist."

" Oh, my God ! "

" Kenneth," said Betsy, " I will not have you saying that."

" It's simply an insular prejudice. On the Continent——"

" I don't care. I won't have it ! It's a bad habit."

" Oh Christ ! "

" Kenneth ! "

" Don't repress him, mother," put in Eliza. " You shouldn't repress an adolescent. It only makes them worse."

Kenneth looked as though he was going to say something really outrageous when the parlourmaid came in to say that Lord St. Mullins wanted Betsy on the telephone. There was, immediately, a significant silence. Eliza became very busy with her haddock. Kenneth and Daphne stared at their mother. As soon as she was out of the room Kenneth exclaimed :

" There ! You see ! "

" Can't anybody ring anybody up ? " asked Eliza.

" Not twenty times a day.

Daphne was bursting with a question but she dared not put it to either of them. If her mother became Lady St. Mullins, would she then be the Lady Daphne ? Or the Hon. Daphne ? She feared not.

In the chilly quiet of the drawing-room, Betsy picked
up the telephone and heard an anxious voice repeating :
" Hullo ! Hullo ! Hullo ! Hullo ! . . ."
Max always did this, when kept waiting at the telephone,
for fear that the exchange might cut him off.
" Hullo, Max ! "
" Hullo ! Hullo ! Lord St. Mullins speaking. Can I
speak to Mrs. Canning ? Hullo ! Hullo ! Hullo ! . . ."
" Max, it's me ! It is Betsy speaking."
" Oh, hullo, Betsy ! Is that Betsy ? "
" Yes, it's me."
" Oh, Betsy ! "
There was a long pause. Max had a way of dying
suddenly on the telephone ; to get through to any-
one exhausted him so much that he had nothing to
say.
" Yes ? " said Betsy.
" Oh, Betsy, how is your toothache ? Is it worse ?
Hullo, Betsy ! Are you there ? "
" Yes, I'm here."
" How is your poor tooth ? "
" Bad. I'm going to the dentist this morning."
" Oh, my dear, how awful ! Poor Betsy ! How dread-
ful for you ! I am sorry. Are you dreading it ? "
" Yes, I am. Silly of me, isn't it ? "
" No. It's not at all silly. I can't bear the dentist
myself. When are you going ? "
" Eleven."
" To Abercrombie ? "
" Yes."
" Shall I go with you ? Would that make it better ? "
" No, no. That's nonsense."
" Somebody ought to. You shouldn't go alone.
Wouldn't you like me to . . . ? "
" No, Max. It's nothing to make a fuss about. I
don't suppose he'll hurt me," said Betsy, already beginning
to feel more cheerful.

" Somebody ought to make a fuss. You might faint or something. I'll be there at eleven."

" No—but, Max, I really . . ."

He had rung off.

His sympathy touched and cheered her. Here was, at least, one person who felt and said the proper things. Nobody else cared what became of her. The children were utterly selfish. Her friends had lost interest in her wrongs. None of them seemed to realize how lonely she was.

Again, for the hundredth time, she hopefully inspected her feelings for Max. He was so good and so kind and so fond of her. If she discovered in herself the smallest impulse of reciprocal emotion, anything at all spontaneous, she need not hesitate for a moment. But, lacking that impulse she could not possibly marry him.

Nor could she send him away, since she so often felt herself just upon the verge of loving him. And every month of this indecision made it more difficult, for he could not keep his devotion to himself, and people would soon say that she was treating him badly. This was most unjust, for it was a desire to treat him well which made her hesitate. She would not marry him without love. And it was his fault, not hers, that the affair had become so public. He was continually ringing her up and sending her flowers. Wherever she went, there he too contrived to be ; so that now they were often invited to meet one another as a matter of course and were thus perpetually seen together.

No, she thought, I won't have them say I exploit him. If Isobel Pattison gets to know this about the dentist she'll make a tale of it. It's not fair.

But she did not know how to get hold of him and prevent him from joining her at Mr. Abercrombie's. She rang up Hornwood, his house in Sussex, and he was not there. She rang up his club and he was not there. At last she was obliged to ring up Isobel Pattison, in case he might be staying with her, in Thurloe Square. Isobel had not the faintest idea of her brother's whereabouts and was so offensive that Betsy nearly said:

"Don't think I'm running after your wretched little brother. I'm trying to stop him from running after me."

Nothing could be done, and she must resign herself.

By the time that she reached Mr. Abercrombie's doorstep the sight of Max's car, already drawn up by the kerb, could scarcely distress her. She was too much terrified. On this doorstep she had been used to stand with Alec once every three months, and he would always slip an arm under her elbow while they waited. In five minutes, or less, she would be in the chair, feeling herself tilted back. The drill would be turned away at first. He would begin by probing between tooth and tooth, until . . . ah! here's a cavity . . . open a little wider, please —now I won't hurt you—and the drill would be swung round . . . medium, please, nurse . . . a thing like a gramophone needle, picked out of a drawer . . . open, please . . . brrrrrrrrr . . . if it's at all sensitive, just raise your hand . . . how can I raise my hand when I'm clinging to the chair! I must cling, in case I jump, in case I jump . . . how I'm sweating . . . open just a little wider. Ah, I shall faint! I shall be sick! It's going on to the nerve. I know it will. It's going on to the nerve, *right on to the nerve*, and I shall jump, I shall jump, it will slip— how can he stop it slipping if I jump? It will cut my tongue in half . . . brrrrrrr. . . .

The grey-haired parlourmaid opened the door. No hand beneath Betsy's elbow pushed her onwards. She had to get herself inside and along the hall. But Max was waiting for her in the room with the magazines and the Hogarth prints. He came and squeezed her hand in an agony of sympathy, murmuring:

"Oh, Betsy, if I could only bear it for you!"

His earnest, wizened little face was quite green; she could not have suffered more herself.

" Would you like me to go in there ? " he asked.

" Oh, no," said Betsy, so firmly that he did not persist.

He was so much wrought up that she had to comfort him. When the parlourmaid reappeared and beckoned to her, he groaned aloud.

MOTHER AND SON

DAPHNE skated very well, and Kenneth was improving rapidly. But Eliza was hopeless. She had no natural balance and never dared to go out into the middle of the rink, but went round and round with the melancholy procession of incompetents at the sides. She wobbled solemnly, her head poked forward, numbed by the chill of the ice, that cold which is so unnatural indoors because it should be long to the freshest of fresh air.

The band swung through a glamorous tune. Far out in the middle Daphne skimmed and spun, her kilted skirts flying out like a wheel. The Hon. Daphne Canning—Lady Daphne Canning—one of next Season's most interesting debutantes—skating at St. Moritz. She wished she had been on the rink at Grosvenor House. Such common sort of people came here ; anybody could come. At school nobody mentioned skating unless they had been to Grosvenor House. Of course my mother, Lady St. Mullins, belongs to the club.

Kenneth had no business to go out into the middle among the adepts. He tried to do elaborate figures and fell down so often that people began to laugh. At length, humiliated and bruised all over, he decided to become less conspicuous. Since competition with Daphne was impossible he might at least console himself by patronizing Eliza. He looked round the rink and saw her shuffling along within clutching reach of the side. Confidently he sped towards her.

" Cross hands with me," he said, " and we'll get on a bit faster."

He took her a little way out. She found that the
quickened pace improved her balance so that she almost
began to enjoy herself. She told Kenneth that he was
much better than the instructor, which pleased him. They
flew harmoniously round and round. Presently he
said :

" Does Daph know . . . what we think ? "

" I shouldn't think she could help it. You say such
horrid things about him."

" He's a perfect little abortion. Isn't he now ?
Honestly ? "

" Oh, I don't think he's bad. Why do you mind the
idea of it so much ? "

" I mind because in Paris she said she never would.
I asked her. I had to know, after all those lies Joy had
been spreading. She swore there wasn't a word of truth
in it and that she would never marry him. So now, if she
does, she must have been lying herself."

" I don't see that," said Eliza. " Couldn't she have
changed her mind ? She may have felt like that in Paris,
and now feel differently."

" She couldn't change her mind about a thing like that."

Eliza realized that it was useless to argue with him.
Nor could she understand how badly he needed to be sure
of his mother's integrity. She knew nothing of that time
in Paris, of how great a strain had then been put upon his
young nerves. After a few more turns, she said :

" Well, anyway, you needn't have been so cross to her
this morning, when she was frightened."

" Frightened ? "

" Of the dentist."

" Oh, rot ! Old Abercrombie never hurts anybody."

" No, but she can't help it. She's got a sort of panic
—she just can't bear it. Like some people are with
cats. Father told me. You remember he always used to
take her."

Kenneth was so much surprised that he fell down,

dragging Eliza with him. When they had picked themselves up they staggered to the balustrade and clung on to it. He demanded :

" Why didn't you tell me before ? I'd have gone with her."

" I think she hates anyone knowing."

" If he used to go with her, then it's my place to go now. I shall go along there at once. You and Daph can get yourselves home."

He hobbled off the rink and began to remove his boots.

Eliza looked on approvingly, feeling that she had done a good deed. It was not unpleasant to know that two households depended upon her common sense and sweet temper. Neither her father nor her mother could really get on without her, first-rate creature that she was. And, though she passed anxious moments, trying to decide which of them needed her most, these deliberations were extremely complacent in tone. Her regret for the past had almost vanished. She no longer pined for the days when she had been an unimportant member of a united family.

" If you go quickly," she advised, " you'll catch her before she comes out."

He looked up into her kind, complacent little face, and said bitterly :

" You do look smug."

Whereat she looked less smug and turned away, back to the rink.

There was no meeting ground for them. They had travelled too far apart during the year that they were separated. Eliza had made a place for herself in the new order of things. She had accepted the inevitable and was learning how to make the best of it. She had grown harder, more domineering, more inclined to believe herself infallible.

Kenneth, on the other hand, had remained in a state

of mental disintegration. He accepted nothing and pitied himself hysterically. He felt a grudge against the world because it had turned out to be a less pleasant place than he supposed. In fact, he was suffering from a moral breakdown.

The first shock—the crude discovery of his father's lust—had been aggravated by every subsequent turn in the quarrel between his parents. He had known all about it ; far more than Eliza knew. During that month in Paris his mother, half-insane herself, had told him everything. He heard about Chris Adams, and about the mean lies which Alec and Joy were spreading. He believed that his mother was entirely blameless, a victim whose life had been ruined by a vicious man. In a dirty world she remained pure and pitiful. He clung to that faith and would have died rather than distress her by any revelation of his own sensuality. She must never know that he had such a gross side to his nature, or guess that the idea of his father's depravity could so shamefully excite him. He listened to her, soothed her, and consoled her with a tenderness beyond his years. He made extreme efforts to be patient and gentle. But these turbulent passions had to find a vent, and his nerves might have given way altogether had it not been for the maid in the flat, a good-natured wanton, who seduced and consoled him in a motherly way.

Yvonne was kind, but she could not do much for his sick imagination and he was too young to appreciate her. He needed stimulus from somebody more like himself. He went back to school a ready prey for Beddoes, or any-one else a little older and a little more experienced. Yet he still, despite the confusion of his mind, desired to be worthy of his mother. He felt himself to be her only protector and he never meant to let her know of his other life. If, at any time, his association with Beddoes should threaten her peace of mind he believed himself capable of dropping the whole business quite easily.

Recalling his ill-temper that morning, he blamed himself very much. He hurried out into the frosty sunshine, full of good resolutions. She had been frightened and lonely, and he had allowed an unpardonable suspicion to cross his mind. Ten minutes brought him to the dentist's doorstep. He asked the maid to let her know that he had come and turned into the waiting-room, which was, by now, full of people, since that house was shared by several doctors.

A smouldering exasperation pervaded the room, for Lord St. Mullins, unable to sit still, racked the nerves of all his fellow-victims by pacing up and down and groaning audibly at intervals. He was in the middle of a groan when Kenneth walked in. But when he heard why his young cousin had come he bared all his teeth in the widest of smiles.

" Come to look after your mother ? Good old chap, that's right ! So did I."

" Oh," asked Kenneth dangerously, " why ? "

The onlookers had by now abandoned their magazines and were listening with frank enjoyment.

" I thought she ought to have somebody with her," explained Max.

" She's got me with her now. I shall take her home."

" My dear Ken, I'm glad you take such care of her ! We'll both take her home, shall we ? "

Kenneth, to this, made no reply whatever. He sat down, took up a magazine, and became absorbed in it.

The audience now watched the door, hoping to get a sight of Betsy before they were called away to their own appointments. The sympathy of the room was with Kenneth, for Max's groans had been intolerable and nobody thought that he would make an attractive stepfather. Now he was pacing up and down again, breathing sharply through his teeth as was his habit when confronted with a problem. And Betsy's children were undoubtedly a problem. By some means or other he must secure their regard.

" And how," he inquired genially, " is Beccles ? "

Kenneth raised a perfectly blank face.

" Beccles . . . your friend . . . didn't you go to Sweden ? "

" Do you mean Beddoes ? "

" Beddoes ! Ah, yes ! I was thinking it was Beccles. Your mother was talking of him. He must be a splendid chap."

" Why do you think so ? " inquired Kenneth.

" From what your mother said. She seemed to like him very much."

" Ah," said Kenneth, " she goes by looks. They count a lot with her. He's tall, you know. Not very tall, but a decent height." He indicated a point some way above Max's head. " And fair curly hair and blue eyes and all that."

Max blenched a little. But he persisted, for he had had plenty of practice in surviving snubs.

" And your other friend, Hannay, how is he ? "

" I haven't the faintest idea. He left school last summer."

" Ah ! Gone up to the University ? "

" No."

" No ? What's he done ? "

" Enlisted as a private in the gunners."

" What ? As a private ? How extraordinary ! "

" I thought you were a Socialist."

" So I am. But . . ."

At this point Betsy appeared and Max bounded towards her with a little moan of sympathy.

" Oh, did he hurt you ? Was it ghastly ? "

" No, no ! " She was radiant. " Only two little stoppings. I hardly felt it. Why, Ken . . ."

She looked from one to the other in dismay. Kenneth, advancing, took her arm and firmly marched her out of the room saying that he had come to see her home. Max followed them. On the doorstep he said, as pleasantly as he could :

" I'm sorry, old man. But I want your mother to come out to lunch with me. I want her advice about some curtains I have to buy. Betsy ! Can you spare me the time ? "

" You're coming home with me, aren't you ? "

Kenneth's eyes were stormy as he turned to his mother. She began to be annoyed with him.

" This concern for me is very sudden," she said. " You didn't show much this morning. I'm sorry you gave up your skating, but I'm afraid I'm not coming home just yet. If you want to be really useful you can drive the car back to Well Walk for me."

Max had already opened the door of his own car, and she got into it without looking at Kenneth again. But as they slid off down the street, and while Max was still arranging an enormous fur rug round her knees, she glanced out of the window and saw her son standing on the kerb. His white, despairing face unnerved her.

" Oh, dear," she said, " now I've hurt him. He's so sensitive."

" Are you never to think of yourself ? Those children make a perfect slave of you."

" But it was really rather sweet of him to come."

" It was sweet of me, too," said Max, with unusual spirit. " And I got there first. I do want you to come and help me to buy some things."

Betsy, who loved spending money, smiled and prepared to listen. He explained that he was going to do up Hornwood, which had not been touched for fifty years. When she learnt how many thousands of pounds he meant to lay out she could not repress a small thrill. The sum took her quite by surprise, for Max, in spite of his wealth, had not the manner of a rich man. He could himself have been very happy on a few pounds a week if only people would like him as much as he liked them. Money meant very little to him and he assumed that it meant nothing to Betsy.

INTERIOR DECORATION

DUSK found them, grimy and excited. in the attics of Hornwood. Betsy had declared that she could not give any advice about curtains and carpets until she had seen the rooms again, and they drove straight down to Sussex, arriving in time for a late luncheon. Ever since then they had been exploring. For the first time she got a chance to go over the whole house and to inspect every room. It was far larger than she had supposed. To make it habitable would be the work of months.

Externally it was a perfect house, nobly proportioned, solid and graceful. Ample wings flanked the central portion, with its tall pillars running up two stories to an elegant plinth. A steep wooded slope rose behind it ; in front there was a park with an extensive lake. The line of the South Downs decorated the horizon. But. even outside, much had been done to quench beauty and character. Monkey-puzzle trees had been planted wherever they could catch the eye, and a jungle of moribund bamboos disfigured the shores of the lake. Neat drives, of bright orange gravel, wound through acres of rhododendrons.

" Pull up, root out, and cut down," said Betsy, standing on the front door steps. " Let's have it all looking a little bit shabby."

Then she went indoors and walked through room after room, exclaiming :

" Everything here must go."

The drawing-room was a nightmare of gilt and Parian marble. The mahogany in the dining-room was all of the wrong date. The library smelt of dry-rot. In the ante-

room there was actually a cosy corner of Moorish fretwork.
The only room on the ground floor which might be left
alone was the billiard room, for Betsy, who did not play
billiards, hardly counted that as a room at all.

Upstairs there were only two bathrooms, immense,
draughty places, without even hot pipes for towels. The
bedsteads were mostly of brass; the jugs and basins on
the wash-stands were designed either for giants or dwarfs,
and no dressing-table was adequately lighted. There were
wardrobes as large as cottages, furnished with immense
pegs instead of rails for hangers. The same picture
seemed to hang in every room, on every wall: a brown,
smudgy picture of a mountain, a lake, some mist and
three cows in the foreground.

Betsy's spirits began to sink under this mass of in-
convenience and ugliness. She had enjoyed herself at
first, attacking each room with gleeful enterprise, but
eventually she complained that she was losing her eye.
She could not see the house for its monstrous trappings.

" Isn't there," she asked, " anything nice anywhere ? "

" I think there are some nice old things up in the
attics," said Max. " When Uncle Jim's father did the
place up in the 'forties I believe he stored a lot of things
up there. Uncle Jim did it over again in the 'eighties or
'nineties, and threw out everything his father had bought.
But I don't think he ever realized there were such things
as attics. Anyway, he never bothered to go up there."

He led her up some echoing, uncarpeted stairs, explaining anxiously that he had no taste and that she might
think the attic furniture was rubbish. They came to a
long passage, dim in the fading afternoon, and full of
doors. He opened the nearest and took her into a good-
sized, darkish room, crammed with furniture, like an
auction gallery.

" There must be about eight rooms like this," he said.
" But we'll just look at one or two. You mustn't tire
yourself. You've been far too good already——"

" Oh, Max . . . be quiet ! I mean . . . this is . . .
incredible. . . ."

Her eyes, growing accustomed to the light, travelled
from one treasure to another. She could not see half of
them. From room to room she darted, breathless and
exclaiming. She found Sheraton chairs and Hepplewhite
chairs, delicate *chinoiserie*, lacquered cabinets, little elegant
four-post beds still hung with faded and exquisite quilting,
graceful sofas upholstered in frayed striped silk, Recamier
sofas, Ingres drawings, Cozens water colours, and one or
two Adams mantelpieces, which must have been removed
in favour of the massy marble ones which prevailed
downstairs.

" They're all museum pieces. Somebody in your family
must have had taste, Max. Will you look at the things
in this cupboard—egg-shell porcelain, this celadon bowl
. . . and that's peach glaze. . . . We'll have them all down,
throw everything else in the house on to a bonfire and
furnish it with these."

" Will they be enough ? " asked Max. " There seems
a lot up here, but won't they look rather lost downstairs ? "

" They'll do for a start. They'll keep my eye in.
We'll go right back to what the place must have been
when your Uncle Jim's father got at it. With these
things to guide us we can't go wrong ; we can't make the
mistake of getting anything else less good. Though, of
course, we must buy a great deal."

The whole beauty of Hornwood had seized her mind,
and she now saw exactly what it ought to be like. She
longed to get to work. Such a task would keep her happy
for years.

" Come and look at this glass," she said, bending over
a table. " It's Waterford. . . ."

Max came to look. In the silence behind her she heard
an odd thumping noise, and realized that this was his
poor heart which had a way of beating far too loudly

when he was much moved.   She saw how excruciating to
him her plans must be, how tormenting the half-promise
of a future together when she said *we* must do this and
that.

He is going to ask me again, she thought in a panic.
And she walked quickly out of the room before he could
speak.

The last attic, across the corridor, was full of books,
some in cases, and some stacked in dusty piles on the
floor. Max did not follow her there immediately. He
was trying to quiet himself, ashamed of his noisy heart
and afraid lest Betsy should have heard it. His body
was always betraying him like this. It would not take
the fences which his soul so easily could have cleared.

When, at length, he went to find her, she was standing
by the window, looking out over the tree-tops at the
watery winter sunset. It was growing too dark to see
much more, but, by the last streaks of light, she was able
to examine a book which she had picked up from the
floor.

" Crebillon," she murmured, " with engravings. These
are very good. This must be valuable."

As she turned the leaves he peered over her shoulder.

" How many petticoats they wore," she said after a
while.

All the pictures were full of petticoats. Plump little
ladies, their mouths perpetually rounded to a shriek which
could not have been very loud, swooned into the arms of
bland little lovers, no larger than Max himself. Nothing
interposed between these fortunate men and their bliss
save vast, billowing layers of petticoats. Max thought
how easy things were for some people. He breathed
sharply through his teeth and said :

" Extremely pornographic ! "

He would not look any more, but stared out of the
dusty window at the long shoulder of a hill and an etching
of bare trees against the saffron streaks in the west.   His

heart sank down and down into a tarn where the sun had
never shone. He felt quite hopeless.

I shall never get her away from him, he thought.

It was as if the shadow of Alec had suddenly fallen
between them—the man who had taken her in her youth,
so easily and so competently. Max believed that his own
passion glowed with a far purer flame ; his devotion was
manly and noble. But the power to transmit the current
was denied to him. His eager soul could never escape
from a body which had neither strength nor dignity.

Betsy continued to turn the leaves of the book. Max
had been right in his comment on these engravings ; for
all their fantasy, they were subtly disturbing. And she,
too, thought of Alec and of her youth, and of many things
that would never come again. To no other man could
she give what she had given to Alec. She would never
love anyone again in that old, light-hearted way. She
had been mad to think that a young heart would come
back to her, now that she was free. She was thirty-nine.

" Let's go," she said. " It's too dark to see any more,
and it's cold up here."

The corridor was so dark that they had to grope their
way along, and at the stairs he took her arm to guide her.
She said, as she felt with her other hand for the bannisters :

" I'll marry you, dear Max, if you really want it. I
don't love you in the way I loved Alec. I shall never love
anyone like that again. But I'm very fond of you and
I think we might be happy. Oh, do be careful ! "

For in his rapture he had nearly lost his balance and
flung them both down the steep flight of stairs.

" To look after you . . . take care of you ! To see that
nobody ever hurts you again ! He never loved you as
I do. And you must love me, or you wouldn't marry
me. I shall die of happiness."

They were covered with dust. Their hands had been
perfectly black before and now, in his frantic embraces,
the grime of a hundred years had got spread over their

necks and faces. When they emerged into the light of
the lower gallery Max gave a yelp of dismay. Betsy
laughed, but he dabbed disconsolately at her face with a
large pocket handkerchief, complaining that this sort of
thing was bound to happen to him.

"It mayn't be your most sacred moment, Betsy, but
it's mine."

He took her to one of the two bathrooms and stood
outside when she had bolted herself in, calling inquiries
through the door. Had she everything she wanted?
Had she towels and soap? Was the water hot?

"Boiling!" shouted Betsy untruthfully. "You go
and wash, too. I don't want to see you again till you're
clean."

She heard his reluctant steps going away along the
passage. In an incredibly short time he had washed and
was back again, fidgeting about on the landing and
calling out to ask why she was so long.

Betsy powdered her nose as well as she could in that
dim light. She combed the curls into order behind her
pretty ears, and made up her mouth.

Here goes, she thought, unbolting the bathroom door.

HAPPINESS

HE was in the seventh heaven. It was wonderful to know that she could mean so much to another person; she could not but be moved to a responsive warmth. As they drove back to London, after dinner, she caught him to her with real ardour, whispering words of love and consolation. He lay, stunned and silent, pillowed on her breast, while she watched the head-lights cleaving the darkness in front of them. Ghostly trees and hedgerows sprang for an instant into the white glare and vanished again into night.

It was not impossible to love him. This tender compassion would carry her a long way. It would satisfy him, and, if he was satisfied, their marriage would be a success. She would make up to him for all that he had missed. She would share in his good works, steering him away from the eccentricity and the violence which had so handicapped him in the past. Out of his eager idealism she would help him to build up something practical. She would teach him to cultivate equanimity, that first necessity of public life.

He might make a very good Minister of Education, she thought.

And then they would make Hornwood into a wonderful home for the children. Kenneth could bring his friends there. He and Daphne and Eliza would grow up in an atmosphere of space and leisure, and they would belong to a far more distinguished world than any which she could have provided for them in Well Walk.

For, when she had made Hornwood presentable, she

meant to entertain a great deal. Her social ambitions
were not crude or vulgar. They were extremely romantic,
but she had never had a chance to realize them until now.
She craved for distinction. She wanted ease, smoothness,
elegance, and to escape for ever from having to tolerate
anything or anybody second rate. She wanted the best,
and she believed that she could achieve it if only she had
the opportunity. All her life she had deplored the waste
of her taste and talents. In the rag-tag and bobtail of
Alec's world she had had no chance. The second rate
never worried him ; his undiscriminating geniality had
quite swamped her finer aptitudes. Even now she felt a
shiver of irritation when she thought of all those shape·
less, noisy parties where distinction and mediocrity were
flung together, pell mell, and nobody listened to anybody
else. As Alec's wife her task had simply been to see that
there was enough food and drink ; she was not even
required to know everybody by sight. But as the wife
of Max, as mistress of Hornwood, she would get a chance
to show her mettle.

If only I am not too old, she mused. I've wasted so
much time giving tea parties to chimpanzees. We'll have
the money. But we've got no position yet. Max isn't a
man of the world, poor sweet, and never will be. Still,
if he was, he wouldn't have wanted to marry me. And
I'm nothing. A middle-class divorcée. Not young, not
beautiful in a striking way, nothing to make people accept
me as somebody who counts. But I am a clever woman.
I know I am. And money helps, say what you like. If
you've got enough of it, and we really shall have enough,
you can know whom you like, if you're clever. But
I think Max ought to be in the Cabinet. How can I get
him into the Cabinet ?

Max, cradled in her arms, began to talk. She listened
to him with half her mind while, with the other half, she
ranged luxuriously about in the future.

" I can't believe it," he was saying, " even now. I

know that people laugh at me and I used to mind frightfully when I was younger. But then I made myself see
that the skies wouldn't fall, even if they did laugh. It
didn't matter : it didn't stop me from making friends.
I didn't let it. And it didn't stop me from getting things
done. It would have if I'd let myself mind. But what
I couldn't bear was the thought that I might have lost
you because of that. I thought you might have married
me if I wasn't always making such an ass of myself. You
know, darling, you'll have to think if you really can stand
it—seeing me cut a ridiculous figure, I mean. I can't
help it. It's partly because I'm rather short. And I
know I've got a bad manner. I get too much excited
and my voice is too high. I said an awful thing last
week, when I was speaking on disarmament. I said
' overwheloping ' when I meant ' overwhelming.' But we
got through our resolution just the same, though I did
make such a fool of myself. Only there it is. You'll
have to sit on a platform and hear me say things like
that."

" You won't say things like that when we're married,"
said Betsy comfortingly. " It's nerves. Your nerves will
be better."

" I believe you may be right. I think losing you had
a lot to do with it. When you married Alec I seemed to
lose confidence in myself. I never could get over the
feeling that you might have cared for me if I'd been as
tall and as . . . well . . . presentable as he was."

She was thinking of his Irish castle which had been
burnt down in the Trouble. Perhaps they might rebuild
it some time. In the formation of new friendships it
might be useful. Hornwood could serve as a sort of
clearing-house. A vast horde of people could be invited
there for week-ends, tried out, inspected, and then the
pick of them might be asked to Mullingar for a fortnight
or more. Two houses were really necessary for her plans
—one near London and one very far away. As for a town

house . . . she was not sure. They would need a small flat, for the sake of convenience, but she did not mean to entertain in London till she was very sure of herself.

" I shouldn't wonder," said Max hopefully, " if people began to take me a lot more seriously."

" They do now, darling. You said yourself you do manage to get things done."

" Simply by making a nuisance of myself, worrying the life out of people until they are done. I never told you, did I, what a job I had over the sanitation at Little Craneswick ? I went down and saw the principal landowner . . . do you know, in the whole of that village there are only three water-closets and two are out of order ? "

" No ! " said Betsy. " How scandalous ! It's *not* true."

" It's a fact. I've seen them myself. Oh, my God ! Telling things to you is simply heaven. To think that I'm going to have you to talk to for ever and ever ! Where was I ? Oh, yes ! I went and saw the landowner, a very decent chap as a matter of fact. And I . . . Hallo ! Is this Putney Bridge already ? Look, shall we pop in for a moment at Thurloe Square and tell Isobel ? "

" No," said Betsy decidedly.

" Why not ? She'll be so pleased."

" We'll settle to-morrow how and when we tell people."

" Betsy ! You won't change your mind, will you ? "

" No. But I'm not sure how many people I want to tell. Isobel . . . of course . . . relations . . . and very intimate friends, but the world in general . . ."

" You mean not put it in the newspaper ? "

Max was disappointed. He wanted to tell the glorious news immediately to as many people as possible. Of the part that he had played in the Canning divorce, of the gossip which had coupled their names, he knew nothing at all. He had been abroad all that year and was at no time well informed as to current scandals.

" People will be hurt if we get married without telling them," he protested. " They'll all be so delighted."

For her part she could not think of anyone who would be delighted. His friends would think that he had been caught. And her friends would probably accuse her, behind her back, of duplicity and ambition. They might even do her the crowning injustice of asserting that she had meant to marry him all along. Her old partisans would all turn aginst her.

But she needed them no longer. She would marry Max and she would never see any of them again. For she meant to detach herself from everyone whom she had known in her earlier existence. Susie Graham and Angela Trotter had been very kind through her trouble ; their shrill support had put heart into her, and she was grateful, but she had never felt that she had much in common with them. She did not want them at Hornwood. Nor did she greatly care what Max's friends might say among themselves. They, too, were destined for the scrap-heap along with the gilt chairs and the Moorish cosy corner. He had involved himself with far too many dowdy bores and moth-eaten philanthropists. She would find other and better cronies for him.

As they flew up Fitzjohn's Avenue she pushed him gently away from her. Holding him for so long had made her shoulder quite stiff and her hat was crooked.

" It's to be hoped," she said as she tidied her hair, " that the children will have gone to bed. I'm sure I don't look fit to be seen."

And when they had let themselves into the hall at Well Walk she asked anxiously if she looked awful.

" I've never s-s-seen you look more b-beautiful," stammered Max.

Indeed, she did look very well. The plaintive shadow was gone from her face, which was no longer pinched and bleak. For now she had a future. Now she was able to look forward and to plan. She was young, serene and kindly. Max ran at her and seized her awkwardly, so that she had to stoop a little.

He must never kiss me standing up, she thought. I must find a way to stop him. We must look silly like this.

Kenneth, standing unperceived in the drawing-room doorway, thought them not only silly but grotesque. To him it seemed that they must be doing it on purpose, that they must know of the rage and anguish which had devoured him all day, and now they were bent on showing him how little they cared. Betsy's quick cry of dismay when she saw him sounded false and foolish.

" Kenneth ! Aren't you in bed ? "

" No," he said wearily. " I waited up for you."

" Then you'll be the first to know," exclaimed Max. " Come in here. We've got something to tell you."

" I don't need to be told."

But Max pushed them both into the drawing-room. He was determined to make an immediate appeal to Kenneth's better nature.

" My dear old man," he said, " you can scowl at me as much as you like. I quite understand your feelings. I may not be the stepfather you'd have chosen, but you must try not to be selfish. Try to look at it from your mother's point of view. You love her very much, don't you ? You want her to be happy ? And if I can make her so, oughtn't you to sacrifice your own feelings ? Think of all that she has sacrificed for you ! "

Kenneth listened, with icy attention, until Max ran down. Then he said politely :

" I'm sure it's a very good arrangement. Please accept my congratulations."

" That's a good chap," said Max, beaming.

" It's been very sudden," put in Betsy. " We've only just settled it. If anybody had told me at breakfast that I should be engaged to be married by tea-time I should have said they were mad."

" But," suggested Kenneth, " nobody will be very much surprised, will they ? "

She flushed and looked quickly at Max. But Kenneth's words had no sting for him.

" I think they will," he said simply. " I know I'm surprised myself. Of course they may have guessed what I feel for her. That's a thing I could never hide. But . . . I think it is rather surprising that she should care for me."

His voice trembled a little. His single-mindedness shone out so clearly that even Kenneth perceived it. He was candid, happy, and full of goodwill. Betsy felt suddenly that she would be willing to sacrifice everything, herself, her own future, her credit even, rather than allow his peace of mind to be destroyed. Her eyes implored Kenneth to spare him.

" Everybody . . ." began Kenneth, and then stopped.

He gave his mother a reassuring, contemptuous little nod. She need not be afraid that he would ruin this fool's paradise. If she thought she could protect the love that she had exploited, then let her do so. Her conscience was her own affair.

Betsy was begging Max to go, and he was endeavouring to do so, now that things had been put on an amiable footing. But to walk straight out of a room had always been impossible to him. He could only get himself gradually towards the door as he told her that she was tired, that she must go straight to bed, that he would ring up early in the morning, but not too early because she must sleep, or perhaps she had better ring him up as soon as she was awake, that he would be at his club and would not go out until she had telephoned. She was obliged at last to take him out and thrust him into the night almost by force.

The first radiance was gone. She looked a little pinched and sour again when she came back to the drawing-room to reproach Kenneth for his unkindness.

" Unkind ? How have I been unkind ? "

" Why do you grudge me happiness ? I've had such a lot to bear. I've been so lonely."

" My dear mother, I don't grudge you anything. I've congratulated you, haven't I ? What more do you want ? "

" I know you don't like him much, but . . ."

" I don't dislike him. I did, but I don't now. In fact I'm rather sorry for him. He's so sincere."

" Kenneth ! "

" But you needn't tell me that you didn't mean to marry him all along," said Kenneth as he went off to bed, " because I shan't believe you."

THE TURNING POINT

THE Merricks had a country cottage in Wiltshire and they had found a pleasant house in the same village which they were urging Alec to buy. For it was, they thought, high time that he should settle down, face the future, and begin to make a new life for himself. A removal to the country, to quite fresh surroundings, might act as a tonic.

He had married Joy on the day after Betsy's decree became absolute, but this did not seem to affect their makeshift manner of life. They continued to be homeless, perching here and there in cheap furnished flats and making no plans. They were like people in a waiting-room at a railway station. They asked nobody to visit them and they went about very little.

It was astonishing that the once popular Alec should have dropped out of the world so completely. The alienation of some of his closest friends had embittered him, so that he was not such good company as he had been. People found that he lowered their spirits, and this is a difficult thing to forgive. Not one in a hundred knew or cared about his divorce, but word went round that he was turning into a moody bore, that his new wife was impossible, that he seemed to have a grievance. To entertain him might be a good and loyal deed, but there was no pleasure in it, and good deeds are easily put off. His breach with Johnnie Graham did him a great deal of harm. It was known that Johnnie objected to meeting him, so that he was not asked to parties where Johnnie was likely to come. All this gave him the impression

that he had been universally dropped and cut. It was
not so. Very few friends dropped him on purpose. Most
people meant to invite him and Joy later on in the spring,
in the summer, when they should have time and energy.

Also he was short of money. He had done no work
for fifteen months, and he was now living on his share of
a recent film sale. When that was exhausted he would
be nearly penniless, for most of his savings had been
handed over to Betsy. He said himself that he had not
the slightest idea of how he was going to earn a living.
He could write words for Johnnie's music and that
was all.

The kindly, anxious Merricks had done their best to
drag him out of this splenetic inertia. But they could not
combat his dread of the future. It was as if he welcomed
impermanency as a shield against the inevitable. He
preferred to remain unsettled, and so, unluckily, did Joy,
who feared that she might lose him altogether if ever
they came out of their waiting-room. She was wildly
jealous of anybody who might possibly come between them.
She worshipped him with a solemn, fanatical absorption
which left no room for other interests or associations, and
which was the more fierce because it was entirely one-
sided. She did not wish to see him on terms with the
world. Her resistance to any hint of change was silent
and stubborn. It prevailed against the efforts of his
friends, and, if Eliza had not forced the issue, they might
have continued for ever in their melancholy isolation.

Eliza's letter came one evening by the last post. Alec
did not open it immediately, for he was finishing a cross-
word puzzle, an occupation which took up more and more
of his time.

" What do you make of this ? " he said to Joy. " *Third
thoughts* in four letters, beginning with an S."

Joy, pleased at being spoken to, began to search her
mind. There was nothing in it, and she had no suggestion
to make. But she looked eager and intense until he got it.

" *Stet!* " he said, writing it in.   " That's rather clever, isn't it ?   Third thoughts . . . stet. . . . Very neat."

She made an assenting noise.   He looked across at her. Of course she did not know what *stet* meant : she had not the least notion of the point.   He opened his mouth to explain, felt that it was too much trouble and said nothing.

The clock struck ten.   It was time for the baby's bottle. She abandoned her evening occupation of sitting on the opposite side of the gas-fire and watching him do his cross-word puzzle.   Her knitting, which got on very slowly because she was obliged to look at Alec so much, was thrust away into a yellow bag.

" Going to bed ? " he asked hopefully.

" No.   Only to give baby his bottle.   I'll be back after."

If she went to bed first he would sit up half the night reading a book or something.   The only way to prevent that was to go back and sit watching him until he was driven from his chair.

She went into the bedroom next door, lighted the gas-fire and warmed up the bottle.   The baby began a drowsy whimper, but the bottle teat, thrust into his mouth, soon silenced him.   She sat with the child in her lap, in a low chair by the fire, waiting stolidly until he had finished. If anything could have surprised her she would have been surprised that she did not love him more, for he was Alec's child, the fruit of Alec's passion.   But he belonged to the present, and she had no interest in the present.   He had not been there when she was in Provence with Alec. He could not remind her in any way of those few lamentable weeks when she had had what she wanted.   Every word then spoken, every caress, was indelibly recorded on her mind.   She would go over every moment of that time again and again in a mournful reverie.   He had desired her then and he did so no longer.   For a short time they had been swept away, quite out of their depth, on a tide of extraordinary and violent sensations. They had abandoned themselves to it, each fiercely snatching at all the other could give. And then, for him, the tide had ebbed as quickly as it rose. In less than two months it was all over and he wanted no more.

He was uniformly kind to her, but she did not ask for kindness. He made little jokes ; he was friendly ; he had not been so in Provence. She wanted to get him back as he was then, angry, untender, and always physically aware of her. But her attempts to revive that vanished flame only seemed to drive him further away.

She could hear him walking up and down in the next room. He must have finished his puzzle. She wanted to go back and watch him walking up and down and she gave an impatient little jerk to the baby, who was taking the bottle slowly.

Presently Alec came into the bedroom. Something unexpected had happened. He looked excited and wide awake.

" The most extraordinary thing . . . Eliza has written. . . . Betsy is going to marry Max after all."

" Well," said Joy, " we always knew she would."

" I suppose so."

Yet he had never been quite sure. There were times when he wondered whether he had been grossly unjust, whether he had behaved as badly as Betsy said that he had. Now it was a relief to know that his case against her had always been a perfectly good one. And yet in some ways he would rather have been the only person to blame. It would have made the whole thing seem less accidental, less of a muddle.

" So Eliza says she will come to us now at any time we like. She is quite clear what she wants to do, and she has no scruples any more about leaving her mother."

" Oh . . . yes . . ." said Joy.

" So what about the Devizes house ?   We'd much better take it if Eliza is coming to us.   Shall I write off to Charles now? I could catch the evening post. I think it's still on the market."

Joy stared at him while her slow mind absorbed this news and all its implications. At last she said:

"It's an expense. We haven't got very much money. You keep saying so. Why should we have to support Eliza? Betsy got all your money to keep the children with."

"Oh, that can be arranged. I must really get down to brass tacks and find some work to do."

"I don't see why we've got to have Eliza."

"There's no got about it. We want her, don't we?"

"No," said Joy.

It was the first time that she had said so, but he had always known that she did not. Only the vagueness of Eliza's promises had prevented them from having it out before. His face hardened and he said:

"Well, she's coming. And that's all there is to it."

"You care for her more than you care for me," asserted Joy sullenly.

"I do, in a way."

Since they were about it he felt that they might as well have it out thoroughly.

"I can't feel about you as you feel about me," he said. "I'm very sorry, but I can't. I never pretended that I could. If we are to go on together we'd better face it."

"I wish I were dead," she muttered. "I shall kill myself if you bring Eliza to live with us."

"All right! All right! You are utterly selfish. . . ."

"How am I selfish? I think of nothing . . . nobody else. I worship the ground you stand on."

"Then for God's sake, woman, worship something else. Think of something else. Leave me alone. I'm sorry . . . it's brutal to talk like this . . . but I can't stand it. . . ."

"What am I to think of?"

" Anything . . . anything ! You never read. I never see you with a book. You have no friends, no interests. I believe the baby bores you. You've only one idea in your head, and that . . ."

" I'll kill myself," she repeated. " I'll do that for you. I'll kill myself and the baby too. And then we'll be out of your way."

" A lot of help that would be. That would be the end of me if you like. We could make something of the future if you'd help, but you won't. You won't lift a finger. We've made a wretched mistake. The whole thing is a mess, but it's a mess that we could clear up a little if we tried. We could work out a sort of compromise . . . learn to get on together . . . if we put our backs into it. But you won't. I've done my best. I've married you. But you don't try to adapt yourself. I can't stand it any more. I can't stand it, I tell you. . . ."

He flung out of the room, and a few seconds later she heard the front door slam. Once or twice before he had gone out and walked about half the night rather than remain in the flat with her.

She sat on by the fire with the baby in her lap. The threat to kill herself had not been idle. She meant to do so now, before he came back. The maid came by the day, so that she was alone in the flat, and she meant to go into the kitchen and put her head into the gas oven. She would take her child with her. Alec should find them both dead.

If the child had remained asleep she would have held to her purpose. But when she rose to go into the kitchen she saw that it was awake and staring at her. Suddenly it smiled, a friendly, toothless smile, and yawned contentedly.

She sat down again on the bed, clutching it. She did not love it, but she could not kill it. She did not know what to do. She began to pray, hardly aware that she was doing so.

" Help me ! " she kept saying, over and over again.
" Help me !   Help me ! "

As a ship becalmed starts and shivers at the first light
breath of wind, so an impulse, beyond herself, took charge
of her.   Imperceptibly she changed her course, veering
round in a new direction.   At no point did she form any
resolution.   Her own struggles came later.   The wind
carried her onwards, and after a while she had turned
her face away from death.   She put the child into the
cradle and went back to her chair by the fire.

Now to-morrow was in front of her, and another day
after that, and all the rest of her life.   She must do something to save herself.   Exhausted with the crisis through
which she had just passed, she leaned back in her chair
and wished that somebody would bring her a nice cup
of tea.   But there was nobody, and she was too tired to
move, too tired to go to bed.

To-morrow, she thought, I will tell him that I want
Eliza to come.   If she were here she would bring me some
tea.   And I will begin to do all that I ought ;   I will show
him that I want to help.   *You never read.   I never see you
with a book.*   That's quite true.   I'll read a book to-
morrow.

Once, long ago, she had been a great reader.   She had
prided herself upon her culture and wrote papers for a
local literary society.   It was hard to believe it now, after
this long interval of stagnation.   She tried to remember
how she had felt and thought, three years ago, before she
fell into this captivity.   She had been very young then
and she was young still.   Experience had taught her
nothing ;   she had taken no step towards maturity.   All
her life since then had been vitiated by a sense of guilt
which stultified growth.   She had lost her self-respect,
and with it the power to undergo any valuable experience.
It seemed as if, until half an hour ago, nothing of any real
importance had happened to her since she was nineteen
and haunted the public library in the town where she

lived. She could remember the smell of that place better than anything, a clammy reek which always pervaded the books which she borrowed. The doors swung draughtily, and shabby, depressed men turned over the newspaper in the reading-room. She searched for her lost self, coming and going there, a bouncing, sanguine girl with a volume of Shaw's plays under her arm. For that was what she had been reading then. George Bernard Shaw had been for ever on her lips and in her heart. She had written a paper about him.

Now that she thought of it, she remembered having seen a volume of his plays in the sitting-room bookcase. So that she would have a book to read to-morrow. She went to find it and took it to bed with her. Forcing her eyes from one word to another, forcing the sense into her brain, she began to read. She had opened the book at random in the middle of a play which she had never read before, and which she would have considered frivolous if George Bernard Shaw had not written it. The print was small and unattractive. It hurt her eyes. She still longed for a nice cup of tea. But she persisted upon the gritty path of well-doing, and presently fell asleep.

She did not wake when Alec came in, just after three o'clock. He came softly to the bedside and saw, with astonishment, the book that had fallen from her hand on to the coverlet. He would not have thought that *You Never Can Tell* could convey anything to her at all. But he had not the heart to wonder what she was about, or to guess at the turn which their fortunes had taken. Of all that still lay before him he knew no more than the baby, asleep in its cradle by the window. Moving cautiously, he undressed, switched off the light, and climbed into bed beside her. Between to-day and to-morrow, so alike and so hopeless, lay a little space of oblivion. He sought and soon found it. All three slept.

TRUTH

" MY poor darling ! " Max kept saying. " My poor,
poor darling ! "

The waiter, who had handed him an enormous *Carte du
Jour*, retired tactfully out of earshot, and Betsy's melancholy redoubled. She was hungry and she wished that
she had allowed Max to order food before she asked for
sympathy.

" How can I comfort you ? "

" With oysters," she said, smiling bravely.

" Oysters ? Would they really ? Would they ? "

His look brought the waiter hurrying back.

" How many could you manage, darling ? A dozen ?
Splendid ! You are the very bravest person in the world,
the way you take things. That you can . . . no, waiter !
Don't go ! What would you like to have after, dear ?
Something off the grill ? A steak ? "

If food would do her good he could not give her too
much of it. Her plea for a caviare omelette hardly satisfied
him.

" You're sure that's all you want ? Quite sure ? Very
well, it will do to go on with. All right, waiter ! A dozen
oysters and a caviare omelette afterwards. Bring them
quickly. Now is there anything I can do ? Would you
like me to write to Eliza ? That's all right, waiter !
Hurry up ! "

" You haven't ordered anything for yourself, Max ! "

" Oh, haven't I ? "

" You don't like oysters. Have some smoked salmon."

" No. I'll just have one dish. Anything that's ready.
I don't care . . ."

"*Sole à la maison* is very nice," murmured the waiter. "With grapes . . . and a little taragon . . ."

"I'll have that. Of course I could see Eliza as soon as I get back from Germany. I could go down to her school. That might be better than writing."

"No, Max. I don't want her to be influenced in any way. I shan't say one word to dissuade her. She has a perfect right to choose as soon as she is sixteen, and she seems to have been thinking it over for months."

"But to do it in such a way! To wait till she had gone back to school and then to write to you!"

"I dare say she wanted to spare us both a painful scene. If she cares most for her father she is quite right to go to him."

"But how can she? How can she?"

This was exactly what Betsy felt, and she was comforted for a moment to hear Max say it.

"I can't conceive of anybody not adoring you. You've been such a mother, such an angel to them. Oh, good! Here are your oysters. That's right! I can't bear to think of what you must suffer. But I know, I do know, how you are feeling."

He does not, thought Betsy, as she dropped minute portions of red pepper into each oyster. He hasn't the faintest notion of my feelings, unfortunately.

She wanted sympathy, and it was exasperating to see so much of it lavished upon an imaginary wound while the real sore was left untended. For sympathy is like a salve : it does no good unless it is applied to the right spot. She had had occasion to discover this before. Once, when she was a little girl, she had sat on a wasp when out paying a call with her mother. She could not help crying, but modesty had prevented her from revealing before so many strangers the true nature of her injury. So she pleaded toothache as an explanation for her tears. The pity and petting which she received for the toothache did not assuage the pain of the sting in the very least. And another

time, when she had interpreted her chagrin at not winning
a Scripture prize as grief at the death of her grandfather
she had experienced the same frustration. For a very
short time the mere fact of attracting attention, of being
the object of pity and concern, could soothe her ; but a
desperate emptiness lay behind it.

In the whole of her conversation with Max there was
an uneasy obliquity. Everything that she said was
perfectly true and yet not the truth. Like an unskilful
tight-rope walker she could only keep her balance for a
few steps at a time.

" To be quite frank," she said, taking a courageous
plunge forward, " I've never got on very well with Eliza."

And that is true enough. I don't terribly mind losing
her. It's the mortification I mind. I'm mortified that
she should prefer Alec, and now everybody will know it.
Then why not say so to Max ? And whose fault is it that
we haven't got on ? Mine. I've never loved her quite
enough. Not like Ken . . . oh, Ken ! Why do you break
my heart ? But I mustn't think of that. I couldn't tell
anyone about that. *Not even Alec* . . .

" Max ! You mustn't, you must *not*, take so much
salt ! "

" I like salt."

" But it's barbaric to ladle it on like that, in a place like
this, where the cooking is so good. It's the worst insult
you can offer them. It's salt enough already. If you
had any discrimination you'd know that."

" I'm afraid good food is wasted on me. You think
that's dreadful, don't you, dear ? "

" Yes, I do. What's the use of . . ."

What's the use of having so much money when he
appreciates none of the things that money can buy ? He'd
eat any provender that was set before him and never know
what it was. It's very noble, I suppose, to have a soul
above these things. All saints are barbarians. He'd be
just as happy on the dole.

" What's the use of what ? " Max was asking.

" Of coming here if you don't enjoy the food."

" You enjoy it. That's a very good reason for coming."

" I suppose you despise me for enjoying it ? "

" Despise you ? " Max looked at her in astonishment.
" Why should I ? For knowing more about these things
than I do ? What nonsense ! You know, there's one
comfort—I don't think little Daphne will ever want to
leave us."

" Oh, no. I don't think she will."

" She has quite accepted me, I think. And she really
seems to look forward to coming to Hornwood. She
was asking me if there would be riding. We might get her
a pony, don't you think ? "

" You mustn't spoil her, dear. She's a selfish, grabby
little thing."

And what a snob ! Fancy asking me if she would be
Lady Daphne ! Where she gets it from I don't know.
At school, I suppose. She's never come across that kind
of snobbery at home. Well, here goes ! I'll tell him.
I simply can't go on being ashamed of the truth.

" . . . and a lamentable little snob, poor sweet ! You'll
laugh, Max, but she really is thrilled at having an earl
for a stepfather."

" Oh, that's natural at her age," said Max easily. " All
children are snobs. Why do you look so worried, my
darling ? There's something the matter that you don't
tell me. I know there is."

" Oh . . . my worries are so mean, so ignoble. I'm a
base creature really, Max. I'm mean and low and petty."

" We all are. Here's your omelette. It's rather small."

" It's just right. Now listen to how mean I am. I'll
tell you just exactly what's on my mind."

" Yes. Go on ! Tell me ! I want to share everything
with you. You must tell me everything. It's not really
anything to do with Eliza, is it ? "

" No," said Betsy, surprised at his penetration.

" It's . . . it's something to do with Alec."

" Max ! How did you know ? "

He looked very sad for a moment.

" I just know. That's all. Tell me what it is."

" Well . . . last night I saw Susie Graham, and she said, she told me, that Alec and Johnnie had had . . . a . . . sort of reconciliation. They met somewhere, and Johnnie was friendly to Alec . . . and now they have started work again."

" Good ! That's good news, isn't it ? "

" Very good. I'm very glad. I never wanted them to quarrel."

No, I did not. And I should be glad if Susie hadn't been so catty. Of course I could see what was behind all those affectionate congratulations. And pretending to be so surprised ! Johnnie has turned against me. That's what she wanted me to know. He never liked me. And now that I'm going to marry Max they have all gone over to Alec's side. They all think I . . . even Kenneth . . . he went back to school . . . went back without a word . . . but I must not let myself think of it.

" But it's sweet of you to be glad, Betsy. I don't see anything mean or petty in that."

" No, but . . . only the best bit of me is glad. I can't help being just a little bit hurt. I mean, one can forgive a wrong for oneself, but one has a mean feeling that one's friends ought not to forgive it quite so easily. They ought to go on resenting one's injuries just a little longer."

" Well, I can quite understand that. I must say I think Graham must be a bit insensitive if he can feel quite the same about Alec as he did before."

" Why . . . you see . . . what he resented was the thought that Alec had ruined my life. Now he knows that my life isn't ruined because I'm going to marry you. So he doesn't feel so angry with Alec. It's very natural."

" I think that's a very just and generous way to put it."

Betsy drew a deep breath and tried to right herself.

" No.   But I minded.   I minded that . . . little affront
. . . more   than   I   minded   getting   Eliza's   letter   this
morning."

He reflected for a while and then explained this for her.

" Isn't that because you love Eliza ?   Therefore it was
less of a struggle to be just to her.   What you call *minding*
is really the struggle to be quite fair."

Oh, devil take you, Max !   You're no good.   No good to
me at all.   Why can't you know exactly what I'm like,
how despicable, and still love me and want to help me ?
Then perhaps I might grow better.   What's the use of all
this devotion to an imaginary woman ?   I want . . . I
want . . .

" Don't let's talk about me any more, Max dear.   Let's
talk about you.   How long shall you have to stay in
Germany ? "

" That's the worst of it.   I can't be sure.   Of course
I'd never have agreed to go if anyone else, at all likely to
be effective, could have been found.   But there doesn't
seem to be anyone.   It's maddening to have to go at this
moment."

He was off that afternoon on behalf of a very old, very
admirable, Jewish editor, said to be dying in a concentration camp.   Max and his friends had been trying to get
him out for months, and now there was a possible chance
that he might be released if a determined person were on
the spot to bring the right pressure.   It was a clear duty
to go, and Max saw no alternative, although it meant the
postponement of his marriage.

He was, as she often told herself, a far finer man than
Alec :   braver and more energetic, more ready to sacrifice
comfort and security.   Unlike most philanthropists, he only
hated his fellow-men in the mass.   The atrocities and
oppressions which he denounced were all the work of
people whom he had never met.   Towards individuals he
was full of charity.   Those with whom he had actually
talked and dealt might be mistaken but were never wicked.

In personal contact he was always ready to infer the best and to suppose that his opponent must be anxious to do right.

And it was, perhaps, this instinctive good will which made him so effective and so difficult to outwit. The best weapon against dishonesty and self-interest is the power to make it ashamed of itself. Betsy sometimes wondered if he was able to produce in everyone the moral discomfort which he produced in herself, a sense of obliquity and the desire to be truthful. She did not believe that these people, whom he would interview on behalf of his Jewish friend, would have a very comfortable time of it. They would find themselves volunteering admissions and confidences which would lead to a definite promise. And the strength of Max was this : having obtained a promise, he did not go away as people hoped he would. Never doubting their good intentions, he continued to haunt his victims, like a mosquito, until the promise was carried out.

" Have you ever," she asked him suddenly, " disapproved of anyone so much that you were publicly rude to them ? "

Max looked a little rueful.

" Yes," he said. " I was once. I cut a man in the club because I thought he was an *agent provocateur* in the sale of armaments to South America. He looked fearfully taken aback, poor fellow, and well he might be, because he wasn't the man I thought he was. He was a perfectly innocent chartered accountant. I've never cut anybody since. It was a lesson to me."

Betsy laughed.

It was strange that he should worship her for qualities which she did not possess, while she so deeply respected him for virtues of which he was unaware. Their life together was going to be an oddly syncopated business and far more difficult than she had at first supposed. Living with him would mean living up to him. He was not nearly as malleable as he had seemed. Less and less was she able to imagine that she could renovate him along with Hornwood, or to hope that a place in the Cabinet would exhaust his moral energies. She might prevent him from making blunders, but she could never stop him from doing what he believed to be right. It might well be that his conscience rather than her common sense would rule their joint lives.

Because he was so simple, so open, she had thought that she could read him like a book. And so she could, but the book had unexpected chapters. She turned each page with a growing uncertainty as to what the next would reveal.

Nothing could have surprised her more than his next words. They had been silent for some while, sipping their coffee, each engaged in a private train of thought. He said suddenly :

" Your friends the Blochs seem to be in a bad way."

" The Blochs ? Have you been seeing them ? "

" No. But I've had a letter from him. They're in Paris, but they've got to leave France in a fortnight's time, apparently. They've been there as long as their permit allows and they can't get it renewed. And they've got nowhere to go. It's a nightmare, really, the lives of these people who have no country."

" What did he want ? " asked Betsy apprehensively.

" Well, he could come to England again if somebody invited him, on a personal visit. One can see our Government's point of view. We can't have a lot of starving refugees unloaded on to us, with no means of support. It wouldn't be fair to our own people. If he comes to stay with a friend it's another matter. And if he could once get over here he thinks he might find work."

" He wants you to invite him ? "

" Yes. I wrote and told him that there was plenty of room at Hornwood for the lot of them. And I sent him a formal invitation that he could show to the authorities."

" Oh, Max ! "

" Why ? Don't you approve ? He's the sort of man

one ought to help : a very good artist and a good European. We might find him some work to do at Hornwood, don't you think ? "

" I don't like him. I don't like any of them. They weren't friends of mine. It was Alec who brought them to Pandy Madoc."

" We shan't have to see much of them, if we go to Ireland after the wedding. They'll have found their feet by the time we go to Hornwood."

" Oh no ! If once they get in you'll never get them out. I told you I didn't like them, Max. I told you so ages ago."

" Yes, I know. But I didn't feel I could refuse the poor fellow. It's life and death to him and only a little unpleasantness for us."

" I simply cannot have the Blochs at Hornwood."

" They can have their own rooms. You need never see them."

" I won't go to Hornwood if they're there."

Max expressed the greatest concern that she should dislike the idea so much, and apologized a great deal. But he showed no readiness to cancel the invitation.

" No, it's too much," she burst out. " If you loved me as you say you do, you wouldn't ask it of me. I not only dislike them but they are connected with a most unhappy part of my life, with a lot of things that I want to forget. I can't see them again."

" Ought you to let personal considerations . . ."

" We've had to put off the wedding, because you thought it was your duty. And you can't say that I wasn't very nice about it. I didn't try to stop you from going to Germany, though most women would have thought it was a moment when they ought to come first. But this is too much, if we aren't to have our own house to our- selves. I simply won't marry you, Max, if I've got to put up with this sort of thing all the time. I mean it."

Anger gave her courage to take the risk. If she could

not rule him now she would never be able to do so, and life would be intolerable unless she held the reins.

" Betsy ! You can't mean it ? "

" Yes I do. If you force the Blochs on me just now it means that you are quite insensitive to my feelings and that you don't really care for me."

" Oh Betsy ! Oh my darling ! How can you say that ? "

He looked so much agitated that she grew calmer.

" I don't say you are wrong to ask them," she said. " I quite understand why you did. But I just can't bear it. I'm sorry. I wish I hadn't such strong feelings. I'm not as noble and as altruistic as you are, Max dear, and I never shall be. I'll always do my best to support you, but there are some things which are too hard for me. And if I feel that you are going to force them on me, if I know that I shall always be sacrificed to your conscience, I can't face it. And we'd much better not marry."

" Oh Betsy. Oh, this is ghastly ! "

But she was adamant and, before they parted, he had promised to sacrifice the Blochs. The idea of losing her was more than he could bear.

She went with him to the station and saw him off. Having gained her point she was gay and affectionate, but her blandishments did not raise his spirits. He looked more wizened and shrunken than ever and he said, for him, astonishingly little. He despised himself for having given way to her, but not more than she, in the depths of her heart, despised him.

THE ESCALATOR

WHEN he was gone she was so lonely, she missed his daily attentions so much, that her misgivings vanished. She began to long for his return, their marriage and the beginning of the new life. Never before had she felt herself to be so alone and so friendless. Well Walk was empty and silent without the children. She had nowhere to go, nothing to do, and nothing to think of. All ties with the past were broken. Such friends as she had in London were all agog over the news of her engagement. Their felicitations were either too warm or too cool and she shrank from meeting them. She lived in a queer kind of pause, hardly speaking to a soul from morning till night.

In these days she had become very cautious about spending money. Why this was she did not exactly know. Possibly she was influenced by some kind of superstition, the fear of tempting Providence. She had never been extravagant, but now she counted every penny. In a few weeks she would be a very rich woman, but, until she actually was so, she would not anticipate any of the pleasures of wealth. These must be saved up and enjoyed as a set off to any possible drawbacks in her new life. In this mood she decided against an elaborate trousseau. Max would never notice it if she did buy new clothes. What she had would do very well until the spring, when she would go to Paris and dress herself properly.

And, in this mood, she took to travelling by tube, a thing which she had always hitherto refused to do. Having secured a good offer for her car she had sold it and was managing to exist without one. But she grudged the expensive taxi fare out to Hampstead. There was a certain piquancy in knowing that, so soon, such a sum of money would mean far less to her than did the tube fare now.

Some such thought was occupying her mind when she went into the tube station at Oxford Circus after a long afternoon at her hairdresser's. It was not yet the rush hour and the escalator was almost empty. She sailed down it complacently, smiling to herself, and clutching a bunch of little parcels.

Far down below her, on the ascending staircase she saw Alec.

As he rose higher no shadow of doubt remained. It was certainly Alec, a little fatter than she was accustomed to remember him, older, shabbier, less good-looking. He rose rapidly. She began to tingle all over with sheer astonishment.

He had not seen her. He was looking at the advertisements on his wall of the staircase. He was not going to see her. He, too, carried a parcel, an odd-shaped one, like a torpedo. She found herself wondering what was in it.

He turned his head sharply, as if someone had called him. He saw her. He was gaping, frozen into the same astonished rigidity. Now they were level. Only the little trough of the emergency stairs lay between them. Now, borne by a power which knew nothing of their plight, they had been carried past one another. The distance was widening.

Each turned at the same moment, she to stare upwards and he to stare down. The slight movement broke the spell of their surprise. Expression came back into their faces. Alec smiled broadly, not a smile of greeting or of courtesy, but as if he could not help it. Their glance was intimate, unreserved ; such a smile as they might have exchanged at any time during their married life, if something had happened that they both thought ridiculous.

" How like us to manage our first meeting like this ! "

ran the message in his eyes. " And what are you doing, my girl, chuff-chuffing in the Underground ? "

And her eyes said :

" Don't laugh, Alec ! This isn't funny."

She sank. He rose. Soon there would be the whole length of the staircase between them. They were too far off to smile. He was right at the top and it seemed to her that he had taken one step backwards, as if to defy the power of these stairs to carry him away. But nothing came of it. The escalator discharged them at either end and they lost sight of one another.

She went home in a daze. So often had she pictured to herself their first meeting, placing it sometimes in one place, sometimes in another, in a theatre, at a restaurant, possibly even at a party. She had known that it was bound to happen, sometime or other, and she had thought that she was fully prepared for it. For some reason she had imagined that he would be the more embarrassed of the two, and she had resolved exactly how to look and what to say so that he might know that all was forgotten and forgiven. But she had never foreseen anything like this and she was disconcerted.

She wondered what was in the parcel and where he was going. Where was he now ? Was he at home too, and was he thinking of her ?

For nearly eighteen months they had both been living in London, each living through every minute of every day, within a few miles of one another. But she had never thought of it in that way before, or wondered what is Alec doing now ? What is he thinking ? For a long time he had hardly seemed like a real person at all. Her anger, and the indignation of her friends, had made a two-dimensional figure of him, the outline of a villain. Even after she forgave him she never thought of him as being as much alive, as much a person, as he had been when he was her husband. He merely became a target for generosity.

Now she was wild to know all about him, and what his life was. She could not tell why she felt like this. She supposed it was because their encounter had taken them both off their guard. Their eyes had said too much and their tongues nothing at all. After exchanging such a look they could never again pretend to be perfectly indifferent to one another. They were friends. Oh yes, they were still friends, not two lay figures making civil noises ! They had things to tell and to hear. She wanted to know what was in that parcel, it was such an odd shape, and he used to make a fuss about carrying parcels. She wanted to know if he had really taken that backward step, if he too felt that there was something unfinished about this meeting. What had he wanted to say to her ?

All that evening, and next morning, when she woke up, she was waiting as if for some further word from him. She had arranged, that day, to go to Oxford and see her mother, but, on a sudden impulse, she telephoned that she was not coming. It would be such a pity if Alec made some move to get into touch with her and found her gone. For she was sure that he must be feeling the same disquietude and curiosity. He could not simply have met her, in that extraordinary way, smiled, and gone on without another thought. He must have passed just such a night as she had, and he could not but know that something more was bound to happen.

As the day passed, and no word came from him, her spirits sank to zero. She listened for the arrival of every post and each time the telephone rang she made sure that, this time, it must be he. She could not understand his silence. And the next day, and the next, were as bad. Perhaps her answering smile had not been kind enough. Men can be so stupid, so slow to guess. He might be longing, all this time, to hear her voice, and not know, poor fool, how it was with her. But he must be the first to make a move, just as he had been the first to smile. This was not a thing that she could manage at all.

A week went by and she was almost in despair. Yet she could not make up her mind to go to Oxford. She kept putting it off. It was not, indeed, very wise to leave the house even, in case he might suddenly take courage and ring up. She stayed indoors and wandered from room to room. The weather was very bad and that was a sufficient excuse for not going out. It rained and it blew. She spent a great deal of time in the room that had once been his study, standing at the window and looking at the stormy sky. It was a bedroom now. She had changed all the furniture and sent his papers and books away. She felt sorry that she had done so : she might have had more ruth for the past and let a little of it linger on. His desk and table might still have been there. In all the house there was nothing of his left except an old pullover which she found thrust away in a cupboard. She knew this, because she had been walking about from room to room, hunting for something that had belonged to him.

She took the pullover upstairs with her to the bedroom. She discovered that, if she dropped it lightly on the bed, it would for a moment fall into round lines and creases, the shape of his body, before it fell flat. She amused herself by doing this two or three times, before she went back to her staring out of the window. In fine weather there was a wonderful southward view of London, but now it was all hidden under a wrack of cloud and fog. He must be down there somewhere. among those dim domes and towers and chimney pots, living through the hours of this long week. She must wait. That was all she could do.

One day, when she was passing through the hall, she heard the telephone bell ringing. Before, when she heard it, her heart would beat very quickly and she would tremble between hope and fear. Now it stood still, because she was quite sure. This time it *was* Alec. She was certain of it. The tumult and the agitation died down. She went into the drawing-room and took up the receiver.

"Can I speak to Mrs. Canning?" he said.

"It's me, Alec. It's Betsy speaking."

"Betsy? It's Alec."

"I know."

"Betsy . . . I've a great favour to ask of you?"

"Yes, Alec?"

"I want you to do a very kind thing. I know I've no right to ask it. But I feel you'll do it when I explain."

"What is it?"

"My mother is very ill. In fact . . . I'm afraid she's . . . I'm afraid there's no hope."

"Your mother? Oh . . . I'm sorry!"

"I'm speaking from Bedford Gardens now. Her mind isn't . . . she's wandering a good deal. And she keeps asking for you. She seems to be worried about you. You see . . . she's quite forgotten . . . everything that has happened. She doesn't seem to remember the divorce and she's distressed that you don't go to see her . . ."

"And you want me to come?"

"If you would, Betsy! They think . . . nurse and the doctor think, that she might be quieter if she could see you. You know how it is when people are . . . very ill. If you could possibly bear to come . . . just for a few minutes . . . could you, my dear? I'd be so grateful. It would be good of you. It's so terrible to see her so restless and not be able to soothe her. It's probably the last thing that we can do for her."

"I'll come," said Betsy. "I'll come now. This minute."

DECREE ABSOLUTE

ALEC stood at the drawing-room window in Bedford
Gardens, watching to see Betsy come. But his
thoughts were not of her. His mother was dying and he
could think of nothing else.

The irrelevance of death bewildered him as it bewilders
everybody ; so seldom does any life end in a full close.
Ten days ago, last week, she had been doing the things
that she had always done, squabbling with old Maggie,
gossiping with her friends, starting a new piece of tapestry,
behaving like a woman who is going to live for many years.
Nothing in last week led on to this. Old age, which should
be a prelude to the end, has not the accent or the modu-
lation of a final scene ; it does not fully prepare the mind
for silence. Old and young depart without farewells,
leaving everything unfinished, a broken sentence, an
unanswered question.

Now he felt the universal remorse. He was consumed
by a sense of stupidity and pitiful waste. It was not so
much regret for their recent misunderstandings that he
felt, or the realization of her bitter loneliness which he
might have assuaged and did not, or the knowledge that
he could never now atone for his unkindness. Nor was it
those tender memories of the past, of his own childhood,
though these haunted him continually. The burden of his
remorse was rather for all those things in her life of which
he knew nothing and could now guess nothing. They were
a book at which he had glanced ; a country viewed from
some hill top where he had always meant to go. Now the
chance was gone.

There was so much to which he had no clue—things that had happened long ago, before his own life began ; the fears, the hopes, the joys of a young girl, of a child. There was a whole world which had lived in her memory alone and which would vanish with her. To know so little, to have cared so little, to have left so much locked in her heart forever unsought and unvalued, was to be a partaker in her death. He felt now that he might hold her back from oblivion if he had known all, everything about her, all that she had felt and heard and seen so as to make her memory his.

He peered back over the long road which she had travelled, lit here and there by a few brief flashes, sentences, all that he could remember of the thousand things she had told him. He tried to conceive of her on this solitary journey, stumbling towards a goal foreseen but never accepted. The hills of Cumberland rose green about him and he saw the track by Drummond Water where she used to go to school. He had been there with her once and had listened inattentively while she chattered of the past.

" . . . Not a school really, but I liked to think that it was. I shared a governess with some other children. . . . I used to take my lunch, my *piece*, in a little basket . . ."

He did not try to see the child who had skipped, so long ago, over the ruts and puddles. He wanted rather to know what it was like to have been that child, to have been Emily Lewthwaite, nine years old, running to school with her piece in a little basket, running towards her death on a wild, windy afternoon sixty years later.

The clink of a taximeter drew his eyes to the street below. It was Betsy arriving, huddled against the wind in the same coat and hat that she had been wearing when he saw her, so surprisingly, on the escalator at Oxford Circus. He ran downstairs and opened the door to her before old Maggie had toiled up from the basement.

" Betsy," he said, " this is very good of you."

The wind rushed in before he could get the door shut and blew all the letters off the hall chest. They stooped to pick them up and Betsy marvelled to see that they were the same letters which had always been there ; a Dutch bulb catalogue, some circulars, and several bills, which got left lying unopened on the hall chest for days because Mrs. Canning did not like having to pay them. It was strange to think that life in the Bedford Gardens house had been going on just the same all this time. Maggie's tearful face appeared at the top of the basement stairs and she greeted the old woman kindly.

" Very well, thank you 'm," said Maggie, pausing uncertainly, not knowing if it was right, in the circumstances, to ask how Betsy was keeping.

" This is very sad for you," said Betsy.

Maggie's face immediately crumpled up and she vanished down the kitchen stairs.

" Is it quite hopeless ? " asked Betsy, turning to Alec.

He jerked his head despondently and led the way up those familiar stairs where she had gone so often, tense with the determination not to be bullied by her mother-in-law.

Here were the Chinese prints, which were not as good as Mrs. Canning thought they were, and the draughty half landing with the telephone. But already the personality was shrinking from the house. These were just pictures, not emanations of Emily Canning. She could no longer fill this shell of her life. All that she had been, all that she had meant to Betsy, was shrunk now to a little grey face on a pillow in a hot, quiet room : a tiny face, like a child's.

The nurse at the bedside shot a warning glance at them over her knitting.

" It's my . . . it's Mrs. Canning," whispered Alec. " Is she awake ? "

A flicker of excitement and curiosity crossed the woman's face. But she composed it quickly to a professional blankness.

"I think so," she said, getting up. "But she mayn't know you. She's been very restless."

She took her knitting over to the window and Betsy sat in the bedside chair. The face on the pillow remained motionless. Presently, with closed eyes, it spoke:

"Is that Betsy?"

"Yes! I've come . . . how do you feel?"

"I'm not at all well, dear. Such a headache! When I get home, back to Drummond Dale, I shall be better. But I'm not quite well enough to travel. I shall go home to-morrow."

"That's how she's been going on," said the nurse in a gusty whisper. "I keep telling her she's at home."

Mrs. Canning opened her eyes to shoot a glance of lively hatred towards the window. Then, the spark of vitality waning, she scanned Betsy's face.

"Tell me . . . how you are getting on . . ." She panted. "I can't talk. Tired. You talk."

"I . . ." said Betsy, "I . . ."

"Did you get those chairs?"

Betsy looked round at Alec who murmured:

"Launceston Place."

That had been their first house. She remembered suddenly about the chairs, a dining-room set which she had refused to buy because Mrs. Canning was determined that she should.

"Yes, yes," she said hastily, "I got them, after all."

A faint smile crossed the wan face.

"But you . . . mustn't . . . do too much, dear. Bad for you. Up and down those stairs. Wait! When I'm better . . . I'll help . . ."

Kenneth had been coming when they moved into Launceston Place. She did not look at Alec again.

"I'm taking great care of myself," she promised.

"That's right . . . was worried about you. I'm so pleased . . . so happy . . . think about it so much. Tell me . . . about the wall papers."

Betsy tried to remember. It was all so long ago. They had only been married a few months, and they had not been in Launceston Place for long because the war broke out, and Alec joined up, and she went to her parents in Oxford. Four years of their youth had been lost, years of terror and disorder which had, at the time, seemed endless, but which, in retrospect became curiously perfunctory and insignificant. She had not lived, during that time; she had merely sat about, waiting for the war to stop. And Launceston Place, on the far side of that dreary passage, belonged to a vanished world. She could not remember the wall-papers, only the freshness, the excitement of having her own house, battles with Mrs. Canning, and feeling sick sometimes, and Alec coming home in the evening to find her all dusty, the glow, the warmth of their love, and the possession of time, all time before them, the conviction that life would be kind.

" White and green for my bedroom," she said.

She had recalled, suddenly, the room where Ken was born ; where she woke to hear a baby crying and crying, and wondered where it came from.

Mrs. Canning's eyes were shut again. She seemed to sink away from them for awhile. The nurse knitted, clicking her needles softly. Betsy moved a little and glanced at Alec, wondering if she might go now.

But a louder, much sharper voice startled them :

" Yes. I wanted to see you. Where's Alec ? "

" Here, mother ! I'm here."

He came and stood beside Betsy. His mother's eyes were wide open and frightened.

" Has Betsy come ? Oh, yes ! Henrietta Hewitt was here this morning. She said you had quarrelled. I can't attend to it now. You oughtn't to worry me like this when I'm so ill. It's not right."

Excited, she tried to raise herself. The nurse came up.

" Now, Mrs. Canning, my dear . . ."

" Oh, do send that woman away ! She annoys me. It's

not right. It's your fault, Alec. You must look after
Betsy and make allowances. A husband ought to . . .
ought to cherish his wife. She's very silly . . . a very
silly woman . . . but she's fond of you."

" Yes, mother. It's all right. Really . . ."

" I've been so worried. It's made me quite ill. I
thought it might be my fault . . . something I'd said.
There was something. . . . It isn't true, is it ? She
hasn't gone off anywhere ? "

" No, no, mother dear ! Look ! She's here . . . come
to see you."

" Ah, yes . . . she ought to have come before. She
ought to know what is due to me . . ." The excitement
died away. " I can't attend to it now. I'm very tired."

And she closed her eyes again murmuring :

" Give her some tea . . . tea, dear ! I expect she's
tired, poor child. I shan't see her again . . . before I go
back to Drummond Dale."

Betsy bent to kiss her and whispered good-bye, but she
did not seem to hear.

Outside the door her tears, long pent up, poured down
her cheeks. Alec put an arm round her shoulders and led
her down to the drawing-room, trying to console her and
tell her how good she had been to come.

After long years, after an age of emptiness and fighting
shadows, she found herself in his arms again. He drew
her down on to the sofa and held her against his heart
until she had finished crying and lay at peace in the dusky
firelight. For a long time they lay there in silence.
Neither dared to move or to speak. They had found one
another ; they were together. As long as this moment
lasted they would remain so.

The slow tick of the clock on the stairs was a threat.

And she said, with a mournful sigh :

" I'm sorry I ever . . . was unkind to her."

" I know."

" All those things don't seem worth while now."

" No."

" Oh, Alec! How has this happened? How did we ever let it happen? We must have been mad."

" Yes."

" It's all a mistake. It was my fault."

" It was mine."

The moment was over and she wanted to hear him say the next thing. But he did not say it, and already they seemed to have moved a little way apart. Panic clutched at her and she whispered:

" Is it impossible . . . ? "

There was a pause, between one tick of the clock and another, before he answered:

" Quite impossible."

He put her gently away from him and stood up. He repeated:

" Quite impossible. We have . . . other obligations."

" You mean . . . Joy? Would she mind very much? "

" She's my wife now. And she's doing her best. She's a good creature. She tries very hard; she has been very unselfish about having Eliza. She didn't want her at first. But then she seemed to pull herself together . . . to make efforts. I can't desert her after that. I must do my best too."

" But I can't be alone, Alec! I can't! I'm so lonely."

" You could marry Max."

" I could never be happy with him. I should always feel I was your wife, not his."

" Well, my dear, you must make up your own mind about that."

" You talk as if . . . as if it wasn't your concern."

" It isn't," he said, with a heavy sigh. " It mustn't be."

Now they were miles apart. She jumped up and came to him but she knew that it was no use.

" Alec! Oh, Alec! "

" You must go now, dear. And I must go back to my mother."

" Then this is . . . really . . . where we part ? "

" I suppose it is."

" Good-bye, then."

" Good-bye, Betsy. God bless you. Try to . . . to . . ."

He meant to say try to be happy, but he said be brave instead.

" And . . . marry Max. . . . He'll look after you. It's quite true you oughtn't to be alone. Tell him everything. He'll understand. And . . . and do your best for him."

" Yes," she said indifferently. " Yes."

After she had gone he stood again at the window, watching the ragged clouds racing over the chimney pots. From the inclement North the wind tore over the land, thundered through the woods, sent the smoke swirling over towns and cottages. There was no rest or peace for anybody. Even the lamp-lighter, staggering up the street, could hardly stand against it. He wished that he had not had to thrust her forth into such a gale.

But she is not more alone, he thought, than anybody else. We can never touch another mind. We are alone. . . .

Nor could he tell why the windy street was eclipsed by a sudden vision of green grass, an apple tree in blossom, and some happy ones walking there in the sunlight. That memory was not his. He had never seen it. Some mind, not his, had brought it, some wandering mind, free from the chain of space and time. But such peace, such ecstasy, came with it that he knew it at once to be *the place*.

There, he thought, we shall be happy. We have been happy there. . . . It is there and we go back . . . go back. . . .

It was gone and he was alone in the darkening room. Maggie was peering through the door. She switched on the light, so that the day outside ended suddenly and night leapt at the windows.

" Oh, sir," she said, " I thought you were upstairs."

" I'm just going, Maggie."

He went up to the drowsy room above. A final, profound repose held sway there. The nurse whispered :

" She's just slipping away, Mr. Canning. Perhaps we'd better send for the doctor. I don't think she'll rouse again."

" Did she say anything else . . . after we'd gone ? Did she ask for me ? "

" No. She just smiled and muttered a little. She was wandering. She said something about an apple tree. . . ."

PART IV
TIME AND CHANGE

KENNETH

IN a shallow, sleepy hollow, between two ridges of downland, lies the village of Abbot's Markham. A great high road to the West runs along the top of the lower ridge : from it a narrow lane twists downhill to a steep little bridge and goes up on the other side through a long street of warm Cotswold stone. The ruins of a fine abbey lie scattered in the meadows beside the river. But it is not for the sake of the ruins that so many cars turn off the high road and come nosing down the lane and over the bridge. Their goal is the Raven Inn, four hundred years old, and kept by the famous Bruce Blackett whose flying exploits were news from Harbin to Cape Town until a disabling crash drove him to another trade. Travellers pause and take a meal at the Raven, on their way westwards, in the hope of seeing him : but they seldom do so, for he spends most of his time in the kitchen showing the local wenches how to clear soup. He is an inspired cook and only keeps an inn so that he may indulge in his darling hobby.

There were already a string of cars drawn up in the street when Beddoes drove over the bridge, one evening in August, so that it was not easy to find a parking space. He should have gone up the hill to the little square by the church, but he would not take the trouble. He simply left his car in the middle of the road, across the bonnets of several others. But, of his three companions, Kenneth was the only one to protest.

" You'll never be allowed to park it there. Those others won't be able to get out. And there's no room for anything to pass."

Beddoes took no notice. Hastings and McCrae, who sat behind, grinned at one another. Young Canning had been asking for trouble, all the way from London, and there was trouble coming to him if he did not look out. He was the youngest of the party, but he seemed to think that his standing with Beddoes, their host, gave him the right to run the show. To bait him was one of the standard amusements of the trip. When Beddoes had asked them to come with him to Cornwall he had hinted that his little friend would be disagreeably surprised, for the tour had been planned as a *tête-à-tête*. Kenneth's long face, when he first saw them in the car, had been excruciatingly funny, and it had been a great joke to invent all sorts of absurd reasons for refusing to let him drive.

They were not St. Clere's men. They had got to know Beddoes at St. Moritz and the acquaintance was continued in London during the Easter holidays. They were older than he was, by a year or two, but they had no money, and he had plenty, and they were ready to let him call the tune as long as he gave them a good time. He liked to have plenty of hangers-on. They all understood one another very well.

" They'll only haul us out in the middle of dinner to move it," Kenneth was protesting.

" Well then, that'll be a chance for you," said McCrae. " You've been howling for a chance to drive all day."

" I'm damned if I do."

" Shut up," said Beddoes, " and come along."

They climbed out of the car, slamming all four doors violently, shattering the sleepy quiet of the street Beddoes shouldered his way into the Raven followed by his admiring friends and Kenneth sulkily brought up the rear. They invaded the dining-room. They looked round them with a long disparaging stare, bullied the waiter, and eventually suffered themselves to be conducted to a table. By the time they were seated, everybody

there, and the room was very full, had taken a strong
dislike to them.

Before the end of the meal Kenneth's prediction was
justified. A waiter came up, a little nervously, and
addressed himself to Beddoes, who had ordered the food
and seemed to be the leader of the party. Would he be
so kind as to move his car, as another gentleman wanted
to get out ? Beddoes took not the slightest notice. He
helped himself to cheese with a perfectly wooden face, as
though the man had not been there at all. Hastings and
McCrae followed his example. But Kenneth could not
help saying :

" I told you so ! "

Whereat the waiter turned to him.

" The gentleman wants to get off, sir. He's waiting."

" It's not my car," said Kenneth, flushing.

Beddoes appeared to see the waiter for the first time
and told him to bring watercress if they had such a thing.
The man hesitated for a moment and then went off to find
his employer.

" You'll have to move it," said Kenneth.

Hastings and McCrae began to make bets as to whether
Kenneth would move it or not.

" I didn't put it there. Beddoes did. It's his funeral."

" You'll do what you're told, my little man."

" No, he won't ! He can be led but not driven."

To all this Beddoes said not a word. He went on eating
cheese, but there was an ugly look in his eyes. Presently
Bruce Blackett appeared and a mild stir went through the
room. At every table the diners turned and stared as
the wiry, one-armed man made his way towards the group
which the waiter had pointed out. Odious young men
were no novelty to Blackett : he dealt with them as part
of the day's work. His quick eye took in the four. He
noted the brutality of Beddoes's mouth, McCrae's spots,
and the black shadows under Kenneth's eyes.

"I'm afraid," he said pleasantly, "that you will have to move your car."

There was a pause. The room was silent and everybody was listening. Beddoes tried, for a few seconds, to treat Blackett as he had treated the waiter. But he had not the strength of will. His haughty blankness crumbled under the silent impact of a stronger personality. He was obliged to look at Blackett.

"What?" he demanded.

"You heard what I said," replied Blackett.

Beddoes turned to Hastings with a shrug.

"What did he say?"

"We—we've got to move the car," mumbled Hastings.

"Oh?" Beddoes stared again at Blackett. "Why?"

"Because it's a nuisance where it is."

"Really? You keep an inn and you don't let your customers park outside it."

"Not so as to block everyone else."

"We'll move it after dinner."

"No. You'll move it now. If you don't, I shall report you to the police for obstructing the road."

Beddoes glanced at Kenneth, and said:

"Cut along."

The whole room was looking at Kenneth. Crimson, choking with humiliation, he rose and went out to do as he was told. As he went he heard McCrae snigger.

In the street an angry little knot of people was gathered round Beddoes's car. As soon as Kenneth appeared they turned upon him furiously, demanding how he had ever come to park it in such a place. He had become a scapegoat for all the hostility which his party had created. Without a word he climbed into the car and tried to manœuvre it out of its awkward position. Even for a good driver the task would not have been easy, as a large lorry had come down the hill and was waiting to get past, so that the turning space in the street was limited. And Kenneth was not a good driver at all. He ground the gears, roared, reversed, shot forwards and backwards, mounted the pavement, and bumped the other cars. His incompetence was exhibited before all these angry and contemptuous people. Bruce Blackett, a man whom he had idolized for years, before whom he would most have wished to appear creditably, stood by and watched it all.

After five minutes, which seemed like fifty, the car was in a worse position than ever. Blackett was obliged to come to the rescue. He waved aside the frantic onlookers, who were all shouting contradictory instructions to Kenneth, and climbed into the driver's seat himself. Steering with his one arm he straightened the tangle in less than sixty seconds. The lorry crawled past and a clear passage was left for the indignant travellers. Without a word or a look at Kenneth he got out again and was going back to the house when the boy called after him :

" I'm sorry we've given so much trouble, sir. It was a rotten place to leave it."

This was a sign of grace. Blackett nodded. Something in Kenneth's voice, something in the " sir " conveyed a little of his shame and mortification.

" Did you leave it there ? " asked Blackett.

" No."

So much of the story was told in one word that Bruce Blackett hesitated for a moment as if he would have liked to say more. But it was not his business. He nodded again and went back into the inn. Before returning to the kitchen he went to his office and made a note of the number of Beddoes's car. He had taken to doing this whenever motoring customers gave any sort of trouble.

Kenneth did not follow him. To go back and face the taunts of the other three would be intolerable. He wandered off, up the village street. The light had changed while they had been dining. The sun had set, but a glow lingered on the stone walls and cottage gardens as if its legacy of warmth was not all spent.

A cart track led downhill, between frothy banks of cow

parsley, to the river in the valley. It was very quiet down there, so silent that he could hear, a hundred yards away, the murmur of shallow water sweeping over a pebbly reach. The ruins of the abbey lay tumbled about under the elm trees. Though the sky was still all bright there was darkness in the air: night was distilled, drop by drop, as the minutes passed. Dusk gathered under the trees and crept like a mist up the golden ridge across the valley.

Kenneth sat on a stone by the whispering river and buried his face in his hands. His cheeks burnt no longer, but he was sick at heart. The fatigue of the day was heavy on him, the roar and stink of the journey, its vexations and disappointments.

He did not want to go on to Cornwall. It would all be like this; they would treat him like this, like a dog, all the time. But he had nowhere else to go. His mother was married to Max St. Mullins and they had gone to Geneva, to some kind of conference. They had offered to take him and Daphne but he had rejected the offer. Nor would he stay at Hornwood for the summer, for he did not wish to regard Hornwood as his home. For him there was no alternative save Cornwall with Beddoes, whom he hated, who treated him like a dog.

It was difficult to believe that he had become so much bound to a person whom he hated. At no time had he really liked Beddoes; but in the beginning there had been a queer excitement, a nervous obsession, which took the place of sympathy. And he was, at that time, so full of pity that he liked to think of himself as going to the bad, as driven to the devil by a world which had ill-treated him. It was more than half a pose. For, though the morbid attraction had gained upon him rapidly, he always believed that he could, if he pleased, free himself at any time. The belief that he had not gone too far, that he could break away at will, had given stimulation to the whole queer business. It was like playing a dangerous game.

The submission of a weak nature to a stronger one can be made almost unconsciously. Slowly and imperceptibly, as if sapped by some drug, his will had been drained and warped. He knew now that it was impossible to break away. Yet, like a drug addict, he still hoped that circumstances might enable him to free himself without effort. He dreamt of waking up one morning and finding himself cured.

He had money in his pocket and could, quite easily, have returned to London then and there. There was a railway station not three miles away. For a time he played with the idea, not as a means of escape but as a gesture of defiance, a way of impressing his tormentor. He would show that he was not going to be treated like this—like dirt, like a dog. Beddoes would have to pursue him and apologize. There would be a scene but there would not be a break. He could stage a quarrel and assert a purely imaginary independence. But they would both know that he could be whistled back. He would carry his chains with him wherever he went.

He sat there while the dusk deepened, his head in his hands, until a shout among the ruins disturbed the quiet valley. It was Beddoes, coming to look for him. He made no answer and remained where he was.

Presently Beddoes appeared and asked angrily what the hell he thought he was doing.

" It would have served you right if we'd gone on without you. It's past nine o'clock."

" All right," said Kenneth, in a voice which was, he hoped, cool and calm, " go on. I don't mind. I'm going back to London."

" Oh, shut up, and come along ! "

" I won't. I've had enough of it. Why should I move your bloody car ? "

" I didn't make you move it. You didn't have to."

" I'm sick of you. I never want to see you again. I'm not going on."

" Oh, really ? "

When Beddoes lost his temper he became cheerful, almost jocund, as if some burden had been removed from his spirits.

" What are you going to do ? " he asked blithely.

" I shall stay here."

" Oh, right ! Right ! You shall—all night—till they find you in the morning."

He had got Kenneth down and pinned him with one knee, wrenching his arms behind his back.

" Want to be tied up ? This scarf will do nicely for your arms and your tie will do for your ankles. Don't worry. You shall stay here."

Kenneth writhed and gasped and bit the grass. He was terrified : too terrified to struggle much or to consider that a tie and scarf could not bind him effectually for long. Beddoes had tied him up before, and he could not bear it. With his mouth full of dirt he began to plead and apologize.

" No, don't ! Beddoes, don't ; I didn't mean it A joke . . . I was joking . . . don't ! Don't ! Let me go ! I'll come on : I'm sorry. It was a joke. . . ."

" This is a joke, too," muttered Beddoes.

Then, suddenly, he paused and listened, still pinning his victim to the ground. Somebody was coming along the river path.

" Beddoes . . ."

" Ssh ! Get up ! "

Kenneth was jerked to his feet. His arm was seized and he was hurried away up the hill, between the drifts of cow parsley.

The street was empty and there were lights in some of the cottage windows. They looked mild and friendly. Kenneth wished he could be another person, some boy who lived in one of these houses, shut securely away into a different life.

McCrae and Hastings were lounging beside the car,

which now stood solitary before the Raven. They said nothing, but they stared oddly at the other two hurrying towards them. Bruce Blackett watched them from the inn doorway, just beyond the great pool of light cast by the headlamps.

" Get in," said Beddoes curtly. " You two behind. Canning can drive."

Once more the quiet street echoed with the slamming of doors and the roar of their departure as they tore off into the gathering night.

Blackett watched their headlamps swing round as they went over the narrow bridge. Kenneth had taken the curve far too quickly. That boy can't drive for toffee, he thought. I wonder how many people they'll kill before to-morrow morning !

MARK

LATE that night a young servant girl, bicycling home from the Pictures in Salisbury, was knocked down and killed by a car which did not stop. Her sister, who rode a few yards in front, heard a scream and saw the car rush past, but had no time to take the number. She thought that it was a large open car full of men. The police made inquiries. Such a car had stopped for petrol just beyond Salisbury, and the man who served it thought that he could identify its occupants. There were four of them; he had noticed the driver particularly as being almost a schoolboy, and quite obviously the youngest of the party.

Some account of this was published in the newspapers next morning. It was read by Bruce Blackett, who pondered awhile and then examined his pocket-book for the number of a car. Later in the day he rang up the police.

It was also read by Mark Hannay, now an acting bombardier in camp on Salisbury Plain. And immediately, automatically, a picture of Kenneth and Beddoes popped into his mind. There was no reason for it, except that this was just the sort of thing that they were likely to go and do. The picture came and stayed there, so insistently, that he was troubled. He began to wish that he knew where Kenneth was, so as to be sure that he was not mixed up in this affair. It was absurd to take such a presentiment seriously, but he could not get the thought of Kenneth out of his head; it continued to return and plague him all through a busy morning. He drove it off but never for long.

He had gone, with three recruits newly arrived from the depot, to the top of a hill some five miles from the camp. Their task was to select an artillery position and to make a sketch map of the ground within range. The burden of it fell upon Mark, since none of the others had ever done such a thing before. They had been taught the theory of map-making, but it did not seem to have made the slightest impression on their minds, and they had minds so different that he was obliged to talk a different language to all three.

To one of them, born and bred in the slums of Rotherhithe, the country-side spread out below them was as strange, as unfamiliar, as the mountains of the moon. It meant nothing at all to him. He was handy with his pencil, the neatest of the four, but he could see no difference between a poplar and an oak, between a haystack and a cornrick. Nor was he disposed to agree with Mark about the use of the compass, in spite of the instructions that they had received upon the subject. He had learnt, he said, that the top of a map is always North, and from this he argued that he could face in any direction that he liked and the compass points would settle themselves.

The second, a swarthy young poacher from the fens, half gipsy by the look of him, saw more than Mark would ever see. He could tell oats from barley in a field five miles away, he knew where the North was without a compass and the time of day without a watch. He was extremely intelligent. But to translate what he saw and knew into pencil marks upon a piece of paper was utterly beyond him, and his idea of distance could not be disentangled from that of time. A place was far off if it would take a long time to get there, near if it could be reached easily. A mile of good road was, to him, much shorter than a mile of ploughed fields and fences, and should be shown shorter on the map. So that his idea of scale was fantastic.

The third could not be induced to take any interest

whatever in maps and map-making. His name was
Lambourne and he was the butt of the battery. That
was all that Mark knew about him until to-day, when it
turned out that he fancied himself as an archæologist,
and regarded this expedition as an opportunity for collecting little pieces of flint which he pronounced to be arrow
heads.

Mark argued with each of them in turn and argued
with himself about the unlikelihood of Kenneth's being in
England at this time of year. It was much more probable
that he and Beddoes were running over people in Spain
or Hungary.

" You ask any educated person," repeated Lambourne,
" and they'll tell you the same as what I do. It would
surprise you to know what there is to be learnt from
stones. What's stones to some is history to others. Now
this little piece of flint may look to you like a perfickly
ordingry——"

" All right," said Mark, " all right. Smithers'll be along
in a minute. You tell him about 'em and see what he says."

Smithers, the officer out with the party, was at the
moment, at the bottom of the hill. But he would soon
be bumping up on his motor-bicycle to see how they were
getting on.

(And for all I know, thought Mark, he mayn't be with
Beddoes at all. It's a year since I've heard anything of
either of them. Beddoes may have chucked him by now.)

" Smithers wouldn't know," said Lambourne scornfully.
" When I say an educated person, I mean a person that's
studied it. There was an old gentleman I used to work
for, old Mr. Pusey, that was a fair masterpiece with all he
knew. He used to take me out, down Wantage way,
digging up these barrows. . . . You've no call to say that,"
he added reproachfully to Gyppo Smith, who had muttered
a severe reflection upon both the intelligence and morals
of Mr. Pusey, " he may of been old, but he wasn't silly,
nor yet he wasn't——"

" Oh, put a sock in it," advised Mark. " We ought to be over at Clandon Spinney by now."

" That's quite right," agreed the Cockney, who had been revolving slowly with his compass and had now arranged it so that the letter N lay at the top of his map. " He must of been batty if he didn't know the difference between barrows and arrows. At his age too ! "

" Of course he knew the difference. I never said——"

" That's not the North," stormed Mark. " Look at the needle pointing away over there ! "

" Oh, that," said Harris contemptuously, " that's stuck or something. It's gone funny. Keeps pointing West."

Mark's rejoinder was forcible, but scarcely to the point, and Harris, who was a clever mimic, bleated plaintively :

" You've no call to say that."

His imitation of Lambourne was so good that Mark and Gyppo laughed.

" But how are we to get to Clandon Spinney ? " said Mark to the gipsy. " Shall we go along the hill and then down ? There's no lane, and we can't take our bikes across the plough at the bottom."

Smith was first-rate at getting quickly across country. He always knew where there would be a gate and how a lane would run. His black eyes roved across the fields below and he gave advice in his curiously gentle voice :

" You go down that here. See the farm close down ? There's another, see, about half an hour across north-west. You'll find a lane there you can get the bikes along."

" I don't see a lane."

" That's there, but you can't see that. There's a double hedge there, look."

Mark looked, scanning the bright spread of fields, woods and farms, and filled with contentment because the sun was warm and the day was fine. He was enjoying his life in camp very much ; he had begun to enjoy it as soon as he had learnt to endure it. For the first few months he had suffered from a continual sense of anxiety, watchfulness and strain. He had been like a person who is learning to ride a bicycle, or to skate, or to practise any art which requires unconscious balance and adjustment. Everything was so new, the unexpected pitfalls were so many, that he could not afford to relax for a moment. He never ceased to be aware that he was no longer head of St. Clere's College, but a private in the Gunners. And though he made no bad mistakes, though he found his feet, to all appearances, very quickly, there could be no enjoyment while his nerves remained so taut. Then, like a skater, he got the knack quite suddenly. Balance and impetus arrived of their own accord and he ceased to be aware of himself.

Now he often experienced a kind of mental satisfaction which he had never known before. It was as if he had formerly led two existences, one of thought and the other of feeling, and all the impacts of life had a double echo, neither of which rang quite truly. Nothing ever completely happened to him. He had known pleasure often enough, but he had never possessed the single-mindedness which is the principal condition of enjoyment, and which comes so much more easily to those who do not think.

He looked where Gyppo pointed and saw now where a lane ran between two clumps of buildings. His eye took in everything that was to be seen : the sheep on the chalky slopes below, two men with a cart in a turnip field, a line of willows crossing the meadows which must betoken a stream, and a sudden flash from a road where the sunlight glanced from an unseen car. More than a mile away a tiny figure was crawling across a field by a narrow footpath between two stiles. It might have been a man or a woman, for all that he could see, yet for three seconds he felt perfectly sure that it was Kenneth. In just such a manner had Kenneth been moving about the landscape of his mind all the morning. He mocked at himself, and dismissed the idea ; but, for all that, he

resolved to get news of Kenneth, as soon as possible.
There might, or might not, be something behind this obsession, and he would not be happy until he had found out.

It was indeed Kenneth; he was looking for Mark and
making his way, as well as he could, towards the camp.
He reached it in the middle of the afternoon. When he
asked for Acting-Bombardier Hannay, the sentry at the
gate referred him to the Sergeant of the Guard, who
directed him to the hutments of Hannay's battery. He
spoke to a number of young men who seemed, to his
exhausted perceptions, to be as much alike as the buttons
on their tunics. They all appeared to be the same age
and the same height, all ruddy, well set up, plebeian and
self-possessed. Presently he saw another one, coming out
of a hut and putting on his tunic.

" Hullo ! " said the soldier, and it was Mark.

So completely was he just another one that Kenneth
stared.

" What's up ? " asked Mark.

One look at Kenneth's face convinced him that any
other remark would be a waste of time.

" Is there anywhere," asked Kenneth, " that I can
speak to you alone ? "

He had intended to say this at once, as soon as he found
Mark, so he said it, although the Mark he was seeking
had vanished.

Mark looked up and down the lines. They were pretty
well alone in this broad avenue. Nobody could hear what
they said. But one or two men, standing in the doorways
of huts, could see them, and Kenneth was looking very
peculiar.

" We could go up to the playground," he said. " There's
no match on. We could be alone there."

" No," muttered Kenneth. " Inside somewhere."

" Oh, well, come into the hut for a moment. Everybody is out. I was just going out myself. If you would
wait we'll go out together, anywhere you like."

Kenneth followed him into the hut, which was empty
save for Lambourne, who was arranging his collection of
flints on the box at the foot of his cot. Mark sat down at
a table and collected some papers that were scattered
there.

"If you'll just wait till I've finished this," he said.
"There's some notes I was writing up. I'll be done in a
minute, and then we can go."

He bent, frowning, over his map.

Kenneth sat down on a box nearby and surveyed him
curiously, trying to make out why he looked so different.
It could not simply be the effect of the uniform. Something had happened to the whole of his body ; he seemed
to have grown so much more compact. He spoke with less
emphasis and moved with more precision. His face was
less expressive and his regard more observant. He had
grown, somehow, shorter and thicker, and, as Kenneth at
last decided, more ordinary looking.

Lambourne, having stowed away the flints in his box,
went out, softly whistling "Annie Laurie." As soon as
they were alone Kenneth burst out :

"I'm in the most ghastly trouble. I don't want to be
seen. We must be careful where we go. The—the police
are after me."

"Umhum," said Mark, busy with his pencil.

"I want to get out of the country if I can."

"All right. I'll be done in a minute. We can take
my motor-bike off somewhere."

"Oh ? You've got one ? You've got a motor-bike ? "
"Umhum ! "

"Can you go out ? Have you got leave ? "

"I'm out on pass for the rest of the day. Don't talk,
old man. I must give my mind to this."

Kenneth's spirits rose, in spite of the blinding headache
which turned every physical impression, every sight and
sound, into a twinge of pain. If Mark had a motor-cycle
they might perhaps get down towards Southampton. He

wanted to get to the sea, but had been afraid to take a train, afraid to go anywhere among crowds of people. Once at Southampton he could easily find a ship. . . .

" You look damn' ill," said Mark, folding up his papers. " Come down to the canteen and have some coffee or something before we go."

But Kenneth shook his head with a vigour that sent dizzy throbs all down his spine.

" You didn't listen to what I said. Have you finished ? The police are after me. I've got to get out of the country if I can. I want you to give me a lift down towards Southampton, as far as you can . . . they'll be watching the railway stations. . . . I must run for it, because nobody will believe me. There are three witnesses——"

" Don't start telling me here. Anybody might come in. I'm ready. Come along."

On their way towards the cycle-shed Mark inquired after Eliza.

" She's all right, I think. I haven't seen her since Christmas. She's living with my father now, somewhere near Devizes."

" Devizes ! "

" Yes. Pandy Madoc has been sold. He's bought a house in Wiltshire."

" But Devizes—that's not thirty miles from here ! "

" Is it ? I suppose so."

" Why . . . " began Mark, and changed his mind. He asked, instead, how Kenneth's mother was.

" She's married again."

" So I heard. How is she ? "

" Very well."

" Where is she ? "

" At Geneva. With . . . her husband——"

" I see."

Mark rode for three or four miles to a place where a grove of beeches spread a shade on the downland road. Here he stopped his engine and said that they could talk.

But Kenneth, on fire to reach Southampton, objected to the delay. He would not sit with Mark on the grass under the trees, but stood in the road, looking anxiously up and down for signs of pursuit.

" There's nothing more to tell you," he declared. " Only that I've got to get out of the country."

" Unless you tell me the whole thing," said Mark, " I shan't go on. What have you been doing ? "

" Nothing. I've done nothing."

" Then why are the police——"

" They wouldn't believe me. They think I've done something and I haven't."

" What do they think you've done ? "

Kenneth stood in the glare of the road and shook his head obstinately.

" Is it," asked Mark, taking a long shot, " anything to do with that car that killed a girl and didn't stop ? "

This went home. Kenneth span round in a panic.

" Christ ! How did you know ? "

" It was in the newspapers this morning."

" Was it ? Oh, my God ! Then they know it was us ! Did they say it was me ? "

" No, no ! They haven't traced the car yet. Were you driving ? "

" I wasn't. I swear I wasn't. I was when we stopped for petrol, just before. But then I was sick, and Beddoes drove. But nobody'll believe it wasn't me. I was driving when we stopped for petrol. And when we had some parking trouble, at Abbott's Markham, I drove. Everybody saw me. It's hopeless."

" You say Beddoes was driving ? "

" When we knocked her over, yes ! I swear he was. And he wouldn't stop. I kept begging him to stop. I said I know we shall be caught. But he wouldn't. And the others——"

" Who were the others ? "

" Hastings and McCrae. Nobody you know. Not

college men. Friends of his. They told me to shut up.
So I said, well you'll have to stop sometime, and when
you do I shall go to the police. I won't be responsible,
I said. And so Beddoes said . . . you do believe me when
I say he was driving, don't you ? "

" Of course I do. Did he threaten to say you were ? "

" Yes, yes ! And the others backed him up. They
said if I split to the police they'd all swear it was me.
Nobody will believe me. I've got three witnesses against
me. And all the people who saw me driving. I haven't
a chance, have I ? "

" I don't know about that. What happened next ? "

" Can they bring it in murder ? They can sometimes,
can't they ? Especially if the car didn't stop."

" I don't think so. Tell me what happened next."

" We went on arguing and arguing, and I said they'd
catch us, because I think our number was taken at Abbott's
Markham. And suddenly Beddoes lost his temper, and
he stopped the car and pushed me out and drove on."

Something of the desperation which Kenneth had felt
when this happened seemed to overcome him again, and
he dropped limply on the grass beside Mark. When he
spoke again his voice was flat and weary :

" I didn't know what to do. I started walking back
along the road. I walked most of the night, but sometimes I rested. The more I thought about it the more
frightened I got. I didn't dare go to the police. I didn't
know what to do. Beddoes was . . . awful. He frightened
me."

" How did you get here ? "

" I thought I'd better get out of the country before
they traced the car. It got light and I kept on walking
and resting and trying to think what to do. I couldn't
think of anyone who'd help me. Then I realized I was
on Salisbury Plain and I remembered you were in camp
somewhere about here. So I set off to look for you. I
thought you might help me to disguise myself. That's all."

Mark chewed a bit of grass and looked at his watch.

"That's all," said Kenneth again. "Hadn't we better be getting on?"

"I'm not sure," said Mark slowly, "what's the best thing to do."

"You'll take me to the coast? Mark! Mark! Don't let me down. You promised——"

"Don't be a bloody fool. You'd certainly be caught, and then things would look black, if you like. No! We can do one of two things. We can go straight to the police at Salisbury——"

"Mark! You won't . . . I refuse. . . ."

"Or I could run you over to your father, if he's really at Devizes. I'd much rather we went to him. You ought to have proper protection and advice as soon as you can. I don't believe Beddoes and Co. will stick to their story when it comes to the point. I think they were only bluffing; trying to scare you into holding your tongue. But they might. And you must get into touch with your guardians as quickly as possible."

"He's not my guardian."

"But you say your mother is abroad. There'd be some delay before you could get hold of her."

"He's not my guardian. I haven't seen him for two years. I don't want to have anything to do with him."

"That's nonsense. As I said, I'd much rather go straight to him. The only thing that worries me is that every moment you delay before going to the police will make your case rather worse. It will make their story look more true. If you'd had the sense to go first thing this morning . . . however . . . you didn't, so that's that. The really important thing is for you to go and give your account of it before they are traced and questioned. And I'm wondering if it's wise to spend time going up to Devizes."

"I won't go to the police and I won't go to my father.

I refuse. I didn't come to you for advice. I came for help. If you won't help me, I'll get along by myself."

Mark said nothing. He continued, silently, to weigh the alternatives. If they went to Salisbury Kenneth might be detained. The boy seemed to be so crazy, so unstrung, that this might well terrify him out of his wits. He might say anything.

" You don't seem to realize that you may be helping to hang me," asserted Kenneth excitedly.

" Oh —— ! " said Mark, getting up. " Come along. We'll go to your father."

" Nothing will induce me to go to him."

" It's that or the police."

" I won't."

" Then I shall."

" You ? You will ? You . . ."

Kenneth flew at him with a shriek of rage. But he was too weak and dizzy to do more than shower a few feeble blows and when Mark pushed him away he fell cursing on the grass.

" All right," he panted. " Go to the police. Go ! But you won't find me when you come back. You'll never find me alive."

" I shan't let you out of my sight," said Mark calmly. " I see a car coming along the road and I'll send a message by it to the police in Salisbury. That is, if you won't go to your father."

" I'll see you in hell first."

" All right ! "

Mark went into the road in readiness to hail the approaching car. Kenneth called out :

" Very well. Have it your own way. I'll go to Devizes."

" All right," said Mark again, and returned from the road.

When the car had gone past he said :

" Come along. And mind, no funny business on the way. No trying to jump off the bike, or anything like that. If there's any of that I shall hand you straight over to the police."

"I'll pay you out for this."

Starting up was the most unpleasant part of it. Mark did not at all like setting off with this lunatic behind him and half expected to get a blow on the head at the outset. When once they were off he meant to go so fast that Kenneth would be afraid to do anything. As he bestrode his machine he said, over his shoulder :

"Pity about St. Clere's, isn't it ? "

"What ? " came a quavering voice behind him.

"Oh yes, you wouldn't have seen. It was in the papers this morning," said Mark, starting up.

"Why ? What's happened ? "

"Burnt to the ground ! "

"Burnt ? St. Clere's ? "

Mark blithely shouted some details as they shot off down the road. Kenneth pelted him with questions which he answered whenever they were obliged to slow down at all.

ALEC

IT had been agreed, at the time of the divorce, that Well Walk and all its contents should be handed over to Betsy, while Pandy Madoc remained Alec's property. So that Alec and Joy imagined, when they moved into their new house near Devizes, that they must have sufficient furniture for their needs. Pandy Madoc had been sold early in the year, and its contents had been stored for a time. This was before Eliza, with her practical ways, had joined her father's household. If she had been in charge of affairs she would have insisted upon making an inventory of the furniture before it was stored, so that they might know exactly how much of it there was. But Alec was too lazy and Joy too feckless to think of doing such a thing.

A disconcerting shock lay in store for all of them when the goods arrived at the Mill House. There was scarcely enough to furnish a labourer's cottage. For Betsy, in that autumn when her fury was at its height, had labelled as her property any object to which she could lay the faintest shadow of a claim ; and Mrs. Trotter, who helped her, had tied surreptitious labels on to anything which she thought that Alec really ought not to be allowed to have. A vast number of things had been, it appeared, wedding presents to Betsy, and much that was not had been bought, so she said, with her money. Alec could not remember if this was so, or not, and would not have disputed it if he could. But he was disagreeably surprised to discover that his share consisted mainly of cups without saucers, jugs without basins, beds without mattresses, kitchen chairs and pedestal cupboards.

He was depressed by this aftermath of a quarrel which had long ceased to exist. Condemnation of Betsy, though unspoken, filled every heart. Joy, Eliza and the Merricks were shocked at this evidence of meanness and spite, and he was powerless to defend her. Nor could he deny that she had once been spiteful; but he knew that she was so no longer and it wounded him to see her thus betrayed to people who did not love or understand her.

The move into the Mill House, therefore, was accomplished in the trough of a depression. Instead of marking the beginning of a new life it became a last chapter of the old. New furniture had to be bought in a hurry, and, since there was no real concord or harmony of ideas between the three of them, they all set to work on different lines. A polite deference to one another's wishes was the rule during those first weeks, so that there was no unity of plan.

Alec's idea was to order all that he needed from Maples and pay for it when he had the money. Eliza inclined to extreme economy. The redecoration of the Mill House had cost a great deal and she now proposed that they should picnic for a while, with a bare minimum of chairs, tables and beds, until they could afford to furnish properly. Joy, intent upon being a true home-maker, was all for picking up old pieces in little shops. Gradually the house became full to overflowing with lavish suites, ordered by Alec, worm-eaten joint stools and rickety dower chests picked up by Joy, deck chairs, camp beds and wicker work chosen by Eliza.

Saturation point had been reached when three vans suddenly arrived containing all the spoil from Pandy Madoc and a great deal from Well Walk. Betsy had only just learnt what was happening and she was greatly shocked. This late fruition of wrath disconcerted her as much as it did Alec. Her own mood, when she had gone about Pandy Madoc, tying on labels, had so completely vanished that she refused to believe it had ever existed. Moreover, she did not want the furniture. Very little of it was up to Hornwood standards.

All these possessions were unloaded on the lawn because there was no room for them inside the house. Alec looked at them, groaned loudly, and announced that he was going away for a week to stay with Johnnie Graham. It was all one to him what they did with the things, and his women must dispose of them as they thought fit.

He went away. When he came back it was to a dictatorship. The house was looking very nice indeed; the furniture from Pandy Madoc and Well Walk had been tastefully and sensibly arranged in all the principal rooms. There was, fortunately, a large loft which had been part of the old mill buildings, and in this had been stored everything that he and Eliza had bought. Joy's treasures seemed to have disappeared altogether. They were too full of worm to be put safely with anything else.

All this had been done by Eliza, and henceforward Eliza ruled the family. This was inevitable since, of the three, she had by far the strongest character. She had insisted upon leaving school at Easter, so that she might help them with the move. There was now very little idea that she should ever go back. Alec, only anxious to get on with his work in peace, let her do exactly as she pleased. And Joy's attempts at self-assertion were no great matter. Throughout the spring and summer Eliza gained one point after another until her autocracy was complete. She kept house, paid the bills, ordered the meals, and even seemed to think herself responsible for the baby. She was so quick and practical that it would have been difficult to gainsay her. Joy, hampered by the desire to please Alec, and never quite certain of what she wanted, soon gave up the unequal battle.

Whenever possible, Eliza saw to it that her stepmother was simply not there, not in the house where she only existed as a regrettable intruder. Her methods were high-handed but effective, and it was wonderful how many little banishments she invented. If shopping had to be done in Devizes, Joy was sent to do it. The car took her there and plenty of time elapsed before it was sent to fetch her away again. She was instructed to return all the calls made on them by neighbours within a radius of twenty miles, and later she played in all the tennis tournaments at these people's houses. The Village Institute was another very useful place of exile. Joy found that she had become one of its most active members and Eliza was always pledging her to join new classes. She protested occasionally, but never for long.

While Mark and Kenneth were struggling on the road under the beech trees, and while Beddoes, tracked down near Helston, was making his first statement to the police, Joy was complaining that she did not want to learn how to make raffia hats.

" But I told Mrs. Stevens," said Eliza, as she handed her father his cup of tea. " I said you were certainly coming. So we'd better put supper at eight-thirty."

" I can't go this evening. It's Helga's night off. I've got to put Peter to bed."

" I'll put him to bed. Mrs. Stevens said they were counting on you."

" I wish you hadn't said I'd go."

" Well, naturally, I thought you would."

Joy looked, from habit, towards Alec. But he did not appear to be listening. She hardly knew what to say. If Eliza would put Peter to bed there was no reason, really, why she should not go up to the Institute. In fact, she quite enjoyed going there, and hearing herself called Mrs. Canning so often that her marriage seemed to be as solid as anybody's else marriage. But she did not like to be sent there by Eliza.

" I don't think I'll go," she said nervously.

" Then," said Eliza, " you'll have to let Mrs. Stevens know. Because she's going to bring round a lot of posters for you and she'll have all her trouble for nothing."

Mrs. Stevens was not on the telephone. Eliza had had reason to be thankful for this before. A message to her would mean that Joy must go up herself, and she would certainly take an hour to make up her mind, by which time it would be too late.

" Do you think I ought to go ? " said Joy, appealing at last directly to Alec.

He was obliged to emerge from the abstraction into which he had so cleverly retired and ask what she meant.

" Don't go," he advised, " if you don't want to."

" Why don't you want to go ? " asked Eliza.

Joy, who was not at all sure, complained that it should not have been settled over her head.

" Oh well," said Eliza crossly, " please yourself ! "

This was a vain command. Poor Joy had no self to please, as they all knew. She sighed and, hearing Peter begin to cry in his play-pen out on the lawn, wandered off to attend to him. Eliza rang the bell for tea to be cleared and muttered :

" It's just because *I* arranged it."

Alec looked round quickly.

He had heard this said before, in almost the same tones. He had heard his mother say it, hundreds of times, when any of her benevolent schemes had been thwarted. Eliza got her bossy ways from both sides of the family.

" It's not really your business," he said dryly. " Joy will, I hope, do exactly as she pleases."

Eliza nodded unconcernedly and began to stack the cups up on the tray. His reproof did not discompose her. Sometimes he said things like this, and she accepted them as a concession to propriety. She knew that he would go no further in support of his wife. He would not, for instance, force her to go up to the village herself and tell Mrs. Stevens that she had made a mistake. He could not have done so. She would have defied him.

To rule her would have been impossible for anyone who was not of the same mettle, as young, as crude, as ruthless as herself. Nor was it likely that such a conquest could be concluded without a considerable amount of passion on both sides. She would yield nothing unless forced to a complete surrender, and must probably be possessed before she could be controlled.

"Supper," she said to the maid who came in for the tray, "will be at half past eight. Mrs. Canning is going to the Institute."

She picked up some rose leaves that had fallen from a bowl and put them into the waste-paper basket. Then she glanced at her father with an eye that suggested that he ought to be getting back to work. She made the cat get out of a chair and shook up the cushions. She glanced at Alec a second time. She re-arranged the newspaper and folded it up neatly. Her third glance galvanized him. She was quite right. He ought to go off now and put in a solid two hours before supper. He was working against time, for he had promised the whole script to Johnnie before the end of August. It was merely an innate disinclination to effort which kept him sitting there.

He got himself out of his chair and went off to his study, obedient to the glance of a commanding woman. All his life it had been like this : first his mother, then Betsy, and now Eliza had taken charge of him. He would never have got anywhere or done anything without them. During the period when Joy had been his only steerswoman he had just sat doing crossword puzzles. And he had put on two stone. Eliza was his salvation.

The scribbled sheets on his desk engaged his mind at once. He came to grips with his task and had finished an important section of it before six o'clock.

The moment's lull, before he began again, was the time when he most felt the discomfort of new surroundings. He missed the wall at Pandy Madoc, where he used to go out and smoke a pipe. At Hampstead there had been the whole of London stretched smokily away beneath his window. He liked standing there and looking out. He

liked working with a view close at hand, and here there
was none. He had his old desk, his chair, his books, but
the window looked out on to a lawn and trees. No doubt
he could get used to it. Already it worried him less.
But it still put him out when he paused in his work, and,
since he had no view, he was getting into the habit of
strolling down to the river for a few minutes to stare at
the patterns on the water. They were a good substitute
for horizons.

He lit a pipe and wandered out on to the lawn. The
baby's pen was still there, and some garden chairs. Somebody would have to fold them all up and put them away
in the summer house. Some chuff-chuffing woman would
come and do it before nightfall. He never thought of
doing it. He ambled across the lawn to the trees on the
edge of the river.

Joy came out of the house, carrying a large cretonne
bag full of raffia materials. Evidently she had made up
her mind to go to her class. She plodded lifelessly towards
the gate.

No longer could she be described as a beautiful girl.
Youth and beauty had departed from her like an extinguished flame. Her yellow hair was lank, she was pinched
and pallid, there was no more resilience in her. But he
had grown so used to seeing her like this that he had
almost forgotten the golden girl who came bounding over
the heather at Llyn Alyn, who brought him his bathing
shoes and gave him a look.

Instinctively, not wanting an encounter, he drew back
among the trees. But she had seen him. She paused
for an instant and then went plodding on. At the gate
she paused again. Perhaps she was resting for a moment,
before climbing the steep hill to the village. Perhaps she
was too stupid to realize how little she was wanted at the
Mill House.

Poor Joy ! he thought. How we treat her !

For he knew, perfectly well, that she was not as stupid

as all that. And he came out of the trees, making as if
to catch sight of her for the first time.

" Hullo ! " he called.

A faint hullo came from the gate. He crossed the grass
and joined her.

" Going to the Institute after all ? "

" Yes," she said. " There wasn't time to send a
message."

" Like an arm up the hill ? "

He repented the offer as soon as he had made it. He
ought to be working. He would lose nearly an hour going
up to the village and back. And her scarlet flush of
pleasure made too much of the concession. She asked for
so little nowadays : when he gave her any attention she
took it with such an ecstasy of dumb gratitude as always
made him feel that he should have given more. But the
thing was done now. He opened the gate, took her work-
bag and gave her an arm up the steep lane. It was hot
and airless, and they panted uphill in silence.

He knew that her fatigue, her lifelessness, came from the
exhaustion of unremitting effort. Every day and every
hour she was forcing herself to leave him alone, to make
no demands, to pursue her own life apart from him. For
his sake she endured Eliza. For his sake she read books,
played tennis and learnt to make raffia hats. He knew it,
but he did not know how to help her. They each had
their own weary burden to bear and neither could lighten
it for the other. Once he had asked her if she would like
to have another baby. But she said no, and she was
probably right, for she had never been able to care very
much for the child that she had.

At the top of the hill, where the slope became less steep,
he thought of something to say. He asked what the
posters were that Mrs. Stevens was bringing for her.

" About Peace," said Joy. " For the meeting next
week. I said I'd take them round to farms and places
and get people to let them be put up on their walls."

" Oh ! Is it League of Nations ? "

" Oh, no ! " she said contemptuously. " I wouldn't walk a yard for the League of Nations. I'm against it."

" Oh, are you, Joy ? Against it ? Why ? "

It did not, she said, do any good. Her meeting was to advocate total and unilateral disarmament. He argued with her for a few minutes, but there is a point beyond which idealism is impregnable.

" Yes," she said, " if another country attacks us we should just have to die. People who die for what is right can't really be defeated. Every person who does it helps the moral force of the world. One martyr can conquer thousands, millions of people. Think of Christ ! Think of Joan of Arc ! "

" She was a good soldier all right. No disarmament for her ! "

" She did more for the world by her martyrdom than she ever did by fighting. There is good and there is evil, always fighting in the world. If you want to save yourself, then you stand for evil. If you stand for good, then you must give yourself up, even your life. People, individuals, have done it. Why not a whole nation ? "

" It never would," was all that Alec could say.

" People probably said that to the early Christians, and they conquered the world."

" Not the world, only the Roman Empire, which was founded on force, on what you call evil. They would never have been heard of outside Asia Minor if St. Paul hadn't been a Roman citizen. They have never conquered the East, for instance."

" Oh, well, Buddhism is so much more spiritual," declared Joy.

" Than what ? "

" Than Christianity. Anyway, if the only thing you can do for good is to die, then you'd better die. Why should it be so fearfully important that we should stay alive ? "

He seemed to remember that he had been through this argument before and had given it up at this point because it was too much trouble to think out a reply. He wondered who it could have been. Then he remembered and laughed.

" You never met Max, did you ? " he asked.

" Lord St. Mullins ? " She looked startled. " No, I never did. Why ? "

" Only you and he are just a pair. You'd get on like a house on fire."

They turned into the village street, where women by twos and threes, all carrying bags full of raffia-work, were making their way towards the institute. He left her at the gate and sauntered back down the lane, back to the calm and comfort of the Mill House, which he was coming to accept as his home.

He was like a convalescent who, after a long and desperate malady, has forgotten what it is to feel perfectly well. His life was so much more tolerable than it had been that he was resigned to its inadequacies. He had his work again, and renewed contacts with the world, and, thanks to Eliza, an orderly household. Nothing very difficult or energetic was now likely to be required of him, and he could continue to take the line of least resistance. A gigantic moral decision was behind him. He had, in grief and anguish, rejected Betsy's offer to return to him because he believed that Joy had a stronger claim. He had taken that fence and now he need do nothing more. Eliza would make him work and see that he did not drink too much.

Johnnie and Susan were coming to stay later in the month. It would be pleasant, like old times, to have the house full of friends. Much had been lost and spoiled, but a very creditable imitation of old times might still be produced. Only he must exert himself to see that the diving board by the river was mended, for that sort of thing could not be trusted to the women.

A motor bicycle was propped up against the fence by

the gate, and he could see a soldier talking to Eliza on the lawn. He was surprised, but not perturbed, or apprehensive of inroads upon his own peace. Whatever the soldier wanted, Eliza would deal with it. She would always stand between him and any kind of worry.

He advanced confidently across the lawn, wondering why the young man looked so familiar, and prepared to be amused if anything at all amusing had occurred. But as he drew closer to them a faint premonition disturbed him. Eliza seemed to be strangely agitated. She did not look as though she were settling anything. As soon as she caught sight of him she began to run and to wave. Her first words were ominous :

" Oh, father ! You must do something ! At once ! "

In the confusion of the next few minutes, while an incredible story was poured out to him, while he disentangled the details and identified their visitor, self-commiseration was his strongest sentiment.

Oh, lord, lord ! he kept thinking. No peace ! Not even now. . . .

If he could have told Eliza to see to it he would have done so. But he could not. An appalling plunge into action lay before him. He must make decisions, accept responsibility, assert himself, and it must all be done at once. They kept on saying that there was not a moment to lose, and he very soon saw that this was true. Both Eliza and Mark were looking at him anxiously. In spite of his dismay he was not a little stung by a touch of doubt in their regard. They were wondering, these little whippersnappers, if he was up to the job. In Eliza this was excusable ; but he did not relish it in young Hannay.

" Where is Kenneth ? " he demanded.

" In the drawing-room," said Eliza, " lying down. He has a most ghastly headache. He didn't want to come. Mark had to bring him almost by force. He had to invent a story about St. Clere's being burnt down to keep him quiet on the way."

Alec went into the house. But he did not go immediately
to the drawing-room. He first paid a visit to the dining-
room, where he mixed himself a double whisky and soda.
It fortified him, but not as much as he had hoped. He
went at last to find Kenneth, feeling that it was all too
much for him.

Kenneth lay upon a sofa with his eyes shut. Standing
beside him, looking down at him, Alec was able to see all
that two years had done to his son. The shock provided
him with the necessary stimulant, for he grew very angry
and extremely anxious to see Beddoes. He swore, under
his breath. Kenneth opened his eyes hazily, saw who it
was and frowned.

" They've told me what's happened," said Alec. " I'm
glad you've come. It's a bad business."

" Mark made me come," said Kenneth. " He forced
me to. You needn't think I'd have come of my own
accord."

" I dare say not. Where is this Beddoes now ? "

" I'm not going to say anything more to you, or the
police, or Mark, or anybody. He's let me down. I
wouldn't have told him if I'd thought he'd treat me like
this."

" But you must, Kenneth. I can't help you unless . . ."

" I don't want your help."

" That has nothing to do with it. Who maintains you ?
Who pays for your education ? "

" Mother does."

" Out of provision made by me. There are certain
things which, as your father, I'm bound to provide for
you whether you like it or not, as long as you are a minor.
It's not a matter for you to decide."

" You're not my guardian."

" Don't you think that your mother would, in these
circumstances, tell you to obey me ? "

Kenneth could not deny this, so he asked sulkily :

" What to you want me to do ? "

" Tell me where to find Beddoes. We must get hold
of the police at once, and you must make your statement
to them. You aren't fit to move. I shall telephone for
them to come here. You must give them your account
and undertake to remain here, in case they want you
again. Then I'll go and see this Beddoes. . . ."

" It's no use. He'll say . . ."

" He won't, after I've seen him."

Alec's face and voice as he said this brought enormous
reassurance to Kenneth. He gave an impression of real
formidability and Kenneth knew that Beddoes could never
stand against strength. Bruce Blackett had shown him
up in thirty seconds.

"Perhaps he's said it already. They may have traced
the car."

" Then he'll take it back, or one of the others will.
I'll see them all, and I'll get proper legal advice for
you."

Alec hesitated and then asked :

" You were in Sweden with him last year, weren't
you ? "

" Yeah."

" I can deal with him more effectively if I know the
whole story," prompted Alec, upon whom certain hints
from Mark had not been lost.

" You do, don't you ? "

"Not all." Alec sat down on the end of the sofa.
" What made you take up with him at all ? He seems
to be a pretty fair cad."

" I don't know. Can't I have friends ? "

" You've known him for some time. You must have
known what he was. Didn't you ? "

" Yeah."

To get the whole story was not difficult, for Kenneth's
resistance was exhausted. He answered in grunts and
monosyllables, but Alec was satisfied that he was getting
the truth.

" You meant to drop him and then found that you couldn't ? "

" Yes."

" I see. Well, I'll deal with him."

" I suppose you think I'm a rotter."

" I'm afraid I do rather."

" If I am, I expect I take after you."

" I expect so," said Alec gravely. " We both have weak characters. We let ourselves be dominated by stronger people. It's a bad fault. But it can be cured."

" Weak ! " cried Kenneth in amazement. " You ! "

He gasped. Never had he thought of his father as weak. His fantasy had been quite otherwise. He had always imagined Alec as a bold, unscrupulous villain who did what he pleased and cared nothing for the suffering that he caused. This interpretation of events bewildered him.

" Weakness," said Alec, " has made hay of my life. I have always meant well, and I've generally seen quite clearly what I ought to do, but I've seldom had the strength of mind to do it if it meant a struggle with anybody. You are young, and you haven't quite done for yourself yet. There's hope for you if you pull your socks up."

He got up to go and telephone to the police.

" I don't think we're alike in the least," declared Kenneth. " I should never have thought you were weak."

" Then you'd better think again," said Alec, rather grimly as he went out.

ELIZA

MARK helped Eliza to put away the chairs and the play-pen on the lawn. After the first burst of question and answer, when he had told her all that he knew of Kenneth's predicament, they fell silent and had nothing more to say for a time.

Mark was preoccupied, wondering how the interview between the father and son was going off, and if there was anything more that he could do.

Eliza was dumb with shyness and dismay. The change in her friend, apparent even to Kenneth's distracted eye, was overwhelming to her. Everything that she had admired in him seemed to have disappeared : his air of distinction, his arrogance, even his beauty. She found him indescribably altered and coarsened. He smiled at her, quite often, in a friendly way, but his smile was the most disconcerting thing about him. The rare smiles of the old Mark had been bestowed with a full consciousness of their value. He had never given this impression of unassuming geniality.

She had known that he was in the army ; Kenneth had told her so at Christmas, opining that some kind of socialistic bee had got into his bonnet. She had been puzzled, but impressed ; she thought of it as a most romantic sacrifice and beheld Mark as a saint, a hero, who must make an immediate impression upon everybody who met him. His new surroundings would be, no doubt, uncongenial, but they could never change him or quench his power to seem different from other people. Sometimes she decided that his companions would persecute him, sometimes that they would worship him. She pictured the mystery which would surround this interesting young recruit, the speculations of the officers, the rapid promotion.

And now this heroic creation was shattered by a commonplace, alert young man with a pleasant smile and a ruddy blob of a face. She wanted to ask a thousand questions, but she did not know how to talk to this stranger. And besides, he was, to her eyes, quite grown up—a man, not a boy any more.

" You can keep Ken here now ? " he asked when they had carried the chairs into the summer-house. " You've got a bed for him, I mean ? "

" Oh, yes ! Heaps of beds. We've three spare rooms."

" Good. Then I think I'd better be getting off again. There's nothing more I can do."

" Oh ! " said Eliza forlornly.

She had not the courage or the words to dissuade him. She turned away to pick up a bundle which she had left on the floor of the summer-house. He picked it up for her, saw that it was a bathing dress and towel, and exclaimed :

" Oh ! Is there bathing here ? Where ? '

" In the river. Just down the garden. I was going when you and Ken came."

A dazzling hope inspired her and she suggested that he might bathe too. He said that he would like nothing better. He was hot and sticky from his ride and he still enjoyed a bathe beyond any other pleasure. So she found him a towel and a spare suit belonging to Alec and took him down to the mouldy little bathing hut under the beech trees. It smelt of fungus, people, and river mud, and it was divided into two cells by a low partition.

When they were each shut into a separate cell Eliza's shyness departed. This semi-solitude reassured her, and now that she could no longer see him she could talk to him. They shouted over the partition, their voices occasionally muffled by the clothes that they were pulling off. She bombarded him with questions.

" How do you like being in the army ? "

" Very much. I'm enjoying it very much."

" I didn't think you would somehow."

" Nor did I quite as much as I am."

" What especially ? "

" I like the work. I like some of the men I'm with, and I like the life . . . the . . ."

His shirt was over his head and she could not hear.

" The what ? "

" The freedom."

" The *freedom* ? "

" I know it sounds funny. It's not very easy to explain."

" I should have thought it would be a sort of strain to live boxed up with a lot of other people."

" It's not so different from St. Clere's. We had a pretty communal life there."

" But isn't it . . . don't they . . . don't they think you're . . . sort of . . . odd ? "

" I don't know. They may ; but if they do it doesn't worry me."

" They don't rag you, then ? "

" Not now."

" They did at first ? "

" A bit. Some people didn't like my accent and thought it meant I wanted to give myself airs. You'll always find some people in any community who will dislike anyone who is different from themselves. They'll give you a bad time if you don't stand up to them, or if you lose your temper. It's the same everywhere. You've got to establish your right to be what you are. If you are singular in any way it isn't quite such easy going."

" But most of them didn't ? "

" Oh, most people are pretty tolerant as long as you aren't offensive. They won't stand up for you, if you let yourself be ragged, but they'll let you alone as long as you leave them alone."

He was going out of the hut as he spoke, and the last words were shouted over his shoulder. A moment later she heard a splash.

When she came out he was swimming up and down in the dappled sunshine. His black hair was plastered down over his eyes, so that he looked exactly as he used to look when they went swimming in Llyn Alyn. She jumped in too, relaxing her body to the smooth current which carried them both rapidly beyond the garden.

" There's more current than you'd think," he said, catching at a branch.

" Yes. The nice thing is to swim right up, as far as you can, to the bend. It's weedy after that, and not safe. Then you float down."

They did this blissfully for half an hour. It was very hard work to swim up to the bend, where a great beech tree spread layers of leaves over the water. The reward came when they lay on their backs and drifted gently out of the green shade into the sunshine, down between meadow banks and alders to the garden again. Mark always got to the beech tree first and held on to a branch, with the current frilling round his neck, till Eliza joined him and they could float down together.

" You said freedom," she said, as they were carried down for the second time. " I don't understand that. You mean freedom from responsibility ? "

" Partly, perhaps. But it's more a kind of mental freedom you get when you are living under a definite discipline. If none, or very few, of the details of your life are settled by your own choice—what you do, what you eat, who you are with, and all that—it sets your mind very free. What you are and feel and think don't matter. They don't signify. So you can feel and be and think what you like quite light-heartedly. Almost frivolously."

" I don't quite see. In that case a servant or a slave is freer than his master."

" He often is. He doesn't have to take himself so seriously. When you are your own master your preferences matter a great deal because you arrange your life to suit them. You spend your time wondering what they really are. You're burdened with a number of choices and decisions. If you have toothache it's a very serious matter. There's something wrong with the way the world has been made. If a slave has toothache it hurts, and that's that."

They had come to the end of that float and could not talk while they were swimming up. But Eliza thought over what he had said and, when next they came down, she argued :

" But in that case everybody had better be slaves."

" Not exactly. A slave doesn't live under discipline but at another man's caprice, which must damage his self-respect. And I said the freedom is enjoyable. I don't know if it's entirely admirable. I think it may have its uses in making the mind more supple, but suppleness is not the only virtue."

After a while they went and lay on the bank in the long grass. Mark fetched some cigarettes from the hut and smoked. But he did not offer one to Eliza, and she felt a little ruffled that he should still so clearly regard her as a mere schoolgirl.

" May I have one, please ? " she asked, smiling.

He looked surprised, but gave her one and lit it for her in silence. She had an uncomfortable feeling that he knew she had never smoked before.

" Well," she said, " but doesn't being at St. Clere's, all your education, make any difference ? "

" Yes," said Mark, grinning, " it does. I got into hot water right away with the Education Officer because my handwriting is so bad. It is said to be quite illegible and worse than Gyppo Smith's, who can hardly write his own name."

" I mean . . . don't you . . . sort of miss intellectual companionship ? Have you got anyone to talk to ? "

" Plenty of the men have most interesting minds, and lots to say that is worth hearing. Of course none of them could get a Balliol scholarship to save their lives, but that's only one way of judging people's minds. And a rather narrow way. One reason . . . the chief reason why I didn't go to the University . . ."

" Yes ? " said Eliza eagerly.

He paused, wondering why he was talking so freely to her. Since his conversation with Parkin on River Cliff he had never explained himself so fully to anybody. Well, he wanted to tell her. It was one of those frivolous impulses in which, as a free man, he could indulge.

" I mean . . . my education was all a preparation for a certain mental virtuosity, a very hard, clear, reasoned way of thinking, and examining evidence, and defending a logical position. I was taught to regard anybody who didn't bear the hall-mark of this training as woolly-minded and half-educated. It's a useful training in its way as far as it goes. But . . . I say, Eliza, do you really like eating gold flakes ? Does that one taste nice ? "

Eliza, blushing deeply, buried the mangled remains of her first cigarette in the grass.

" But," he continued, " if you really want to find out what other people are thinking, and how they've reached their conclusions, it's no use at all. You can argue the hind leg off a donkey, but that won't teach you any more about donkeys. Whatever method you may have used in forming your own opinions, you must understand other people's methods before you can hope to get anyone to agree with you. You'll never induce a man to change his mind by making him look silly. You merely put his back up."

" Then you want to get people to agree with you ? What about ? "

But now she had asked too many questions. He said

that he did not know, and asked if she had any idea of the time.

" I'm glad," she said, " that you don't believe in arguing so much. I think everybody at St. Clere's is just silly about it. Do you remember when you said the river flowed uphill at Pandy Madoc ? "

" When did I say such a thing ? "

" Don't you remember ? You and Ken got lost, and you went on and on up a stream expecting somehow to find the sea at the top. And when I told you that water can't flow uphill you started to argue. You made me feel like a perfect idiot, telling me everything I said was a *non sequitur* and I'd got an undistributed middle, till you'd actually forced me into admitting that water can flow uphill. But I *knew* it didn't. I thought then all this arguing is stuff, and it makes people more stupid instead of less."

He laughed and got up to go into the hut. She was sorry to see him go. She asked quickly :

" Then you're glad you went into the army ? It's been what you wanted ? "

He considered for a moment, stretching his arms above his head.

" I'm enjoying it much more than I expected. Perhaps I thought it would be more of an experience, somehow. Make me different. It hasn't done that."

" Oh, but it has."

" You think so ? How ? "

" Why . . . you are more . . . composed."

" Composed ? What a funny word ! "

" I dare say it isn't the right one. Anyway, you never know you are having an experience until you've had it. A real one, I mean. It isn't till afterwards that you see what a difference it's made."

He laughed again and went into the hut.

She did not immediately follow him. She lay, chewing grass, and wondering what she had meant by composed.

Also she was beginning to feel that there had been some-thing lacking in this most pleasant conversation. It did not follow quite smoothly upon their last one, when he had told her that she was a first-rate creature. For any thing that he had said to-day he might never have made that momentous remark. Yet her whole life, ever since, had been moulded by it. Belief in herself, as a first-rate creature had given her strength to make painful decisions and had upheld her in the management of her father's household. She had never doubted but that all her actions would have earned Mark's unqualified approval. And she felt now that she would like to hear that approval restated, so as to forge some link between this meeting and their memorable parting upon the head master's doorstep.

For he was changed. He judged now, possibly, by other standards, and it was not so easy to guess what he was thinking. It would be disaster if he no longer found her admirable. She did wish that she had not tried to show off about that cigarette. He might have got quite a wrong idea of her, and then he had had no chance to know of her recent good deeds. Before he went away his attention must certainly be called to all that she had endured and performed, for she would die unless she was certain of his good opinion. The change in him, if change there was, did not alter that fact.

She went back into the hut.

" I'm living here now, you know," she called over the partition, as she stripped off her bathing dress.

" Always ? All the time ? Not sometimes with your mother ? "

His voice came back with a reassuring note of interest.

" Always. She can get on without me, you see, but they can't."

No reply came to this for a long time. Mark was sitting on a bench winding on his puttees, a job at which he never excelled. She stood stark naked and gazed forlornly at

the mouldy boards between them. Presently she heard
a muffled :

" Why ? "

" Well, I have to run everything. Joy is head duffer
of the world. Father simply wouldn't get any meals if
I wasn't here."

" Didn't he get any before you came ? "

" I don't think so. She's perfectly helpless."

" What happens when you go to school ? "

" Oh, I've left school. They can't do without me."

" I say ! That's not such a bad break for you, is it ?
You always hated school."

She tugged at her suspender belt. Something was going
wrong, and her first-rate qualities were failing to penetrate
the partition. She supplied further details of her sufferings
and struggles, and presently she heard him open the door
of his cell. He was going out. She burst into indignant
protest.

" Oh, you are selfish ! You've told me all about yourself, and when I start telling you my things you go away."

" Well, you kept asking questions. And why did you
wait till I was nearly dressed before you started on the
story of your life ? I can't stay here. It's smelly. Hurry
up and come out and tell me all about it."

She dressed quickly and went out. On the river bank
she found again a pleasant young stranger in khaki.

" Well ? " he asked kindly.

She pretended not to understand.

" Well . . . what ? "

" What about you ? "

" Oh, I don't suppose it would interest you particularly.
Why should it ? "

He said nothing for a few seconds. Everything about
Eliza interested him, though he had never thought about
her very much. Somewhere, buried in his heart, lay the
germ of an intense feeling for her. He half guessed this
and wanted to keep it buried. What they were to be to

one another must be left to time. To anticipate it would be to belittle something that might turn out to be grave and important.

He ignored her half petulant, half provocative tone, and said gently :

" It does. Start and tell me everything that has happened since . . . since you went into the head master's house."

Eliza turned quickly to look at him. She grew quite pale. Then he must remember what he had said ! She could not speak. They walked on towards the house in silence, both staring at the ground.

Her pale, shining glance was a shock to him. He had never supposed that she could be conscious of anything special between them. That idea should have been entirely his own, something which he meant to explore fully when the proper time came. Until he had made up his own mind, Eliza had no business to dream of such a thing. She was too young. They were both too young.

Their silent, ecstatic progress was interrupted by Joy, who came dragging across the lawn with her bag of raffia and a great roll of posters. Eliza was too much distracted to introduce Mark, so he introduced himself and reminded Joy that they had met at Pandy Madoc.

" Oh ! " was all that Joy could find to say.

" Ken is here," said Eliza abruptly.

" Ken ! Why . . . how . . . how did he come ? "

" On Mark's motor-bike."

Joy turned towards the house, and Eliza added :

" Don't go into the drawing-room. Ken's there with father and they don't want to be disturbed."

" Has . . . has anything happened ? " asked Joy.

" Oh, yes," said Eliza wearily, " thousands of things. Ken will be staying here. You might tell them to make up the bed in the . . . no . . . perhaps he'd better have the little room next yours."

Mark listened impassively. They might all, he thought,

be back at Pandy Madoc. Here was Joy meekly taking orders, not from Betsy, but from Eliza, who was getting to look and to speak more like her mother every minute.

" And tell them there'll be two extra for supper. You'll stay, won't you, Mark ? "

" I think I ought to be getting back," he said.

" Oh, but it's practically supper-time now ! You can stay a little longer, can't you ? "

Mark looked at Joy. But she said nothing. She just stood there in a dazed way and then went plodding off towards the house.

" I don't think I'd better stay," he said, when she was out of earshot. " Mrs. Canning didn't seem to be very keen on the idea."

" Joy ? Joy ! She wouldn't think of asking you."

" Then I shouldn't think of staying."

" But I've asked you."

" I know. But she didn't, and it's her house after all."

" She never would. She's as dumb as a fish. I'll bring her back and make her ask you."

" No, Eliza ! No ! "

He caught her wrist and held her back when she would have started after Joy.

" You don't understand. I run the house."

" That must be nice for her," he observed, dropping her wrist.

" It's not that she doesn't want you. Only it's about twenty-four hours before she takes anything in."

" Then we'd better leave her to take Kenneth in. That should be quite enough for her . . . if she's got to put up with the two of you. . . . I'm off anyway."

He was not smiling and pleasant any more. His eyes were quite hard, and he looked at her as if he thoroughly disliked her.

" Say good-bye to them for me," he added, " and thank you for the bathe. It was nice."

He turned and walked away to the gate. A moment

later the sound of a motor-cycle starting up echoed through the valley. It rose, roared and died away in the distance.

Eliza stood where he had left her. The whole of her world came tumbling down about her ears. Her words to Joy, so bullying, so contemptuous, came back to her, and she heard them as he did. Nothing that she had ever done seemed good any more. She was despicable because he thought her so.

NOBODY else noticed that he had gone.

Joy found the house full of policemen who had arrived while Mark and Eliza were bathing. And then it was discovered that Kenneth's temperature was one hundred and two, so they put him to bed. A doctor was summoned who diagnosed shock, exposure and slight sunstroke. Alec departed for Cornwall in the middle of the night, and, next morning, newspaper reporters began to telephone and to call at the house. Joy answered their questions, but she could not tell them much, for nobody had told her what it was all about. The fact that Kenneth was the son of a peeress seemed to excite them a good deal. They were interested to learn that Betsy was Kenneth's guardian, that she had gone abroad, leaving him to his own devices, and that he had not seen his father for two years. They thanked Joy very much for telling them that. It was, as one of them observed, a very human story.

It was unlucky that Eliza should have selected that particular moment to abdicate from the management of the house. She would probably have been less communicative. But she remained invisible for the greater part of the day, shut up in her room, leaving Joy to her own devices.

Late that night, after everybody had gone to bed, Alec returned. Joy had been listening for him and went to the head of the stairs.

" How is Ken ? " he asked when he saw her.

" Better. Dr. Grainger thinks he is decidedly better this evening."

" Good. Everything is all right, you'll be glad to hear."
She was glad, though uncertain of what he meant.

" I'll just get a drink and come up," he said, going into
the dining-room. " It's been the hell of a day. Go back
to bed, dear, and I'll come up and tell you."

There was a creak of a door and Eliza, pale and tearful,
peeped out of her room.

" Everything's all right," Joy told her.

" How ? What's happened ? "

" I don't know yet. But he says it's all right."

" He's made them tell the truth ? "

" Yes, I suppose so," said Joy, wondering who " they "
were.

Eliza sighed and vanished again. Joy looked into
Kenneth's room and found him awake. She repeated her
cheerful formula.

" I don't believe it is," Kenneth muttered. " Of course
he'd say that."

They heard Alec on the stairs and Joy called to him
softly. He came in and stood by Kenneth's bed, looking
tired and grim.

" You don't have to worry," he said without elation.
" They've all admitted that Beddoes was driving."

" Did you make them say so ? "

" I didn't have to. It had all come out before I got
there. They got hold of Beddoes and Hastings near
Helston, yesterday afternoon. They both swore that you
were driving and that they had held their tongues for your
sake. . . ."

" They did ? They did ? " cried Kenneth, starting up.

" No, it's all right. McCrae seems to have quarrelled
with them that morning and parted company with them.
He went to the police at Exeter, late last night, and volun-
teered a statement which entirely corroborates your
account of the matter. The police interviewed them again
early this morning, before I got there ; they tried to bluff
it a bit, but they both ended by admitting that McCrae's

story was true. You'll be blamed for not reporting the accident as soon as you possibly could, but not seriously, I think, since you were the youngest of the party."

" Then . . . then I'm out of it ? "

" You may have to give evidence at the inquest, I'm afraid, but that will be a very simple matter. The date for that isn't fixed yet."

" Shall I have to see . . . Beddoes . . . again ? " asked Kenneth with a shiver.

" I expect you will, for a few minutes, But I shall be there. You'll have nothing to worry about."

Alec's tone was flat and gloomy and his manner was not reassuring.

" You don't sound as if it was all right."

" I've had a tiring day."

Kenneth's feverish eyes searched his face and he was forced to add, more cheerfully :

" You're out of the wood all right, Ken. In a few days you'll be able to forget about it."

Alone with Joy, in her room, he gave vent to his depression.

" It's a stinking business. They all show up so badly. McCrae comes best out of it. But it's a shocking thing that Ken should have been going about with such a crew. It's a black mark against us all. If he'd been properly looked after, it wouldn't have happened."

" It's not your fault," said Joy.

" Oh . . . I don't know. I'm dreading the inquest . . . the publicity."

" That poor girl ! It said in the paper to-day that it was her birthday."

Alec gave a groan.

" I know ! I know ! That's what one ought to think about. I stopped in Salisbury, on my way back, to see the inspector, and ran into the poor girl's mother, who was at the station. I felt such a brute. Here is this child dead, and when one thinks what it means, what an agony of grief for her wretched parents . . . and all we've been thinking of is how to shift the blame, how to avoid responsibility. Those four young brutes drive on with no thought in the world, apparently, except their own skins, and leave her lying in the road."

"You'd have thought," agreed Joy, "that Mark Hannay would have behaved better."

"Hannay? But he wasn't there."

"Oh, wasn't he? I thought he was. Why did he come here then?"

"He brought Ken. He . . . by the way! What happened to him last night? I never saw him again, never thanked him."

"I don't know. He went off just before supper I think."

"I must see him again. We must get him over here again. If it hadn't been for him, God knows. . . . He insisted on Kenneth's coming to me, you know."

Joy did not know. He found that she knew nothing except what she had read in the papers. A little shocked that such a state of things could exist, he began to tell her the whole story. His room opened out of hers and he undressed as he talked, leaving the door open. He generally slept there, but, by the time that he was ready for bed, he had not half finished. So he got into Joy's bed, switched off the light, and continued to talk in the dark.

"It's not so much what to do at the moment," he said. "I think we can get him out of this, all right, and he won't ever see any of them again. But I'm worried about his future. He's in a bad way, physically and mentally. Nerves all in pieces. . . ."

Their voices rose and fell in low murmurs, just audible to Kenneth who lay tossing next door. He listened resentfully. It occurred to him that his mother and Max were also lying in bed, somewhere, jawing away, completely absorbed in their own concerns. The idea made him feel lonely and desolate.

How they can do these things, he thought. How they can ! I don't understand any of them.

At last the sounds died away into silence.

There was no more excitement or mystery about his father and Joy. They were just a married couple. His picture of them as a guilty pair, indulging in illicit passion, had been as fantastic as his belief in his mother's inviolable truth. They were all of them quite incomprehensible to him, and he would never know what they thought, how they felt, or why they had acted as they did. He only knew that he was very miserable. The night was going to be endless and to-morrow would not be any better because there was still that inquest in front of him.

An hour later he was knocking on the wall. Joy heard him and slipped out of bed very carefully, so as not to waken Alec.

" This room's haunted," complained Kenneth, " I've seen a ghost."

" Oh, nonsense ! "

" A thing came out of the wall, like an enormous white cigar, six feet long. It's here still, only it keeps just out of sight."

" You've been dreaming. Have a drink. Have some barley water."

She shook up his pillows and gave him a drink. He caught at her hand, begging her not to leave him alone with that thing, until she promised to stay for a little. She brought a chair to his bedside, and wrapped herself up in his eiderdown.

He dozed and muttered, still clinging to her hand. Whenever she tried to move, his grasp tightened. So she sat on for hours in a house so quiet that she could hear the faint whisper of the mill race, out in the night.

In the grey of early morning he woke and lay looking at her attentively. He was struck by the stern gravity of her expression.

" Why do you look so sad ? " he asked.

She started from her reverie and turned to him.

" You're feeling better ? "

" Yes. Yes, I am. Why do you look so solemn ? What are you thinking about ? "

She coloured slightly.

" I wasn't sad," she said. " I was thinking about something very difficult. About a paper I've got to write. I was planning what I was going to say."

" A paper ? What for ? "

" For the Institute. They've asked me to read a paper to the literary group, on the tendencies of Modern Drama."

" Oh, really ? " asked Kenneth with a faint grin. " And what shall you say ? "

" Well, I shall say that he was the first dramatist who really had a message. Before that, the drama was simply for entertainment."

" Who is ? "

" George Bernard Shaw."

" Oh, yes. What other dramatists will you talk about ? "

" I shall mention Ibsen, of course, because he influenced Shaw."

" I don't call them moderns, exactly."

" Perhaps not Ibsen. But Shaw is still alive."

" Then you think people are modern until they are dead ? "

" Of course they are."

" Who else will you talk about ? "

" I don't believe I'll have time for anybody else."

Kenneth would have loved to argue with her, and to fluster her thoroughly as to the true meaning of modernism. But his head ached too much.

He made up his mind, however, to be at the Mill House when Joy read her paper on Shaw. That was something which he could not possibly miss. He carefully memorized their conversation, so that he might be able to repeat it, word for word, to Eliza who would certainly agree with him that it was gloriously funny.

But in this he was disappointed. Eliza, when told of it, would not admit that it was funny at all. She said at once that they ought not to laugh at Joy, who had been so nice to them, and that it could be no fun for her to have the house full of stepchildren who got sunstroke and mocked her. But she said it without much spirit. So low had she sunk in her own estimation that her reproofs sounded like timid suggestions. Kenneth proceeded to demolish her.

" You can argue the hind leg off a donkey," she told him. " But that won't teach you any more about donkeys ! "

" I know all I want to know about donkeys."

Her strange state of mind would have been more noticeable if the household had been less preoccupied. Joy had talked a great deal too much to the reporters, as was evident when the newspapers came next morning. There happened to be a dearth of news that week and the Press made the most of the story. Headlines announced that the son of a peeress and a distinguished writer had been implicated in the Salisbury car mystery. The divorce was recollected and received far more publicity than it had had at the time. There were hints of a dramatic reconciliation at the Mill House, when the terrified boy went to consult the father from whom he had been alienated for two years. It made pleasant reading in a million homes, but the Cannings felt that they could never look at a newspaper again without feeling a little sick.

Alec was still more worried than he cared to admit, and had secured Counsel to appear on Kenneth's behalf if necessary. He knew the ways of coroners and was aware of the intensity of popular indignation. The more he learnt about Beddoes the more he dreaded the effects of any public inquiry into the boy's character. It was possible, he felt, that they might all be on the edge of a pretty scandal in which Kenneth's name might suffer irreparably.

But of this he said nothing to anyone. His whole care

was to seem as calm as possible and to keep Kenneth
steady. So that he had little attention to give to his
daughter, and was surprised when Joy said :

" I wish I knew what has upset Eliza so much. She
doesn't seem a bit like herself somehow."

" Isn't all this enough to upset anybody ? "

" No, but that grouse really was too high to eat."

" The grouse Johnnie sent us ? Was that Eliza's
fault ? "

" Not exactly. Gladys asked her when she should cook
it, and Eliza told her to ask me, and I didn't know, so it
got hung too long. I mean, Eliza won't settle anything
any more, or say what is to be done. She even asked my
leave to change Peter's smock."

" Sounds like an improvement. She's inclined to be too
bumptious, generally."

" Yes. But she's unhappy."

There was no malice in Joy. She had suffered a good
deal at Eliza's hands, and she had resented it, but she did
not like to see the girl unhappy. For Eliza to become,
suddenly, very much nicer might be, she felt, a pleasant
change for everybody except Eliza herself. People, in
Joy's experience, did not become nicer at this pace without
some violent and painful stimulus. To improve at all is
uphill work. But it is better to toil heavenwards upon
aching feet than to be blown up by a charge of dynamite.
She felt this so strongly that she was moved to do something which she had never done before : she proffered
wifely counsel.

" You mustn't," she said, " get too sort of wrapped up in
Kenneth."

" He happens to be a full-time job at the moment."

" I know. But when this is over . . . I mean . . . we
made a great fuss of Eliza coming . . . she is our child,
too. When . . . if Ken is with us now, a lot, it will be a
bit hard for her to take a back seat, when she has always
been so much to you."

" Very good for her. You know, Joy, if you agree, I think I'll try to take Ken somewhere as soon as *Byron* is produced. He ought to have a thorough change. I'm not sure about his going back to school for this last year. I want to get him right away. Bobby Malcolm is always asking me to go over and stay on his ranch in Mexico. What do you think ? "

" I think it would be splendid. But couldn't you take them both ? "

" Eliza too ? Lord, no ! "

" Then you must give her some sort of change as well. She's too young just to settle down here and vegetate. Perhaps she might like to go abroad and work at her music."

" But then you'd be all alone here, for some months."

" I don't think that would matter. I have a lot to do at the Institute. And . . . if you wouldn't mind . . ." she hesitated " . . . I should very much like to ask my mother to stay."

He was surprised. She never talked about her mother, never, indeed, talked very much about anything connected with her past life. For him she had always been a creature singularly without background ; he had no picture of her home or her childhood, no glimpse into all those memories and incidents which go to make up personality. But the personality was there, all the time, and now it was beginning to shine out, a little uncertainly, like the sun behind a mist.

" But certainly," he said. " Do ask her."

He was so much absorbed in his own troubles that he scarcely realized what was happening. Afterwards he used to think that Joy and he had never really got on together very well until that frightful business over Kenneth. He supposed that it had brought them together.

MAX AND BETSY

ON the day of the inquest Alec and Kenneth departed early for Salisbury. It was a very hot day, and an unnatural quiet seemed to descend on the house after they were gone. Eliza and Joy sat waiting for news. Nobody came down to see them from the village. The maids hid in the kitchen, alert but silent.

After luncheon Eliza went up to her bedroom, unable any longer to bear with Joy, who kept fidgeting and exclaiming and wondering what was happening now. She lay down on her bed, had a little nap, and was awakened by a tap at her door.

"What is it?" she cried, starting up as Joy came in. "Has any news come?"

"No, no! Not yet. But there's something awful happened. Lord St. Mullins is downstairs."

"Max! But I thought he was in Geneva."

"Well, he's here. Whatever shall we do? I was lying down, too, and Clara brought up the message. He says he wants to see me."

"He must have seen all this about Ken in the papers and come to find out what's happened."

"Somebody ought to go down. You go, Eliza."

Eliza began hastily to pull a comb through her curls. She was so sleepy and dazed that she had not quite grasped the situation. Habit reasserted itself and she was prepared to go down and, as her father's spokeswoman, settle Kenneth's business with Max. But, a moment later, her trouble raised its head. She remembered that she was miserable, and why, and she turned quickly to Joy.

" No, old dear. I don't think it would do if I went.
He asked for you."

" Clara said he asked for Alec, and then, when he heard
Alec was away, he asked if he could see me."

" Then you must go. I expect he has come to take Ken
away."

" Oh, Eliza, I couldn't. You go, for goodness sake."

" But I can't go and discuss Ken as if I was a parent
or something."

" I'd be so terrified."

" You mustn't be. You're the head of the house.
Father would be awfully upset if you didn't see him."

" But what shall I say ? They can't have Ken.
They've neglected him terribly—and now Alec has so
many plans——"

" Just tell him anything he wants to know. He's quite
nice. Very kind and simple. And tell him he must wait
and see father. And offer him tea and all that. . . ."

" Oh, but you'll come too. You must."

" I'll get you into the room and introduce you. But
then I shall melt away while you talk about Ken. It will
look better. Powder your nose before you go down, my
dear. That'll make you feel braver."

Eliza's powder advertised the fact that the poor girl
had no mother to guide her. It was of the wrong colour,
far too light a shade for her warm brown skin. She
liberally dusted her own face and that of her stepmother,
and they both went nervously downstairs looking as if
they had just emerged from a flour mill. Even Max,
who seldom noticed externals, thought their appearance
rather strange.

" You know Joy, don't you ? " said Eliza, when she had
greeted him.

Then, crimson with shyness, she endeavoured to intro
duce them formally.

" Lord Canning . . . Mrs. St. Mullins. . . ."

It was a most awful thing to have said. But neither

of them noticed anything wrong. They were too much taken up with their own embarrassments.

Max shook hands with Joy, very earnestly and gravely, as if to convey a deep personal respect which might console her for having been, at one time, in an unfortunate position. His customary benevolence was at work and he had begun to believe the best of her. Up till that moment she had been, to him, a wanton and a home wrecker. Now that he had met her she became a poor girl who had given everything for love.

She was not at all what he had expected. Betsy had talked so much about her beauty, quoting it as an excuse for Alec's rash folly, that he had imagined a much more attractive woman. His surprise and her shyness kept them quite incoherent for some time. He apologized repeatedly for being there. She apologized for Alec's not being there. And so they went on. Had Eliza been in any condition to notice them she must have laughed.

At the end of five minutes they had got no further than this : that a telegram had been sent from Geneva which had never reached the Mill House.

" How unfortunate ! How very unfortunate ! " Max kept exclaiming. " Then you weren't expecting us at all ? Naturally, as soon as we had seen the English newspapers, we thought we ought to come at once, that you would expect it. But we wired. . . . How very unfortunate ! This is the first time I have ever known such a thing to happen."

" But even if we had got the wire Alec would have had to go to Salisbury," Joy was saying. " You see he had to go. It is the inquest to-day. Would you like to go there after him ? Or would you like to wait ? I am so sorry. So very sorry. . . ."

" We'd have been here much sooner if the flying conditions hadn't been so bad. Oh yes . . . we flew. But of course we wired to warn you. . . ."

Eliza was now so far recovered that she could take

notice of what they were saying. It struck her that Max
was not, apparently, alone.

" But is Mother here ? " she exclaimed.

" She . . . she's in England . . . yes . . ." said Max,
hesitating. " She came back with me."

And he looked exceedingly guilty, for Betsy was, in
fact, only half a mile off, looking at the tombstones in
the churchyard. She had declared that she did not want
to go to the Mill House unless her presence there was
absolutely necessary, in which case he was to send for her.
Otherwise her being in the neighbourhood was to be kept
a secret. But, in his confusion, he had not chosen his
words well.

" Where is she ? " asked Eliza, upon whom his guilty
looks had not been lost. " At Hornwood ? "

" No."

He turned in a panic to Joy and actually came to the
point, driven to it by the need to escape from Eliza's
questions.

" What is all this about Kenneth ? What has happened ? "

Eliza, ignoring Joy's appealing eyes, slipped out of the
room.

A large car, which had brought Max from the
aerodrome, was standing outside the front door.
Eliza looked into it and saw a woman's tweed over-
coat.

" Is Lady St. Mullins up in the village ? " she asked the
driver.

" Yes, miss. At the church."

" Can you just run me up there ! I've got a message
for her."

She jumped into the car, smiling at her own cleverness
and acumen. But, by the time that they got to the lych
gate of the church, her confidence had leaked away again.
She wondered why she had come. Her mother did not,
apparently, want to see her ; nor could she be sure, when

she came to think of it, that she wanted to see her mother.
They would have nothing to say to one another.

She walked slowly up the flagged path through the
churchyard, and in the porch she paused, half minded to
slip away again. Yet there was something wrong, something a little unpleasant, about the idea of that. It gave
her a sensation of roughness and discord ; as if things
had not been done quite properly.

I'll just go in and kiss her, she thought, and come away
again. That's all I want to do, really. Just to kiss
her.

There were quick footsteps on the pavement inside the
church and Betsy appeared.

" Eliza ! "

" Oh, Mother ! "

Now we kiss. You are my mother. I am your daughter.
What does that mean ? Does it mean anything ? You
gave me birth ; you carried me once in your body. Have
you forgotten ?

" Darling, how did you know I was here ? " demanded
Betsy uneasily.

" Oh, I guessed. Max didn't let on, but I saw your
coat in the car so I asked the driver. And I thought I'd
just pop up and see you."

!' Oh ? Oh yes . . . then nobody else knows ? "

" Nobody."

" I see." Betsy looked relieved. " But my dear !
What on earth have you done to your face ? "

" My face ? "

" It's all . . . oh it's powder ! My *dear* Eliza ! "

" Of course it's powder. You wouldn't like me to have
a shiny nose, would you ? "

" My child ! If you must use powder at your age, do
at least find a more becoming shade. What possessed you
to put dead white on a skin like yours ? "

" It's not dead white," muttered Eliza furiously. " It's
Rachel."

" Try Ochre next time. I'm sorry, darling, but you look a perfect little guy."

Eliza was not grateful for the hint, although she took it the very next day. Furtively rubbing her nose with a handkerchief, she followed Betsy out into the churchyard where they strolled about, looking at the tombstones.

" Malachi Miller," spelt out Betsy. " This is a quaint one !

> " In perfecte hilthe I wente from Home
> Nor littel guessed myne houre was come . . ."

What is all this about Ken ? What *has* he been doing ? "

While Eliza was telling her she sat down to rest on a low box tomb. Sometimes she looked at her watch and sometimes she exclaimed.

" But how silly ! How stupid of him," she kept saying. " Really he has no sense at all ! "

She was very much annoyed with Kenneth. When Eliza said it was all Beddoes's fault she said no, it was the fault of the public school system.

" If I'd thought then as I do now I should never have let him go to St. Clere's. Max has a horror of public schools."

When Eliza had finished she said :

" So it's all right then ? He isn't seriously involved ? We didn't know what to think from the accounts in the newspapers. But I told Max that Alec would see to it, whatever it was. Only Max insisted that we ought to come, and of course he is quite right. We are responsible for Ken. But it's all most annoying. Max has to make a most important speech to-morrow. I do hope . . . you say this inquest is going on now ? "

" Yes. We've been waiting all day to hear the verdict."

" W can't go back until . . . we must wait to hear, I suppose. Just in case anything . . . But there would still be a chance if we flew. . . . Max is going to ask if your father can keep Ken for a little while now, till we are back in England and can settle things. Of course, if it's not convenient, we must take him to Geneva with us. But we're both so busy, this conference takes up all our time . . . we couldn't look after him much and he'd probably get into mischief. Still . . . we could engage some kind of tutor for him. What do you think ? Would he like to stay here, do you suppose ? Would your father be willing to keep him ? "

" Oh yes," said Eliza. " I think he wants to."

" Then that will be all right. I hope Max is arranging that now. You say he's talking to Joy ? It's a pity he couldn't see Alec."

" I'm sure she'll tell him that we . . . that she and father want Ken to stay."

Betsy got up again and continued her wanderings. She stopped to examine the little gravestone of Lucy Jane Godden, born in August 1741 and died in January 1742.

" Poor little thing ! " she sighed. " Only "—she counted on her fingers—" five months."

" You've got a hairpin sticking out," said Eliza.

This was a *quid pro quo* for the powder, but Betsy, tucking it in again absentmindedly, did not seem to appreciate that. She gave the impression of caring very little about her appearance. That she should be somewhat battered and blown about, after so long and rapid a journey, was perhaps natural. But travel stains could not entirely account for the alteration in her looks. As Eliza now noticed, she was more carelessly dressed than she used to be. Her clothes were good and expensive, but they looked as though they had been bought and put on without much thought. As Lady St. Mullins she was far less elegant than she had been as Mrs. Canning. And her skin looked older. It was a trifle red and rough and there were a number of new lines round the mouth and eyes, as if she had begun to neglect that unremitting rearguard campaign against time which a woman of forty must undertake if she wishes to remain beautiful.

" Max has been so extraordinarily good about this,"she said presently. " I do feel it's hard that my children should take up his time and attention, just at this moment."

" Couldn't you have come without him ? "

" I wanted to. But he wouldn't let me take the journey alone. And, as he says, we do share one another's responsibilities. That is part of marriage."

" Then why didn't you come to the house ? " asked Eliza. " Didn't you want to see father and Joy ? "

" I . . . I thought . . . as Max was here . . . that it might be more comfortable for all of us . . . if I didn't."

" Not even Ken ? Didn't you want to see Ken ? "

Betsy gave her a haggard look. Do be careful, it said. Oh do be careful and don't say anything that will hurt me too much !

Eliza realized that this flustered inconsequence, the staccato manner, the spasmodic interest in tombstones, were symptoms of terror. It was not that her mother did not care about Ken. She cared too much. She hardly knew what she was doing.

" But Ken and father are both away in Salisbury," she urged. " There's only Joy and me. Do come and have a cup of tea."

" No," said Betsy uncertainly. " I don't think I will. It's not that I bear any grudge. You understand that, don't you, dear ? It's . . . I can't explain . . . later on perhaps we can all meet more comfortably. . . ."

No ! She did not want to see the house where Alec was living now, or to have him brought close to her in any way. That was why Max, who understood her as nobody else did, had insisted upon coming with her and taking the painful interviews on his own shoulders.

To see Alec or Kenneth, to see anything connected with them, might cast her back into that abyss from which Max had only just rescued her. He had hauled her out of it,

on to a dry, bleak little island. He had said : Marry me
and help me with my work. And so she had, and was
now, if anything, the more active worker of the two.
Their island was bleak but it was not barren ; there was
shelter there and some flowers grew. Max's astonishing
tenderness and generosity made it habitable. That she
should have inspired such feelings no longer surprised her,
for she felt that no human being could ever be quite
worthy of such love.

"It's such a nice house," said Eliza. "I wish you
could see it."

"Yes. I'm sure it is. I'm glad it's nice."

"It's funny that it should be a mill. So was Pandy
Madoc. We seem to run to Mills."

"Yes. You do. Don't you."

You do, she said. Who was she talking about ? What
group of people ran to mills ? Eliza had meant that the
Cannings did. But who were the Cannings now ?

They wandered round behind the church and Betsy
looked into a little shed full of brushwood brooms and
grave-digger's spades. Eliza quite understood now that
she wanted to hear nothing about their life—nothing at
all. She was keeping her mind upon little things, close
at hand. She would not even look up at the line of the
downs or the trees, or at anything belonging to these new
horizons.

"Darling . . . you won't say anything about my being
here ? I don't want to hurt their feelings."

"No. I won't say anything. How is Daph ? "

"Oh Daphne. She's been rather tiresome."

"Doesn't she like it in Geneva ? "

"We'd made a delightful plan to send her to one of
those International Holiday camps : a lovely place in the
Salzkammergut. You know . . . the idea is that school
children of all nations should meet and mix and grow
friendly. But after three days she wrote and begged us
to take her away. She complained of the food and the

beds and I don't know what. And didn't like the other children. So she came back to us in Geneva. But I was too busy to take her about, so I engaged a very nice girl, a Jewess, a refugee as a matter of fact, who was badly in need of a job. And that was a grievance. Why must she go about with a freak ? The poor girl couldn't help her looks. She was most intelligent and interesting. And now Daph wants to go to some kind of holiday school she's heard of, somewhere near Lucerne, where girls, according to her, have a lovely time. I don't like what I hear of it. She seems to have read an account of it in the *Tatler* or the *Bystander*, or one of those papers. It all sounds horribly snobbish to me. But Max says she will be well looked after and I'd better let her do what she pleases. The rest of you have."

Have any of us ? wondered Eliza, as she gradually and finally realized that the Cannings were not a family any more. They were five individuals with no corporate existence. Somehow she had never quite accepted this before ; the habits of a lifetime were too strong and she had persisted in thinking of herself, her parents, Kenneth and Daphne as a unit, as a group which had been dispersed temporarily and by accident.

The thought saddened her so much that she wanted to be alone with it. This wandering about among the graves was more than she could bear.

" I think," she said, " that I ought to be getting back. Some news may have come from Salisbury. Father said he would telephone."

Betsy kissed her affectionately, but made no effort to keep her.

" You're growing very pretty," she said.

" Am I ? " asked Eliza sadly.

For a moment she hid her face on her mother's shoulder.

" Darling ! You're not crying ? What is it ? "

" Nothing. Only . . . it's all very sad . . . isn't it ? "

" Yes," said Betsy harshly. " But there's no use crying over spilt milk."

" No. No, there isn't."

Eliza ran out of the churchyard, jumped into the car, and drove back to the Mill House.

Max and Joy had, she thought, been a long time alone together. But she was anxious not to appear officious. So she went and listened outside the drawing-room window, to find out how they were getting on. She heard Max say:

" And what sort of response do you get from the agricultural labourers, hereabouts I mean ? "

" Oh," came Joy's voice, " the ones I've talked to are all against war. But only for rather selfish reasons. They are afraid they will have to go and fight."

" Ah ! But still . . . one can understand that. . . ."

Eliza looked in at the window and saw them cosily sitting together on the sofa, studying some of Joy's pamphlets. They were, as Alec had prophesied, getting on like a house on fire. Joy was pinker and more lively than she had been for two years.

" Any news ? " asked Eliza through the window.

They started and looked a little guilty because they had forgotten the crisis which they were supposed to be in. There was news. Alec had telephoned. The inquest had gone off without accidents and the verdict was Death by Misadventure, since it was proved that the poor girl had been riding with no rear light. Beddoes was to be charged with not stopping and with failure to report the accident, but Kenneth had not been blamed at all, and Alec's mind seemed to be at rest.

" I must be getting back," said Max, recalled to the affairs of the moment.

Joy cordially pressed him to stay to tea, but he would not do so, though he took a long time, and said a great deal before getting himself out of the house. It seemed that he had settled everything with Joy. Kenneth was to be left in his father's hands and the trip to Mexico was to be put before Betsy.

He climbed into his car and drove off towards the village with such a conspiratorial air that Eliza was diverted.

" How nice he is ! " exclaimed Joy, as soon as he had gone. " I wasn't a bit frightened of him after the first."

" Yes," said Eliza, " he is nice. I told you he was."

" He has got such interesting ideas. They are going to have a sort of house-party at Hornwood in the autumn— leaders of the Peace Movement from all nations. I think it will be wonderful. Some miners are coming from the depressed areas. He sort of . . . half asked me to go. I should have loved to, but I said no. I don't think I could, quite, do you ? "

" There's an idea going about," said Eliza cryptically, " that we all do as we please."

" Still," said Joy regretfully, " it might be rather awkward for Betsy. You know, I can't help being surprised that Betsy married him. I wouldn't have thought he was her sort at all. Doesn't it surprise you ? "

" Nothing surprises me any more," said Eliza.

" Because he really is . . . though it's not very kind to say it . . . he really is rather peculiar looking. Just at first, till you get used to it. Not an attractive man, I mean. l just can't think how a woman who was married to Alec could ever . . ."

Max was saying very much the same thing to Betsy as they drove back to the aerodrome.

" A thoroughly nice woman. I liked her immensely. Not very intelligent perhaps. A little muddle-headed, and she expresses herself crudely. But she's got hold of the right end of the stick and she seems to be doing good work down here."

" I'd never thought of her as being interested in that kind of thing," commented Betsy.

" Oh, she's fully alive to the importance of it. But

I made one awful bloomer! I forgot, for the moment,
who she was, and asked her to come to our Agapemone at
Hornwood."

" Max! You didn't ? "

" I did. However, she grew rather pink and said she
was afraid she couldn't, and then, of course, I remembered."

Betsy laughed.

" It would have puzzled the Blochs," she said. " I
almost wish she would come, if only to see the Blochs'
faces."

For the Blochs were at Hornwood after all, packed away
in a cottage behind the stables. Somehow or other they
had got themselves there during the spring, when Betsy
had been plunged too deep in her abyss to care what anybody did. And now, just as she had said, it was going to
be impossible ever to get them out.

" I had expected her to be prettier somehow," said Max.

" Oh! Didn't you think her very beautiful ? "

" No, not a bit. How Alec could have done what he
did for her sake I don't know."

" I've told you how that was."

" I know. But I wouldn't have called her an attractive
woman. As good as bread, no doubt, but not charming.
How any man who was married to you . ."

A slight quiver in her face warned him to break off.

They drove in silence through the Wiltshire lanes and
over canals and rivers. Betsy did not look about her.
She kept glancing at her watch and making calculations,
and speculating about the flying conditions. What with
cars and aeroplanes, she still hoped to get him back in
time to make his speech.

A sudden exclamation from him broke in upon her
thoughts. He had turned and was looking after a car
which had just passed them on the road.

" That was Alec and Kenneth."

" Oh, was it ? "

She turned to look, in spite of herself. The little car,

with two heads sticking up in it, receded rapidly along the straight road and vanished round a corner.

"They must be on their way from Salisbury," he said.

"Did they see us?"

"I don't think so. Would you . . . like to . . ."

"No, no . . . Let's get on, Max. We must hurry. We haven't a moment to lose. . . ."

MARK had been invited to come over to the Mill House whenever he liked. Alec not only wished to express his gratitude, but felt, too, that he was a good friend for Kenneth, whose former hero worship had flamed up again.

He came twice. The two boys rode and bathed together and began once more to be friends. But on neither occasion did he see Eliza. The first time she remained upstairs all day with a headache. The second time she was away, spending a week-end with the Hewitts. Mark was sorry, and said so. He expected to be ordered to Gibraltar very soon, and did not know if he would be able to come again. He would have liked to see her to say good-bye.

" We told her she'd miss you," said Kenneth. " She could have gone to Oxford any other week-end. I shall tell her that you think she is extremely rude."

" No, don't say that. Tell her that I wanted to say good-bye to her."

Kenneth, however, forgot to give the message. When she came back from Oxford it was to learn that she would not, probably, see Mark again. She need invent no more pretexts for avoiding him. He was going to Gibraltar and her suspense was over.

The Grahams came to stay that day and the house was very full. Sometimes it seemed strange to her that her sorrow should not be apparent to all of them. They could talk and laugh and eat and drink, with this pain sitting so close to them, as if a ghost had sat at the table. But she was glad that it was so, for she had not the slightest wish to tell anybody of her trouble.

Joy gave her a queer compassionate look sometimes, as if she half guessed. Their friendship was growing very fast ; it was an alliance which the arrival of Susie Graham had done much to promote. They both resented Susie's sharp eyes and sharper tongue, and were determined that the Mill House should not provide her with material for a tale.

One evening they sat together making a smock for Peter. All the others had gone for a walk on the downs and would not be in till supper-time. When Eliza heard the sound of a motor bicycle, chugging along the lane, her heart fluttered anxiously. She wished that Joy would say :

" Isn't that a motor bicycle ? Didn't it stop by the gate ? Is it somebody coming to see us ? "

But Joy only lamented the fact that she had forgotten the difference between feather-stitching and herring-boning. She did not even seem to hear Clara going to the front door.

But it's all nothing, thought Eliza. I've been through this every time I heard a motor cycle.

The door opened and Mark was ushered in, smiling and quite at his ease.

" Oh ! " cried Joy in distress. " Alec and Ken have just gone out. Only just. Would you like to try and catch them up ? "

But Mark, as he shook hands with her, said that he would rather stay and talk to them. Then he turned and held out his hand to Eliza, asking if she had had a nice week-end at Oxford.

" Oh," said Eliza. " Yes, yes, I did. Yes."

" You'll stay to supper ? " asked Joy.

" Thank you. I'd be delighted, if you can do with me."

He took a seat beside Joy and began to ask her about

Byron, how it was getting on and when it was to be produced. Nothing could have pleased her more, though she had not very much to tell him. She had not read the script, but she was able to report some theatre gossip about casting, and once or twice she said " we " as though she habitually took part in Alec and Johnnie's deliberations.

Eliza kept her eyes on her work. Her heart had stopped banging about, but she wanted to be sure that she had entire control over herself before she tried to move. In a few minutes she would get up, quite casually, and smile, and ask if she could tell Clara that there was one extra for supper. Then she would get out of the room and upstairs, where she would stay until the others came in. After that she could manage easily not to speak to him again until he took his leave.

Presently she felt that the moment had come. She put down her work and rose. But she could not have done it quite as casually as she had meant, for Joy and Mark stopped talking and looked at her.

" Are you going to bathe this evening ? " asked Mark at once.

" No, no, I'm not. I bathed this morning. Joy . . . shall I tell Clara there's an extra person for supper ? "

" Oh, yes," said Joy, ringing the bell. " Don't worry to go. Clara will come." And she added to Mark : " Would you like a bathe ? "

" Not by myself. If either of you . . ."

And when neither of them took the hint he began to ask for music.

" Do you never sing now ? " he asked Eliza. " Every time I've been here I meant to ask you, but you weren't there. Do you remember how we used to sing at Pandy Madoc ? "

" Oh, she's come on a lot since Wales," said Joy. " She really does practise very hard."

" Shan't we sing now ? I see a lot of the same books."

He was edging her towards the piano, which was open,

and he picked up a volume of Schubert from the music stool.

Clara came in and Joy gave some orders about supper. At the same instant Eliza heard a murmur at her elbow.

" Make it up, won't you, Eliza ?   Forgive me ! "

If he had suddenly floated up to the ceiling she could not have been more surprised.   What had she to forgive ?

She sank down weakly upon the music stool, and he said as he turned over the pages :

" What was it we used to sing together ?   *Death and the Maiden.*   Here it is."

" Her voice has come on enormously," said Joy, who had finished talking to Clara.

" Has it, Eliza ?   Sing up ! "

Eliza began to sing and immediately came to grief over the accompaniment.

" Calm yourself," advised Mark.   " Don't go at it like a bull at a gate.   That's too hasty and terrified altogether. Look here !   Before you do your bit, give me a little practice with my bit, for I'm not sure that I remember the words."

She began to play the noble chords of Mark's bit, and tranquillity returned to her.   Joy beamed at them through the horn-rimmed spectacles which she wore when sewing.

" Now ! " said Mark.

Eliza sprang once more at the opening, and this time she sailed through it triumphantly.   A great access of strength and power came to her, into her hands, into her voice and into her mind.   It flowed through her like an ecstasy, so that she and the song seemed to be one thing. Mark was amazed, so much amazed that he was a little late in coming in with his bit.

At Pandy Madoc he had only hummed, but now, stirred and uplifted by Eliza's performance, he sang aloud, in a fine and resonant bass which served him very well until the last profound note.   The song ended perfunctorily, with a shrug from him and a laugh from Eliza.

" That was very pretty," said Joy. " Do sing some more."

And as they passed from song to song she fell into a pleasant reverie.

This is very nice. Music . . . and people staying . . . like it used to be at Pandy Madoc. It is going to be a real home for him now that he has Ken. It hasn't been all for nothing . . . all that time when I tried so hard . . . I used to think it would never . . . but he is ever so much happier now. And they are all very nice to me . . . even Susie . . . though sometimes she says little things . . . it was on purpose, that what she said about Betsy's bed being in the spare room . . . no . . . perhaps it wasn't. I mustn't be unjust. But I do like Margaret Merrick better than I like Susie. How well Eliza sings ! . . . how pretty she is ! . . . I do appreciate good music. I have intellectual interests. It isn't as if I had nothing in common with him. I really enjoy listening to this very much. And I can understand what these songs are about. I understand German. I have been very well educated. Le⁺ me see . . . *nun bin ich manche stunde*. . . . Now I am many leagues away from that place. How sad that seems somehow ! I must be a great deal happier, or I wouldn't be enjoying a sad song like this."

" Now," said Mark, " as we are singing about trees, let's have *Nussbaum*."

Eliza began to search in the volume of Schubert, forgetting, as many people do, that *Nussbaum* would not be there. He said :

" No, darling. . . ."

And then stopped, as though he had come to the edge of a precipice.

The word fell into their hearts like a little stone into a pool. It vanished, but ring after ring spread out to the very edges of thought and feeling.

He had not meant to say it, but, now that he had, he was ravished. He would not pass it over or slur its importance. He waited, fixing his eyes on Eliza, forcing her to look at him.

She did so at last, raising her eyes slowly from the music on her knee. And he saw what moved him more than he had known to be possible ; he saw that she was frightened—that she had lost herself. It was as if that one word of his had come to her only as a sound, as if she had heard a rider in the night, the cry of a new-born child, the rattle of stones and earth in a grave. In the noisy tunnel of the years these fatal, irrevocable undertones are heard but seldom. They break like waves upon a hidden strand ; but no thunder-clap can wake so long or so haunting an echo.

Joy turned in her chair. She had heard nothing save a long pause which disturbed her meditations.

The slight movement recalled them. Mark said quickly : " No, not Schubert. Schumann."

He found the song and set it before Eliza, who shook her head.

" I can't sing it and play it at the same time," she told him.

" Then play it. The accompaniment is so lovely."

She played.

And he thought rapidly of many things : that he was going away for a long time, that he could not leave her, thus lost, and that it might not be easy to see her alone again. He must say more ; he must say exactly what was in his heart. For they had strayed by accident into a kingdom which they were too young to claim. They must not attempt to usurp it. They must be as wise as they were lucky.

It's all or nothing for us, he thought. In two years, three years, I'll come back and marry her. But till then it must be nothing. I won't see her again till then. I won't write to her. She's not a woman yet. It's not fair to treat her as if she was, to wake those feelings in her. I must leave her alone. . . .

There were voices outside the window. The walkers had returned and Joy went to greet them. He had a moment before they all came in.

" I must talk to you a little before I go."

She nodded, still playing.

" I shall go at ten. Can you slip off early and go a little way up the lane so that I can catch you up ? "

" Yes."

Then all the others were in the room, and he did not speak another word to her for the rest of the evening. Alec, who came in first and caught a glimpse of their faces, took especial note of that. In fact, to Alec's mind, they overdid their detachment. They were incredibly unconscious of one another. Mark's cool, alert glances were for everybody but Eliza, and she was the only person who did not laugh when he said something amusing. She hardly spoke at all and he talked a great deal more than usual. His high spirits infected them all. They made much of him because it was his last visit, and Kenneth was anxious that he should impress the Grahams. Supper was a lively meal. Even Joy said one or two good things.

How didn't I guess, wondered Alec, that there was something between those two ? Joy has been saying something was the matter with her ever since the day Ken came, when, of course, he came too . . . and was alone with her some time . . . but . . . had they been meeting before ? . . . how . . . when he came again did he see her ? . . . No . . . she had a headache . . . she was at Oxford . . . that's why she insisted upon going to Oxford . . . they quarrelled that day ? And now he has taken us by surprise because . . . they've made it up now, anyway.

The discovery disturbed him, although he tried to believe that it could not mean anything very serious—a boy and girl affair, which had best be ignored. To be a father to Kenneth was more than he had bargained for ;

it was going to take up the greater part of the autumn.
It was too much if Eliza was also going to turn herself
into a problem. Yet he was uneasy. He wondered what
Betsy would think. Mark was an unusual boy. And
perhaps Joy was right in maintaining that Eliza had been
neglected. She had been through more than most girls
of her age, and she had been treated by everybody as
though she was grown up. She was not, but for their
own convenience they had treated her so, unable or un-
willing to face the complications of her youth and their
own responsibility. They had relied upon her unusual
maturity, and now perhaps she was paying them out.

For there had been a look about those two, conferring
there by the piano, which he could not forget. It was an
odd, settled look, as if a very great deal had already taken
place between them—everything, in fact, which can take
place between lovers. For a moment he had been appalled,
until all that he knew of Hannay occurred to reassure him.
And he was still very glad to think that the boy was going
to Gibraltar.

If he wasn't off so soon, he thought, I'd have to have
a talk to him. I'd have to tell him it isn't fair. She's
too young and he's got no business to play about with her
feelings. Let him come back in a year or two. Nothing
would please me more . . . in a year or two . . . she
wants keeping in order, and he'd be the man to do it.

When the men rejoined the women after supper, Eliza
had vanished. They said she was tired and had gone to
bed. Mark took his leave at ten o'clock. They all
wandered out into the garden to see him off the premises.

A round harvest moon had risen over the hill, and the
night was balmy. Their laughter, their farewells, echoed
under the shadowy trees, as Mark started up his cycle.
When he had vanished along the lane, their light, brief
voices sank into comment and discussion. Kenneth was
demanding admiration for his hero friend. The Grahams
gave it readily enough. Susie thought him too attractive

for words, and Johnnie muttered something about an able fellow and a pity.

" Why a pity ? " asked Kenneth, instantly on the defensive. " He's only going to be with the colours for three years. After that he'll be in the reserve, but he'll be able to go into politics, as he's always meant to."

" Politics ? " sniffed Johnnie. " What ? Labour ? Communist ? "

" I don't know. I don't think he much minds as long as he gets a name for himself and gets himself known."

" But what does he want to do ? "

" Has he got any money ? " asked Susan.

" Lots. But he's never going to live beyond six hundred a year. None of them are. Everything else they've got, and everything they earn over that, will go into their fund. He says you must use money to get power, not let it get power over you."

" What fund ? Who are you talking about ? "

" Oh, some more people, some friends of his. Two Americans, and a French boy he's talked about, and some others they've collected. They've all agreed never to live like rich men, because then they'll be free, and all have one standard of life, so if a poor man joins them he won't be corrupted. You should hear the way he goes on about Labour leaders who dine with duchesses."

" But what do they want to do ? " asked Alec and Joy and Johnnie and Susan.

" Oh," said Kenneth airily, " run the world."

At their laughter he protested :

" A very few people, a small group, could run the world in the state it's in now. Everybody is frightened and nobody knows what they want. A group of people who knew exactly what they wanted, and didn't care about money, and weren't afraid of anything, could easily get a lot of power. Think of the Jesuits ! "

" Six hundred a year ! " said Susan. " They won't stick to that for long. Why, they'd never be able to marry ! "

" Lots of people do on less.   Lots of people would think it a fortune."

" You wait till they want to get married."

" Oh, they're all going to get married young," explained Kenneth, " so as to break their wives into the idea of not wanting money.   And to settle the problem of women in their lives.   They don't want to be bothered with women."

" But did Mark really say that he intends to run the world ? " asked Alec.

" Oh, no.   But I say so.   I think he will."

" And you are one of them, I suppose ? "

" I'd like to be," said Kenneth, flushing, " if they'd have me.   But they won't take anybody.   Only people who are prepared to give up the whole of their lives, and who they think will be really useful.   He thinks they'll get all the recruits they want, in time.   He's expecting to get them in England and France and America mostly. He says there's nothing for a young man in a civilized country to do but sit and watch the ship go down, and everybody is sick of it.   I think they'll begin by forming a party, each in their own country, and then, when they are strong enough, they'll join up and make it inter-national."

" A sort of moral force ? " suggested Joy hopefully.

" Ye-es.   And the other kind of force too, if necessary : lots of it."

He saw that they were impressed, and began to improvise further details of Mark's scheme to run the world.   Actually he had very little to go upon.   He knew that Mark and his friends had worked out a plan of life for themselves, that they had renounced the standards of the middle classes, that they all meant to go into politics, and that some kind of international agreement was their goal.   This had set fire to his imagination and he had built many airy castles ; some of them were of Fascist design, others were Communist but all of them were strongholds for dictators.

"Moonshine," sighed Johnny—"moonshine! If he'd gone to Oxford they'd have got the nonsense out of him. He'd have gone into a profession and settled down."

"I think it would be a nice idea, as long as they only use moral force," said Joy.

Susie could not get over the suggestion that they were not going to be bothered with women. She took it as a personal affront.

"Ho, ho!" she prophesied darkly. "You just wait!"

Alec had not said anything for some minutes. His only anxiety was to be sure that their dynamic young guest had really gone. It had seemed to him that there was something wrong with the noise of that departing motor-cycle. It had not died away as it should have done. Unless his ears deceived him it had stopped very suddenly.

Without a word he detached himself from the group in the garden and strolled off up the lane. Near the top of the hill he found what he had expected : a motor-cycle parked against a gate into a field. He looked over the gate and thought that he saw the glimmer of a light dress against a hedge on the other side of the meadow.

He started towards it and then lost it, but he went on over the short, dewy grass, his moon shadow running before him. As he had hoped, they came out to meet him from their shelter under the gloom of the hedge.

"Eliza!" he said. "Mark! I thought so!"

Eliza took one arm and Mark the other. They seemed quite content to have his chilly, middle-aged, disillusioned body between them. He began to walk them back towards the gate, feeling all the warmth of their youth, their ecstasy, on either side of him, and feeling himself quite powerless to insulate the current. It went on through him as if he had not been there. But he did his best to ignore it, and sought for words which should put both him and them back in their proper places.

"Well . . ." he said at last, ". . . you absurd little creatures . . ."

" I know ! " said Mark and Eliza together.

And Mark added :

" We shan't be seeing each other for at least two years, so you don't have to worry, sir."

" Or write, or anything," said Eliza. " We've just settled that we shouldn't."

" That's a comfort, anyway," murmured Alec, who felt that his attitude had been insincere and a little ridiculous.

" Because, you see, we haven't really anything more to say . . . till . . ."

Her voice died away on a sigh of happiness.

" If that's the case, I commend you," said Alec. " You see, Mark . . . I expect I worry about her more than I would . . . if . . . if her mother was here. I've everything to learn about daughters. I expect it's all right . . ."

" I quite understand," agreed Mark. " We've both got a lot of things to attend to at present. And we have all the time there is."

At that Alec pushed them away from him, partly because they had come to a patch of thistles where it was difficult to walk three abreast, and partly because he remembered that once time had appeared in this fashion to him. He felt suddenly so sorry for them that he would proffer no more counsel.

" You ought to be off," he said to Mark. " I'm going home. I give you five minutes. If at the end of that time I don't hear your cycle starting up, I shall come back with a horsewhip."

He scrambled over the gate again and hurried off down the lane. As he reached the garden gate the bicycle began to thump away on the hill. This time it made a really effective departure. He could hear it for a long time, throbbing through the quiet night, till it was no louder than the ticking of a watch.

Everyone had gone back into the house except Johnnie Graham, with whom he lingered on the lawn, waiting for

Eliza. Presently he saw her coming, quickly and silently, in and out of the chequered patches of shadow. She went past them towards the house, moving steadily forward, like a sleep-walker, invested by some power not her own. Her face, in the moonlight, looked strange to him, yet familiar ; he felt that he might have seen it long ago when he too was young, and knew nothing, and took the light of heaven for granted. And now, after many years, he saw again that face, that fabled face of happiness, up-lifted to the quiet sky, before she passed by him and was gone.

Johnnie turned with him to look after her.

" She reminds me," he said suddenly, " of someone. But I can't remember her name, after all this time."

" I don't suppose you ever knew it," said Alec.

" Oh, yes. I knew it all right," said Johnnie morosely. " Wilcox, or Wilkinson . . . or it might have been Blenkinsop. It's funny . . . a funny thing ! I can never remember their names."

" Their names," said Alec, " *we know not nor shall know.*"

He paused, unable to recall the end of the quotation. Johnnie, surprisingly, finished it for him in the disgusted manner which he reserved for poetry and for all expressions of sentiment.

" *Like the lost Pleiad* . . . ugh ! . . . *seen no more below.*"

A frog, in the reeds by the river, set up a dry little croaking like an echo.

THE END